Women and the cinema

Illinois Central College
Learning Resources Center

WOMEN
AND THE
CINEMA

Karyn Kay has a B.A. in English from the University of Wisconsin, and has done graduate work in film at Northwestern University and Columbia University. She teaches Women in Film at Livingston College, Rutgers University. She is the author of *Myrna Loy* (1977), and has contributed to various cinema periodicals, including *Film Quarterly, The Velvet Light Trap, Cinema, Women and Film,* and *Jump Cut.* She helped organize the Chicago '74 Films By Women Festival and the Second New York International Festival of Women's Films (1976).

Gerald Peary is completing his Ph.D. dissertation, "The Rise of the American Gangster Film," at the University of Wisconsin. He lectures on Film in the English Department of Livingston College, Rutgers University. He is coeditor of two anthologies on the American novel and the movies and author of *Rita Hayworth* (1976). He is associate editor for *Film Heritage* and *The Velvet Light Trap* and book editor of *Jump Cut.*

WOMEN
AND THE
CINEMA

A Critical Anthology

Edited by
KARYN KAY
and GERALD PEARY

A Dutton Paperback

E. P. DUTTON   NEW YORK

PN
1995
.9
.W6
W65

Library of Congress Catalog Card Number: 77-71301

ISBN: 0-525-47459-5

Published simultaneously in Canada by Clarke, Irwin & Company
Limited, Toronto and Vancouver

10 9 8 7 6 5 4 3 2 1

First Edition

To the sisters, with love—

Gail, Linda, Myra,
Paula, Laura, Tanya—

and to Dorothy Arzner

List of Illustrations

Contents

Preface

The raising of consciousness through the women's liberation movement has led feminists to the profound knowledge that women's roles are cultural rather than biological and that these are molded, stereotyped, caricatured, reinforced—consciously as well as subconsciously—by the mainstream (read: "male values"-dominated) media. Yet while finding our culture impossibly weighted with patriarchal values and with sexism, women keep discovering hidden pockets in which vestiges of "female culture" have grown—usually unnoticed, or condescendingly ignored, by this male media majority. One such place is the cinema.

The more women really delve into the vast vaults of filmmaking, the more awesome the findings: new heroines to champion, new artists and artisans to admire, new women (real and fictional) to claim as "sisters," an assortment of works (traditional and experimental, feature length and shorts, narrative and documentary) that offer discovery and dialogue to womankind. For instance, there exist a tiny group of Hollywood films directed by women. And a high percentage of these—by Lois Weber around World War I, by Dorothy Arzner from the late 1920s to the 1940s, by Stephanie Rothman in the 1970s—prove subversively feminist in spirit and covert values, if not always in outward design. Movies such as Arzner's *Dance, Girl, Dance* (1940), properly grasped, can make women today "stand up and cheer" just as inevitably as the macho crowd rises at a *Walking Tall*.

Sometimes, even surprisingly enlightened "women's pictures" have emanated from the entrenched Hollywood men's club, made by sympathetic, more often idiosyncratic, directors such as George Cukor, Douglas Sirk, Max Ophuls, Raoul Walsh, or Howard Hawks. (On occasion under the womanly influence of such vigorous screenwriter talents as Leigh Brackett, Zoe Akins, or Ruth Gordon.) But finding these estimable films requires digging: laborious feminist archaeology. And what of today?

Within the industry, things are not so rosy. Female cinematographers are, as ever, excluded systematically from the union. (Has a woman ever photographed a Hollywood film?) Any buoyant invasion of female directors, bursting with women's-movement energy and ideology, has been held at bay. And the (overkill) cheers and huzzahs, "at last there are serious and decent women's roles," for 1974's *Alice Doesn't Live Here Anymore* and *A Woman Under the Influence* have long ago dried up. Seen any good Hollywood-made women's pictures lately? The usual "strong" women's roles are very strong indeed: kung fu and karate types, battling drug dealers and pimps in endless black neighborhood pictures. Otherwise, ERA is Unwelcome to L.A.

Outside of Hollywood women can locate worthy feminist allies making movies—Nelly Kaplan and Marguerite Duras in France, Mai Zetterling in Sweden, Danielle Huillet and Margarethe von Trotta in West Germany, among many others. (Will the brilliant Vera Chytilova, silenced since 1970, be allowed to make films in Czechoslovakia again? Here is certainly a prime case for the human rights' cause.) But it is the independent film, made free of the interference of producers and studio bosses, that is the rallying ground for dedicated feminists in the media.

Shorts in 16mm abound—about birth control, child rearing, rape, self-defense, sex roles, and women's history; these are distributed to schools, hospitals, feminist conferences, women's groups, and television stations. Usually they are made by women more concerned with consciousness raising than with popularizing their individual names. Chicago's Kartemquin Films and the Boston Women's Film Group are two examples of filmmakers who operate collectively to produce fine issue-oriented works for specific community usage.

Certain films can be mentioned in passing as capably demonstrating the immense potentialities of independent film production: Claudia Weill's shorts on ghetto black women and her lushly photographed *China Memoir* (1974), with Shirley MacLaine; Amalie Rothschild's subtle, resourceful family portrait, *Nana, Mom, and Me* (1974); Nancy Porter's model documentary, *A Woman's Place Is in the House* (1975), with Micky Lemle, an openly partisan tribute to state legislator Elaine Noble, a radical lesbian. These are just three of many. Other examples: the works of Maya Deren, Marie Menken, and Storm De Hirsch, pioneers of the American avant-garde; Joyce Wieland and Yvonne Rainer, who have combined feminism with theoretical experiments in "structuralist" filmmaking.

On the rarest occasions, women have gathered enough funds to produce full-length independent works. The results have been startling: *Wanda* (1970), directed by and starring Barbara Loden, remains filmdom's definitive exploration of the lumpen white woman. In *The Connection* (1960) and *The Cool World* (1963), Shirley Clarke went outside "women's topics" and offered among the first cinematic accounts of life inside a Harlem youth gang and within the secretive world of cool jazz and hard drugs. In *A Portrait of Jason* (1967), she presented a unique glimpse at the life and times of a charismatic black male hustler. Another independent director is Joan Silver, who, for *Hester Street* (1975), turned her camera to a beautiful evocation of life on New York's Lower East Side at the turn of the century.

Last, and most significantly, there are a solid number of deeply committed and engaged political films made by feminist progressives: a logical movement from indignation at injustices to women to a call to arms for all exploited peoples. Cinda Firestone made *Attica* (1973). Sarah Maldoror, who once assisted Pontecorvo on *The Battle of Algiers* (1967), came forth with *Sambizanga* (1972), perhaps the greatest of all films on African revolution. Tra Giang directed movies in North Vietnam as American bombs fell. Barbara Kopple told the coal miners' story in the militant *Harlan County: USA* (1976). And Jane Fonda advanced mightily from soft-core victimization, "Floating through the air as Barbarella," she calls it, to her role as indefatigable fighter for peace in Vietnam, for the freeing of the thousands once held in Thieu's prisons.

It is to this last group that this anthology is especially inscribed.

Finally, a note about the strategy of this anthology. We realize that the movement away from role-model studies and impressionist, personal criticism and toward structuralism and psychoanalytic theory wins converts by the day among feminist film critics. Although we recognize the exciting potential of applying the latest "scientific" methodology to feminist studies, we also know that much of the best writing is yet to come. Rather than attempt an anthology of theory, we feel a more immediate need to explore the expansive history of feminist cinema writings. For this very first collection concerning women and film, we wish to present as many types of engaging essays as possible, from the avant-garde to the antiquarian, from unapologetic "bourgeois feminism" to subjective reaction pieces, to simple factual-historical articles, to interviews, to autobiographical essays, to Marxist declarations, to, finally, texts of a developing feminist theory.

Contradictions leap out from one article to another. Methodology lies helter-skelter. But let the reader peruse and choose at leisure among the abundant pickings—and from these choices, let ideology and theory grow, as well as a deeper sense of women's mighty contribution to the cinema.

We want to express special thanks to Dorothy Arzner, Peter Brunette, Bonnie Friedman, Molly Haskell, Bill Horrigan, Ruth McCormick, Catherine Plumb, Reid Rosefelt, Roger Shatzkin, Charles Silver, Phil Susswein, Charles Swartz; Elizabeth Dalton and the Wisconsin Center for Film and Theater Research; Jonas Mekas and the Anthology Film Archives; Betty Moss and New World Pictures; The Museum of Modern Art Stills Collection; Les Robley and DKA, USC Chapter; Betty Woolner and Dimension Pictures; and to our editor, Julie McGown, for staying with us so patiently.

KARYN KAY
GERALD PEARY

I
Feminist Perspectives

A Short Manual for an Aspiring Scenario Writer*

Colette

Introduction

At various times in her life the French novelist Colette wrote film criticism and commentary, subtitles for foreign films, scenarios and additional dialogue. Her voluminous correspondence testifies to her continuing and passionate interest in the movies, and we know from the faithful Maurice Goudeket that in her final years, invalided and wheelchair-bound, Colette often asked to be taken to "the dark rooms." When this was no longer possible, a place was made—"at the expense of the books"—in her famous Palais-Royal apartment for a television set. Nevertheless, in an access of literary snobbery, she eliminated most of her writing for and about the cinema from the edition of her complete works issued in 1948—six years before her death.

The excerpts below are from a series of four short articles published in 1918 under the title "A Short Manual for an Aspiring Scenario Writer." They no doubt reflect her sobering experience as screenwriter for the 1917 silent version of her novel La Vagabonde, *for which the director insisted on imposing his conception of feminine behavior and psychology. Continually in need of money—*

* Translated by Stanley Hochman. Reprinted with permission from *Colette au cinéma*, eds. Alain Virmaux and Odette Virmaux (Paris: Flammarion, 1975).

Colette later wrote the dialogue for Marc Allégret's Lac-aux-dames
(*1934*) *and both the scenario and dialogue for Max Ophuls's* Divine
(*1935*). *She also contributed dialogue when her novels became
films:* Gigi (*1948*) *and* Chéri (*1950*).

S. H.

I. THE FEMME FATALE

A sensational film owes the public a "presentation," in enormous
close-ups, of its principal characters.

The presentation of the sympathetic heroine has few specific requirements. On the other hand, that of the femme fatale is a shatter-
ing revelation, and from the very first minute we know what we can
expect from her.

Q: Why?

A: Because (1) the femme fatale is almost always in décolleté;
(2) she is often armed with a hypodermic or with a flacon; (3) she
sinuously turns her serpent's neck toward the spectator; and more
rarely (4) having first revealed enormously wide eyes, she slowly
veils them with soft lids, and before disappearing in the mist of a
fade-out, risks the most daring gesture that can be shown on the
screen . . .

Q: Easy, now . . . !

A: . . . What I mean to say is that she slowly and guiltily bites
her lower lip.

Q: You had me worried there. . . . Is that all she does?

A: That's all, but it's enough.

Q: You don't mean to imply that the characterization of the
femme fatale is limited to that?

A: Unfortunately not. She also uses other weapons, such as the
dagger, the revolver, the anonymous letter, and finally, elegance.

Q: Elegance?

A: I mean by elegance that which the woman who treads on
hearts and devours brains can in no way do without: (1) a clinging
black velvet dress; (2) a dressing gown of the type known as "exotic" on which one often sees embroidery and designs of seaweed,

insects, reptiles, and a death's-head; and (3) a floral display that she tears at cruelly.

Q: What does the evil woman do when she is alone on the screen?

A: She lights a cigarette and stretches out on the divan. Or else she slyly busies herself writing. Or she rereads letters and "documents" that she withdraws from an unsuspected hiding place—the base of a lamp, a parrot's cage, or the sixth square of the parquet. Or she goes to the window, draws aside the curtain, and raising her arm, sends forth some mysterious signal.

Q: And what happens to the femme fatale at the end of the sensational film?

A: She dies. Preferably on three steps, covered by a rug.

Q: And between the apotheosis and the fall of the femme fatale, isn't there room on the screen for numerous passionate gestures?

A: Numerous, to say the least. The two principal ones involve "the hat" and "queasiness."

Q: Pretend that I've never seen them.

A: The femme fatale's hat spares her the necessity, at the absolute apex of her wicked career, of having to expend herself in pantomime. When the spectator sees the evil woman coiffing herself with a spread-winged owl, the head of a stuffed jaguar, a bifid aigrette, or a hairy spider, he no longer has any doubts; he knows just what she is capable of.

Q: And "queasiness?"

A: "Queasiness" is the imposing and ultimate means by which the evil woman informs the audience that she is about to weep; that she is hesitating on the brink of crime; that she is struggling against steely necessity; or that the police have gotten their hands on the letter.

Q: What letter?

A: *The* letter.

Q: Is there no other way she can express such different emotions?

A: It's not the custom. "Queasiness" is the thing. . . . The heart thumps. The flanks swell. The staring eyes seem about to pop out of their orbits. The stricken wretch suddenly swallows a flow of saliva. And the handkerchief also rises, from her waist to her lips, and . . .

Q: Enough, enough! I'll give you a good grade for this all-too-faithful evocation, but another examination is scheduled: the Society Woman.

II. THE SOCIETY WOMAN

Q: How can the society woman be recognized on the screen without any help from the script?

A: By the fact that she is less well dressed than the woman who is *not* accepted in society, and by her excessive use of black taffeta. Other signs also prevent any possible error, for example, the bunch of daisies and the victoria drawn by two unprepossessing horses.

Q: But the society woman isn't guaranteed exclusive use of daisies or the victoria, is she?

A: No, but by a subtle convention the demimondaine and the adventuress more often prefer orchids and a limousine.

Q: What is the usual facial expression of the society woman on the screen?

A: She scarcely has any choice but boredom or pain, both of a very distinguished variety. In the movies a true society woman suffers: (1) from a brutal, jealous, and alcoholic husband; or (2) from a youthful error—actually quite honorable—the fruit of which she conceals in a distant province.

Q: What are the consequences of these two sets of circumstances?

A: There is only one: as soon as the other characters turn their attention from her, or she finds herself alone on the screen, the society woman is constrained to raise her eyes to the heavens and sigh.

Q: Is that all?

A: And what more would you do if you were in her place?

Q: You're not here to ask questions but to answer them . . . Doesn't that sigh foreshadow sad events?

A: Sad indeed, and not long in coming. Before six hundred feet of film have been unreeled, the society woman receives a letter, sometimes anonymous, in which the spectator may note a completely unrestrained orthography, the trace of a hasty and literal translation

if the film is a foreign one, and—finally—an absolutely revolutionary syntax.

Q: What happens next?

A: Several cases of nervous prostration in the audience.

Q: Why is that?

A: Because from the first appearance of the Letter, projected *in
extenso* in an enormous close-up, the knowledgeable spectator
abandons all hope. He knows that the society woman, whose fate is
linked to that of the letter, will soon reread the letter, which will
tremble—still in an enormous close-up—between two hands that
are as big or bigger than either of us and that sport black fingernails . . .

Q: *Black* fingernails? You must be losing your mind! A society
woman!

A: . . . black, I say, because the manicurist has colored them red.
This Letter, already twice offered as food for our anxiety, resumes
its normal size, and the society woman, horrified, first hides it in her
bosom and then in a piece of furniture that has a secret compart-
ment . . . Alas, it is only so a servant, dismissed or suborned, a
thief, a suspicious husband, an innocent son, or a detective can
employ violence to get at it some one hundred and fifty feet of film
farther on. He looks for it—he finds it—he reads it; horrors, he
makes us read it, still *in extenso* in an enormous close-up! At this
point the society woman can choose between a swoon, if she is the
fragile type, and a revolver, if she wants to save the honor of her
name. But we, the public, we have absolutely no choice. Whether
the husband brandishes it under her nose or the stricken son sobs
over the fatal paper, we the public will not escape the projection—
in an enormous close-up—of the Letter . . .

Q: I see . . . Would you mind talking about something else for a
while? I'm beginning to feel somewhat upset . . .

A: Impossible. The society woman and the Letter, the Letter and
the society woman, the one hiding the other, the other chastising the
one, will go hand in hand until the very end of the film. We shall
witness the preparations for bed—oh, very discreetly, to be sure: a
society woman never undresses on the screen—of the society

woman who, having scarcely dozed off, awakes with a start, or else sinks into a nightmare, a nightmare that . . . a nightmare whose . . .

Q: What nightmare?

A: I was hoping you would ask that question. The nightmare of the Letter. In a velvet-ringed fade-in, in a "medallion" in the left corner of the screen, there once more implacably appears, in the handwriting of an ambitious illiterate, the Letter . . .

Q: Yes, yes . . . But can't we get back to the society woman?

A: Have we left her for so much as an instant? Not a moment of respite! Now it will be necessary for the eternally damned traitor to flee with the Letter, to put it in a "safe place"—in the movies this means a place from which someone will fish it out moments later. It will be necessary for the society woman, dressed in black taffeta and coiffed with a tiny hat with a flowing veil (she can still be recognized by the fact that she rarely wears a tailored suit or traveling clothes, which are reserved for the femme fatale or "the American woman"), to race after the Letter . . . We shall read the Letter in the hands of the traitor, we shall read the Letter snagged against a cliff and flapping in the wind, we shall read the Letter sealed in a bottle and floating on the ocean, the Letter recopied, the Letter forged, the Letter sold, then the Letter repurchased, the Letter damp with tears, and finally the Letter crushed between the fingers of a dead woman, a saint, a veritable martyr—between the fingers of the society woman.

Q: Ouf!

A: Where are you off to, sir? Are you forgetting that the unconscionable persecutor of the society woman, now prostrated by grief and remorse, will piously pry open the clutching fingers of his victim, smooth out the paper, and read *you* the Letter?

Dorothy Arzner's
*Dance, Girl, Dance**

Karyn Kay and Gerald Peary

INTRODUCTION

This admittedly polemical article was written several years ago by the editors, at a time when Dorothy Arzner's once revered name was barely remembered in América and when the prints of her films were hidden away in archives. To our knowledge, this was the first piece to analyze in detail a single work by this most exceptional director. But since, Arzner's star has risen a thousand times, culminating in a festive tribute by the Directors Guild in 1975, attended by a thousand guests and the reluctant celebrity, Arzner, herself—over thirty years after she retired from Hollywood.

Dance, Girl, Dance likewise has done remarkably well—as an instant classic of women's film festivals, as a 16mm film society staple on college campuses, and as a revival-house standard in New York and Boston theatres, often double-billed with Arzner's Christopher Strong *(1933), starring Katharine Hepburn.* Dance, Girl, Dance *has also emerged as a central text of feminist film theorists who support the political strategies of the Brechtian "entertainment" film over the* cinéma vérité *documentary of most women's movement pictures. (See* The Work of Dorothy Arzner—Towards a

---

* Reprinted from *The Velvet Light Trap*, no. 10 (Fall 1973).

Feminist Cinema, ed. Claire Johnston, London, 1975, for a reading of Arzner divergent from the article below.)

From Edinburgh to Toronto, wherever women have gathered at festivals to reexamine their film heritage, the movie of the year has proved to be an obscure RKO comedy of 1940, rescued from the vaults, liberated from its original put-down by an insensitive and indifferent press, typified by *The New York Times*'s snide summation, "But it's not art." The film is *Dance, Girl, Dance*, the next to last feature of Hollywood's most employed and probably most talented woman director, Dorothy Arzner—herself rediscovered and becoming a new star of the women's movement as she passes through her seventies.

Ms. Arzner deserves the feminist recognition. From her first film, *Fashions for Women* (1927), in which a pushy female street urchin locks a rival in a closet in boosting her own incipient modeling career, to her final film, *First Comes Courage* (1943), in which a woman spy chooses honor over love, Arzner documented the lives of women at all phases of consciousness, wrestling for love, career, independence, integrity. George Cukor, "woman's director," sympathizes with his women characters. Dorothy Arzner, woman director, empathized with hers.

The girl dancing through Dorothy Arzner's *Dance, Girl, Dance* is Maureen O'Hara as Judy O'Brien, ingenue and Cinderella-like stooge to soubrette Lucille Ball's lusty burlesque queen, Tiger Lily White—also known as Bubbles. Stripper and stooge battle over love and career, discovering finally that they have no quarrel at all, their feud an adolescent hangover. The core of *Dance, Girl, Dance* is carefully hidden beneath an extraordinarily embellished plot, featuring romantic intrigues, gambling raids, song and dance, high and low comedy, unemployment, frustrated career opportunities, and a mandatory trial scene. When the excitements are stripped away, the film remains an intensely sensitive portrayal of the competitive yet finally sympathetic burlesque partners' relationship. More, it is the saga of a childlike woman, Judy O'Brien, growing up, conquering fantasy and self-doubt, to stand on the brink of a career as a modern ballerina.

Dance, Girl, Dance begins with Bubbles and Judy as lead dancers in a patchwork chorus line comprised of loyal students from Madame Basilova's faltering ballet school. Basilova, former prima ballerina of the Russian ballet, now grimly refers to herself as a "flesh peddler," because her studio, gone broke, is reduced to selling its dance line to the highest bidder. For this task Basilova depends greatly on Bubbles, the only member of the troupe with "oomph"— and "you can't learn 'oomph.'" So while Judy, the most talented one, choreographs ballet movements in her head, Bubbles, "the hard one," slaps her ass, gyrates her hips, and lands all the jobs.

This is the pattern of the movie: every time Judy wants something, Bubbles gets it. Take the hula job, for instance: Judy learns the steps, but there is no way she can match Bubbles's gut-level charisma. When Judy performs before "Hoboken," the screen's most swinish nightclub manager, he is unmoved by the classic ballerina's dignified rendition of Hawaiian dancing. He smirks, "Very neat— classy, in fact too classy. I'm running a drink and dance joint, not a kindergarten." Then Bubbles arrives. Gowned in furs and beads, she coos to the agent, "I ain't got an ounce of class, Sugar, honest." She flings her purse across the room, drops her stole to the ground, and pulls her skirt down toward her hips. She holds Hoboken's attention with her eyes, then wiggles in an outrageously calculated fashion, not in rhythm to the music, but in time to the simmering mood of the nightclub manager, who practically swallows his cigar watching. (All this time Judy cowers behind the record player.)

Bubbles rises quickly from Hoboken hulaist to featured act for the Bailey Brothers Burlesque, changing her name along the way to the absurd Tiger Lily White, and changing her address too: "I live on the Drive now." That is Riverside Drive, but it also means "the drive of ambition." She achieves fame and fortune while Judy's career seems demolished, over before it has begun. Unlike Bubbles, who never lapses in self-confidence, who is never out of verbal or physical contact with her audience, Judy is hesitant, paralyzed, hampered by nightmarish fears of failure. When given her chance,

Dorothy Arzner consults with Lucille Ball on *Dance, Girl, Dance* (1940). (Courtesy Dorothy Arzner)

an audition with the American Ballet Company, Judy flees in panic on witnessing a company dance rehearsal. "Today I saw what real dancing was," she states in awe. This "real dancing" is much more an expression of artistic maturity than of ability, a manifestation of the growth process Judy must experience before she can become a true dancer in spite of herself.

From the moment Judy accepts the job as Bubbles's stooge, she begins to change. She dances before the taunting burlesque audience night after night, loosening up, subtly discarding her inhibitions, all the while preparing for the moment of adulthood. It comes one night when she angrily discovers that Bubbles has married Jimmy Harris (Louis Hayward), the lover she herself has abandoned in dramatic self-sacrifice. This time Judy does not run away. First she walks onto the stage and stands, arms crossed, sternly reprimanding the jeering audience, "Go ahead and stare . . . get your fifty cents worth . . . I'm not ashamed. . . ." Then she and Bubbles engage in a real fist and hair-pulling fight. Judy sheds forever her role in life as everyone's "second banana." Judy has metamorphosed from passive, waiflike stooge into a forceful, dynamic personality. She is now ready to dance.

Dance. There are three different styles of dance in *Dance, Girl, Dance:* (1) Judy's spiritual classic ballet, the morning-star dance, is played against (2) Bubbles's sensual burlesque routine, and these are finally fused in (3) the futuristic style jazz ballet performed by the American Ballet Company. (The dances in *Dance, Girl, Dance* are not escapist; they are comments on the action of the film, never pure enterainment, although always—and Brecht would approve— entertaining.)

Judy's character is vividly expressed in her dance of the morning star, the one star, according to Jimmy Harris, that "keeps shining after all the other stars have quit." Judy literally sparkles, wearing sequins in her hair. And she is the only trouper from Madame Basilova's chorus line who never quits caring. After the others have gone home for the day, Judy dances jubilantly alone. While the other women sleep, Judy exercises long into the night, her shadow the last eerily moving figure in a darkened, nighttime world. She is magical, moving in exercise rhythms through her fairyland.

In these muted moments, Arzner photographs Judy alone, truly enchanted and beautiful, a transcendent image that counteracts the daytime Judy the Stooge, or Judy the Romantic Child. Yet Judy's problem remains that her dance, no matter how enthralling, is an escape from the world. The morning-star music, the soothing, haunting harmonies, intimate a child's bedtime music, a perfectly ordered and peaceful universe, free of the chaos of life.

Even when Judy steps out into the world, she carries her ethereal image with her. Arzner photographs Judy's reflection through the mahogany piano top in the burlesque hall as she dances her morning-star/stooge number. She looks the quintessential classic prima ballerina in flowing sequinned taffeta skirts. It is an exquisite but intangible image, almost translucent, unreal, as if it would disappear beneath waves of perfectly polished wood. Yet Judy's beauty is misplaced, a fantastical vision glaringly inappropriate to a smoke-filled room of peeping toms. Rather this is Bubbles's native environment, where the second style of dance—bumps and grinds—predominates. Bubbles, the philistine, dances not for artistic transcendence but for the money. She thus offers a complete alternative to Judy's philosophy of dance as she struts and teases and titillates the male audience. She feeds the egoistic male fantasy, enabling them to "play at being the stronger sex for a minute."

But the third style of dance, performed by the American Ballet under the direction of Steve Adams, asserts the notion that dance, indeed any art form, should not be used as escape, by either the dancer or the audience, but should attempt to meet the contemporary world with eyes open. Steve Adams is a brand of futurist. He choreographs jazz ballets about "American life today," about mechanics, aviators, and he insists, "If I ever see another bird dancing, I'll shoot it." He reprimands those art-for-art's-sake choreographers, "Haven't you ever heard of factories, cafeterias, telephones?"

In the jazz ballet Judy witnesses on her traumatic visit to the American Ballet Company, a woman, much like Judy herself, dances among weirdly shrouded figures in a cloistered atmosphere, then falls asleep to awaken in a downtown, urban environment like the New York City to which Judy has traveled. While the ballerina lies in a deathlike trance in the foreground, the other troupers appear wearing modern apparel, the flamboyant stripes and polka dots of the city. The music jazzes from sedate balletic tones into the upbeat tempos of the city: police and fire sirens are underscored by resounding, trumpeted Latin American beats, with an occasional hurdy-gurdy refrain of "East Side, West Side" thrown in (the same "Slaughter-on-Tenth-Avenue"-type music played during a montage sequence when Judy first arrived in the city).

The dancer awakens, looks around in confusion, then trades her ballet outfit for urban wear, including gloves and a feathery hat (although she is still a dancer, for she keeps the ballet slippers on her feet). At the close of the number, she is carried off triumphantly above the other dancers: her victory is because of her chameleonlike ability to adjust to urban life. She sits confidently high in the air atop the sunshiny city setting, thrusting a parasol above her head.

Arzner's counterpoint at the end of this scene is Judy at her lowest, most despairing point. The rehearsal has crushed her: she is barely able to speak as she scurries out of the ballet company offices. She walks into a pouring rain, without umbrella, without a dime (she literally crawls into a metaphoric gutter, fishing for a last, lost coin). As she stands soaked in the rain, adding a cold to her miseries, she seems irretrievably distanced from her jubilant dancer persona inside the theatre.

Songs. The singers in *Dance, Girl, Dance* function as balladeers, using the songs refrained through the film as narrative comment about Judy. "The Morning Star" song, for instance, is crooned in the background on Judy's last, fateful nightclub date with Jimmy Harris. The words, "We flew too high; now it's time we descended," float over their conversation, foreshadowing their imminent breakup. The song also provides turgid comment on Judy's morning-star existence. Her head is in the stars, literally and figuratively, and she must descend to earth. The song also tells her "You are alone now," and Judy soon finds the truth of pronouncement when she leaves Harris forever to his drinking, partying, and estranged wife.

Bubbles's songs during her burlesque act are also indirect musical comments on Judy. Bubbles's song "Jitter Bug Bite" concerns a proper-speaking, dehumanized woman who has mastered her Dos and Don'ts: "I never, never slip . . . I try to be a lady day and night." Yet underneath lies a figure of sensuality who can be aroused by melody. ("When I hear music, I get the jitterbug bite.") The message for Judy is to allow music to melt her rigid, reserved exterior. She must merge herself with the pulsing beats of the modern city.

Bubbles's second song, "My Mother Told Me," taunts Judy the bewildered child: "My mother told me what to do, but she didn't tell me how." Madame Basilova, like the mother in the song, told Judy, "Dance, dance, dance," as she was dying, but she didn't hand over the important details of how Judy should realize her career.

Judy, like the confused woman in the song, doesn't know what to do "when the cold wind blows." She runs away rather than force her destiny.

But there is another Judy in development. When she first is humiliated as the clown of Bubbles's act, Judy thinks only of escaping. But, in a moment of striking resolve, Judy decides to stay on, learning to take her "boos and hisses as part of the game." Immediately after this momentous decision the most incredible montage sequence of the movie begins: Bubbles's press releases stream together with shots from Judy's proper ballet juxtaposed against Bubbles's steamy strip number. In the midst of the montage, this melodic line on the sound track leaps out at the viewer: "My mother told me, always count to ten. And if that doesn't do the trick, start over again." Here, in a musical phrase, is Judy's answer to "what to do." She must follow the sound advice of that age-old saying: "If at first you don't succeed, try again."

This line from Bubbles lays bare the narrative structure of Arz-

Dorothy Arzner directs Maureen O'Hara in the courtroom scene of *Dance, Girl, Dance* (1940). (Courtesy Dorothy Arzner)

ner's movie, which is an exact working out of the film's most elemental theme: trying again. *Dance, Girl, Dance* is divided into two
distinct and parallel parts, the second repeating, with important
variations, the events of the first. The first section is a chronicle of
Judy's failure to succeed as a dancer, while the second half shows
Judy's journey toward adulthood and career. In many instances, the
events in the second part of the picture are an improvement for
Judy on the corresponding happenings of the first half. In no case is
the second event a regression, as Judy is growing constantly
through the movie, becoming better able to cope with her problems.

First Part

1. Judy harassed by someone
in the audience: Jimmy rescues
Judy and protects her. He passes
the hat among the raiding police
so she and the other chorines
will be paid for their work.

2. Jimmy leaves with unex-
pected woman: He meets and
talks to Judy but leaves the
nightclub with Bubbles.

3. Apartment scene: Eleanor
Harris, in the process of divorc-
ing Jimmy, comes home late at
night to find him sleeping in her
apartment after his date with
Bubbles. She offers him a drink;
they quarrel; he leaves without
drinking. Her maid is present.

4. Bubbles gets something
Judy wants: Bubbles gets hula
job for which Judy auditioned.

5. Traumatic experience:
Madame Basilova dies. Judy left
alone must take a leap toward
adulthood and independence.

Second Part

1. Judy harassed by someone
in the audience: Jimmy rescues
Judy and protects her. He chastises the burlesque audience for
laughing at Judy.

2. Jimmy leaves with unex-
pected woman: Bubbles thinks
she will leave with Jimmy, but
he sneaks off with Judy.

3. Apartment scene: Jimmy
Harris, the night his divorce is
complete, comes home to find
Eleanor sleeping in his apartment, after his date with Judy.
He offers her a drink; they
quarrel; she leaves without
drinking. His butler is present.

4. Bubbles gets something
Judy wants: Bubbles marries
Jimmy.

5. Traumatic experience:
Fight with Bubbles on the burlesque stage, marking the death
of the child Judy.

6. Scene at the offices of the

6. Scene at the offices of the American Ballet Company: Judy runs away from audition believing she has no talent, then runs away from Steve Adams, who tries to pick her up on the street. She doesn't know he's the manager of the company.

American Ballet Company: Judy almost runs away but doesn't. She is about to become a professional dancer. She is last seen cradled in the arms of Steve Adams. She learns his true identity: as manager of the ballet company and her teacher.

Running away. Claude Lévi-Strauss makes a comment about myths in *Structural Anthropology* that is pertinent to the repetitive form of *Dance, Girl, Dance:* ". . . the question has often been raised why myths . . . are so much addicted to duplication, triplication or quadruplication of the same sequence . . . [T]he answer is obvious: repetition has as its function to make the structure of the myth apparent."

Dorothy Arzner relates her story about "not running away from yourself" following this strategy of reiteration. She contrives six incidents in which Judy is faced with the decision of running or staying. The increasingly intelligent manner in which Judy keeps solving this dilemma shows vividly and simply the way toward maturity: (1) Judy runs away from the dance studio after witnessing the rehearsal. (2) Judy runs away from Steve Adams after their encounter on the street. (3) Judy almost runs away from Bubbles, but stays on. (4) Judy *correctly* runs away from Jimmy Harris. (5) Judy almost runs off the burlesque stage, but stays on. (6) Judy almost runs away from the dance studio, but stays on.

The first two incidents occur in the first half of the film and prove erroneous decisions. Judy flees the dance studio without even attempting an audition, then she escapes from Steve Adams, which is symbolic of deserting her career. The other incidents occur during the second half of the picture, and the decisions of Judy inevitably reveal improved judgment. She decides to remain on with Bubbles that first night as stooge, the ramifications of which have been discussed. She wisely departs from Jimmy Harris because he continues to love his estranged wife. She almost runs off the burlesque stage after discovering Bubbles has married Jimmy Harris, but stays to deliver her blistering attack on the audience. At the end Judy almost regresses and runs away again from Steve Adams and the dance studio, but she endures, finally ripe to tackle her dance career.

Cinderella. The quasi-fantasy sequences revealing Judy alone at night dancing and wishing on a star are incredibly similar in texture to a Walt Disney fairy tale, almost mistakable for animation despite the live woman and the real settings. The reason for this strange resemblance makes perfect sense when it is realized that Arzner's movie is a kind of fairy story, and that Judy is undeniably a modern cinderella figure. She pines not only for a Prince Charming gallant lover, but also for a platonically perfect dance career, the latter equivalent to promenading eternally around the floor of the king's ballroom. Bubbles, the foil of Judy, is akin to the two wicked stepsisters rolled into one, jealously grabbing away Judy's men and exploiting Judy's talents while making sure her genteel "little sister" rival remains hidden in the background.

Cinderella (at least in the Disney movie version) dances with the mice in the attic while her wicked sisters cavort at the ball. Judy dances alone in Madame Basilova's attic while Bubbles hulas upward toward her burlesque career. Yet miracles happen: the fairy godmother spies Cinderella's secret dance and transforms mice, rats, and pumpkin into coachmen, silver white stallions, and golden coach so that Cinderella can attend the ball. Madame Basilova, who clandestinely watches Judy's private choreography, telephones the American Ballet Company and arranges an audition for her star pupil.

After cautioning Cinderella to be home by midnight, the fairy godmother vanishes into air. Madame Basilova advises Judy, "dance, dance, dance," before dying after being hit by an automobile. Cinderella participates in full glory at the ball, dancing and beguiling Prince Charming, yet fleeing on orders at the stroke of midnight (and losing her famous slipper in the frantic dash out the castle door). But Judy watches her "ball," the ballet rehearsal, from the sidelines, behind a protective door. And when Judy flees, it is out of personal fear, not necessity; she leaves hanging not only her dance career but also her Prince Charming, Steve Adams, who is forced to chase her throughout the rest of the movie. The camera focuses on Judy's fleeing feet as she runs, panicked, down the street. The only element missing is Judy's shoe falling onto the pavement!

In the end of the fairy tale, Cinderella and Prince Charming are reunited, of course, embrace, and live happily ever after. The slipper fits Cinderella's dainty foot. But Arzner's conclusion offers no such simple and perfect ending. The embrace of Judy and her Prince Charming is bittersweet at best, as Judy laughs and weeps simultaneously, slumped exhausted onto Adams's shoulder. Is this person Judy's absolute romance, her true Prince Charming? Will Judy become a great dancer, succeeding at "the ball"? Arzner reserves answers. There will be neither wedding bells nor a command dance performance in this movie.

The tortoise and the hare. The rivalry between the slow, plodding Judy and the flashy, meteoric Bubbles is reminiscent of another folk tale—Aesop's race between the tortoise and the hare. The hare, of course, sleeps along the path to the finish, and the tortoise, the crowd's sentimental favorite, wins the race. Arzner's conclusion differs sharply, but rather generously, from that of Aesop. Although Judy closes the gap and threatens to take the lead in this battle for fame and fortune, Judy and Bubbles still end in a triumphant tie (that is, after the climax in blows) rather than as winners and losers. Dorothy Arzner could allow for no other way. The director's indulgent attitude toward Bubbles comes close to matching in affection her deep feelings for Judy.

Structurally, Bubbles is set up to be the villainess of the piece. Yet Arzner clearly is seduced by Bubbles's flamboyant manner: the way she slinks and swaggers and smirks, leading with her hips, swaying her shoulders, a parody of sexuality that is, nonetheless, sexual. She is enamored of Bubbles's steamy sauntering across the burlesque stage, kneeling over the ramp to chat with the men in the crowd with the easy intimacy of one inquiring for a match.

Bubbles also displays tremendous talent, another reason she deserves admiration. She is a burlesque star not only because she can flirt with style, but because she can sing, dance, and knock hell out of an audience by her inspired trouping. These positive traits take the edge off Bubbles's hard, calculating side as an out-and-out gold digger who uses men mercilessly for dollars and career.

Just as Dorothy Arzner photographs Judy's private moments with persuasive empathy, so too she offers favorable intimate peeks into Bubbles's character (these remain masked from the other persons in the movie). Bubbles's self-proclaimed role is to be ruthless, selfish, soulless, a woman hating, and hated by, others of her sex. But the film audience knows that Bubbles's totally witchy persona is qualified, even contradicted, by rare but genuine moments of virtue. If she exploits her female cohorts without blinking, Bubbles also is shown by Arzner secretly paying the other women's rent and asking Hoboken to hire not only herself but all the dancers in Basilova's troupe.

Dance, Girl, Dance thus offers, in effect, two heroines, a good one and a bad one. (Judy is the center of the film; Bubbles is slightly off-center—as well as being off-color!) And they both try, try, try and ultimately succeed in getting what they want. Judy wins a career (and maybe a lover), and Bubbles gets fatty rich, hauling away fifty grand in an alimony settlement. At the end of the film Bubbles is about to apologize to Judy for her crude behavior, an incredible show of trust in rendering herself vulnerable. But Judy is too much of a pal to make Bubbles reveal anything humiliating. So, with almost nothing said, everything implied, they part, bound together in an adult friendship at *Dance, Girl, Dance*'s finish line.

Coming of age. Dance, Girl, Dance belongs to a significant group of movies that have dealt with the "coming of age" theme, showing a young woman's rise to independence and maturity in terms of the quest for a dramatic career. The constant theatrical setting for the action of these films is not too surprising. Film studios have avoided controversy by keeping women struggling in the one profession that has accepted them as equals, more or less, since the eighteenth century. Yet despite their conservative base, the theatrical "coming of age" films belong to a genre type rich in possibilities, capable of allowing for great varieties of experience and subtleties of message within its form.

All films of this type, however, build from the same stirring central image, that of the single woman "making it" on the stage by stepping through to success over the literally dead or dying bodies of those who held the spotlight before her. The actress/dancer learns to sacrifice everything personal that might hold her back from her career, not stopping for lovers or friends. She conquers her own fears and childish sentimentality, seizing all opportunities without regret. And though this way to the top may seem cold and cruel, she cannot look back or stop along the way.

At the end of *Morning Glory* (1933), Katharine Hepburn is told, "You belong to Broadway, to lights . . . You've got to think of yourself now and not of anything or anyone else in the world." In *Stage Door* (1937), an actress on the verge of suicide because Katharine Hepburn has won away her role, comments with histrionic stoicism, "I've had my day in the theatre, now Kerry deserves her part." Even as the actress's body is carted off to the morgue, Hepburn's Kerry steps into the spotlight without missing a beat and recites the coveted lines, a necessary act of courage approved and cheered by everyone in the theatre.

All such films gradually push to a philosophical theme beyond the coming of age one. When Hepburn proves so dramatically that "the show must go on" in *Stage Door,* she also demonstrates that "life must go on," rejuvenating itself through the young and talented who keep performing, going on after the crippled and dying have vanished. In Ingmar Bergman's *Summer Interlude* (1950), Maj-Britt Nillsen continues dancing even after her young lover has smashed himself by driving onto the rocks, finally purging herself of the terrible memory of his death. And Diana Ross's Billie Holliday keeps singing the blues after Piano Man has been murdered. (Sometimes the party on the decline bravely pushes the sad transition along. James Mason walks into the sea, allowing a star, Judy Garland, to be born. And most beautifully and profoundly of all, when youthful Claire Bloom, literally a flower in bloom, pirouettes into the *Limelight* [1952], it is old age, the old way, the old star, Charlie Chaplin, who succumbs in the wings to allow her unhampered room to breathe and grow.)

Dance, Girl, Dance fits squarely into this long line of female coming of age in the theatre movies. Judy moves step by step through the initiation process before being sworn in, as it were, to the sisterly ranks of womanhood, a process of maturation seen metaphorically through Judy's increasingly serious concentration on achieving her dance career, overcoming adversity and death along the way. Judy learns: (1) to put her dancing before loyalties, leaving behind the less talented and dedicated Basilova troupe; (2) to place dance before love, dropping the romantic dabbling with Jimmy Harris; (3) to make unpleasant sacrifices to advance her career, like dancing in the burlesque house; (4) to move forward despite the death of Madame Basilova; (5) to put dance before any sentimentality, rendering that magical moment with Bubbles only a moment, for she must return to her dance lessons.

If Arzner adheres to the basic narrative pattern of the coming of age movies, endorsing the central thematic point that "work should come first," there is also a parting of company from the mainstream meaning. Normally all artistic endeavors—singing, dancing, playing the violin—are interchangeable pursuits. The form of expression is not important: acting Shakespeare is more or less equivalent to tap-dancing. What is taken seriously is only the metaphor itself of Young Woman as Artist. Not only does the show go on, but art goes on, life goes on. Artists die, but art is immortal, passed from generation to generation by the female bearer, carrying forward the Olympian torch.

In the usual coming of age in the theatre movies there is a supreme moment, the last evocative visual image, with the woman finally alone on the stage, reciting her lines or dancing a lush and lovely solo. It is a moment out of time, the visual moment of maturity. However, *Dance, Girl, Dance* ends unexpectedly with the more ambiguous image previously mentioned: Judy, laughing and in tears, in Adams's arms. In a traditional theatrical movie there would be a dissolve to a final shot of Judy twirling in a Keatsian ode to timeless, ahistoric art. For Arzner, such is nonsense. Immortal art is for the birds, the dancing-bird balletists whom Steve Adams threatened to shoot. Likewise, Arzner would sneer at the irrelevant thunder-and-lightning melodrama in which Hepburn "carries on" so nobly in *Stage Door*, just as she rejects Judy's closet ballet. What must be judged is the particular nature of the chosen career. More important than immortal art is today's art, a career not in touch with the gods, but with the contemporary world. That is what Arzner tells us in all her films.

In her celebrated early sound Paramount film, *The Wild Party*
(1929), Clara Bow, a silly wastrel jazzing and flitting through college, is advised that "real freedom" (like Judy's "real dancing") can
be won only through serious work. Ultimately, however, Bow and
her anthropologist professor lover leave behind the rigid ivory
tower, bastion of aesthetics, to journey out into the field where
genuine learning can be accomplished. (Who else but Arzner has
ever put forward a serious conception of the nature of education
within the context of a Hollywood film? Already in 1929, she was
presenting a radically Rousseauian vision to contemplate: to be
educated means to participate in life, not to sit back in a university
and swallow other people's knowledge. And true art demands the
same active involvement by both creator and audience alike.)

Seen in this context, Judy's contemptuous put-down of the burlesque audience is more than an antimale speech. It is a startling,
pointed rebuke to those who misuse art as a decadent mode of escape. Each night Judy confronts a searing, hideous image: anonymous faces in a darkened burlesque hall, gazing with erotic longing
at women whom they know they cannot possess. The voyeurs goggle
and dream, the only break in their passivity occurring when they
erupt into derisive catcalls aimed at Judy or whoever else plays the
stooge. On this particular night, the hostility goes too far.

When the strap breaks accidentally on Judy's top, the audience's
juices flow. While she attempts to fix it, they chortle, "Don't you
think we can take it?" And when Judy's problems are compounded
by a mannequin prop falling on her head, the audience cackles
maliciously, "Are you going to cry now little girl? Are you going
home to Mother?"

Judy neither cries nor runs away. She turns—wry, cool, very de-
liberate—and stalks to the end of the runway, the place where she
never has dared venture. She folds her arms before her, stares
straight at her hecklers, and launches her attack:

> Go ahead and stare. I'm not ashamed. Go ahead and laugh, get
> your money's worth. We're not going to hurt you. I know you want
> me to tear my clothes off so you can get your fifty cents worth.
> Fifty cents for the privilege of staring at a girl the way your wife
> won't let you. What do you think we think of you up here with your

silly smirks your mothers would be ashamed of? It's a thing of the moment for the dress suits to come and laugh at us. We'd laugh too, only we're paid to let you sit there and roll your eyes and make your screamingly clever remarks. What's it all for? So you can go home and strut before your wives and sweethearts . . . play at being the stronger sex for a minute? I'm sure they see through you just like we do!

This utterly remarkable and abnormal speech is not only a phenomenon coming forth from Judy, but without parallel in the whole history of cinema. There is little wonder that it is followed by shocked silence by those sitting in the burlesque audience, perhaps surpassed only by the amazement of those in the film audience upon hearing the burning, articulate words on the screen.

When the quiet is broken, the deed is performed appropriately enough by a woman, who stands up in the burlesque house and applauds the accuracy of Judy's rhetoric. Certainly the man-hating surface of the speech appeals most instantaneously to another woman, and this feminist bond cannot be denied. But probably more important, the woman fan is an employee of the American Ballet Company; her approval shows that Judy is acknowledged to be ready for her big break, to become that "real" dancer long prophesied but never yet realized.

Unbelievably, Judy still manages to entangle herself in the fist-fight with Bubbles, a trip to night court, and a stay in jail before finally being ushered through the portals of the American Ballet Company. She walks past secretaries and into the inner office as if her being there was the most natural thing in the world, her destiny and sovereign right (no one seems to remember her missed appointment of many months earlier, when Judy ran frightened and perhaps forever from this same office).

As Judy stands at long last at the end of the maze, she comments, "If I had only known how simple things could be . . . I've just got to laugh." And Judy begins to cry, recognizing the heavy irony of her statement.

The intricate paces of maturation required by Dorothy Arzner are so enormously demanding and complex that they seem hardly containable in one film. But they are contained in *Dance, Girl, Dance.*

The Divided Woman:
Bree Daniels in *Klute**

Diane Giddis

INTRODUCTION

In their manifesto film, A Letter to Jane *(1972), Jean-Luc Godard and Jean-Pierre Gorin mock Jane Fonda's tortured facade as Bree Daniels in* Klute, *deeming it a disingenuous Hollywood spectacle, the combined distortion of "Stanislavsky and show biz." They accuse Fonda of focusing indiscriminate attention on the strikers of* Tout va bien *(1972), the villagers of North Vietnam, and the cop of* Klute. *Yet feminist filmmaker-critic Michele Citron found a different significance in Fonda's face—not the castrating stare of American imperialism felt by Godard and Gorin but an important mirror to feminist struggles. "*Klute *was the first film that made me cry in five years," Citron stated bluntly in* The Velvet Light Trap. *Diane Giddis sides with Citron in considering Jane Fonda's characterization both emotionally stirring and intellectually provoking. As she stated in prefatory remarks for her original essay, "*Klute *seems to me to have more to say about women (and men) than any film of the last two or three years."*

. . . Bree Daniels is not self-consciously "liberated," or even struggling with self-definition. If anything, she is going in the opposite

---

* Reprinted from *Women and Film*, 1, nos. 3 and 4 (1973).

direction: from a brittle but genuine self-sufficiency to love and dependence on a man. Yet in her tormented journey she succeeds in embodying one of the greatest of contemporary female concerns: the conflict between the claims of love and the claims of autonomy. For the emotional tug-of-war that Bree acts out—between the urge to give and love on the one hand and the fear of loss of self on the other—is a very common female conflict, and one that seems particularly appropriate to our time.

More than a contemporary reworking of the private eye movie —as some critics have seen it—*Klute* (1971) seems closer to the psychological suspense thriller, with most of the action going on inside the central character's head. *Klute* is told from a highly

Jane Fonda and Donald Sutherland in discussion with Alan J. Pakula, director of *Klute* (1971). (Courtesy Warner Communications)

subjective viewpoint, and the other characters, although "real," can be seen as projections of the heroine's psyche. The film functions on both levels, as a straight suspense story and as a dramatization of intense inner conflict, but it is from the second level that it derives its power.

The first shot of the film is of a tape recorder, innocuously eavesdropping on a lively, sunny dinner party where a man and his wife warmly toast each other. This happy scene immediately yields to a shot of the same setting, now dark: the man, who is believed to be somehow associated with Bree, has disappeared. The credits that follow are superimposed over a shot of another tape recorder, from which Bree's voice issues. Bree is thus immediately linked with the opposition of light and dark, love and fear.

The girl of the tape recorder—the prostitute—materializes as an aspiring model; we first see her in a lineup at an audition for a commercial. We later see her, having failed to win the job, arranging an appointment with a john via telephone. With these opening strokes the filmmakers establish the acute ambivalence, the unremitting conflict that is Bree's motif through the rest of the film.

Bree articulates this conflict in a later scene with her therapist, where she confides that the only time she feels she is exercising any control over her life is when she is turning tricks. Only by controlling clients can she feel she is controlling herself. Yet part of Bree needs to give up control, too; hence her attempts at modeling and acting, at escaping "the life." But these gestures of escape only engender helplessness and vulnerability, which in turn must be counteracted by turning tricks: the audition followed by the phone call. Bree equates losing control with danger, a danger she nonetheless constantly courts; as director Alan Pakula has pointed out, although Bree is a frightened girl, she lives in a rooftop apartment— with five locks on the door.

When Klute, a small-town cop investigating the disappearance of his friend, enters Bree's life, her conflict intensifies. Klute's arrival signals the possibility of a different way of life for Bree, but it also brings the anonymous threat that stalks her into sudden, palpable life. In fact, that threat, Bree's potential killer, can be seen as the incarnation of the emotional danger presented by Klute. From the beginning the two men are almost always shown in juxtaposition. The morning after Bree receives a "breather" call from her tormentor, Klute makes his first appearance in her life. He is preceded by a curious shot: of the skylight on the roof above Bree's apartment—the roof, that, along with the telephone, is the concrete locus of her fears. But several factors neutralize the shot, strip it of ominous overtones: the skylight is photographed from *inside*, its white lines (as opposed to the black of the outside) form an almost abstract pattern, and it is morning. Nevertheless, the juxtaposition implies a connection, which is strengthened by Bree's first sight of Klute through the peephole, his face distorted by the view.

Typically, Bree's demeanor on this bright morning is in marked contrast to her lonely vulnerability in the dark of the night before. She peers at Klute from behind a chain on the door, hostile and arrogant. (The lock that protects her from physical danger keeps out Klute as well.) Pakula emphasizes the antagonism Bree feels toward Klute with constant crosscutting between the two. Klute counters by tailing her, spying on her—"getting the goods" on her so she will cooperate with him in the investigation. Although his intentions are the opposite of her pursuer's, his methods are the same.

The two men are identified with each other throughout the film. The second time Bree and Klute meet, the killer is shown watching them through a gate ascending the outside stairs from Klute's basement quarters to her apartment inside. He is always shown to us or heard by Bree in conjunction with Klute's appearance in the scene.

Many reviewers have noted this correspondence between Klute and the killer (whom we later learn is Peter Cable, the missing man's employer), but not in the light of their respective—and parallel—roles as lover and killer. Yet no matter how one interprets the film, it is undeniable that the physical danger Bree is in increases in direct proportion to her involvement with Klute. As her attachment to Klute grows, Cable progresses from disembodied (and silent) telephone presence to anonymous voyeur and rooftop visitor to a fully materialized (and vocal) would-be murderer. The closer Bree gets to losing control emotionally, the closer she gets to losing her life.

For Bree, losing control *is* losing her life—as she knows it. Bree equates giving with giving up (of self), dependence with danger, love with death. She can only counteract by trying to kill what wants to kill her: at the point when the physical danger is closest, she attacks Klute with a pair of scissors.

That Klute is the real focus of Bree's fears is indicated in several scenes. In the course of their search for the missing man Klute and Bree visit Arlyn, once a friend of Bree's when both were full-time call girls. The sight of Arlyn, now strung out on drugs and clinging to an equally hooked boyfriend, horrifies Bree, driving her out of the apartment and later out of the car in which she is riding with Klute. She runs wildly away, only to turn up later at a former hangout, a discotheque patronized by her old friends and her ex-pimp, Frankie. When she walks in, she is stoned, sweaty, disheveled —looking very much like Arlyn did earlier. She crawls into Frankie's arms, staring defiantly back at Klute, who has followed her there. (The abrupt close-up of Klute looking at her is truly frightening; the distinction between Klute and Cable is never more blurred than at this point.) Her return to a life that now appalls her—that, in fact, apparently led to the scene from which she flees—can only be understood as an act of self-assertion, of denial of what Klute promises/threatens. The image of Arlyn, desperate and dependent, is to Bree a vision of what will become of her if she yields to a man. Arlyn is associated with dependency, and dependency with death: Arlyn is eventually killed by Cable (later Cable plays for Bree a tape recording of the murder).

Bree makes a later, more serious attempt to return to her former existence after her apartment is almost literally raped by Cable. Klute walks in to find her preparing to go off with Frankie. Again Bree stares defiantly back at him. In a previous scene we saw her in bed with Klute after the incident, stonily turned away from him as he calls her name. Frightened though she is, instead of clinging to Klute she repudiates him, seeming to hold him responsible for what has happened to her.

But if Klute can be seen as a projection of Bree's simultaneous need and fear of losing control, Cable can be seen as a projection of the need to maintain control. Cable, like Klute, serves a dual function: he is both what she fears and what she is, or would like to be. There are several parallels between Bree and Cable. As Jonathan Stutz has pointed out in *The Velvet Light Trap* (no. 6), both seek power and detachment, both divorce "the sexual act . . . from its emotional charge by turning it into an act of will." Cable is emotionally numb; Bree tries to be. At the height of her involvement with Klute, she tells her therapist that she would like to "go back to the comfort of being numb again." Their sexual impulses bring them both to violence—Bree against Klute, Cable against Bree and two other women. After Bree comes home to her mutilated apartment, the voice on the other end of the telephone is not Cable's, but Bree's (which Cable had captured earlier, by tape recorder). Their voices are virtually interchangeable.

But Cable's most striking similarity to Bree is his apparent urge to endanger himself. He engages Klute to find the man he himself has murdered, thus reviving an investigation that had reached a dead end. He watches Bree from the roof while Klute is there, provoking a rooftop-to-cellar chase in which he is almost caught. He thrusts himself more and more conspicuously into Bree's life as Klute gets closer to uncovering the identity of the murderer. Like Bree, Cable needs as much to lose control as to maintain it.

As much as the two principal men in the film, the whole pattern of *Klute* reflects Bree's duality. The loving or vulnerable Bree is shown constantly alternating—and sometimes coexisting—with the manipulative or defensive Bree. Frightened by a noise on the roof, she comes down to Klute's basement room, and they later make love. But having exposed her vulnerability, she must now reassert her detachment: she informs Klute that, like the rest of her johns, he has failed to satisfy her. As before, she assumes the role of prostitute when threatened. Yet the sequence doesn't end there: her exit from Klute's apartment dissolves to a shot of her lying in her own bed again, alone and miserable.

Images of death follow images of love: Klute ascends in an elevator to the storage section of the morgue, where he inspects the possessions of a dead woman; Bree gazes tenderly at Klute from across the room, drawing him over to her bed; Arlyn's wrapped body is fished from the river.

The use of Bree's voice is especially effective in revealing her divided impulses. Bree's words often belie her actions. We hear her tell her therapist that her fear of Klute makes her angry, makes her want to manipulate him, while we watch her returning his caresses. Later, in bed with Klute, she warns him not to "get hung up on me," as she embraces him. Bree's voice also contradicts itself: her discussions with her therapist, often heard in voice-over, offset the tape recordings of Bree as call girl that Cable obsessively plays. The hesitant, searching voice of the former, signifying growth, is answered by the sure, controlled voice of the latter, signifying inertia. (The tape recordings, variations on a theme, could have been made at the same session—and probably were.)

Most paradoxically of all, as Bree—through Klute's influence— moves further away from her life as a prostitute, she gets increasingly closer to it—again through Klute. With him she revisits several places and people from her old life, including a madam who tells her, "You'll always have a home here." Her two escapes to Frankie are in each case both a flight from reminders of that life and a return to it. As she tells her therapist, "I was trying to get away from a world I had known . . . and found myself looking up its ass."

But this circular flight represents ultimate progress, for it leads Bree to a confrontation of her fears. Her first real gesture of commitment to Klute begins the succession of events that brings her face to face with Cable. From a vantage point outside her apartment window, we hear her turning down a prospective john on the telephone while Cable (her own hovering fear and doubt?) watches from behind the gate. Bree and Klute are then shown on a leisurely shopping trip in the most extended scene of mutual tenderness in the film, a tenderness ruptured by the return to Bree's violated apartment. Later, Bree attacks Klute when he tries to stop her from leaving with Frankie. She rushes out and eventually seeks refuge in a dress factory, looking for one of her clients, a gentle old man. But he is gone, and after everyone else leaves, Cable tracks her there.

Bree Daniels (Jane Fonda) crossing a New York street in Alan J. Pakula's *Klute* (1971). (Courtesy Warner Communications)

Just as he is about to kill her, however, Klute rushes to the rescue, and Cable falls out the window.

Klute—the healthy, giving, loving side of Bree—appears to have triumphed over Cable—the malignant, fearful, unfeeling side. Cable's death signals the start of a new life for Bree. At the end she is leaving New York for a small town in Pennsylvania with Klute, apparently giving up prostitution for good. She seems to have emerged from her dark night of fear unified, whole.

But Bree remains stubbornly ambivalent to the end. The shot immediately succeeding Cable's leap out the window is of the skylight, again from the inside, again white and ambiguous. This is followed by the image of Bree sitting at Klute's feet. Perhaps the conjunction implies that Klute has exorcised the demons. But again the voice-over contradicts: Bree is explaining to her therapist that she has told Klute it wouldn't work, that she could never settle down and live his life, etc. That, of course, is negated by the final image of her departure with Klute from her apartment. But the voice-over persists—"You'll probably see me next week"—and, most interestingly, she is wearing the same clothes at the end that we saw her in at the beginning, when she made that first phone call.

Klute, then, is the story of a woman and her battle not *for* love but *with* love—and, as such, would seem to have particular relevance for women today. Yet most of the critics have ignored this aspect of the film; while recognizing Bree's emotional odyssey as its main concern, they have largely interpreted it in moral terms—that is, the "good" woman triumphs over the "bad." Although this is a valid reading of the film on one level, it ignores the psychological basis of Bree's conflict and its wider application. For *Klute*, whatever its conscious purpose, seems nothing less than a metaphor of the intense struggle many women go through when they find themselves getting involved with a man, usually (but not always) in the initial stages of a relationship.

When it occurs, this battle between opposing emotional forces is one of the most dramatic in a woman's life. On the one hand is the progressive invasion of another's identity that seems to jeopardize one's own (as Klute jeopardizes the Bree who is in control of herself and of others); the conscious and unconscious modification of one's personality (her apartment, which is closely identified with Bree, twice progressing from wild disarray to order; her first refusal of a trick); the painful acknowledgment of need (her difficult admission that she is going to miss Klute); the gradual exposure of the self and its blemishes (Bree allowing Klute to see her "mean," "whorey," "ugly"); the giving and taking of trust and concern (Bree accepting Klute's care in the aftermath of her self-destructive night with Frankie; later, on their shopping trip, entrusting herself to him, following his lead as she tugs at his jacket).

On the other hand is the fear of loss—of self-control, independence, wholeness (Bree's various flights and retreats); the dread that the need, allowed to assert itself, will never be fully satisfied or reciprocated (her question, "You're not gonna get hung up on me, are you?," is really a warning to herself); the doubts about one's worthiness to receive love (Bree's disbelief that Klute can accept her after seeing her at her worst). And all the various forms of reaction: wild anger, willed detachment, hysterical self-assertion, blind denial of the legitimacy of another's reality.

This is putting it all in extreme terms, of course, and most struggles are seldom so overt, or even so conscious, as Bree's. In most women, I suspect, the resistance takes one or more disguised forms: sexual inhibition (the most common); sexual infidelity, with another or several men; irrational jealousies (which are in effect a repudiation of the man's belief that the woman is worthy of serious, exclusive attention). Or it may take the guise of some "external" obstacle, like family opposition.

The avenues of ultimate retreat are also devious: marrying another man; leaving town; or driving the man away—either by delivering an ultimatum he can't or won't meet ("Marry me or else!") or fighting him long and hard enough—that is, becoming a "bitch." And there is always the most insidious and classic cop-out of all—the sudden or gradual loss of interest, the short-circuiting of the emotions. This is an extreme but popular resolution: it has the virtues of being unconscious, unanswerable, and usually irreversible.

Of course, self-awareness aside, not every woman experiences the conflict to the same degree. But whatever its nature and extent, the struggle *is* primarily a female phenomenon. Most men just don't seem to go through the agonies, the violent oscillations of emotion, the frightened givings and retractions that women do—at least not in the same way and certainly not with the same frequency. It's partly a matter of style: a man generally practices a more passive kind of resistance, dropping out for a while either physically or emotionally. But mostly it's a matter of intensity— the struggle is not as dramatic because it is not as vital. For men, however much they may love, simply do not have to make the kind of commitment women are called upon to make; they are not expected to give, and therefore to lose, as much. Or to give *up* as much. Apart from the deeper emotional investment, a woman parts with much more of her identity than a man does. This involves more than the obvious concessions—going where the man goes, living *his* life-style, sacrificing her job to his when necessary. More insidiously, a woman's personality tends to get absorbed in the man's; to a greater or lesser degree, she suppresses —or represses—those aspects of her personality that don't happen to fit his. This is seldom a conscious process; very few women are aware of their assimilation in the man, although they may observe it in others. But women *sense* this potential in a relationship, this possibility of being swallowed up, and it is an important factor in their resistance to involvement.

In any relationship, of course, a certain sacrifice of autonomy, of self-determination, must be made by both partners, but even in the age of dawning liberation the balance between men and women is still way off. And the more a woman has a life or mind of her own, the greater the sacrifice seems. In a sense, her identity is more precarious; it is a thing arrived at. A man's identity is more established; it is not as "cultivated," as solicitously hovered over. Small wonder if, like Bree, women associate losing their identity with accepting love, for when their "Klute" wins out over their "Cable," they give up part of themselves in the process.

This is certainly true for Bree at the end of *Klute*. Granted that Bree's surrender, tentative as it is, represents a positive growth on her part—surely it is better to be loving and feeling than to be exploiting and exploited—the film's facile assumption that Bree should be the one to follow Klute into the sunset is revealing. After all, as Bree herself admits, what is there for her in Tuscarora (Klute's hometown)? Certainly her chances of realizing herself there are almost nonexistent. Why didn't the filmmakers end the movie with the couple going off, say, to San Francisco, where Bree might have a better chance of making it, not only with Klute, but with herself? The answer is that Klute's life is in Tuscarora; if Bree can't make a go of it there—well, that's her failure. In the movies, as in real life, it's still a man's world.

The film's final image says it all: Bree turns down a john, presumably for the last time, picks up her belongings, and walks out the door with Klute. The last shot is of Bree's bare room—totally stripped, except for the telephone, of all reflection of Bree.

Belle de jour*

Kathleen Murphy

INTRODUCTION

For film critic Joseph McBride, the "glacial beauty" of Belle de jour *is "an ironic cloak over a cesspool . . . Buñuel's disciples go into ecstasy when the impeccably pure Deneuve is pelted with cattle dung . . . , for the story is nothing more than the gradual lapse of a creature of seeming purity and elegance into a world of insane violence and seeming degradation." (*Montage, *Madison, Wisconsin, November 19, 1970)*

Interestingly, some feminists have defended Belle de jour *against this interpretation of Buñuel's misogynist purposes. Joan Mellon stated in* Film Heritage *that "It is extremely difficult to think of . . . fine films about women—films which treat women with dignity and respect and yet are well-made. At the top of any such list I would have to place . . .* Belle de jour, *which examines the origins of the damage inflicted upon the psyches of us all." The essay below by Kathleen Murphy takes a softer, more casual feminist line. Far from McBride's brilliant, excitable reading of* Belle de jour, *Murphy offers a becharmed appreciation of Buñuel's erotic insights—taking us almost inside the sensitized skin of the heroine, Deneuve's Séverine.*

* Reprinted from *Movietone News,* no. 39 (February 27, 1975).

Belle de jour (1968) is a circular film, curving its way surely and urbanely through fantasy, memory, and whatever reality one can distill from Luis Buñuel's surrealist solution. Probably the first bone of contention among critics of the film is how much reality, how much fantasy, and where each sector is located in this suave Buñuelian landscape. Depending on the reading, Catherine Deneuve's Séverine/Belle de jour may have fantasized the whole of the film with no anchors in reality, she may be engaged in an act of exorcism that finally leads her to a kind of normality, or she may have ultimately ruptured the fragile barriers between her conscious life and the world that shapes itself out of the darkness behind her brain. Whether Buñuel is hypnotist or mesmerizer is moot; whether he has plunged his heroine into the darkness of insanity or caused a sunrise, a coming to terms with reality, is also open to question. Considering the bland banality of Séverine's "reality," itself a kind of madness that Buñuel has never ceased to send up with a discreet but nonetheless devastating charm, can acceptance of such a life be considered enlightenment? Her fantasies may be kinky but they're certainly more fun, more richly devised and experienced, than anything that home, hearth, and hubby can provide. Perhaps what Buñuel has mesmerized Séverine (and us) into is a serenely crazy delight with the complete dissolution of distinctions like reality and fantasy into a rich warm soup blended of both. Buñuel knows what kind of spell movies may cast, and that we as viewers are not unlike Madame Anaïs's clients who buy the opportunity to frame and move and light their most private, cherished fantasies. Like Séverine, we turn from the peephole and exclaim in righteous disgust, "How can anyone sink so low!," a half-smile of perverse fascination playing about our lips. We should not feel diminished for all that, for Buñuel's discreet and amiable charm is all-encompassing; he subjects no one's fetish to contempt, only to the good-natured amusement of an old roué who is surprised by nothing, but is endlessly delighted with the conventions of bourgeois perversity. Consequently, we do not move from scene to scene in *Belle de jour* impelled by a sense of urgency that Séverine "get well" or go crazy with a vengeance; rather, we are satisfied with permission to participate in the picaresque sexual adventures she either fantasizes or realizes in her pilgrimage from neurotic innocence through exotic sin to that ambiguous "endgame" played within her mind.

From the moment that coach comes jingling down that autumnal landscape, we are seduced by Séverine's (and Buñuel's) vision of things: the coach moves slowly, but inexorably, toward us, taking a long time, but finally picking us up as it passes and carrying us on with it. It's all so plausible, and therefore well within the amenities, that this nice young couple who seem to be at sexual odds should suddenly begin to act out a pulp-fiction version of de Sade. In those brief moments of dialogue we are already a little contemptuous, exasperated with Pierre's insufferable "kindness," his wilting in the face of his ice-princess's frigidity. Secure in her little red dress of impeccable cut, porcelainized and remote, Séverine invites violation, mussing up. We cast our vote entirely with Séverine's unconscious, with its solution to her adamantine virginity. Dragged, stripped, whipped, and raped by the coachmen, Séverine apologizes to Pierre (at a figurative peephole) "It's not my fault"—what? her frigidity or the mode of her pleasure? "Don't let the cats loose," she begs— which under the circumstances verges on the hilarious, but also makes irrational sense since cats, in dream analysis, are associated with passion and sexuality.

Just when we're hoping that Pierre will indeed let the cats loose, we find ourselves ensconced in comfortable reality where Pierre goes dutifully off to his single bed and his little china doll gives him the clue to their sexual contretemps: "Forgive me, you're so kind." Husson, Pierre's friend, would get the message: as he ogles pretty girls at the ski lodge he muses "What punishments I am missing!"; and later, when his unacknowledged visit inspires Séverine to imaginatively replay this same scene, he will accompany her under the table with a broken bottle, the better to seduce her, while Pierre nervously inquires as the table bumps up and down, "What are they doing?" But then, Pierre is a Boy Scout, and Husson is . . . the Devil, perhaps, tempting Séverine out of her compartmentalized neuroses into the actualization of her sexual fantasies. (In his next movie, *The Milky Way* [1969], Buñuel would appropriately cast Michel Piccoli—Husson—as the Marquis de Sade.) That (real or imagined) movement is traced from fantasy (Séverine's legs, her

nylons pulled down about her ankles, dragging through a drift of
autumn leaves) through reality (her feet beside some spilled per-
fume) to memory (the little girl Séverine's legs, up which the
camera rises to view her passively receiving a workman's caresses)
to her smartly shod feet mounting the stairs toward Madame Anaïs's
establishment—which, according to interpretation, may or may not
be a real event.

Real or not, Séverine's ascent to the genteel brothel lets loose the
cats for her as Pierre's paternal tuckings-in never could. Almost
everyone at Madame Anaïs's place gets Séverine's number at once:
"What you need is a firm hand," says Anaïs, and shoves her back in
to Adolphe the candy manufacturer, who turns her on with some
"rough stuff." ("Forgive me, Pierre, you're so kind.") Ritual bath
and bra-burning over, Séverine dreams happily of black bulls (who,
like cats, have names like Expiation and Remorse). Husson inquires
of her husband "How's the soup?" and Pierre querulously replies,

Séverine (Catherine Deneuve) joins the women in Madame Anaïs's
(Geneviève Page, right) brothel in Luis Buñuel's *Belle de jour* (1968).
(Courtesy Allied Artists)

"It's cold and I can't warm it." "How's your wife?" Cut to steaming dung being shoveled into a can; soon Husson is slinging shit over the white-clad Séverine who assures Pierre (as usual) "I love you." Sex is all bound up with sin and pain for Séverine; in order to warm up, she must be besmirched, her passivity must be attacked and violently breached. Thus, she's badly cast as sadist to the gynecologist's masochist; even he is a much more active participant in his humiliate-the-butler scenario, egging "the marquise" on with bug-eyed confessions of broken vases and secret lechery, entreating her to step on his face, etc.

After Adolphe, who bears the gift of a spring-action snake-in-the-box, comes a smiling Oriental (with a Geisha Club credit card!) who further contributes to Belle de jour's sexual education with a mysterious something, also in a box, that buzzes. Whatever it is (and Buñuel allows our imaginations full rein), it draws blood, causing the little maid Pallas to murmur sympathetically to the prone Belle de jour, "I'd be afraid too. It must be painful sometimes." Séverine's pleasure-bleared face comes up from under that mane of blonde hair and, smiling secretly, she retorts, "How would *you* know?" She segues luxuriously into a full-fledged fantasy of necrophilia and incest, "a very moving religious ceremony" in which the cats almost get loose but the host fends them off by humping solitarily under his surrogate daughter's coffin. Home again, clad in her virginal, little-girl's nightgown, she crawls into bed with Pierre, who worries about *imposing* on her.

Marcel the thug, whose prop is a knife in a cane, marks a turning point in Belle de jour's fantasy life. He is more autonomous than any of the other characters. We see him at large with Hyppolite, free to act outside of the limit of Séverine's perception. Also, he is a fake, a failure at being a genuinely sadistic stud. His whole performance during their first encounter, his strutting arrogance ("Many would like to be in your place"—that is, in bed with him), his rejection of her because of her birthmark, is calculated to get him off the hook of actually having to *perform*. His vulgarity and sloppy dandyism stands in strong contrast to her upper-middle-class, impersonal chic. As he becomes more enslaved (remember Husson's reason for liking the brothel atmosphere: "women there are completely enslaved"), she begins to become more her own person, to behave with more animation and verve, almost as though she had created him as a kind of lightning rod to draw off some of her own obsessions and compulsions. Appropriately, after Husson's discovery of her secret life, it is Marcel who will force the collision of both worlds—if indeed they do collide. The quality of the sequence in which Marcel shoots Pierre and then does running battle with the police is pure melodrama, bad *Breathless* (1959), and might well be the sort of thing that Séverine would conjure up in her bourgeois mind's eye. I suspect that Marcel's appearance in her home (territory of the normal) dislodges some keystone of sanity in Séverine. The first shot after the hospital sequence is of a building that dissolves into banked autumn trees (the only dissolve in the film), that landscape in which Séverine's first fantasy of rape and humiliation took place. Inside a rain- (tear-?)streaked window, Séverine, dressed in a chic little nun's dress with a tiny white collar, ministers to her vegetable husband. Is this the expiation so devoutly wished for? "Since your accident I've not been dreaming," she tells him in his wheelchair. When one is wholly taken by the dream, then of course one would cease to believe one was dreaming. Husson's therapeutic truth is delivered while a clock chimes—always a signal that Séverine's perceptions may not be entirely in touch with reality. After Husson's departure, Séverine reenters, the camera following her around the room, Pierre remaining conspicuously out of frame. Finally, the camera reveals what she (and we) have avoided seeing: the effects of Husson's "kind" cruelty, tears wetting the cheeks of that blind face. She begins to do needlepoint (remember Anaïs's eloquent gesture explaining Belle de jour's popularity: "as easy as threading a needle"), then stops and looks at Pierre. Several disjointed, sharply cut shots of Pierre follow as though to visualize some seismographic shift in perception. Séverine smiles, bells ring, and comes the question with which the film began: "What are you thinking about, Séverine?" She continues the litany, "About you, Pierre." A cat meows; Pierre takes off his dark glasses and gets up. They embrace. Séverine goes to the window, serene, and watches the empty coach drive up the familiar avenue. It passes, moves on, and the camera holds on the russet leaves over which it drove. The passing of an obsession? Or the seamless merging of two planes of reality?

Love among Buñuel's bourgeoisie is fantastically convoluted, laced with equal portions of voluptuous sin and sterile virtue. Buñuel's people always seem to be locked within the strangest sorts of proprieties, so that even their breaches in polite behavior result in a kind of institutionalized outrageousness, or perversity. Séverine never sins very mightily, her fantasies are those of a "precocious schoolgirl" who hasn't yet read *The Story of O*. Like Giulietta Masina in Federico Fellini's *Juliet of the Spirits* (1965), Séverine's "problems" seem to have their origins (although far less directly) in her Catholic childhood. But whereas Juliet manages to free her "little girl" from the bondage of the past, thus freeing herself as a woman, Séverine moves from childhood to transitory womanhood and then falls back into playing little girl to Pierre's priestlike father, who at the end offers her a mountain retreat (as he earlier gave a vacation by the sea) as substitutes for excursions into sexuality at home. Sex in *Belle de jour* is always a matter of props and prods: snakes and buzzing in boxes, whips and belts, knives in canes, broken bottles, surrogates for the real thing. Certain proprieties of costume are necessary: keep the bra on; take off the bra, but leave on the pants; keep all your clothes on, dress up or down for the occasion. Each of the principals in this series of sexual vignettes refuses or is unable to get to the heart of the matter, to face and deal with sex unadorned or untricked-up. Even Séverine's tempter is rather put off by her gaffe, her fall from grace, as though he in his own way is just another pillar of the bourgeois community. In such a world, love, sex can only be an unfulfilled wound, and thus Séverine's vision of supreme pleasure always takes the form of mutilation or humiliation. That way you can pay for your pleasure while you're having it.

But Buñuel never savages the participants in this comedy of sexual manners; his camera inscribes circular movements about them like a noncompulsive voyeur with a kinkily cathartic sense of humor. He possesses an inimitable eye for the beauty of banality, the pornography of proprieties, and the sublime madness of civilized life.

Hollywood Heroines
Under the Influence:
Alice Still Lives Here[*]

Janet Maslin

On the evidence of *Alice Doesn't Live Here Anymore* and *A Woman Under the Influence* (both 1974), there is a liberal feminism afoot in Hollywood, perpetrated by hip youngish directors whose tackling of the subject recalls the ease and aplomb with which Lenny Bruce's white suburbanite approached his "colored friends" at parties. John Cassavetes's Mabel Longhetti and Martin Scorsese's Alice Hyatt may not exhibit many direct similarities, but both of these deeply distressed women appear incapable of really helping themselves, and both are presented with a compassion so extreme it's almost abjection. Although neither film attempts much explanation of its heroine's psychic makeup or initial circumstances, it is implicit that neither Alice nor Mabel is quite responsible for her own behavior. Each is depicted as a victim, and each can do no wrong.

I don't think these ably crafted *apologiae* fall within the realm of feminism, and I am therefore dismayed by some of the fanfare both have received. Must a film that simply centers on a female character be so loudly and perfunctorily hailed as a feminist tract? Ignoring their considerable dramatic merits for the moment, I don't like these films' assumptions that their heroines' resources are so meager; I don't like the way both women ultimately toss in the towel and are still somehow commended for their courage. There is, in each in-

* Reprinted from *The Boston Phoenix,* February 25, 1975. Reprinted by permission of the author.

stance, too much self-congratulation in the air, too much pride in what ought to be a less exceptional accomplishment. It's so easy for audiences of either film, but particularly *Alice,* to heave a sympathetic, cathartic "You've come a long way, baby." Maybe the Hollywood heroine *has* come a painful distance, although both of these otherwise excellent efforts demonstrate that she's still got a long way to go.

The moment that disturbs me most in *Alice* comes toward the conclusion. The recent widow of a truck-driving ogre, Alice (Ellen Burstyn) has set out to seek her freedom and fortune. But instead of fulfilling her maudlin show business ambitions—Alice's sickly-sweet dream is to be able to sing like Alice Faye—all she manages to land are a waitressing job and Kris Kristofferson. When, after

Tommy (Alfred Lutter, Jr.) interrupts the tranquillity of his mother, Alice (Ellen Burstyn), and David (Kris Kristofferson) in Martin Scorsese's *Alice Doesn't Live Here Anymore* (1974). (Courtesy Warner Communications)

prodigious billing and cooing, Alice and her beau finally quarrel (he thinks her son, who is twelve, shouldn't talk like a sailor; she thinks her son, who does indeed talk like a sailor, is nonetheless perfect), and when Alice stalks off in a tearful huff, it looks as if she may finally have to come to terms with the facts that (1) the kid *is* spoiled, and (2) so is she. It's a potential turning point and a very loaded moment, but the film fritters it away by making Kristofferson beg forgiveness and promise to change his ways. What on earth has he done? Only gotten tough with her, in a way that director Scorsese—who handles Alice lovingly but much too gingerly throughout—should have attempted to himself.

Alice doesn't have a chance to change in the film because she, her son, and their station wagon glide through the world very nearly unchallenged. People hurt her feelings, sure; bar proprietors are less than thunderstruck by her musical abilities, and Harvey Keitel, as a married though amorous psychopath, threatens to smack her around. But Alice's life is otherwise buffered, and in that sense it's quite cruel because she is so insulated from experiences that might be painful yet productive. The film opens with shots of her as a child, and even by the time it ends we can't be sure she's fully grown.

Ellen Burstyn is a wonderful actress, but she isn't Alice; she radiates too much cynicism and wit in the film's smaller moments to give in as easily as her character does in the big ones. She doesn't seem like a person who'd have so much pluck yet so little self-esteem, who'd be willing to take so much petty abuse. Is there really no professional middle ground between the stage and the hash house? Alice doesn't know; Burstyn comes off as someone who could and would find out. As Cybill Shepherd's tawdry, nihilistic mother in *The Last Picture Show* (1971), Burstyn elicited ten times the sympathy she does here because she wasn't playing dumb; she was a hardened quitter, not a spunky though submissive victim. True, her performance here is superb—the scenes with the son are particularly endearing—but it has to be isolated from the rest of the film to be fully appreciated. There are too many contradictions in *Alice*'s basic conception for the whole ever to measure up to the sum of its parts; regrettably, everything looks better out of context.

This is particularly true of Scorsese's direction. Here, even more than in *Mean Streets* (1973), he achieves some marvelous effects that pale only when one steps back to examine his methods. Alice is too warm a character to require the excessive sentimentality in which her efforts as a chanteuse permit Scorsese to indulge. And although it's as funny as it is touching, the film offers an overdose of cheap humor (e.g., Burstyn and Kristofferson conduct a very intimate conversation in a diner and then receive an ovation from the patrons). It works even though it shouldn't, because of Scorsese's innate vitality and the breakneck momentum he can generate. *Alice* doesn't match the fury of *Mean Streets*, but its very superficiality allows it to be lively and likable. The flaws emerge only in retrospect, after the joyride is over.

Like *Alice,* the graver and more profoundly affecting *A Woman Under the Influence* doesn't take shape until well after one has left the theatre. As with all of Cassavetes's work, it is as excruciating to watch as it is exciting—I suppose it can be argued that Cassavetes's rawest, most startling moments can be achieved only through the use of dull and flaccid episodes to connect them. Self-indulgent or not, he seems to aim almost deliberately at forcing the viewer to nod out every now and then, the better to emphasize the astonishing emotionalism of his methods. You don't so much see a Cassavetes picture as feel it; the visual and temperamental landscape is carved exclusively from the characters' tense, seemingly unstructured interaction. The most revolutionary aspect of his style is not his pretension to naturalism but rather his use of human behavior as a form of dramatic punctuation: the abrupt slaps, sobs, and epithets here serve the same purpose that cuts and angle changes might for a less obsessively humanistic director. Even his reliance upon sudden switches of focus feels more like impulsiveness on the part of the characters than it does a director's self-conscious caprice.

Cassavetes demands—and exacts—a lot of allowances from his audience. Just as his films have an erratic intensity that nearly makes their concomitant monotony worthwhile, the agony and frenzy of *A Woman Under the Influence* almost justify his decision to begin the film in mid-breakdown, with its heroine's madness an inadequately explained given. Perhaps he intended, in keeping the causes of Mabel's collapse obscure, to make hers a nightmare every woman in the audience could understand, with the vague underpinnings of her rage and horror meant to universalize the experience. In any case, it doesn't work, largely because Gena Rowlands—unlike Liv Ullmann or Joanne Woodward, who can sometimes function as Everywoman—is unique, and so grimly persuasive in her lunacy.

I'm still not sure what happens to her. Though the film loosely suggests that the "influence" of the title—of Mabel's husband, her children, her stifling societal role—contributes heavily to her instability, she has already taken one step beyond some ineffable psychic boundary by the time the film begins. Hauling around a spherical

Mabel Longhetti (Gena Rowlands) plays with the neighborhood children in a scene showing disintegration, from John Cassavetes's *Woman Under the Influence* (1974). (Courtesy Faces International Films, Inc.)

radio that resembles a ball and chain, making odd noises, wearing pink socks, and scratching herself with a fork, she is difficult to understand—not just for us, but for her husband, Nick (Peter Falk), as well. Although Rowlands, who isn't onscreen more than half the time, easily dominates the picture, it is the love, bewilderment, and frustration conveyed by Falk that open up the drama, lending it passion and accessibility. Unlike *Alice,* which winds up stereotyping its men in much the same way that less ostensibly progressive films stereotype women, *A Woman Under the Influence* creates a complete, if jumbled, panorama as it acknowledges that feminism and humanism are interdependent and inseparable.

I don't know of another actress who possesses the physical and emotional elasticity to skitter through Mabel's moods the way Rowlands does; the scene in which she finally falls apart, pulled screaming to the floor by her children and then cradled by her uncomprehending husband at the very instant when her mind snaps, is as blood-curdlingly authentic as anything she or Cassavetes has ever done. Yet Mabel is as exhausting as she is dazzling, and so utterly unreachable that I almost prefer Rowlands's repressed, straining characterization in her previous film for her husband, *Minnie and Moskowitz* (1971). Cassavetes's relative coherence in that effort, facilitated by its more mundane concerns, more tangible demands, and more linear structure, has been sacrificed to capture the hysteria of his current subject, a hysteria to which *A Woman Under the Influence* is doggedly sympathetic. There are only a few important moments that ring false, notably the happy-looking ending. We can't simultaneously accept Mabel's pathology and believe in her miracle cure.

Woman's sometimes undue tenderness for and consideration of Mabel are born out of the same excessive reverence that plagues Scorsese and *Alice.* Mabel's madness is given as holy a cast as Alice's Search for Tomorrow, and her failures are cushioned by the same familiar excuses, by the same easy air of helplessness and irresponsibility. How much more wrenching these women would be if they were not strictly victims, and if their weaknesses were tempered by a belief—both their creators' and their own—that strength and self-determination were not perforce beyond their grasp.

The Twilight of Romanticism: *Adele H.**

Michael Klein

Introduction

Three faces of François Truffaut: (1) the popular, beloved, charming entertainer à la Renoir, who adores children and lovesick adolescents who pine for women on a pedestal; (2) the moody Hitchcockian who tells morbid and misogynist tales of doomed, destructive love affairs; and (3) the surprisingly tough political thinker who, like other non-Marxist yet often "progressive" directors such as John Ford, Satyajit Ray, and Akira Kurosawa, juxtaposes his protagonists with the changing tides of history. Jules and Jim (1961) *shows courtship and marriage as mirroring the before and after of World War I Europe.* The Wild Child (1970) *is an almost Marxist tract, a parable celebrating the rise of civilization and the achievement of human progress.* The Story of Adele H. (1975), *far from being an apolitical melodrama of unrequited love, is best understood, as in Michael Klein's astute essay, as the story of women's rights ironically stopped short and suppressed by the great bourgeois antimonarchic revolutions of the nineteenth century.*

Coupled siamese fish swimming in the sad deep water.

—Guillaume Apollinaire

* Excerpted from *Jump Cut,* no. 10/11 (Summer 1976).

Adele H.'s life is an archetypal heroic but self-destructive romantic quest for perfect love in which the role of the male Petrarchan suitor is played by a "liberated woman." This is conveyed by the action, the many passages from her journal, which are spoken in a stream-of-consciousness manner, and by her dreams. At one point she writes "Love is my religion" in her journal. After Pinson continues to reject her she makes an altar—his picture, burning candles, incense—and prays to his image. She continually dreams about her sister's death by drowning with her husband during their honeymoon. Adele is haunted by the ideal of *Liebestod,* in which the identities of two lovers become completely fused: "The newlyweds are buried together—even death cannot part them." She reifies love.

Adele is a romantic heroine who dares to act like a Byron or a Shelley, and appears bizarre because nineteenth-century romantic culture granted this role only to men. Her actions become extreme as she is thwarted by social constraints, as she is driven to the point of madness by internalized cultural contradictions.

PATRIARCHAL ASSUMPTIONS: TRUFFAUT'S RHETORIC

François Truffaut very skillfully guides us to sympathy for Adele. From the early part of the film, when she is in Halifax chasing Pinson, her actions strike us and all the characters within as peculiar. Yet from midway, the characters in the film treat her with increasing respect (a bookseller, the family she is lodging with, a doctor), and we grant her greater significance, although her most bizarre actions (procuring prostitutes for Pinson, wandering about Barbados in a cape like a sleepwalker) occur in this latter half.

This is partially because Truffaut has provided information about the breach of promise. However it is primarily a result of everyone learning that she is the daughter of Victor Hugo that Adele gains respect within and without the film.

Truffaut's rhetoric is masterful. For as we realize our patriarchal bias—the woman becomes significant because she is the daughter of a famous male writer—we at the same time gain insight into the basis of her predicament (internalization of romantic ideals, the social and legal inequalities of nineteenth-century women). A sort of catharsis takes place. As Adele is driven further beyond the limits of normal behavior, we, through the understanding of the typicality of her contradictions, come to have greater sympathy for her.

THE PSYCHOLOGY OF CONTRADICTION

Adele's "madness" is a function of her attempt to achieve liberation within the matrices of a sexist trap, to live a life and forge an identity that is in fundamental contradiction and in turn reflects fundamental contradictions in society.

We have seen how Catherine's [in *Jules and Jim*] contradictions and internalization of romantic values compel her to act in destructive and seemingly extreme ways. In *Two English Girls* (1971) Muriel responds to similar tensions by becoming frozen into a constrained inactive life. After the failure of her early romance with Claude—his mother imposed a test period of separation—she retreats to a semireclusive life. Her attitude toward Claude vacillates between opposites—the apparent "irrational feminine" response has a logic, for it is a reflection of her acute situation. She pledges herself to Claude forever (in chastity). When he writes after six months that he wishes to live a free bachelor life, she replies: "I don't understand that expression. I'm not your sister but your wife. Whether you want it or not." However, before their separation she too resisted the ideal of marriage: "Claude, I love you. Everything is yours except what you ask of me." Subsequently she resolves to attempt to break loose of her total involvement with the memory of Claude: "I will no longer write this diary for Claude. If I do write one it will be for myself . . . I shall never marry." Later she does send her diary to Claude, yet after a very brief affair with him, moves on.

Adele also vacillates between the romantic ideal of complete fusion with her love (on patriarchal terms) and striking out to develop her own identity. On the one hand she pursues Pinson across the ocean, unilaterally offers to support him, unilaterally takes his name and attempts to live a form of *Liebestod* in which she is completely fused with the ideal of her lover. She writes to Pinson (after he has clearly rejected her): "My love . . . In giving

myself to you I become your wife . . . I am your wife evermore."
(This echoes Muriel's: "Whether you want it or not I am your
wife . . . exactly what you want.") Adele tells Pinson: "Do with
me what you wish." She asks her father to write Pinson: "Tell him
I'll be a dutiful wife." She literally throws herself at Pinson. She
adores him and walks through the streets to glimpse him passing.

On the other hand Adele also struggles to assert her identity
through tapping the independent strength that sustained her daring
violation of patriarchal conventions (her aggressively chasing the
object of her desire around the world). At times she taps this source
for entirely nonsubmissive ends. For example, note that Adele regards her journal as an important literary work—one night, in a
flophouse, she sleeps with it under her bed to make certain that it is
not stolen. She composes music, although her father does not en-
courage its publication. She travels incognito to ensure that if she
succeeds in getting Pinson, it will be a result of her own efforts. She
attempts to achieve artistic success in her own right—to liberate her
identity from patriarchal dependency: "I am born of a father completely unknown. I denounce the official records as a fraud of
identity."

Her struggle for liberation of necessity involves inconsistencies.
For example, she writes at one point in her journal: "My sisters
suffer in bordellos or in marriage . . . Let them have liberty and
dignity." Later she vows to come into her own as an artist in four
years, and claims to have rejected Pinson's proposal of marriage:
"My work needs solitude. I would never give up the name Hugo. It
is I who refused to marry him." Yet she goes to Barbados and gives
herself Pinson's name.

The elements of inconsistency and irrationality (her opposition of
the oppressive patriarchal Hugo identity to the submissive patriarchal Pinson identity, her claiming to have literally rejected Pinson's proposal, her many vacillations) are reflections of the acute,
internalized cultural contradictions that circumscribe and fragment
her quest for identity, liberty, equality, and dignity.

Near the end of the film, after Adele has been brought home from
Barbados, Truffaut in semidocumentary fashion moves from the
1860s to the time of her death, in 1915, during World War I—public

photographs of important events in Victor Hugo's life and a view of Adele's clinic take us up to 1915. Then Truffaut superimposes young Adele's face over the Halifax landscape, and has her speak exaltingly to us: "That a girl shall walk over the sea to the new world to seek a lover. This I shall do."

Adele has been portrayed as a heroic figure in a tragic situation: her quest for liberation springs from romantic ideals that, given a certain society, simultaneously stimulate and frustrate, inspire and destroy.

VICTOR HUGO: THE LIMITS OF THE BOURGEOIS DEMOCRATIC REVOLUTION

By the time *The Story of Adele H.* (1975) concludes, Truffaut has placed Adele's predicament in a political perspective: he defines the nature of the culture and society that has structured Adele's situation, that has oppressed her. In previous films Truffaut indicated that he regards certain dates as having some sort of historical significance. In both *Jules and Jim* and *Two English Girls* the World War I period is seen as a cultural watershed. In *Jules and Jim* the tone of the film drastically shifts away from lyricism at this point—the war, somber music, ominous cars, book burnings in Germany, deaths of Jim and Catherine being signs of negative historical development. In *Two English Girls* the film concludes with a somber epilogue that is set just after World War I. Anne is dead, and Muriel has disappeared from our view. Claude senses that he is old, that joy is passing out of life, that a culture that was once radical is waning. This epiphany occurs while he is attending an exhibition of sculpture—he recognizes that neither Rodin nor Balzac is now a revolutionary figure; they have been accepted by the establishment as public emblems of respectability. It is also significant, as we have noted, that Adele Hugo dies in this period, the war again being a point of demarcation.

Although Truffaut's signs are primarily implicit and superstructural, there is a correlation between the negative dates in his symbolic time scheme and what may be viewed as the beginning of the postwar decadent imperialist epoch. In *The Story of Adele H.*, Truffaut's symbolic history is especially clear. The film begins in

1863 and concludes in 1915. We are told by the narrator that 1863 is the period of the war against slavery in the United States. Adele's father, Victor Hugo, is not only the major French romantic literary figure of the century; Truffaut lets us know that he supported the revolutions of 1848, that he fought for the abolition of slavery in the United States and Latin America. During most of the action of the film Victor Hugo is in political exile because of his defense of the French Republic. In a documentary epilogue that concludes the film, Truffaut sketches Hugo's triumphant return to Paris in 1870, lists the political honors awarded him by the new Republic, and shows us a procession of two million people honoring Hugo after his death in 1885.

Truffaut indicates to us that Hugo's literary romanticism is an aspect of his bourgeois democratic world view. He clearly defines Hugo as a leader of the romantic cultural revolution, and as an active leader of the continuing bourgeois democratic revolutions of the nineteenth century. In Halifax Adele is in contact with a doctor and a bookseller—both discover her identity, and speak of her father's literary achievements. Later, after Adele goes to Barbados, an ex-slave recognizes her and writes to Victor Hugo as "a friend of the oppressed." Adele is then brought back to her father in Europe by a black woman who was once a slave.

Because Victor Hugo's links with the struggles of the oppressed and exploited are highlighted by Truffaut, we experience a shock of recognition: the daughter of an abolitionist and leader of the bourgeois democratic revolution is herself unfree. The gains of the bourgeois revolution (abolition of slavery, formal democratic rights in legal and cultural spheres, formal equality in the pursuit of happiness) have not been extended to its daughters.

Near the end of the film Truffaut informs us that Victor Hugo's last words were: "I see a black light." Truffaut gives us this information in context of the disclosure that Adele lived the remainder of her life in a mental clinic, withdrawn from the society that broke her spirit. The "black light" in part is a sign of Hugo's personal (patriarchal) failure, and that the democratic revolutions to which he devoted his life did not encompass the cultural, political, or economic liberation of women.

Swept Away[*]

Ruth McCormick

Raffaela, a rich, spoiled, stunning, Northern Italian blonde, hires a yacht where she is entertaining her bourgeois friends on a Mediterranean holiday. Gennarino, a sullen, hardworking, Sicilian Communist Party member, has been hired as one of the yacht's crew for this excursion. Aside from his resentment of the rich in general, Gennarino is particularly enraged by this strident, opinionated, bossy but sexy-looking female who treats him like a piece of animated furniture there to do her bidding. What happens when, through a peculiar set of circumstances, they are stranded alone on an island together? There have been Hollywood films about two unlikely prospects for romance stranded together on islands before but it's likely there never will be again. No one will ever see *Lifeboat* (1944), *On an Island with You* (1948), or *L'Avventura* (1959) (or, for that matter, *From Here to Eternity*, 1953) again in quite the same way after seeing *Swept Away by an Unusual Destiny in the Blue Sea of August* (1974).

Gallons of printer's ink have been expended in the last few months on Lina Wertmuller. Every major critic as well as a goodly number of feminist, radical, and radical-feminist writers have had their crack at Wertmuller. She's the hottest topic in the culture

[*] Reprinted from *Cinéaste*, 7, no. 2 (Spring 1976).

industry today. Her gift is for broad social satire and equally broad implications of the human tragedy that results from our inability to change society. Herein lies both the strength and the weakness of *Swept Away*.

The first half of the film is high comedy, wherein we cheer Raffaela's sallies against the men of her own class (who, and you have to understand Italian society to appreciate this, are Communist sympathizers), as we do Gennarino's little acts of revenge, like appearing to serve Raffaela's coffee in a sloppy, oversized but clean shirt after hearing her complain about his sweaty clothes. Both are presented as sympathetic, despite their shortcomings. Gennarino, for all his cuddly charm and honest working-class indignation, is a rampant male chauvinist. Raffaela, arrogant, bitchy, and consumerist though she be, is bright and clever—a warm-blooded woman who is a far cry from the frigid, snobbish upper-class mannequins played poorly by Grace Kelly and well by Stéphane Audran. (Even as a "bitch" she's more Roz Russell than Bette Davis.) His complaints about her bossiness lose some of their validity when put in the context of his general opinion of women—it infuriates him that her husband allows her to stay up after he retires, drinking and playing poker. Her anti-Communism loses some of its reactionary character when we realize that she's talking about the only Communism she understands—reformist and collaborationist at best, brutal and repressive at worst, in any case, hypocritical. There's almost nothing Raffaela doesn't miss in her constant talking—pollution, abortion, concentration camps, the Catholic Church, Stalin, Hiroshima. At one point she makes the remark that "The world was changed by people with servants. I'll bet Marx had at least three," in a tone less of irony than of self-defense.

On the ship, and even adrift in the boat, Gennarino and Raffaela play by one set of rules: boss and worker. Once on the island, the master-slave relationship is not negated but merely changes emphasis. Where property rules, its owners make the rules; in a "natural" setting, brute strength takes over. In either case, domination is not natural but determined by social indoctrination. In "civilization," Gennarino obeys Raffaela because he is being paid to do so; it is his means of survival, like it or not. On the island, Raffaela, not only because she is a woman but also because she has always been able to pay others to work for her, is helpless and must obey Gennarino if she is to survive. At this point, they become like comic strip characters and you know exactly what will happen. Even the sado-masochism some critics find so offensive in the film is a game; whereas at first she played "boss," Raffaela now plays "woman." Gennarino tells her, "You are so beautiful when I beat you." She tells him, "You are man as he must have existed in nature." If he seduces her with masterful machismo, she seduces him with flattery. The things they say to one another are things they were conditioned to think long before they ever had the opportunity to say them to anyone and, aside from a little unpleasantness, they seem to be having a hell of a good time.

Raffaela, for all her assertiveness, must have read and heard a

Raffaela (Mariangela Melato) and Gennarino (Giancarlo Giannini) at peace on the island of Lina Wertmuller's *Swept Away* (1974). (Courtesy Cinema 5)

million times, as all we women have, of the joys of femininity and total sexual surrender. Gennarino, on the other hand, sees the winning of Raffaela as expropriation of bourgeois property. The genuine affection that develops between them is the only really natural thing that happens, and that is mistaken for romantic love, both by the two characters and many in the audience.

In a sense, it is probably true that Gennarino represents a Stalinized communist movement that still clings to outmoded notions of authority, and Raffaela, a feminist movement that still speaks only to relatively privileged women. From the way she continually snipes at the male friend who tries to defend the CP, ignores her own husband, and taunts Gennarino, we might gather that Raffaela is not any better disposed toward men than her antagonist is toward women. She may actually hate men as much as he does the rich. Both have their reasons. When she threatens him with arrest, as soon as they are rescued, for "withholding help," he answers that in that case the rich should all be jailed. When he throws the lobster into the fire rather than offer it to her, asserting that "you rich burn food to keep prices up," he's right but she's equally within reason when she objects that *she* didn't do it, so why take it out on her?

Those who object to the film on the grounds that it makes either workers or women look bad are missing the point. Her sarcastic jibes injure him no more than his fisticuffs do her. Although it is true that it is sexual attraction that finally brings them together, there has been a jocularity to their fighting all along. If she is "tamed" by his sexual prowess, he, the tiger, becomes more and more the pussycat. Until the final moments, the film remains basically a farce, although we are always aware of the underlying property relations that made these two the way they are.

In any case, when that crude reality finally intervenes, the real political point of the film is made. Raffaela does not desert or betray Gennarino; it is pure romanticism to suppose that any woman, let alone a rich one, would be able to leave her secure life to devote herself to a penniless worker who will, under Italian law, be forced to give everything he earns to the wife and kids. Escape back to the island? Ridiculous. *Swept Away* is a fable about oppressed people— he, as a worker, she, as a woman. Both are as much victims of their own illusions and prejudices as they are of the society that predetermines their lives. Only an "unusual destiny" brings them together at all, and their idyllic interlude, during which their real false consciousness is never challenged, remains in the realm of dream and in no way serves to change the reality of the world in which they must live.

Wertmuller proposes the problems, not solutions, and attempts to entertain us while stripping away the romantic myths with which we have all been fed. The fact that she has become so popular with those who have no interest in or sympathy with social change, at the same time enraging many of those who do, points less, I believe, to her lack of sincerity than to the fact that she has not yet really succeeded in coming to any conclusions herself. It's also possible that *Swept Away* is too amusing. In her efforts to enthrall and entertain us, Wertmuller, intelligent though she is, appeals more to our guts than to our brains and perhaps thereby suffers more from the emotional responses of her critics than from their rational evaluation. In this sense, a large portion of the audience is as "swept away" as Gennarino and Raffaela and, like them, develop no new perspectives but are reinforced in their old ideologies.

Ten That Got Away

Jeanine Basinger

Feminists generally agree that the average red-blooded American girl grew up at the movies, the place where she found her ideas about love, marriage, and her role as a woman. Much effort has gone into analyzing the negative influences these films have had on several generations of women. Few have talked of the considerable minority of Hollywood pictures with positive portraits—women who remained true to themselves throughout the films' running times. Although these films do not necessarily have happy endings nor are they always overtly feminist, it is possible that some of the courage and energy that has fueled the women's movement may have originated, however subliminally, with them.

In selecting a sample list of ten such works, I have defined a positive portrait as any one of these: (1) A woman who defies conventional roles and redefines her life on her own terms, even if she opts to become a wife or a wife and mother. The process of questioning is what is valued. (2) A woman who defies, more than just convention, society itself, never settling for less than possession of her own life, even if she is destroyed in the fight. A man who fights this way is a hero. Why not a woman? (3) A woman who, by choice or accident, finds herself in a situation or profession that commonly would be restricted to male participation, and she functions ably in this situation. (She must not be caricatured as choosing this endeavor because she is "unwomanly" or "frigid.") (4) A woman who forms and maintains a positive sisterly relationship or a healthy mother/daughter relationship.

National Velvet (1944). As acted by the exquisite, still preadolescent Elizabeth Taylor, Velvet Brown demonstrates the freedom and character young girls possess before sacrificing these virtues to become young women. (Angela Lansbury, playing Velvet's boy-crazed older sister, provides a striking contrast.) Velvet loves to ride horses but she is "feminine," not made into a tomboy. The tomboy character has come to stand for the prefeminine aspect of a woman's life, with a common assumption that, as soon as she matures sexually, she will give up the nonconformity and set her hair in curlers. With Velvet, there is every indication that she will maintain her admirable identity through adolescence and into adulthood.

National Velvet contains a model mother/daughter relationship. Mrs. Brown (portrayed by the formidable actress, Anne Revere) works in the butcher shop alongside her husband and manages the family's accounts. But once she was a champion channel swimmer. In a touching scene, she takes Velvet into the attic where she keeps her mementos and makes her daughter the gift of the prize money she once won. She tells Velvet that everyone ought to have a dream and a chance to realize it.

Velvet Brown enters her horse in the Grand National steeplechase and, when the men desert her, she courageously crops her hair and rides the horse to victory herself. The achievement is all the more striking because, on screen, a female jockey of any age is a rare creature indeed.

The Shocking Miss Pilgrim (1947). Feminists search the filmographies of Hepburn, Crawford, Davis, and Stanwyck for liberated women. None of them thinks to look into the films of the famous World War II pinup girl, Betty Grable. Unlike her Twentieth Century-Fox predecessor, passive Alice Faye, who often was ditched by men and then masochistically awaited their return, Grable took

Velvet Brown (Elizabeth Taylor) and King Charles in Clarence Brown's *National Velvet* (1944). (Courtesy Wisconsin Center for Film and Theater Research)

precious little from the opposite sex. More likely she ran off and left them, after she disarmingly flashed her gorgeous smile and allowed a peek at her famous legs.

One of the most extraliberated women on the American screen is Grable's Cynthia Pilgrim in *The Shocking Miss Pilgrim*. She is one of the first "typewriters" (secretaries) in the United States, and she invades a totally male domain with flowers and smiles, trim ankles and twitching bustle—and ability. Whatever the men can do, Cynthia does better. When her boss tries to ridicule her by setting her up to speak at a suffragette rally, Cynthia goes forward and sweetly, confidently, wins over the audience—boss included. Her male coworkers end up respecting her and her boss falls utterly in love.

Cynthia Pilgrim is as pretty as a box of candy tied with ribbons and ruffled to a fare-thee-well. She dreams about romance. But she defines herself by her profession and does not abandon it. The ending of this pleasant, minor musical finds Cynthia the head of her own business college, cheerfully finding for her former boss a new secretary to take her place.

A Woman Rebels (1936). Katharine Hepburn plays a Victorian girl who defies both her father and the restrictive social conventions of her time. Choosing a bounder (Van Heflin) to be her lover, she becomes pregnant while unmarried. After he deserts her, she is able to survive the personal disaster through her strength of character, although she is conveniently bolstered by family wealth. A series of plot complications enables her to keep and raise the child as if it were her dead sister's. After returning to England, she realizes that girls less fortunate than herself are ruined by similar situations. With consciousness raised, she starts a feminist newspaper and devotes her life to women's rights. She refuses to marry an ardent suitor, preferring to dedicate herself to the causes of liberation and sisterhood. She finally chooses matrimony but on her own terms, not those of romantic fancy. As always, her life is shaped by her goals and ideals.

Westward the Women (1951). This begins as a traditional genre film in which the leading man (Robert Taylor) and the leading lady (Denise Darcel) represent one of the gloomier cinematic examples of macho male dominance over a willing female victim. But within the film is a second and parallel story of a group of extraordinary women who take a wagon train west to start new lives. They are estranged from an eastern society that has brought them pain and disappointment, but their unhappy backgrounds are nothing against the long and hazardous journey in which they must perform "as if they were men." The women cope with weather, hostile Indians, impossible environments, their own sexual natures, personality conflicts, and even Taylor, the woman-hating wagon master himself.

Although their journey is taking them West to become brides, the arrival of the women is a triumph that proves their equality to the men awaiting them. "We'll do the choosing" dictates one woman, and it is clear to the audience that they have earned the right. This

Desperate Rosa Moline (Bette Davis), trapped in the small town of King Vidor's *Beyond the Forest* (1949). (Courtesy Wisconsin Center for Film and Theater Research)

is a truly feminist film, which has broken the conventional Western genre mold.

Beyond the Forest (1949). "You're something for the birds, Rosa," says a character in *Beyond the Forest* to the central female figure. But Rosa Moline (Bette Davis) is a desperate woman who never stops fighting convention or trying to get out of the hick town where she lives.

Rosa is strong-minded and outspoken. However, her horizons are limited. Her ideas of being different from other women are to own a mink coat, to hang her windows with Venetian blinds, to serve chicken à la king at dinner parties, and to initiate a clandestine love affair with a masculine power figure from Chicago. She intuitively knows that being a woman in a small town is a one-way ticket to hell. "Go, go, little fishie," she tells a trout her husband returns to the stream, "get out while you've still got the pep."

Rosa nearly gets away herself, but she is stopped by an unwanted pregnancy. "See it on me?," she asks her husband by way of an announcement of the impending child. "It's the mark of death." Rosa does everything she can to abort herself and finally achieves her goal. Yet by trying to get up too soon after losing her baby, Rosa dies just short of the railroad tracks, still trying to get out of town.

The opening titles for *Beyond the Forest* refer to Rosa as a creature of evil and explain that an audience sometimes has to see evil in order to understand it—to see a woman, scorpionlike, sting herself to death. Modern audiences may feel more like cheering Rosa. Even though she looks a mess, commits murder, and dies desperately, she fights. She never quits. Rosa Moline is a hero.

My Reputation (1946). In one of the most touching portraits of an American woman on film, Barbara Stanwyck plays the wealthy widow of a successful and strong-shouldered man. (He is never seen. The film opens following his funeral.) Her husband's death has left Jessica Drummond lonely and lost. The children are going away to boarding school. What is she to do with herself?

Her mother offers the ritual suggestion. Jessica should put on black, roll bandages for the Red Cross, lunch occasionally with female friends, wait for the children's vacations—and that's that. It was the life the mother, herself once a young widow, accepted—a modern equivalent to the Indian ritual in which the woman throws herself on the funeral pyre. Jessica tries to be a dutiful daughter. But after suffering a near breakdown, Jessica forces herself to take a vacation with friends.

While skiing in Idaho, she meets a raffish Army major, a man who is footloose and fancy free and definitely not approved of by her mother, her social crowd, her children—and almost not by herself. He makes gentle fun of her prudery, telling her that women can be just like men: if they want it, they can have it. She should just let him know.

Jessica Drummond's ultimate decision to tell off those who want her to live by their rules is a positive step, and a kind of liberation. Her decision—she insists on marrying her lover instead of running off with him—is a conventional ending but represents a breakthrough in that she follows her own mind.

(*My Reputation* is similar to Douglas Sirk's great film, *All That Heaven Allows*, 1956, which also concerns a widow "walled up" in the tomb and expected to remain there.)

A Life of Her Own (1950). "Men have been buzzing around me since I was fourteen years old," says Lily James (Lana Turner) in *A Life of Her Own*. "I'm not interested. All I want is a chance to be somebody. To work. To have my own profession." She has worked five years to save up enough money to get out of Imperial, Kansas. "I won't be back," she tells a taxi driver as she hoists her suitcases and boards the train.

On her first night in New York, Lily doubles with a former model

Jessica Drummond (Barbara Stanwyck) visits the home of her strict and stolid mother (Lucile Watson) in Curtis Bernhardt's *My Reputation* (1946). (Courtesy Wisconsin Center for Film and Theater Research)

(superbly played by Ann Dvorak) marked by tragedy: she's beginning to lose her looks and has let her career go in order to be available for a man who has grown tired of her. The model commits suicide shortly after, leaving Lily James her "lucky talisman"—a glass slipper.

Lily James works hard and becomes the number one model in New York. After reaching the top, she finds her life lonely and empty. ("You don't really *do* anything in modeling," she muses. "People just sort of . . . *use* you.") When she meets that inevitable married man (Ray Milland), their romance follows the typical idyllic pattern of movie romances, with a jolly trip to the country, "their" song, "their" place, and champagne and roses. The conventions of the soap opera that are used include Milland's crippled wife, who suffers nobly in her wheelchair. (Milland cannot leave her because he was the one driving the car in which she . . . , etc., etc., etc.)

However, this typical "woman's picture" disintegrates effectively into a gloomy mess, with Lily getting drunk and running amok, and her lover breaking down as they cling hopelessly in a cloud of alcohol and tears.

Working back and forth between soap opera conventions and the reality behind those conventions, the film sinks deeper and deeper into despair. Lily fondles her glass slipper and contemplates suicide. Finally, in a display of remarkable courage, she tells her love that she can't live without him—but that she's going to try. She takes the glass slipper—that fairy-tale symbol of what women once dreamed of from their Prince Charmings—and, symbolically, smashes it.

Lily James achieves a sad and compromised freedom. After trying to let her career substitute for romance, she then tries to make romance itself fulfill her needs. Finally, she abandons both the idea of a career as a substitute for love, and love itself. The film's ending finds her broken, but "liberated."

Mannequin (1938). Joan Crawford was the rags-to-riches queen of the 1930s. Her films are remarkable for their combination of reality-fantasy, dark-light motifs in terms of the woman's role. The first section of this film is a stark portrait of a lower-class girl who

Lily James (Lana Turner) stares across the table at Lee Gorrance (Barry Sullivan). They are on a double date with Jim Liversoe (Louis Calhern) and Mary Ashlon (Ann Dvorak) in George Cukor's *A Life of Her Own* (1950). (Courtesy Wisconsin Center for Film and Theater Research)

makes a bad marriage and is stuck, dependent on a lazy and unreliable man. The middle section presents her courageous rejection of him and her fight to make something of herself. The final section is the dream of escape for the audience—she meets the rich father figure (Spencer Tracy) and finds true love.

Mannequin's most significant contribution is the relationship between Joan Crawford and her mother (superbly played by Elizabeth Risdon). Ma's tight-lipped face, grim and unsmiling amidst the revelers at her daughter's wedding, spells out the future.

In a striking scene the two women discuss the woman's role. Joan Crawford, as Jessica, has returned home from her exhausting job in a factory just in time to help her mother prepare supper for the two couples. It is a hot night and the women struggle over steaming stoves in the kitchen while their two husbands lounge in the outer room (neither man works), calling rudely for their suppers. The mother tells her daughter: "There are some things I've been wantin' to tell you . . . About what you've got and what you want. What a woman gets. A woman's supposed to lead the man's life. *Her* man's life. And women *are* made that way, occasionally. Woman's weakness is supposed to fit in to a man's strength. Her respect pays for the security the man gives her. But now you, Jessica, you've got strength of your own. You can do things. Not just dream about them like . . . like most women."

"What are you trying to tell me, ma?," asks Jessica.

"Make a life for yourself," replies the old woman. "Always remember what it is *you* want. Get it. Anyway you can. If you have to, get it alone."

Happy Ending (1968). Made at the beginning of the surge of national publicity for the women's movement, *Happy Ending* was more or less overlooked. Although not a great film, it is one of the first "new" movies to deal directly with the issue of the disintegrating housewife. Jean Simmons gives an Academy Award–nominated performance as a middle-aged woman whose romantic dreams of marriage (based on remembered images of Elizabeth Taylor in *Father of the Bride*, 1950) have faded into a haze of alcohol and loneliness.

Simmons plays a character who sits around watching old movies on television while she waits for her successful husband to notice her. She spends the rest of her time visiting beauty spas, quarreling with her adolescent daughter, and drinking. She finally gets a grip on herself long enough to become that phenomenon of the late 1960s—the runaway wife.

Her flight takes her on an unrealistic journey to the Caribbean, where she meets an old girl friend who is now the mistress of a wealthy and powerful man. (This couple ends up happily married in one of the film's major cop-outs.) She also becomes involved with an aging gigolo who has his own problems (falling hair, advancing age, etc.). When she returns home, she is sobered up and wiser.

Despite its meandering script and unclear attitudes, *Happy End-*

ing represents what women were thinking and feeling at a key point in history. And its thought-provoking ending is excellent. The heroine stands on the steps outside night school, clutching her books. Her husband (basically a kind man who has seen her through difficult times without judging her too harshly) asks her to return to him. Clinging to the books as if they were life preservers, she gazes at him candidly and asks, "Tell me one thing. If you had it to do all over again, would you still marry me?" As he instinctively hesitates, a small and knowing smile curves her lips—and she turns, walks away, and enters the classroom.

Roughly Speaking (1945). *Roughly Speaking* is a minor film, an example of just one of many forgotten titles that tells a story of a bright and eager woman who couldn't settle for anything other than a world of her own, even if she were married and had a family. Based on the autobiography of Louise Randall Pierson (who also wrote the screenplay and who personally selected Rosalind Russell to portray her on the screen), it is an overly long, episodic, but engrossing story that covers forty years in an American woman's life. The action begins just after the turn of the century when Louise is twelve years old. She is presented as a child of incredible determination, eager to make her own way, intelligent and forceful. She becomes a young woman who lives by the ideals of feminism. She works her way through a business college and plans her career. Temporarily sidetracked into a doomed marriage with a Yale man, she becomes the mother of five children. Her grit and determined feminism destroy the marriage, but she finds happiness with a man who accepts her as an equal, and who understands her need to do something with her life.

Roughly Speaking is sentimental, but it has humor and vitality. Louise Randall Pierson has been described as a woman who "would not have needed the aid of the women's liberation movement." She is not quite all that liberated, but she coped with society's restrictions as best she could.

There are other films that reveal strong portraits of women, many of them. Women courageous under stress in war time (*Cry Havoc,*

1943, *Three Came Home,* 1950, *So Proudly We Hail,* 1943); biographies of real-life heroines (*Madame Curie,* 1943, *Sister Kenny,* 1946, *The Girl in White,* 1952); women who succeed in politics (*Lady from Cheyenne,* 1941, *The Farmer's Daughter,* 1947); films that question the hypocrisy of the feminine role (*What Every Woman Knows,* 1934, *Quality Street,* 1937); films that show adolescent females on the brink of a positive self-discovery (*Home in Indiana,* 1944).

There are more than ten that got away, but, whatever the story, those who did it needed courage, determination, brains, and true grit—even at the movies.

Bibliography

Buñuel, Luis, and Carriére, Jean-Claude. *Belle de jour*. New York: Simon & Schuster, 1971.

Cook, Pam. "Approaching the Work of Dorothy Arzner." In *The Work of Dorothy Arzner—Towards a Feminist Cinema*. Edited by Claire Johnston. London: British Film Institute, 1975.

Cumbow, Robert C. "Une Femme Sauvage." *Movietone News*, no. 49 (April 1976). [*The Story of Adele H.*]

Durgnat, Raymond. "Buñuel: *Belle de jour*." *Movie* (Spring 1968).

Haskell, Molly. "*The Story of Adele H.*" *The Village Voice*, October 27, 1975.

———. "Women in Pairs." *The Village Voice*, April 28, 1975. [*Dance, Girl, Dance*]

Houston, Beverle, and Kinder, Marsha. "Madwomen in the Movies: Women Under the Influence." *Film Heritage* (Winter 1975–1976).

Johnston, Claire. "Dorothy Arzner: Critical Strategies." In *The Work of Dorothy Arzner—Towards a Feminist Cinema*. Edited by Claire Johnston. London: British Film Institute, 1975.

Kael, Pauline. "The Current Cinema." *The New Yorker*, January 13, 1975. [*Alice Doesn't Live Here Anymore*]

———. "The Current Cinema." *The New Yorker*, December 9, 1974. [*A Woman Under the Influence*]

Kay, Karyn, and Peary, Gerald. "*Alice* . . . Waitressing at Warners." *Jump Cut*, no. 7 (May–July 1975).

———. "Women in Film Pick the Ten Best Films About Women." *Film Heritage* (Winter 1975–1976).

Klein, Gillian. *"L'Histoire d'Adele H."* *Film Quarterly* (Spring 1976).

Kopkind, Andrew. "Hollywood . . . under the influence of women?" *Ramparts* (May–June 1975).

Macklin, Anthony. "It's a Personal Thing with Me: Interview with Marty Scorsese." *Film Heritage* (Spring 1975).

Martens, Betsy, and Webb, Teena. *"Alice* . . . A Hollywood Liberation." *Jump Cut,* no. 7 (May–July 1975).

McBride, Joseph. "The Ugliness of *Belle de jour." Montage* (Madison, Wis.), November 19, 1970.

Mellen, Joan. "Female Sexuality in Films." *Women and Their Sexuality in the New Film.* New York: Horizon Press, 1974. [*Klute*]

Rignall, John. "Alan J. Pakula's *Klute." Monogram,* no. 4 (1972).

Rosen, Marjorie. "Film: Who's Crazy Now?" *Ms.* (February 1975). [*A Woman Under the Influence*]

Sarris, Andrew. *"Belle de jour." Confessions of a Cultist.* New York: Simon & Schuster, 1971.

Sayre, Nora. *"Dance, Girl, Dance* Blends Rivalry and Sympathy." *The York Times,* January 29, 1975.

Stutz, Jonathan. "Sex and Character in *Klute." The Velvet Light Trap,* no. 6 (Fall 1972).

Wood, Robin. *"Klute." Film Comment* (Spring 1972).

II
Actresses

On Making Pabst's Lulu*

Louise Brooks

Introduction

Louise Brooks made her great films about half a century ago, at the end of the silent era. "I learned to act while watching Martha Graham dance, and I learned to move in film from watching Chaplin," she told Kevin Brownlow for an interview in The Parade's Gone By *(1969). She worked for James Cruze and Fatty Arbuckle, director, for William Wellman in his classic* Beggars of Life *(1928), for Howard Hawks in his first major "love triangle" movie,* A Girl in Every Port *(1928), and she was the American actress called to Germany for G. W. Pabst's blue-ribbon masterworks,* Diary of a Lost Girl *(1929) and* Pandora's Box *(1929).*

In recent decades she has lived alone in Rochester, New York, cut off from Hollywood except for the historical reruns at the George Eastman House. But whenever the impulse has struck, Brooks has embarked energetically on her second artistic calling: as a vigorous, free-lance journalist, specializing in firsthand think pieces on moviemaking. No teacup pleasantries here. Brooks is as stormy, defiant, and brilliantly unorthodox a writer as she was an actress, and she

---

* Reprinted from *Sight and Sound,* 34, no. 3 (Summer 1965). Reprinted by permission of the author.

tosses off these reminiscences with customary "devil may care" im-
prudence and impudence.

One foul day, Louise Brooks slung her unpublished memoirs,
Naked on My Goat, *down the incinerator. But luckily she has al-*
lowed some of her Hollywood tidbits to be printed—remembrances
of Bogart, Chaplin, Garbo, Gish, Wellman—and also this spicy
memoir on the making of Pandora's Box *in Europe.*

Frank Wedekind's play *Pandora's Box* opens with a prologue. Out
of a circus tent steps the Animal Tamer, carrying in his left hand a
whip and in his right hand a loaded revolver. "Walk in," he says to
the audience, "walk into my menagerie!"

The finest job of casting G. W. Pabst ever did was casting himself
as the director, the Animal Tamer of his film adaptation of Wedekind's "tragedy of monsters." Never a sentimental trick did this
whip hand permit the actors assembled to play his beasts. The
revolver he shot straight into the heart of the audience.

As Wedekind wrote and produced *Pandora's Box,* it had been
detested, banned, and condemned from the 1890s. It was declared
to be "immoral and inartistic." If, at that time when the sacred
pleasures of the ruling class were comparatively private, a play
exposing them had called out its dogs of law and censorship feeding
on the scraps under the banquet table, how much more savage
would be the attack upon a film faithful to Wedekind's text made in
1928 in Berlin, where the ruling class publicly flaunted its pleasures
as a symbol of wealth and power. And since nobody truly knows
what a director is doing till he is done, nobody connected with the
film dreamed that Pabst was risking commercial failure with the
story of an "immoral" prostitute who wasn't crazy about her work,
surrounded by the "inartistic" ugliness of raw bestiality.

Only five years earlier the famous Danish actress Asta Nielsen
had condensed Wedekind's play into the moral prostitute film *Lou-*
lou. There was no lesbianism, no incest, Loulou the man-eater de-
voured her sex victims—Dr. Goll, Schwarz, and Schön—and then
dropped dead in an acute attack of indigestion. This kind of film,

with Pabst improvements, was what audiences were prepared for. Set upon making their disillusionment inescapable, hoping to avoid even my duplication of the straight bob and bangs Nielsen had worn as Loulou, Mr. Pabst tested me with my hair curled. But after seeing the test, he gave up this point and left me with my shiny black helmet, except for one curled sequence on the gambling ship.

Besides daring to film Wedekind's problem of abnormal psychology, "this fatal destiny which is the subject of the tragedy," besides daring to show the prostitute as the victim, Mr. Pabst went on to the final damning immorality of making his Lulu as "sweetly innocent" as the flowers that adorned her costumes and filled the scenes of the play. "Lulu is not a real character," Wedekind said, "but the personification of primitive sexuality who inspires evil unaware. She plays a purely passive role." In the middle of the prologue, dressed in her boy's costume of Pierrot, she is *carried* by a stagehand before the Animal Tamer, who tells her, ". . . Be unaffected, and not pieced out with distorted, artificial folly, even if the critics praise you for it less wholly. And mind—all foolery and making faces, the childish simpleness of vice disgraces."

This was the Lulu, when the film was released, whom the critics praised not less wholly, but not at all. "Louise Brooks cannot act. She does not suffer. She does nothing." So far as they were concerned, Pabst had shot a blank. It was I who was struck down by my failure, although he had done everything possible to protect and strengthen me against this deadly blow. He never again allowed me to be publicly identified with the film after the night during production when we appeared as guests at the opening of an UFA film. Leaving the Gloria Palast, as he hurried me through a crowd of hostile fans, I heard a girl saying something loud and nasty. In the cab I began pounding his knee, insisting, "What did she say? What did she say?," until he translated: "That is the American girl who is playing our German Lulu!"

. . . Pabst's assistant, Paul Falkenberg, said in 1955:

> Preparation for *Pandora's Box* was quite a saga, because Pabst couldn't find a Lulu. He wasn't satisfied with any actress at hand

> and for months everybody connected with the production went around looking for a Lulu. I talked to girls on the street, on the subway, in railway stations. "Would you mind coming up to our office? I would like to present you to Mr. Pabst." He looked all of them over dutifully and turned them all down. And eventually he picked Louise Brooks.

How Pabst determined that I was his unaffected Lulu with the childish simpleness of vice was part of the mysterious alliance that seemed to exist between us even before we met. He knew nothing more of me than an unimportant part he saw me play in the Howard Hawks film *A Girl in Every Port* (1928). I had never heard of him, and knew nothing of his unsuccessful negotiations to borrow me from Paramount until I was called to the front office on the option day of my contract. Ben Schulberg told me that I could stay on at my old salary or quit. It was the time of the switchover to talkies, and studios were cutting actors' salaries just for the hell of it. And, just for the hell of it, I quit. Then he told me about the Pabst offer, which I was now free to accept. I said I would accept it and he sent off a cable to Pabst. All this took about ten minutes and left Schulberg somewhat dazed by my composure and quick decision.

But if I had not acted at once I would have lost the part of Lulu. At that very hour in Berlin Marlene Dietrich was waiting with Pabst in his office. "Dietrich was too old and too obvious—one sexy look and the picture would become a burlesque. But I gave her a deadline and the contract was about to be signed when Paramount cabled saying I could have Louise Brooks." It must be remembered that Pabst was speaking about the pre–von Sternberg Dietrich. She was the Dietrich of *I Kiss Your Hand, Madame* (1929), a film in which, caparisoned variously in beads, brocade, ostrich feathers, chiffon ruffles, and white rabbit fur, she galloped from one lascivious stare to another. Years after another trick of fate had made her a top star—for Sternberg's biographer Herman Weinberg told me that it was only because Brigitte Helm was not available that he looked further and found Dietrich for *The Blue Angel* (1930). To Travis Banton, the Paramount dress designer, who transformed her spangles and feathers into glittering, shadowed beauty, she said: "Imagine Pabst choosing Louise Brooks for Lulu when he could have had me!"

So it is that my playing of the tragic Lulu with no sense of sin remains generally unacceptable to this day. Three years ago, after seeing *Pandora's Box* at Eastman House, a priest said to me, "How did you feel? playing *that girl!*" "Feel? I felt fine! It all seemed perfectly normal to me." Seeing him start with distaste and disbelief, and unwilling to be mistaken for one of those women who like to shock priests with sensational confessions, I went on to prove the truth of Lulu's world by my own experience in the 1925 *Follies*, when my best friend was a lesbian and I knew two millionaire publishers, much like Schön in the film, who backed shows to keep themselves well supplied with Lulus. But the priest rejected my reality exactly as Berlin had rejected its reality when we made *Lulu* and sex was the business of the town.

At the Eden Hotel where I lived, the café bar was lined with the better-priced trollops. The economy girls walked the street outside. On the corner stood the girls in boots advertising flagellation. Actors' agents pimped for the ladies in luxury apartments in the Bavarian Quarter. Racetrack touts at the Hoppegarten arranged orgies for groups of sportsmen. The nightclub Eldorado displayed an enticing line of homosexuals dressed as women. At the Maly there was a choice of feminine or collar-and-tie Lesbians. Collective lust roared unashamed at the theatre. In the revue *Chocolate Kiddies*, when Josephine Baker appeared naked except for a girdle of bananas, it was precisely as Lulu's stage entrance was described. "They rage there as in a menagerie when the meat appears at the cage."

I revered Pabst for his truthful picture of this world of pleasure which let me play Lulu naturally. The rest of the cast were tempted to rebellion. And perhaps that was his most brilliant directorial achievement—getting a group of actors to play characters without "sympathy," whose only motivation was sexual gratification. Fritz Kortner as Schön wanted to be the victim. Franz Lederer as the

Lulu (Louise Brooks) is embraced by the lesbian Countess Geschwitz (Alice Roberts) in G. W. Pabst's *Pandora's Box* (1929). (Courtesy The Museum of Modern Art/Film Stills Archive)

incestuous son Alva Schön wanted to be adorable. Carl Goetz wanted to get laughs playing the old pimp Schigolch. Alice Roberts, the Belgian actress who played the screen's first lesbian, the Countess Geschwitz, was prepared to go no farther than repression in mannish suits.

Her first day's work was-in the wedding sequence. She came on the set looking chic in her Paris evening dress and aristocratically self-possessed. Then Mr. Påbst began explaining the action of the scene in which she was to dance the tango with me. Suddenly she understood that she was to touch, to embrace, to make love to another woman. Her blue eyes bulged and her hands trembled. Anticipating the moment of explosion, Mr. Pabst, who proscribed unscripted emotional outbursts, caught her arm and sped her away out of sight behind the set. A half hour later when they returned, he was hissing soothingly to her in French and she was smiling like the

star of the picture . . . which she was in all her scenes with me. I
was just there obstructing the view. In both two-shots and her close-
ups photographed over my shoulder, she cheated her look past me
to Mr. Pabst making love to her off camera. Out of the funny
complexity of this design Mr. Pabst extracted his tense portrait of
sterile lesbian passion and Madame Roberts satisfactorily pre-
served her reputation. At the time, her conduct struck me as silly.
The fact that the public could believe an actress's private life to be
like one role in one film did not come home to me until last year
when I was visited by a French boy. Explaining why the young
people in Paris loved *Lulu,* he put an uneasy thought in my mind.
"You talk as if I were a lesbian in real life," I said. "But of course!,"
he answered in a way that made me laugh to realize I had been
living in cinematic perversion for thirty-five years. . . .

That I was a dancer, and Pabst essentially a choreographer in his
direction, came as a wonderful surprise to both of us on the first day
of shooting *Pandora's Box.* The expensive English translation of the
script that I had thrown unopened on the floor by my chair had
already been retrieved by an outraged assistant and banished with
Mr. Pabst's laughter. Consequently I did not know that Lulu was a
professional dancer trained in Paris—"Gypsy, oriental, skirt dance,"
or that dancing was her mode of expression—"In my despair I
dance the Can-Can!" On the afternoon of that first day Pabst said to
me, "In this scene Schigolch rehearses you in a dance number."
After marking out a small space and giving me a fast tempo, he
looked at me curiously. "You can make up some little steps here,
can't you?" I nodded yes and he walked away. It was a typical
instance of his care in protecting actors against the blight of failure.
If I had been able to do nothing more than the skippity-hops of
Asta Nielsen, his curious look would never have been amplified to
regret, although the intensity of his concern was revealed by his
delight when the scene was finished. As I was leaving the set, he
caught me in his arms, shaking me and laughing as if I had played a
joke on him. "But you are a professional dancer." It was the moment
when he realized all his intuitions about me were right. He felt as if
he had created me. I was his Lulu! The bouquet of roses he gave

me on my arrival at the Station am Zoo was my first and last experience of the deference he applied to the other actors. From that moment I was firmly put through my tricks with no fish thrown in for a good performance. . . .

In the matter of my costumes for the picture I put up a fight, although I never won a decision. My best punches fanned the air because Pabst had always slipped into another position. Arriving in Berlin on Sunday and starting the picture on the following Wednesday, I found he had selected my first costume, leaving me nothing to do but stand still for a final fitting. This I let pass as an expedient, never suspecting it would be the same with everything else I put on or took off, from an ermine coat to my girdle. Not only was it unheard of to allow an actress no part in choosing her clothes, but I had also been disgustingly spoiled by my directors at Paramount. I had played a manicurist in five-hundred-dollar beaded evening dresses; a salesgirl in three-hundred-dollar black satin afternoon dresses; and a schoolgirl in two-hundred-and-fifty-dollar tailored suits. (It tickles me today when people see these old pictures and wonder why I look so well and the other girls such frumps.)

With this gross overconfidence in my rights and power, I defied Mr. Pabst at first with arrogance. The morning of the sequence in which I was to go from my bath into a love scene with Franz Lederer, I came on the set wrapped in a gorgeous negligee of painted yellow silk. Carrying the peignoir I refused to wear, Josephine approached Mr. Pabst to receive the lash. Hers was the responsibility for seeing that I obeyed his orders, and he answered her excuses with a stern rebuke. Then he turned to me. "Loueees, you must wear the peignoir!" "Why? I hate that big old woolly white bathrobe!" "Because," he said, "the audience must know you are naked beneath it." Stunned by such a reasonable argument, without another word I retired with Josephine to the bathroom set and changed into the peignoir.

Not to be trapped in this manner again, when I objected to the train of my wedding dress being "tied on like an apron" and he explained that it had to be easily discarded because I could not play a long, frantic sequence tripping over my train, I answered that I did not give a damn, tore off the train, and went into an elaborate tantrum. The worst audience I ever had, Mr. Pabst instructed the dress designer to have the pieces sewn together again and left the fitting room. My final defeat, crying real tears, came at the end of the picture when he went through my trunks to select a dress to be "aged" for Lulu's murder as a streetwalker in the arms of Jack the Ripper. With his instinctive understanding of my tastes, he decided on the blouse and skirt of my very favorite suit. I was anguished. "Why can't you *buy* some cheap little dress to be ruined? Why does it have to be *my* dress?" To these questions I got no answer until the next morning, when my once lovely clothes were returned to me in the studio dressing room. They were torn and foul with grease stains. Not some indifferent rags from the wardrobe department, but my own suit which only last Sunday I had worn to lunch at the Adlon! Josephine hooked up my skirt, I slipped the blouse over my head and went on the set feeling as hopelessly defiled as my clothes.

Dancing for two years with Ruth St. Denis and Ted Shawn had taught me much about the magic worked with authentic costuming. Their most popular duet, *Tillers of the Soil,* was costumed in potato sacking. In her *Flower Arrangement,* Miss Ruth's magnificent Japanese robes did most of the dancing. But the next three years of uncontrolled extravagance in films had so corrupted my judgment that I did not realize until I saw *Pandora's Box* in 1956 how marvelously Mr. Pabst's perfect costume sense symbolized Lulu's character and her destruction. There is not a single spot of blood on the pure white bridal satin in which she kills her husband. Making love to her wearing the clean white peignoir, Alva asks, "Do you love me, Lulu?" "I? Never a soul!" It is in the worn and filthy garments of the streetwalker that she feels passion for the first time—comes to life so that she may die. When she picks up Jack the Ripper on the foggy London street, and he tells her he has no money to pay her, she says, "Never mind, I like you." It is Christmas Eve and she is about to receive the gift that has been her dream since childhood. Death by a sexual maniac.

Why I'm Called a Recluse[*]

Greta Garbo

INTRODUCTION

Stark Young wrote of Greta Garbo, ". . . conceive of someone who stays in when she could go out, who could see people but thinks it a kind of communion, peace, rest or right to be alone sometimes! This has made Miss Garbo almost a national puzzle. . . . We must swallow it . . . as a cosmic mystery, this successful star really likes at times to be alone . . ." (The New Republic, September 28, 1932).

Imagine the hostility to Garbo for not being properly gregarious, open, fun loving! The pressure must have been intense from the beginning of her stay in America because, in 1927, Garbo took pen in hand (or was this ghostwritten?) and tried to explain her "strange" behavior to the puzzled public. Her assurance that this introversion was only a temporary condition takes on a certain poignance when we realize that "I want to be alone" has lasted a lifetime, and that the proud, aloof, ethereal Garbo was as intimidated by public opinion as Marilyn Monroe.

I do not like the smack of the word *recluse*, for it is not what I am in reality. I have been amazed to learn that I have this reputation. Let me go back a bit and explain to you how this idea came about.

It was a little over a year and a half ago that I came to America and I have not entirely accustomed myself to American ways yet.

* Reprinted from *Theatre Magazine* (December 1927).

Greta Garbo. (Courtesy Films, Inc.)

My country, Sweden, is so small. It is also so quiet. The women there are entirely different, so inactive, almost placid, I might say. Life flows along like a noiseless stream. The women consider themselves accomplished when they learn to cook and do fine embroidery or perhaps painting. Even the activities of professional women, actresses and singers, are slight. I led in Sweden very much the sort of life I lead here and I was not considered a recluse.

But in America everything is different. The girls here amazed as much as they fascinated me. I found that they led the most active lives and thrived on it. Even if they did not have definite careers, they worked at something, in offices mostly, yet they still found time to go in for sports. They can all swim, play tennis, play golf, ride horseback, dance, drive cars; they keep abreast of the times, read the new books, see the new plays. They also are smartly gowned and have studied themselves so that they know what kind of clothes they can wear to best advantage. And added to all this they still have time to keep up with and to entertain regularly dozens and dozens of friends.

I could not believe that what I saw when I was first taken to the Metro-Goldwyn-Mayer lot was a studio. I found that it covered acres and acres of ground and boasted some twenty stages, each one of which was larger than our entire studio in Sweden. Can you not realize that the enormity of America would astound me? And can you not also see that I would be dazed by the bustle and the high speed of all the work done here?

The more American girls I knew, the more I wanted to be like them. I decided to begin slowly, at first. I started out by learning to drive my car. Then I took up horseback riding, and the days had gone before I realized they had come.

Then I began to work. During my first picture, *Ibañez's Torrent* [1926], it was exactly as if I had to learn the making of motion pictures all over again. I was just beginning to learn the language. My days at the studio were long and difficult. I tried to place people and find out what they were doing. In Sweden the director is everything. Occasionally he has an assistant, and these two plan the sets, assemble the properties, select the costumes, and put the story in screen form. With only a few carpenters, a laborer or two, three or four electricians, the cast, and the director everything is accomplished. That is because the pictures are not an industry as they are here. It often takes six months in Sweden to make one picture, here it takes six weeks.

On the sets there are dozens and dozens of people, each of whom is important. Each does a stipulated amount of work. I toiled and tried to adjust myself. In my spare time I studied English, because working through an interpreter was too trying, and I wanted to learn as much of the language as I could in as short a time as possible.

You may imagine that I had very little time for friends. Perhaps you cannot imagine that, you Americans who can stretch twenty-four hours out indefinitely.

Perhaps it was the nervous tension at which I worked that made me demand eight or nine hours sleep. Everything was more difficult for me. I found that the perfected lighting at the studio here demanded a different sort of makeup. It took me longer to apply the greasepaint and powder than it did the other girls. That is but one example. I had to accustom myself in hundreds of other ways.

Now, of course, things are easier for me. The second picture, *The Temptress* [1926], I found less hard. *The Flesh and the Devil* [1927] fairly spun along, and now *Love* [1927] is going easier still.

The studio does not seem as large as it did. I am becoming used to the bustle and the activity, but perhaps I am not yet entirely acclimated. I find myself weary when the day's work is over. A year and a half is little enough time to entirely change one's mode of living, and I am still far short of my ideal, the American girl. I cannot yet find time to do in one day all of the things that other girls here can do.

And when the day is ended my energy is gone. I then want rest and quiet. I want simply to relax, read a bit, perhaps, write a letter or two, and retire. Meeting many people saps my energies. I do think that I have learned English fairly well; I can read it, speak it, and write it better than I can understand it. The quick conversation makes it necessary for me to be constantly on the alert to follow what is being said. At large gatherings I am at a loss. I am just beginning to feel at ease on the sets where there are so many people. That is why I cannot do my work and be with many people in my spare time. When I am away from the studio, I try to think only of resting and the next day's work. All of my wakeful hours I am thinking of my work.

Friends I certainly have. I have found so many charming and delightful people in America. And they are all so kind. When I first came here, it warmed my heart to find how gracious everyone was in helping me and in teaching me the new ways. The other girls on the lot showed me their makeup secrets. The director was always very patient when I used such bad English. America has been good to me.

Friends, yes! I could not do without them, but I am not yet able to attend large affairs while I am working on a picture. Do you call that being a recluse?

What Maisie Knows: Mae West[*]

Stark Young

INTRODUCTION

Just how seriously should Mae West be taken? With her butterfly collection of body-builder lover boys and her trick bag of sexual double entendres, is she a feminist heroine or an anachronistic retrograde? Is she a major twentieth-century satirist-ironist or only a boisterous swinger and playgirl? Perhaps the best place for research would be the publication of her long hidden away plays. Anyone for Sex? In the meantime Mae West remains an enigma, a parody of a parody, still enjoying herself and her eternal adulation as a healthy octogenarian.

In this 1944 essay, drama critic Stark Young tried his best to pin her down in his typically fanciful prose, but in the end she eluded him also. At the time she was walking Broadway in Catherine the Great, *a rehash of a screenplay she wrote in the 1930s and couldn't peddle to the movies. In her autobiography West talks more of her chorus-line lover than the play. Afterward, she and this young man, "Jeff," broke up. West explains solemnly, "He has, I am told, lived a life of celibacy ever since."*

[*] Excerpted from a chapter in *The Faces of Five Decades: The New Republic 1914–1964*, ed. Robert Luce (New York: Simon & Schuster, Inc., 1965), pp. 298, 300. Reprinted by permission of *The New Republic*. Copyright 1944, The New Republic, Inc.

Mae West. (Courtesy Universal 16)

One of the chief sources of Miss West's interest for us is the extent to which the element of the abstract, as it were, clings about her. She is a performer of great canniness and of incredible, though well-disguised, energy, dogged labor, and an almost insolent amount of skill. But basically she is as abstract as Harlequin, or Pierrot, or the Charlie Chaplin in the films, or Sarah Bernhardt, or one of the pattern figures out of history, like Julius Caesar, stern, martial, conquering hero, who—see Quintilian and elsewhere—when he was a young man, painted his nails and rouged his cheeks and was known as the Queen of Bithynia, because of his relations with its monarch; or like Cleopatra, seductress, wanton, serpent of the Nile, but who, we read, spoke five languages and nine dialects, and was so temperate in her wine that the pious Roman frauds writing their Augustan chronicles had to invent a magic ring supposed to keep the numberless cups from going to her head. So much just here about other people is out of proportion, no doubt, but it is fun and it will serve; for we can come back now to Mae West, a step that is always easy even for those who profess to be bored or horrified. She is, to repeat, as abstract as the figures I have mentioned; or as a song, good or bad; or as the circus.

And one of Miss West's secrets, though whether she knows it is thus and keeps it so I have no idea, is what, outside of business of course, she herself thinks of it all and of herself. How beautiful does she think she is, how brilliant, how dramatic? But no matter what she thinks, there must be few indeed who take this lady for a raving beauty, all curves and damask roses, the serpent of the Hudson, East River, and Long Island Sound, the bird of Fire Island. Nobody believes that she has passed from one romance or passionate episode to another, or would care if she had.

Nobody would say she had great glamour, allure, et cetera—who else in the theatre has, these days? But she does have something to hold your attention, she does create a howling, diverting mythology of glamour; you watch her as you watch an animal in a cage, tigress or cinnamon bear. Her cultural motifs and her ideas go round in a circle; they all come to one conclusion in fact, which seems to be that every woman has the lure and that every man can be had, and which seems dumb and flat only when she fails to insist on it as bold and true and as a theme to be accompanied by her special sway of knees and hips, her pauses, her unerring delivery, and her tone—as a Frenchman once called out at the Paris opera, that nose has a remarkably fine voice . . .

August 21, 1944

Marlene Dietrich:
At Heart a Gentleman*

Alexander Walker

INTRODUCTION

Two entries from her own witty collection of epigrams, Marlene
Dietrich's ABC (*1961*), *offer the best way to introduce Alexander
Walker's essay on Dietrich:*

Army. "*You get a uniform—the most attractive attire a man can
wear* . . . *You learn—discipline, mental and physical. You learn—
to live with other people. You learn—how to take it. You learn—
esprit de corps.* . . . . *You learn—to cook and to peel potatoes and
to bear the unavoidable with dignity.*"

Gentleman. "*A man who buys two of the same morning paper
from the doorman of his favorite nightclub when he leaves with his
girl.*"

If one dwells on how Dietrich was photographed, and how she
sounds, it is because these erotic qualities are ones that predominate
in the seven films which she made for von Sternberg. Save for
Blonde Venus (1932)—a mother's sacrifice story he tried to leave
Paramount before making—every one of the parts has been that of

* Reprinted from Alexander Walker, *Sex in the Movies* (4th ed.; Baltimore,
Md.: Pelican Books, 1969), pp. 88–93. Originally published as *The Celluloid
Sacrifice* (London: Michael Joseph, Ltd., 1966).

Marlene Dietrich. (Courtesy Universal 16)

a femme fatale, a woman who attracts men at the cost of suffering to them and sometimes to herself. How well she knows her own strength is revealed by the story that she refused the leading role in Terence Rattigan's play *The Deep Blue Sea* on the ground that she could never be convincing as a woman who tries to gas herself because she cannot keep her lover or find other men. Vivien Leigh can convey the extremities of sexual despair, not Dietrich. Let her show herself for five minutes at a street window, one thinks, and Mr. Rattigan would have been writing a different play. Though she has been married to one man since her German film days, her husband always keeps himself unfocused, in the background, seldom in her company; so that her public image reinforces the view of her as a rootless one, a femme fatale who travels alone. Of course it is not as simple as this. Dietrich has played many kinds of femme fatale; and the more one examines her career, the more clearly the fact emerges about the men she attracts and the code she lives by on the screen. Loyalty is as much part of it as love, and in some cases a great deal more.

She had been done a great disservice in this respect by her most famous film; for *The Blue Angel* (1930) is the least characteristic role she ever played. The really shocking thing about Lola-Lola, the cabaret singer, is not that she deliberately destroys Jannings as the infatuated pedagogue, it is, rather, the impassive way she watches him destroy himself, throw up social position for sexual bondage, with padlocks for cufflinks on his clown's outfit and a slave's neck-band in collar sizes, and wail out his grief over the footlights at the end in the famous rooster's crow of "Cock-a-doodle-do!" that seems to echo back as "Cuck-old-ed!" This humiliation was a typical invention of von Sternberg's; it does not occur in the original Heinrich Mann novel. Dietrich certainly tantalizes her lover, puffing her face powder into his beard and letting her lacy knickers float down from her upstairs dressing room over his face. But most of the time she stands to one side of him on her "provocating legs," as Siegfried Kracauer called them, and regards him coolly and egotistically. Instead of exploring their relationship, von Sternberg simply keeps on depicting Jannings's physical servility in front of her—forever dropping onto his knees to pick up erotic postcards, or help roll on her stockings. Lolling back cross-legged in cutaway skirt, with black suspenders stretched tightly against her pale thighs, or dangling libidinously loose, Lola-Lola is sex incarnate—but uninvolved. She is more of a narcissist than a femme fatale. What she keeps falling in love with again is her own image: no wonder that song has such a damnably introspective ring!

It is significant that Dietrich's image had to be changed before the American public was allowed to see her. For Paramount, the coproducers of *The Blue Angel,* delayed its American premiere till January 3, 1931, to give von Sternberg time to rush out his protégée's first Hollywood film, *Morocco,* premiered on December 6, 1930. Gary Cooper was the star of it, by virtue of prior American fame, and the story was made palatable to Main Street moviegoers by letting legionnaire Tom Brown leave the foreign heartbreaker in the lurch at the end, staggering off into the desert with her own broken heart, to follow her man on those notorious high heels. By humiliating her, the film appreciably humanized her—made her capable of returning a man's love as well as accepting it. Not till *The Devil Is a Woman* (1935)—her last film with von Sternberg and their biggest box-office disaster—did she go back to playing a fatal woman, "Concha the savage, the toast of Spain," who humiliates her lovers for no motive except the perverse pleasure it gives her. Outside of *The Blue Angel* no more heartless scene exists than the one in this film when she plucks the cigarette out of Lionel Atwill's lips and bestows it on the gigolo he has caught her with, pays the young man for his services with a bill from her protector's wallet, and sends him off with a flower broken off the bouquet Atwill has brought her tucked behind his ear. It is like a public degradation inflicted on a court-martialed officer whose buttons, ribbons, and medals are stripped off on the parade ground.

In this sense, it is the reverse of Dietrich's characteristic passion. For her, love usually goes with loyalty. If not to the man, then at least to the code of life that he and she both observe. It is a military code; and it is the very heart and soul of Marlene Dietrich. With a father in the uhlan cavalry and a stepfather in the hussars, it would not be surprising if she grew up attached to the soldier's virtues of honor, loyalty, and contempt for the pettiness of snug, bourgeois life. (Possibly her military background helped her accept von Sternberg's authoritarian command so completely.) What *is* surprising is the constancy with which such virtues appear on the screen, shaping her relations with men and giving her a comradeship with them that often precedes love and survives it. "I am at heart a gentleman," she was once reported as saying, a Garboesque communiqué the full text of which ought to have been, "I am at heart an officer and gentleman." Soldiers in Dietrich's films are always saluting her—not just out of courtesy, but in recognition that she wears the same uniform as they. And sometimes she does, literally. The male dress she often puts on in her films is not necessarily sexual in its undertones: generally it has a military association, too. Even the rakish clip she gives to her top hat whenever she appears in evening dress is in the nature of a masonic salute. *Shanghai Express* (1932) holds the beautiful surprise of seeing her, clad in an extravagantly feminine stole trimmed with fox fur and fully ten feet long, suddenly clap Clive Brook's army cap on her head just after kissing him—like a gage of loyalty. Even her growling boast that "it took more than one man to change my name to Chung-high-yee Lily" makes one feel that the name is the posthumous battle honor of those who fought over her and fell, like Mons or the Marne.

Her opening remark in *Dishonored* (1931), "I'm not afraid of life, although I'm not afraid of death, either," sounds like the translation of a regimental motto. This film, adapted from a von Sternberg story, uses a ludicrous plot about spying in World War I, and the invention of an even more invisible kind of invisible ink, as a glorious excuse for stating Dietrich's sex appeal almost entirely in military terms. She plays an officer's widow who has turned prostitute and is picked for her work as a spy when cooing "Hellooo?" with cool professionalism at the chief of the Austrian secret service. "I need a woman who knows how to deal with men," he informs her, and her eyes smile cynically at this recruiting euphemism. Her entrance into the secret service headquarters resembles that of a visiting general; a physical thrill stirs the roomful of uniformed men, as if they expect mobilization of some kind to be declared. Later on, when she traps her first traitor, he acknowledges it by surrendering his sword to her. "What a charming evening we might have had if you had not been a spy and I a traitor," he murmurs before shooting himself. "Then we might never have met," she reminds him. Such is the ruthless logic of love and war.

Sometimes her sex appeal is exercised directly through the conditions of war. *The Scarlet Empress* (1934) shows the transformation of a frightened virgin princess into an iron-willed military autocrat galloping up the staircase of her palace in hussar's uniform to confirm the power she has already learned to exercise over her Russian guards in her royal bedchamber. But although love for her is military in its appeal, and often in its trappings, it is by no means patriotic. She is a patriot for the heart, not for any king or country. (Dietrich sometimes makes a point in interviews for newspapers or radio of referring to herself as a wanderer in the world, giving the impression that she is almost a stateless person, with no home to go to.) "Could you help me die in a uniform of my own choosing?," she asks the priest in *Dishonored* when the Austrians who recruited her as a counterspy are about to execute her for liberating the Tsarist spy with whom she fell in love. "Any dress I was wearing when I served my countrymen, not my country," she adds. Understanding man of God!—he brings her her old streetwalker's clothes. She makes up her face in the gleaming blade of an officer's sword, walks professionally out to the firing squad and gratefully utilizes the brief reprieve when the officer in charge breaks down in tears to touch up her lipstick and straighten the seam of her stocking. The scene is absurd in recollection. On the screen it works like a *coup de théâtre;* she is so plainly meeting her execution as if it were an assignation. But the point is, it is a soldier's death she is privileged to die. And one's mind flashes forward precisely thirty years to Stanley Kramer's *Judgment at Nuremberg* (1961) in which she played the widow of a German general executed for war crimes. Dietrich's own sentiments about Germany are well known and it is usually assumed she took the role to help bring the war guilt home to the people who supported Hitler. No doubt this did play a part. But as Abby Mann wrote the character of Frau Bertholt in his screenplay, she corresponds more closely to a pre-Hitler Dietrich. She is a woman whose love for her husband excuses everything—she does not believe him guilty of war crimes—except the manner of his death, which outrages her own devotion to military ideals and dignity. "He was entitled to a soldier's death," she insists. "He asked for that. I tried to get that for him. . . . Just that he be permitted the dignity of a firing squad. You know what happened. He was hanged with the others."[1] No wonder von Sternberg was so angry when Ernst Lubitsch, as production chief at Paramount, insisted on changing the title of his film from *X-27*—Dietrich's code name—to *Dishonored.* The lady, he protested, was not dishonored by being shot; she was merely dead.

---

[1] Abby Mann, *Judgment at Nuremburg* (London: Cassell & Co., 1961), p. 124.

Actress Archetypes in the 1950s: Doris Day, Marilyn Monroe, Elizabeth Taylor, Audrey Hepburn

Janice Welsch

Irwin Panofsky called them "Vamp and Straight Girl," and many other writers on the cinema have approached the subject of basic female film types. The elemental dichotomy of virgin and vamp (or femme fatale) is pointed to by Edgar Morin in *The Stars* (1960), but he suggests that a further archetype, the goddess, brings together the purity of the virgin and the allure and mystery of the femme fatale. Richard Schickel, in his *The Stars* (1962), writes of the virgin and the vamp as personified by Mary Pickford and Theda Bara, equating the former with American heroines while associating the latter with exotic foreign screen images. He goes on to discuss "It" girls, pinups, sex goddesses, the girl next door, and other screen types. Martha Wolfenstein and Nathan Leites, in their study of late 1940s cinema, *Movies: A Psychological Study* (1950), differentiate female protagonists as good-bad girls and masculine-feminine women while also taking into account maternal types. In *From Reverence to Rape* (1974), Molly Haskell mentions the "age-old dualism between body and soul, virgin and whore," before offering various female types such as flappers, superfemales, sex goddesses and sex objects, earth goddesses, bitches, and mothers. She associates the virgin/whore dualism specifically with the 1950s.

The basic virgin/vamp classification of stars can have meaning for any era. Yet the archetypes that have emerged as pertinent to the more popular female stars in the post–World War II era are actually more complex. They are sister, mistress, mother, daughter. These archetypes provide the fundamental structures underlying the films of four stars studied: Doris Day, Marilyn Monroe, Elizabeth Taylor, and Audrey Hepburn.

The image of each of these stars is a concretization of an archetype that gives a unifying structure to her oeuvre. The archetypes, like that of virgin and vamp, are identified principally in terms of the heroine's relationship to the male protagonist and reflect the major emphasis given romance in movies that feature female stars. They describe rather than define. Although elements of several archetypes may be evident in a single persona, it is the archetype that dominates each star image that is of concern here. Thus, Doris Day provides an embodiment of the sister archetype; whereas Marilyn Monroe suggests mistress; Elizabeth Taylor, the mother; and Audrey Hepburn, the daughter. Why these archetypes appealed to an extensive part of the 1950s population—as the box-office status of these movie queens attests—will have to wait for a further study.

Sister. The archetype sister, closely related to the virgin, implies male/female relationships that are marked by camaraderie, equality, and, at times, competition. The girl next door, the female buddy and good joe, the tomboy and the Amazon are all variants of this archetype.

Mistress. The mistress is more closely connected with the vamp than the virgin since she gives sex freely and outside of marriage. But the prototypal vamp is destructive and self-gratifying; the mistress is often kind and even selfless in her relationships with men. She is defined primarily in terms of her sexuality; she is a sex goddess, a temptress, and/or sex object. She is sometimes aware of her sexual allure and consciously manipulates her appeal to get what she wants. Yet she often uses her body and beauty intuitively, sensing but not articulating the power of both.

Mother. The mother is surely the most familiar archetype, the dominant image of adult woman in our society. She nurtures, protects, cares for, encourages. She is home, family, marriage-oriented and generally defines herself and others in terms of the roles each fulfills within the family. In her own case this means the centrality of her functions as childbearer (which she interprets as destiny) and as familial stabilizing force. She enjoys having others dependent on her. Her willingness to sacrifice for them is influenced by the desire to direct their destinies. She can be emasculating as well as nurturing, a bitch and a nag as well as an empathic and encouraging protectress of the household.

Daughter. The filial archetype is the young woman of respectability, learning, and sophistication who is both showpiece and helpmate. Because she is well educated, she is generally associated with the higher social and economic levels and is more apt to depend on reason than on intuition. She is capable and efficient and manages the role of female head of the household with ease, even finesse, whether managing domestic affairs for her father or for her husband. At times she is likely to be willful, spoiled, aloof. She is the female counterpart of "the aggressive, self-confident, autonomous, inner-directed man" defined by Page Smith in *Daughters of the Promised Land* (1970). She relates to others more as individuals than as family members and, although associated with family herself, she manifests considerable independence and self-determination, since her personality is only partly shaped by her role as mother or wife.

DORIS DAY AS SISTER

Doris Day's movie image is defined considerably by her propensity to work and compete in the entertainment and business worlds. Seventy-five percent of her movies present her with a career outside the home, and the majority of Day films indicate that a marriage and career can be simultaneously enjoyed. Alfred Hitchcock's *Man Who Knew Too Much* (1956) implies that Jo's (Day) hysteria when her son is kidnapped is connected with the repression that resulted from abandonment of her singing career for marriage. In the context of the predominant negative attitude toward working wives in the 1950s, the suggestion is a bold one but consistent with the Day persona.

The male/female equality that is part of the sororal archetype is

Doris Day parodying her "good joe" image as Beverly in Norman Jewison's *Thrill of It All* (1963). (Courtesy Universal Pictures)

furthered by the occupations of the Day heroine. The jobs usually are prestigious, equivalent to those of the heroes; and often, especially when the two are in entertainment, the careers are related. In some of the sex comedies (*Caprice*, 1967, and *Lover Come Back*, 1961) there are indications that the hero knows his job better than the heroine knows hers. Even here, the Day woman refuses to be intimidated. If several biographical films focus on male protagonists (*Young Man with a Horn*, 1950, and *The Winning Team*, 1952), more often the emphasis is on Day's career. Because she is occupation-oriented, the Day woman usually lives in a major city, normally New York or Hollywood. However, when she is involved in tomboy activities—such as stagecoach guard, baseball player, or auto mechanic—or farm-related occupations, Day lives in small town or rural settings. The wholesomeness, health, and conservative sexual attitudes frequently associated with these locations are carried over into the Day woman's big-city living.

Several manifestations of the sister archetype are associated with middle-class socioeconomic status and values—the girl next door, the good joe, the tomboy—and it is not surprising to find Day placed here. There is a democratic aura apparent in all her relationships, not only with men. Her movement into the upper or upper middle class, socially or economically, is usually earned by hard work and perseverance combined with talent and a touch of luck. Seldom does upward mobility come from matrimony, since Day usually chooses a spouse close to her own status. The focus of the Day career woman is not economic advancement so much as personal fulfillment. In her sex comedies the lavish production values dictate emphasis on chic fashions and expensive-looking sets, but the connotations of wealth and elegance are mitigated by the star's own down-to-earth, middle-brow attitudes, and comic situations that counteract any elitist pretensions. The Day character often is involved in a muddy or watery misadventure that leaves her a dirty mess, as in *Calamity Jane* (1953), *Billy Rose's Jumbo* (1962), *Caprice,* and *Move Over, Darling* (1963).

Day's image as sister is supported further by the presence of male friends who are not romantic interests (*Tea for Two,* 1950, *Lucky Me,* 1954, *Julie,* 1956, and *Teacher's Pet,* 1958) as well as by the large number of times the central romance develops from an existing platonic relationship (*My Dream Is Yours,* 1949, *Calamity Jane, It Happened to Jane,* 1959) or from a business association. Negatively the archetype is reinforced by the focus on virginity, even frigidity, in a number of the sex comedies, particularly *Pillow Talk* (1959) and *Lover Come Back,* both starring Day with Rock Hudson. In these instances it is implied that attempts by women to compete in the business world and to place themselves on a par with men necessitate sexual repression and lead to a loss of femininity. This supposition is alternately supported and denied in various Day vehicles. In those films that support this notion, careers are given up (usually only at the close of the picture) in favor of marriage and motherhood; in those movies in which she actually functions as a mother and a wife, however, she maintains her ability to think and act independently and at times combines career and family responsibilities. In the two pictures in which she has three or four children (*Please Don't Eat the Daisies,* 1960, and *With Six You Get Eggroll,* 1968), Day mixes homemaking with a full-time job or with school, community, and social activities.

An important element in the Day image, throughout her oeuvre, is her optimism. This quality is implied again in the familiar sister-related types (the good sport, the all-American girl, the good joe) and is grounded in the sense of equality and independence that characterize the archetype. In the Day heroine, optimism is coupled with energy and manifests itself, as already indicated, in a willingness to work hard to achieve a goal. It does not prevent Day from being discouraged, frightened, or sad but it does help assure that she will be so only temporarily. Day optimism is not simply an accompaniment for the happy ending of her movies but a basic attitude toward life that keeps her actively striving and seeking; it is an energy often expressed through song and dance.

Monroe as Mistress

Ninety percent of Monroe's major films place her in careers for which her body is an important asset. Her employment as a fashion model (*How to Marry a Millionaire,* 1953) and a television model (*The Seven Year Itch,* 1955)) depend directly upon her physical attractiveness, as do her many jobs as entertainer, where she is quite literally a "showgirl," on display as much for her figure as for her talent. In Doris Day's musical films, primary attention is focused on the heroine's singing and dancing abilities; but Monroe's curvaceous body, especially breasts and derriere, is emphasized, particularly in the musical numbers of such films as *Gentleman Prefer Blondes* (1953), *River of No Return* (1954), *There's No Business Like Show Business* (1954), *Some Like It Hot* (1959), and *Let's Make Love* (1960).

In only one instance (*There's No Business Like Show Business*) does a Monroe character share the Day heroines' strong desire to achieve success in their careers. Not only do they usually lack the keen awareness of direction and purpose possessed by Day women, Monroe heroines are also without a comparable sense of identity and family ties. In a couple of movies (*Gentlemen Prefer Blondes* and *There's No Business Like Show Business*) Lorelei and Vicky hold tenaciously to their own plans for their future, but ordinarily the Monroe women are easily swayed to change direction (*How to Marry a Millionaire, River of No Return, Bus Stop,* 1956, *Some Like It Hot, Let's Make Love*).

Despite this lack of direction and the focus on their anatomy, Monroe heroines are able to give of themselves quite generously, to be supportive, and to awaken their male companions to unrealized values, emotion, and potential (*Bus Stop, The Prince and the Show-girl,* 1957, *River of No Return, The Misfits,* 1961). Only once (in *Niagara,* 1953) is her sexuality used viciously, as an instrument of

The most famous moment in the Marilyn Monroe oeuvre: "The girl" is ogled by Richard Sherman (Tom Ewell) in Billy Wilder's *Seven Year Itch* (1955). (Courtesy Films , Inc.)

a man's destruction. She is more frequently sympathetic toward men when they are drawn to her sexually.

Because of their innocence and amorality, the Monroe heroines are able to dissociate sex from guilt, not only for themselves but for the men with whom they come in contact. It is Monroe's comedic talent that also makes it possible for her characters to approach their sexuality and its impact lightly, even humorously. The emphasis given her physique and sensuality makes it difficult to ignore either; this continued focus, however, does not prevent the Monroe heroines from becoming more ethereal from film to film. Men are attracted to them erotically at first, but soon recognize other qualities of the heroines: sensitivity, vulnerability, generosity, openness, honesty.

The Monroe heroines are generally aware of their own allure but, even while utilizing it, they seek a chance to relate on other levels as well. Thus Kay (*River of No Return*) befriends a youngster; Lorelei (*Gentlemen Prefer Blondes*) enjoys a strong, genuine friendship with Dorothy (Jane Russell); and Amanda (*Let's Make Love*), for all her onstage sensuality, is actually innocent and simple, devoting her time to knitting, studying, and providing support for others in her company.

Elizabeth Taylor as Mother

Taylor as Martha in *Who's Afraid of Virginia Woolf?* (1966) declares herself to be Earth Mother and in doing so points to the archetype that defines the dominant Taylor image. Even while playing child roles, the star showed a tendency to relate in a caring, mothering way in child/animal relationships. In *Courage of Lassie* (1946) and *National Velvet* (1944), for example, the Taylor characters care for and help train a dog and a horse. As adolescents the Taylor young women tend to be less understanding and more domineering as they attempt to direct their peers' behavior (*A Date with Judy*, 1948, *Little Women*, 1949). Propriety, social position, and roles are concerns not only of the Taylor teen-agers but often of her young and independent adults. Their concerns parallel that of the mother within the family.

Kay Banks (Elizabeth Taylor) is walked down the aisle by Stanley Banks (Spencer Tracy) in Vincente Minnelli's *Father of the Bride* (1950). (Courtesy Wisconsin Center for Film and Theater Research)

The above interests, although not always articulated, are reflected in the characters' inevitable selection of a man of comparable status for their husband. The Taylor women do, in fact, frequently choose their mates and take the initiative in romantic relationships. The men they decide will make good husbands characteristically are men who in some way are immature or weak and who can benefit from the heroines support and mothering. Thus, Mary (*The Big Hangover*, 1950) determines to help cure David's alcohol allergy; Angela (*A Place in the Sun*, 1951) decides to initiate George into upper-class society; and Helen (*The Last Time I Saw Paris*, 1954) tries to assist Charles in his transition from journalist to novelist. After her marriage to John (*Elephant Walk*, 1954), Ruth finds it necessary to help her husband recognize and resolve a paternal love/hate relationship, and Maggie (*Cat on a Hot Tin Roof*, 1958) is called upon to aid Brick in overcoming his psychological hang-ups. Both Louise (*Rhapsody*, 1954) and Frances (*The V.I.P.'s*, 1963) recognize that their happiness is contingent upon their husbands' dependency on them. Men such as Paul in *Rhapsody* and Victor in *The Girl Who Had Everything* (1953) who are more independent and who resist the Taylor characters' shaping influence are ultimately rejected as possible husbands.

The mothering nature of the Taylor heroines at least partially accounts for the emphasis given the family in the star's movies. In her M-G-M pictures at least one parent is normally present; more frequently a second parent, siblings, a husband, children, and/or in-laws are also significant. The presence of kin of several generations suggests the tradition and continuation of the family and reflects the maternal desire to perpetuate it. Not only are the Taylor characters obviously identified with their families, they also consistently move directly from their parental home to that of their husband. For them an intermediate period during which they live away from their families and establish themselves in a career appears unnecessary and undesirable, although, among the heroines portrayed by Day and Monroe such a pattern is common. In Taylor pictures, courtship is depicted as a quick prelude to marriage, the real focus of the narrative. In movies starring the other actresses, courtship often receives the primary emphasis and marriage provides the climax of the story or is pending at the end of the film.

In many of her later films, Taylor delineates women whose maternal instincts have been thwarted. Martha in *Who's Afraid of Virginia Woolf?* is one of these women. To fill the void left by her inability to bear a child she—with her husband—creates an imaginary son to whom she can relate with a tenderness, understanding, and affection she is evidently afraid to reveal to anyone else. In her relationship to her husband she is often devouring, castrating. Other Taylor heroines who are blocked in their efforts to live their mother roles include Maggie (*Cat on a Hot Tin Roof*) and Leonora (*Secret Ceremony*, 1968). In *Cat on a Hot Tin Roof* Maggie is able to find an outlet for her motherliness in caring for her impotent husband, and ultimately, she has opportunity to conceive the child(ren) she wants. Leonora, too, finds a substitute child, someone who even looks like the daughter she lost, but in this instance the relationship cannot be sustained. The women of the later Taylor pictures are middle-aged; most of them have been married for a number of years, but they are generally childless and their husbands strong enough to resist mothering. Some of these women are domineering and shrewish (*Reflections in a Golden Eye,* 1967, *Boom!,* 1968, and *X, Y, and Z,* 1972) and some become mentally deranged (*Secret Ceremony, The Driver's Seat,* 1974).

Audrey Hepburn as Daughter

The Hepburn characters are their fathers' daughters. As such, they place importance on intelligence and education rather than on intuition or emotion. Some Hepburn heroines are students (of music, French cooking, philosophy). Others have jobs or professions (nurse, teacher, secretary, translator) that require formal training or that are related to learning (salesclerk in bookstore). Apart from their specific occupations, however, the Hepburn women are associated with a desire to experience life and are usually attracted to men who hold out the promise of such experience. Thus their fathers, their husbands, and their tutors are all potential sources of knowledge.

Hepburn characters are not only intelligent but also determined and aggressive. Because of their exquisite grace and generally cool self-confident manner, their assertiveness is never unappealing. In *The Nun's Story* (1959) Sister Luke's (Hepburn) strength of will eventually prompts her to leave religious life. In other Hepburn vehicles the characters' decisiveness and aggression do not always lead to independence. She does, in fact, capitulate in *Sabrina* (1954) by leaving for Paris as Linus requests, and in *Breakfast at Tiffany's* (1961) by accepting Paul's evaluation of her life and returning to him.

All of the stars treated are aggressive to some extent, Doris Day and Elizabeth Taylor most notably so. Day's self-assertiveness is usually directed toward career success whereas Taylor's (during her early career) is generally disguised by feminine coyness or wiles and is directed toward securing a husband or maintaining her home. Hepburn's aggressiveness is more subtle than theirs; it is

Joe (Audrey Hepburn) finishing up a song in Stanley Donen's *Funny Face* (1957). (Courtesy Wisconsin Center for Film and Theater Research)

directed toward prospective mates like Taylor's but it is more cerebral than emotive. It is intertwined with gold-digging tendencies, although Hepburn is not ordinarily thought of along those lines (except as Holly in *Breakfast at Tiffany's*), possibly because her natural elegance and charm preclude such association. However, as the central figure in her Cinderella films, she does not wait to be fitted with the slipper but grooms herself with the idea that she will be appealing to the prince if she acquires some of his knowledge and sophistication. Her ploy inevitably works. Her appeal is not only based on her poise and elegance but on their combination with elfin good humor, childlike innocence, inquisitiveness, and intelligence. She dons the trappings of wealth and social prominence without losing her ability to delight in the most ordinary and simple pleasures and without suggesting self-indulgence, snobbishness, or greed.

Hepburn conveys refinement and grace. It is only as Eliza (*My*

Fair Lady, 1964) that the star temporarily sheds her natural restraint and adopts a coarse, loud demeanor in keeping with the requisites of the narrative, which specifically revolves around Eliza's transformation from uncouth flower-hawker to exquisitely refined lady. Hepburn characters are repeatedly taken (or take themselves) from an ordinary, middle-class environment (*Sabrina, Funny Face,* 1957, *Love in the Afternoon,* 1957, *Breakfast at Tiffany's,* and *Two for the Road,* 1967) into the upper echelon of society, and inevitably they assume the deportment of this elite class as though it were natural to them. They combine simplicity with sophistication.

Because of their youth (in only three films are the characters middle-aged) Hepburn heroines are usually not in positions of authority (*The Nun's Story* and *The Children's Hour,* 1962, are exceptions), even though their intelligence, decisiveness, and graciousness suggest they would prove quite capable and efficient.

The Hepburn characters' diverse tracts create a tension that is similar to that produced by Monroe's unique blend of innocence, naïveté, and sexuality, by Day's good nature and occupational willfulness, and by Taylor's combination of propriety and earthiness. Each of the four stars projects a complex image that appealed to thousands of moviegoers during the 1950s and 1960s and that still reflects a multidimensional but clearly recognizable archetype.

from *Brigitte Bardot and the Lolita Syndrome**

Simone De Beauvoir

INTRODUCTION

A character in Simone De Beauvoir's novel The Mandarins (1956) *states that the two most important priorities in life are politics and movies. De Beauvoir is for politics first and then she is an enthusiast of literature. But she also takes moviegoing seriously, making no distinction between cerebral Continental works and American popular films. In* All Said and Done (1972), *she talks of her favorite movies of the last few years: from Ingmar Bergman and Luis Buñuel to* Easy Rider (1969) *and* Five Easy Pieces (1970), *from the political films of Sweden's Bo Widerberg to James Bond to* Bonnie and Clyde (1967), *from Raoul Walsh's* White Heat (1949) *to* The Honeymoon Killers (1970), *from* Les Abysses (1964) *to* Z (1968).

Altogether De Beauvoir seems very open, some would say too casual, in her cinema preferences, never insistent on a correct political line or demanding in a central way about women's roles in the movies she discusses. Her long essay on Brigitte Bardot, excerpted below, is a different story—militant and analytical. She writes as a strong feminist partisan in support of this most maligned

* Excerpted from *Brigitte Bardot and the Lolita Syndrome,* trans. Bernard Fretchman (London: Four Square Books, 1962). Reprinted by permission of New English Library Limited, London.

*of screen actresses—BB, whose haunting and elegant performance
in Godard's* Contempt *(1963) alone is worth other's full careers.*

On New Year's Eve, Brigitte Bardot appeared on French television.
She was got up as usual—blue jeans, sweater, and shock of tousled
hair. Lounging on a sofa, she plucked at a guitar. "That's not hard,"
said the women. "I could do just as well. She's not even pretty. She
has the face of a housemaid." The men couldn't keep from devouring her with their eyes, but they too snickered. Only two or three of
us, among thirty or so spectators, thought her charming. Then she
did an excellent classical dance number. "She *can* dance," the others
admitted grudgingly. Once again I could observe that Brigitte
Bardot was disliked in her own country. . . .

Brigitte Bardot is the most perfect specimen of ambiguous
nymphs. Seen from behind, her slender, muscular, dancer's body is
almost androgynous. Femininity triumphs in her delightful bosom.
The long voluptuous tresses of Mélisande flow down to her shoulders, but her hairdo is that of a negligent waif. The line of her lips
forms a childish pout, and at the same time those lips are very
kissable. She goes about barefooted, she turns up her nose at elegant clothes, jewels, girdles, perfumes, makeup, at all artifice. Yet
her walk is lascivious and a saint would sell his soul to the devil
merely to watch her dance. It has often been said that her face has
only one expression. It is true that the outer world is hardly reflected in it at all and that it does not reveal great inner disturbance.
But that air of indifference becomes her. BB has not been marked
by experience. Even if she has lived—as in *Love Is My Profession*
[1959]—the lessons that life has given her are too confused for her
to have learned anything from them. She is without memory, without a past, and, thanks to this ignorance, she retains the perfect
innocence that is attributed to a mythical childhood.

The legend that has been built up around Brigitte Bardot by
publicity has for a long time identified her with this childlike and
disturbing character. Vadim presented her as "a phenomenon of
nature." "She doesn't act," he said. "She exists." "That's right," con-
firmed BB. "The Juliette in *And God Created Woman* [1957] is

Brigitte Bardot's famous bosom being perused by a leering Frenchman in *The Light Across the Street* (1957). (Courtesy UMPO Pictures)

exactly me. When I'm in front of the camera, I'm simply myself." . . .

All men are drawn to BB's seductiveness, but that does not mean they are kindly disposed toward her. The majority of Frenchmen claim that woman loses her sex appeal if she gives up her artifices. According to them, a woman in trousers chills desire. Brigitte proves to them the contrary, and they are not at all grateful to her, because they are unwilling to give up their role of lord and master. The vamp was no challenge to them in this respect. The attraction she exercised was that of a passive thing. They rushed knowingly into the magic trap; they went to their doom the way one throws oneself overboard. Freedom and full consciousness remained their right and privilege. When Marlene displayed her silk-sheathed thighs as she sang with her hoarse voice and looked about her with sultry eyes, she was staging a ceremony, she was casting a spell. BB does not cast spells; she is on the go. Her flesh does not have the abundance that, in others, symbolizes passivity. Her clothes are not fetishes, and when she strips, she is not unveiling a mystery. She is showing her body, neither more nor less, and that body rarely settles into a state of immobility. She walks, she dances, she moves about. Her eroticism is not magical, but aggressive. In the game of love, she is as much a hunter as she is a prey. The male is an object to her, just as she is to him. And that is precisely what wounds masculine pride. In the Latin countries where men cling to the myth of "the woman as object," BB's naturalness seems to them more perverse than any possible sophistication. To spurn jewels and cosmetics and high heels and girdles is to refuse to transform oneself into a remote idol. It is to assert that one is a man's fellow and equal, to recognize that between the woman and him there is mutual desire and pleasure. Brigitte is thereby akin to the heroines of Françoise Sagan, although she says she feels no affinity for them—probably because they seem to her too thoughtful.

But the male feels uncomfortable if, instead of a doll of flesh and blood, he holds in his arms a conscious being who is sizing him up. A free woman is the very contrary of a light woman. In her role of confused female, of homeless little slut, BB seems to be available to everyone. And yet, paradoxically, she is intimidating. She is not defended by rich apparel or social prestige, but there is something stubborn in her sulky face, in her sturdy body. "You realize," an average Frenchman once said to me, "that when a man finds a woman attractive, he wants to be able to pinch her behind." A ribald gesture reduces a woman to a thing that a man can do with as he pleases without worrying about what goes on in her mind and heart and body. But BB has nothing of the "easygoing kid" about her, the quality that would allow a man to treat her with this kind of breeziness. There is nothing coarse about her. She has a kind of spontaneous dignity, something of the gravity of childhood. The difference between Brigitte's reception in the United States and in France is due partly to the fact that the American male does not have the Frenchman's taste for broad humor. He tends to display a certain respect for women. The sexual equality that BB's behavior affirms wordlessly has been recognized in America for a long time. Nevertheless, for a number of reasons that have been frequently analyzed in America, he feels a certain antipathy to the "real woman." He regards her as an antagonist, a praying mantis, a tyrant. He abandons himself eagerly to the charms of the "nymph" in whom the formidable figures of the wife and the "Mom" are not yet apparent. In France many women are accomplices of this feeling of superiority in which men persist. Their men prefer the servility of these adults to the haughty shamelessness of BB.

She disturbs them all the more in that, though discouraging their jollity, she nevertheless does not lend herself to idealistic sublimation. Garbo was called "The Divine"; Bardot, on the other hand, is of the earth earthy. Garbo's visage had a kind of emptiness into which anything could be projected—nothing can be read into Bardot's face. It is what it is. It has the forthright presence of reality. It is a stumbling block to lewd fantasies and ethereal dreams alike. Most Frenchmen like to indulge in mystic flights as a change from ribaldry, and vice versa. With BB they get nowhere. She corners them and forces them to be honest with themselves. They are obliged to recognize the crudity of their desire, the object of which is very precise—that body, those thighs, that bottom, those breasts. Most people are not bold enough to limit sexuality to itself and to recognize its power. Anyone who challenges their hypocrisy is accused of being cynical.

. . . "I want there to be no hypocrisy, no nonsense about love," BB once said. The debunking of love and eroticism is an undertaking that has wider implications than one might think. As soon as a single myth is touched, all myths are in danger. A sincere gaze, however limited its range, is a fire that may spread and reduce to ashes all the shoddy disguises that camouflage reality. Children are forever asking why, why not. They are told to be silent. Brigitte's eyes, her smile, her presence, impel one to ask oneself why, why not. . . .

Liv Ullmann:
The Goddess as Ordinary Woman*

Molly Haskell

It is not just the publicity releases that are comparing Liv Ullmann to Greta Garbo, Ingrid Bergman, and Jeanne Moreau. Along the length of Bloomingdale's Belt, where *Scenes from a Marriage* (1973) is playing at Cinema I, men can be found wandering in a daze. And some of them haven't even gotten inside to see it. Women are more guarded in their admiration, but most admit that Ullmann is "together" in a way that seems to elude many of us at this transitional moment of history.

What is it about the Norwegian-born Ullmann, aside from the titian hair, and the blue eyes that one must resist translating into purple prose? If I hadn't been shamed by the interviewer from the woman's magazine in *Scenes from a Marriage* who does just that, I would say they have the color and the astonishing pale brightness of a gray sky just turning blue. The color—as it happens—of the telephone she uses several times in the film. The color of the floor-length knit dress she wore the first time I saw her, when she came to Sardi's in 1972 to pick up a Best Actress award (for *Cries and Whispers,* 1972) from the New York Film Critics Circle. Not only the color, but the slight angora-fuzziness of the dress, emphasized her soft contours and ultrafemininity, and suggested the awareness of a woman in perfect harmony with her exterior—and not above displaying it a bit.

I think the popularity of *Scenes from a Marriage*—if it turns out to be a popular as well as a critical hit—is largely explainable by her presence, and an audience's gratitude for what is not just the first real woman in months of drought, but a particular kind of woman—a radiant, soothing Earth Mother who appears to heal the wounds wrought by sexual enmity. I am not sure that the reconciliation isn't as illusory as President Ford's great healing act, but the fact that we grasp so desperately at something that is more than a straw but less than a sexual lifeboat suggests that perhaps our needs have been given too short a shrift in American movies.

In the simplest terms, there is, underlying *Scenes from a Marriage,* an assumption that we are in this together, that both sexes are plunked on this planet without a guidebook, and if we join our heads and hearts and the rest of our bodies, we will probably do better than if we spend all our time and energy trying to prove we don't need each other. If in Bergman's films, men need and revere women too much—thus imprisoning them in their "superior," traditional roles as mothers and nurturers—in American movies the reverse is true. Men, fleeing their own mortality and the love and knowledge that might redeem the pain of growing old, take refuge in greater and greater displays of violence, opting for the short physical spurt of the professional athlete rather than the long imaginative span of the man of wisdom. As has happened so often in the past, a European actress has come to fill a gap in our own culture.

Ullmann is that anomaly, an international star—the only one in Bergman's repertory to make the cover of *Time* magazine—who has yet to make a good film outside Scandinavia. The uncharitable might attribute this to the famous *Time* cover jinx on movie stars, but I think it is rather that Bergman has probed, penetrated, and allowed her to reveal and extend herself in ways that no other director, including Jan Troell, has dared to do.

It is probably true, as she pointed out in our interview at the Pierre—the eventual subject of this piece—that critics have been unwilling to accept her in non-Bergman pictures. "If it's not Bergman," their thinking goes, "it's no good." But it's a little like taking a poor city kid for a few days on the Atlantic Ocean, and then sending him back to play in the fire hydrants of the ghetto. Once we have seen Liv Ullmann speak worlds just by narrowing her eyes or barely parting her lips in a Bergman close-up, how can we tolerate the distance she places between us and a fustian, posing Queen Christina (in *The Abdication,* 1974), who makes a mockery of woman's "search for fulfillment."

Having lived with Ullmann for some five or six years, Bergman knows her moods and contradictions and what it is like to watch television with her and sleep with her and help her wash the dishes, and it is this knowledge that seeps through the cracks of Johan and Marianne's crumbling marriage, filling the narrative frame with feelings and perceptions that are sometimes at variance with the middle-class stereotypes with which it is concerned. Although Bergman gives Ullmann a looser rein than heretofore to "become her own person," the film is ultimately not about Ullmann/Marianne's growth in understanding herself, so much as with Bergman's understanding of Ullmann—her strengths, her vanities, her evasions, her shuffling drabness, her sudden, dazzling beauty. Her gestures toward the women's movement are not particularly convincing, nor does her career seem to play any great role in her life. But her vibrations and metamorphoses as that classical creature, a woman "made for love," have an uncanny aura of truth: the way she becomes more alluring when she has "gotten over" him and is no longer emotionally dependent; her increased sexual desire, and abandon, when she no longer feels possessive toward him, or anxious about what he feels for her.

Ullmann, who once "exchanged identities" with Bibi Andersson in *Persona* (1967), radiates a poise and self-possession that is strikingly unlike Andersson's more tenuously cerebral grasp of herself. The differences between the two, as they have evolved since 1966, are fascinating. Andersson suggests the insecurity of the more complex, intellectual woman, harboring an unresolved conflict between her sensual and spiritual selves. It is Ullmann's self-containment, bordering on complacency, that drives her crazy in *Persona,* and that in *Scenes from a Marriage* galvanizes her into a momentary alliance with her despised husband. In Andersson, we think we glimpse the kind of woman who is constantly in search of something, who is tormented by doubts and driven by spiritual needs. Whereas Ullmann, even when she withdraws from the world in *Persona,* is responding simply, with a peasant sense of survival, by rejecting the world and its unanswerable questions.

As a woman who fulfills herself in love, she demands paradoxically less of men than Andersson, who requires that they engage her mind. Andersson, the challenge, the mind, has sharp edges; Ullmann, the mother, the solace, has none. But in her soft sufficiency, she is invulnerable. The other side of her pliancy is what Johan/ Bergman calls her "white, hard resistance." Perhaps she gives everything . . . and nothing. Only a great artist or a long relationship could uncover such cruel ironies, and with Bergman, Ullmann had both.

Certainly, when you meet her in person, you are likely to decide that even such failings as the screenplay attributes to her are unthinkable. There is nothing hard or resistant in this woman in red pants and top who, when I meet her, is cheerful, voluble, curious, frank, self-critical, and betrays no weariness at having to confront yet another interviewer except to confess that she is sick to death of talking about herself.

When I arrive at their suite in the Pierre, she and her companion Cecillia Drott, who did the makeup for *Scenes* and *Cries and Whispers,* are watching "The Mating Game" with that mixture of amusement and disbelief and dismay that makes American daytime television such a mind-blowing experience for Europeans.

Ullmann is still trying to recover from a show in which the wife, in the presence of the husband, was asked to tell the worst secret of her marriage, and she revealed, to her husband's horrified humiliation, that they had a lousy sex life.

"Yesterday I saw the Merv Griffin show," she said, "where Burt Reynolds and another he-man and a (*Laughing.*) he-girl were talking about what they would do to all the bad critics of their movie. I couldn't take them seriously—they are not like real people. If anyone ever came on a show and acted sincere and normal, he would look fake," she said with amazement. And I remembered all over again that European actors and actresses *are* different, that they are allowed to ply their profession with more dignity and less psychic dislocation—probably because they are treated like artists rather than trained seals.

Ullmann speaks beautiful English, having lived in New York briefly as a child and studied it in school. There is only a slight accent—she also has a Norwegian accent in Swedish—and an occasional marvelous neologism (or transposition of a Norwegian word into English), as when she told me that some poor plagiarist whose book on Harlem had been much praised, had the "unluck" for somebody to discover the original.

I told her I had seen the two-hour, forty-eight-minute version of *Scenes from a Marriage,* as well as the four-hour version (itself cut from the original six-part, five-hour television special), and asked her what she thought had been gained or lost.

LIV ULLMANN: The four-hour version was a compromise of the television version. There were many of the same kinds of scenes, only slightly different. There were moments of relaxation which you need in a TV show but not in a movie. The film shows all the important things that happen, but some of the emotional scenes are cut because you can't watch everything in that short a time.

MOLLY HASKELL: I found myself liking it much better the second time around. It was like watching it on television, getting to know and accept the people. In particular, I found the husband (played by Erland Josephson) more sympathetic.

LU: This happened in Sweden, too. The first time around, people had enormous discussions the whole week. Then the next time around (the whole cycle was shown three times), what you said happened. They had seen more of the husband, and they understood his attitude in the first scene, his arrogance. They came to pity him, and they realized he was acting that way to hide his insecurity.

MH: My male companion (as we say) didn't understand why Johan would leave Marianne. "She's so beautiful and extraordinary," he said. But I think women understand it.

LU: Why he leaves her is that he suddenly feels afraid. He's trying to grab life while it's still there.

MH: It's something we've begun referring to (apologetically) as "male menopause."

(*Ullmann appreciates the term and she and Drott nod vigorously.*)

LU: Yes, men have it harder than we do. We can call it something physical, can get pills, go to the doctor, get pity. But men do all these crazy things—they get divorces, they suddenly turn homosexual, they walk through red lights. They feel lost but they have nothing to prove what's wrong. It is much more difficult.

We are very lucky if we have a relationship where we feel fulfilled, but if we are unfulfilled, the warning lights keep flashing that age is coming on.

MH: In one of the film's most extraordinary scenes, you are interviewed by an elderly woman (actually Barbro Hiort af Ornas, who was the nurse in *The Brink of Life*, 1958) who wants a divorce.

Liv Ullmann and Erland Josephson, wife and husband, in Ingmar Bergman's *Scenes from a Marriage* (1973–1974). (Courtesy Cinema 5)

Suddenly in the calmest possible manner, she confesses not only that she doesn't love her husband, but that she doesn't love her children, has never loved them; and that she feels her senses failing her—when she hears, sees, touches something it is remote, the "sensation is thin and dry." You start to say something, but then are silent. What was it?

LU: Bergman never told me, but I think it is that the woman touches a nerve in me, something that I am used to hiding.

MH: In the first scene you and Josephson (the reader will forgive me for not always distinguishing between the actor, the character, and the person, particularly in Ullmann's case. The ambiguity, I think, belongs) are being interviewed by a reporter, Mrs. Palm, from a woman's magazine. Some of the scene has been cut for the theatrical version.

LU: Yes, she runs and snoops around when they've left the room, she even peeks in the bedroom. It's a very funny moment, but you know she is that kind of woman without showing that scene.

MH: She reminds me of so many interviewers, when she pushes her glasses back on her head, and opens that enormous, all-purpose sack, the way she intimidates you with her clickety-click professionalism.

LU: All the interviewers for the gossip magazines in Sweden are like that, with their little skirts and big belts, always snooping.

MH: And you feel stupid because you can't respond in their terms, can't think of something cute and quick and "profound" about love and marriage. Having just endured a similar experience, I really appreciated that part, and the whole notion of the Happy Couple feature, which is predicated on the assumption that each partner was a cipher or a half-person until the marriage, which miraculously completed and transformed them.

But there are other things that have been cut, like our discovery that Mrs. Palm was an old schoolmate of yours. To me, it seemed an allusion to *A Doll's House,* and the scene when Christine comes to see Nora.

LU: (*thoughtful, then delighted*): Yes, you're right. I never thought of that. I don't have anything to say to the interviewer, I don't feel friendly. I try to move away, and yet I never quite got the bit of business when we were shooting the film. But then, when I was doing *A Doll's House,* I suddenly remembered this feeling and I used it, I moved away from Christine more decisively. I believe I felt at the time (of *Scenes*) that if I ever have the opportunity, I will use this gesture. And with *A Doll's House,* I remembered it and used it.

It's like when I was watching a production of *A Doll's House* a long time ago. It was a bad production, but a friend of mine, a good friend, was playing Nora. In the scene when she is decorating the Christmas tree, before Torvald is coming home, she suddenly starts decorating herself! At the time, most of us didn't understand, but when I came to do the scene, I started doing it, I started decorating myself. This is a woman who is always putting on masks for her husband.

MH: Another interesting, and related, factor is that Mrs. Palm is addressing most of her questions to Johan. When she asks you one that you *can* respond to, and you finally open up, she immediately interrupts and calls for a photograph! This becomes especially ironic when you know that she is an old friend of yours, and seems to confirm something that Johan says later, in a semifacetious diatribe against "women's lib," when he claims that all women are out to get each other.

LU: Yes, but interviewers do that to men, too. With Bergman, they always interrupt him just when he is going to say something interesting, because they can't handle it. It doesn't fit, like a person suddenly acting natural on your TV game show. The interviewers come to get what they want to give their readers, so it is fake to begin with. It's like a bad director. When you at last find the right action or motivation, he will talk it out so much that you'll never find it again.

MH: Why do Johan and Marianne consent to the interview?

LU: Why does anybody? Because they think it will be fun. They've never done it before.

MH: What is Bergman's attitude toward the Bibi Andersson character? The scene seemed rather harsh on her.

LU: He likes her. I think he likes her. He feels sorry for the man, but sympathy for her. He finds a kind of hope in the woman. Women are stronger than men.

MH: I think the fact that Marianne blossoms after the separation is proof of that.

LU: It's funny. One woman critic wrote that it was unbelievable—the man got more and more wrinkled and sad while she was lovelier than ever, but that's the point of the story. This is always happening in real life, women becoming more attractive after their husbands divorce them, or die.

MH: I think it's partly just discovering that they *can* make it alone that gives them strength. I also love the scene when, after they are separated, he comes for dinner. She brings out the journal that, at the encouragement of her psychiatrist, she has started to keep. (With that wonderful insight into her female vanity, Bergman has her wishing she hadn't stayed up till three on *that* night writing in it, as it has made her look tired.) She begins reading it to Johan, and he falls asleep.

LU: I've heard men say, heard Bergman say, they just want to leave when women go on and on about emotional things. This is a difference between women and men—men are tired, but women are always ready to go on about emotional things. That can be exhausting for a man. They are on another level where everything is not that important, and when you start up they say, "Oh, there you go again." He sees her like that.

MH: Yes, but she never does go on and on. Johan is always criticizing her for faults you never show.

LU: I agree, they say it about her, like when at the end he is surprised that she is jealous. He thinks she is not jealous. I don't know where he got that idea. It's not written in the character, but so what, let them say it about her.

Everybody has his own interpretation. It's like your friend saying, how could he leave her? I identify so closely with the woman, I felt it very natural that he should leave her. She's wearing those glasses and that nightdress, she looks terrible. She takes the marriage for granted and he wants somebody who doesn't. She's plain and very uninteresting. It's all in what you see at the time.

MH: There's a scene in the published screenplay that is one of my favorites, that has been cut out of the shorter version. It's when he's leaving her and they are discussing the details over breakfast. She mentions she'll have to tell the old housekeeper and he stutters and finally says, you don't need to—she already knows. Marianne looks surprised, and shamefacedly he explains that there had been a change of her schedule that he didn't know about, and he had brought his mistress home—the only time—and the housekeeper walked into the bedroom the next morning. On her face there's this incredible pain mingled with an attempt to see the absurdity of it.

LU: Yes, to me that's one of the most horrible things that happens to her, maybe the most horrible—more than the humiliation of finding that all of her friends know. The fact that the cleaning woman is such an old friend, and that the husband brought his girl to her home. But men don't feel it that way. Bergman had to choose between the two scenes, and he kept the one with her on the phone, where rage comes for the first time. The other one is actually worse. But the way the man is talking about it, he doesn't know how terrible it is. If a woman had written that scene, she would have made the lines more cruel, to bring out the horror of it. But the way Johan is talking, neither the man who acted it nor Bergman understood the impact of it. That's what makes the whole thing so interesting.

MH: How much freedom does Bergman give you?

LU: A lot. He gives you a direction: you pass through a room. But the freedom of expression is yours.

MH: I liked it when you just pulled the covers over your head, to make the whole thing go away. Did you think of that? It seemed such a reflex.

LU: I don't remember. It was probably something I had done or would do.

MH: And packing the husband's suitcase?

LU: I wouldn't have done that. But I have a friend (*She says a name and turns to Cecillia Drott, who nods.*) who always helps her husband pack when he goes on his affairs.

MH: In the very last scene, there's a sequence in which you

confess to Johan that early in your marriage you had affairs. That's been cut.

LU: I'm glad. I never saw her as having affairs. I guess Bergman wanted to think she was more exciting and open to adventure than she was, that she had been exciting all the time. I didn't want to say the line, so I asked Bergman if I could say it as if I were lying. That's what I'm trying to do. Now afterwards, Bergman has been very nice about it in interviews—he admitted I didn't want to say it.

MH: The abortion scene has been cut, but frankly I don't miss it.

LU: There's a lot of life left out.

MH: I would have liked to see the scene, cut from both versions, between you and your mother.

LU: So would the woman who played my mother. I feel very sad about that. At first I didn't have the heart to tell her it had been cut, but I guess I will have to now.

MH: I miss, too, the scene in which Johan admits to hating the children.

LU: Well, there are always things cut from every picture that disappoint you. As a matter of fact, I miss more in *The Abdication* than in *Scenes from a Marriage*. If you really care for a picture, there will always be those scenes on the cutting room floor about which you say, "There's where I really show this other side of my character."

(*Having now seen* The Abdication, *she may be right. I'd like to think there were some footage somewhere that would show Ullmann as something other than a neurotic, posturing soap-opera queen who makes decisions of state on whim, and religious conversions out of displaced sexual longing.*)

MH: What was it like doing *Persona,* your first film with Bergman?

LU: At first I was terrified. I blushed whenever Bergman said a word. If I had not had Bibi there—I lived with her and her then-husband—I wouldn't have gotten through. Slowly I understood that he was kind and nice. Then he got excited about the rushes and I got confidence. Bibi was nervous, too, at the beginning, and broke

Alma (Liv Ullmann) and Elizabeth (Bibi Andersson) in a somnambulist sequence from Ingmar Bergman's *Persona* (1967). (Courtesy United Artists 16)

out in nervous spots. Bergman knew very little about me, he had only seen me on the stage. And there I was this young girl who was always blushing, playing a mature woman. Bibi and I heard later that there was a lot of talk during the first week about canceling the whole project.

We went to the island of Faro and redid all the scenes done in Stockholm. We had a wonderful time, always joking. We just thought we were making this small film on an island and nobody would ever see it, and then it became a classic. Bergman experimented a lot and let us be a part of it. The scene with the faces coming together, we didn't even know what was up until we went to the rushes. Bibi said, "Liv, you're marvelous." I said, "Bibi, you're fantastic." Then we saw the faces merging—it was the most frightening thing I ever saw in my life. Everybody has one good side and one bad side, or at least two different sides, one not as good as the other. Bergman had taken the worse side of each of us. To see this woman, moving her lips, and half of her is you! It's what schizophrenic people must feel. There were things like that all the time.

With *Cries and Whispers* you never had a somber atmosphere. Harriet Andersson was running around and making jokes in this little nightgown, and I was really getting worried, but when the camera said go, she looked dead.

MH: What about the character you play?

LU: She isn't really a sympathetic character. Someone says she's the kind of woman who goes through a room and never shuts the door after her, very selfish. When her sister needs her, she can't give. And yet everybody still thinks she's sweet and nice—the audience, too. That's why she's dangerous.

Some people criticized and said Bergman is so bad what he does to me. I'm so stupid, I just thought it was the part's bad character, not mine. There is this streak of selfishness in me, though, that I wish weren't there.

MH: Although you were highly praised for your role as the pioneer woman in the Troell epics, I always think of you as contemporary, as belonging to a world of people and particularly, men.

LU: Actually, I've done mostly period things, except for Bergman. Classical movies like *The Abdication* also reflect modern people. I like that mixture, although I guess I'd like to do more modern stuff.

MH: What about your American movies? One I haven't seen is *Zandy's Bride* [1974].

LU: I loved Gene Hackman. He is fantastic, very inventive. He played an unsympathetic character but he did wonderful things with him.

MH: One male critic told me he found you at your most attractive and most womanly in *Zandy's Bride*.

LU: Then he must be a misogynist, because I was asked to look thin and haggard. I was a mail-order bride, after all, and no great catch. The first thing he says to me is you lied about your age.

MH: *Forty Carats* [1973]?

LU: I'd do it again, willingly. Only with a little more control.

MH: I didn't quite see you as the "older woman."

LU: If I'd only had Cecillia to help me. What happened is they were so afraid I wouldn't look old enough, that they made me look ugly instead of older. The boy would have easily gone off with someone forty but more attractive. Only in Greece did I look OK—I had a scarf on my head. I'd really like to do more comedy. I have a disadvantage of working in the Bergman pictures. All the critics think if it's not Bergman, then it's wrong. It's unfair that I have to do seven American pictures that are as good as the Bergman pictures before they will accept me.

MH: The difference between you and, say, Garbo and Ingrid Bergman, was that they came here first, and their myths grew out of their American movies, whereas you . . .

LU: If I'd come here first, then nobody would have *ever* heard of me. Bergman and Garbo came at a time when they still made pictures for women in America. Joanne Woodward is the only actress who has scripts written for her. All anybody wants to see is Paul Redford.

(We yelp with delight at this slip.)

MH: I'm afraid it's women as much as the men who go to see *The Sting* [1973]. They get two for the price of one.

LU: I guess women don't want to look at other women over thirty with the same problems.

MH: Why is the situation different in Europe, in European films?

LU: In Sweden, in Europe, they make more movies about women because they feel more interest in women's inner soul. On commercials here, nobody talks about the inner side of woman. They only do things to their outside, to their smell, their hands, their hair, for the husband when he comes home. That's their idea of attractiveness in a woman, while a man reads newspapers, does other things. They've made a myth of the American woman everybody wants to get away from.

MH: What about European commercials?

LU: In Sweden they don't have them at all. In England there is not the same emphasis. You don't have the same theme that all women must be this way. Here, it is really effective propaganda.

When I watch for a while, I feel I have to go out and get that shampoo. They talk even in a certain kind of voice because they know it works. There is this image of the sophisticated woman which very few of us are. All of us have to face the problem of what to do with ourselves, and what we are.

MH: What about the women's movement?

LU: I don't like the real militants. Their idea of what a woman is is just as rigid. They have a fixed image that is even more frightening than the commercials. Everyone is afraid to show woman to herself. They think nobody will love her if she grows for herself.

MH: I was electrified at that point in *Scenes from a Marriage* when we see snapshots of you as a child and a teen-ager, just seeing what you looked like. Marianne's voice-over says she has always lived for others. Is that true of you?

LU: Very much. I have spent most of my life and still spend most of it living for other people, doing what is expected of me, being scared of doing my own thing. I've wasted oceans of time doing what other people didn't care about my doing for them, while they were doing the same thing for me.

In fact, Bergman got hold of these pictures without my knowing it, and his insights were a revelation to me. Like the one where I am all dressed up with the hat and the pocketbook and the big bosoms. That was taken when I was seventeen and I went to London to study acting. I lived at the Y.W.C.A. with older girls, only by about two years, but they seemed much older. All the time, I was trying to be grown up, wearing a hat, and padding my bust, all these things that had nothing to do with me, just to be accepted by the older girls.

Then there's a picture with me lying on the beach, and the speech says I was obsessed with sex. I certainly didn't think of myself that way, but I look at the picture and it proves it. After years of padding, I have finally started to get a bust, and I've crossed my arms to make the crease show. There again, I was preoccupied with sex so people will accept me, so early on we get into these things.

MH: How much of *Scenes* is your story, the story of you and Bergman?

LU: It's not my story. I was terrified everyone would think that, but everyone thinks it's *their* story. A producer here in America who had divorced his wife told Bergman that once she invited him home during the separation and that she started telling him she had gone to sleep with her psychiatrist, and about her soul-searching, and he fell asleep, exactly like in the movie.

Men have a facade. One part of women's nature is to be open to these emotional things, so they can see a film like this and fit it in, face it, but men aren't able to deal with it as easily. A man, a journalist, came here, he was very stiff and formal, but in talking about the movie he suddenly broke down. He had had a similar situation, and was shattered by the film. He was so attractive when he broke down.

One reason a lot of women relate to it is that I've drawn from so many women, from this friend and that one, I steal bits and pieces like a drawing. Things I've kept and collected I've used in this picture.

MH: The divorce scene becomes extraordinarily violent although Johan's actual hitting you occurs below the frame.

LU: Erland didn't want to do it, he didn't want to hit a woman. He just felt he couldn't do it and he felt sick beforehand, but when he got into the scene he lost himself. It wasn't that he lost control but suddenly he felt it was right for his character. It took a long time to get to that part, twelve minutes. But we start with hating, so we are already at a high level. He will be able to do a lot more now. That's why it's important to have a director like Bergman who will allow you to do anything.

(*I don't know. I remember the story of Gregory Peck not being able to bring himself to hit Lauren Bacall when they were doing* Designing Woman *[1957]. She told Bogey and the boys when she got home, and they were supposed to have gotten a big laugh out of it, but I always thought Peck was the hero of that story. Of course, American violence and Swedish violence are two different things.*)

MH: The jobs seem unreal, subordinated to the relationship.

LU: Because love is more important than the job. You throw yourself into a job when you can't do other things, but deep down we want to talk about the human condition. Their story is really their marriage story, and that's also the reason the children—who wouldn't have changed what was between them one way or the other—are left out. It's *their* particular story. Some other couple, the children might have come between them.

MH: Isn't it really about a relationship rather than a marriage?

LU: Yes, it's very important that it's a relationship. Homosexuals also think it's their story. It's about a relationship and a longing for it, so even people who have never had one understand it.

MH: How long did it take to shoot?

LU: A very short time—eight weeks shooting. It was very hard, because there was a lot of dialogue to learn. We shot it in sequence, rehearsed for one week, then shot for a week. We couldn't have gone on like that much longer. There was no improvisation, for almost the first time with Bergman, who lately is very free. We were not allowed to depart one word from the script. This was important because there was a lot of silly, banal talk. If we had been let loose we would just swim out into sheer banality.

It was an extraordinary experience, fighting and crying. We got to know each other so well, we skipped all kinds of shyness with each other and with everybody on the crew. We worked intimately and discussed the scenes. Working on the island was so much fun, very relaxed. You had to walk for miles to a toilet and there is only cold water. We would meet in the evenings by the fire and drink and talk.

MH: Bergman, too?

LU: No, without him; he's a recluse in the evenings.

MH: And how is it now, since you have broken up?

LU: Much easier. Before, if we had an argument at breakfast, I would be upset all day in my womanly way. Now we have the best part of a relationship. (*She hesitates.*) Or almost. The best thing you can have with somebody you lived with—friendship and working together.

Bibliography

Barthes, Roland. "Garbo's Face." *Moviegoer* (Summer 1966).

Bogdanovich, Peter. "Miss Dietrich Goes to Denver." *Pieces of Time.* New York: David McKay, 1973.

Braun, Eric. "Doing What Comes Naturally." *Films and Filming* (October 1970). [Mae West]

———. "One For the Boys." *Films and Filming* (November 1970). [Mae West]

Brett, Simon. "Audrey Hepburn." *Films and Filming* (March 1964).

Brooks, Louise. "Charlie Chaplin Remembered." *Film Culture* (Spring 1966).

———. "Gish and Garbo." *Sight and Sound* (Winter 1958/59).

———. "On Location with Billy Wellman." *Film Culture* (Spring 1972).

Brownlow, Kevin. "The Stars." *The Parade's Gone By.* New York: Ballantine Books, 1969. [Louise Brooks]

Card, James. "The 'Intense Isolation' of Louise Brooks." *Sight and Sound* (Summer 1958).

Corliss, Richard. *Greta Garbo.* New York: Pyramid Publications, 1974.

Counts, Kyle B. "America's Favorite Misunderstood Commodity: Doris Day." *Take One*, 5, no. 1 (1976).

Dietrich, Marlene. *Marlene Dietrich's ABC.* New York: Doubleday & Co., 1961.

Durgnat, Raymond. "B.B." *Films and Filming* (January 1963).

Essoe, Gabe. "Elizabeth Taylor's Career." *Films in Review* (August–September 1970).

Eyman, Scott. " 'I've Always Done Everything I Wanted!'—Mae West Interviewed." *Take One*, 4, no. 1 (1974).

Guiles, Fred Lawrence. *Norma Jean: The Life of Marilyn Monroe*. New York: Bantam Books, 1970.

Haskell, Molly. "An Interview with Doris Day." *Ms.* (January 1976).

Hotchner, A. E. *Doris Day: Her Own Story*. New York: William Morrow, 1976.

Israel, Lee. "Rise and Fall of Elizabeth Taylor." *Esquire* (March 1967).

Kinder, Marsha. *"Scenes from a Marriage." Film Quarterly* (Winter 1974–1975).

Luce, Clare Booth. "What Really Killed Marilyn." *Life*, August 7, 1964.

Mailer, Norman. *Marilyn*. New York: Grosset and Dunlap, 1973.

Maurois, André. "B.B.: The Sex Kitten Grows Up." *Playboy* (July 1964).

Mellen, Joan. "The Mae West Nobody Knows." *Women and Their Sexuality in the New Film*. New York: Horizon Press, 1974.

———. *Marilyn Monroe*. New York: Galahad Books, 1973.

Monroe, Marilyn. "I Want Women to Like Me." *Photoplay* (November 1952).

———. "My Beauty Secrets." *Photoplay* (October 1953).

Nordberg, Carl Eric. "Greta Garbo's Secret." *Film Comment* (Summer 1970).

Odets, Clifford. "To Whom It May Concern: Marilyn Monroe." *Show* (October 1962).

Pabst, G. W. *Pandora's Box*. New York: Simon & Schuster, 1971.

Rosten, Norman. *Marilyn: an Untold Story*. New York: Signet, 1973.

Sargeant, Winthrop. "Dietrich and Her Magic Myth." *Life*, August 18, 1952.

Shipman, David. "Doris Day." *Films and Filming* (August 1962).

Silke, James R. "The Tragic Mask of Bardolatry." *Cinema* (California), 2, no. 2 (1962).

Silver, Charles. *Marlene Dietrich*. New York: Pyramid Publications, 1974.

Steene, Brigitta. "Freedom and Entrapment: *Scenes from a Marriage*." *Movietone News* (April–May 1975).

Sternberg, Josef von. *Fun in a Chinese Laundry*. New York: The Macmillan Co., 1965.

Taylor, Elizabeth. *Elizabeth Taylor*. New York: Harper and Row, 1964.

Trilling, Diana. "The Death of Marilyn Monroe." *Claremont Essays*. New York: Harcourt, Brace and World, 1963.

Tynan, Kenneth. "Garbo." *Sight and Sound* (April–June 1954).

Viotti, Sergio. "Britain's Hepburn." *Films and Filming* (November 1954).

Walker, Alexander. "Star Syndrome: Elizabeth Taylor." *The Celluloid Sacrifice*. London: Michael Joseph, 1966.

Waterbury, Ruth. *Elizabeth Taylor. Her Life, Her Loves, Her Future.* New York: Appleton-Century, 1964.

Webb, Teena. "*Scenes from a Marriage.*" *Jump Cut,* no. 5 (January–February 1975).

West, Mae. *Goodness Had Nothing to Do with It.* rev. ed. New York: Manor Books, 1970.

Young, Stark. "Film Note: Greta Garbo." *The New Republic,* September 28, 1932.

Zolotow, Maurice. *Marilyn Monroe.* New York: Harcourt, Brace & Co., 1960.

III
Women in American Production

Alice Guy Blaché:
Czarina of the Silent Screen[*]

Gerald Peary

I

Alice Guy Blaché is an exemplary subject for feminist film research.
An amazingly prodigious director, she made as many as 270 films.
And, bypassing even Mary Pickford's presidency of the United
Artists Corporation, Alice Blaché was the most powerful woman
executive ever to work in the film industry. She owned her studio,
the Solax Company, from 1910 to 1914, and ran it with the kind of
total authority that leads to theorizing about "the studio head as
auteur." Furthermore, Alice Blaché was noticeably successful, both
as a businesswoman and as an artist.

Alice Blaché's secret was to make her mark in film before the
barriers against women came into existence, indeed before there
was such a thing as a film industry. Born in Paris in 1873, Alice Guy
joined the Gaumont organization as a secretary in her early
twenties, but suddenly switched positions to become Gaumont's
first and only movie director—all this before the turn of the century.

A reporter who talked to Alice Blaché in 1912 described her contribution: "Mr. Gaumont was absorbed with the scientific department of production of merely engaging in photographing moving
objects. She inaugurated the presentation of little plays on the

* Reprinted and abridged from *The Velvet Light Trap,* no. 6 (Fall 1972).

screen by that company some sixteen or seventeen years ago, operating the camera, writing or adapting the photodrama, setting the scenes and handling the actors . . ."

Were some of those little playlets, produced in the garden of her boss's home, actually made before Méliès? That is what the ninety-eight-year-old woman, then still alive in a nursing home in America, told Francis Lacassin for his remarkable article, "Out of Oblivion: Alice Guy Blaché," printed in the Summer 1971 *Sight and Sound*.

Lacassin, who has made a particular study of the French phase of Madame Blaché's career, described works in every kind of genre among the 200-odd one-reelers she directed at Gaumont through the autumn of 1905. Alice Guy made "fairy tales and fantasies . . . saucy comedies . . . trick comedies . . . religious subjects."

She ended her career at Gaumont with superproductions in late 1905 and 1906, *Esmeralda* from Hugo's *Hunchback* and a *Life of Christ*, then worked in successful collaboration with scriptwriter Louis Feuillade before his celebrated directing debut. But in 1907 Herbert Blaché, her husband, was made general manager of Gaumont's New York office, and Alice Guy accompanied him, giving up her directing career to be a wife and mother.

. . . Mrs. Blaché began to get bored with her placid existence. Says Lacassin,

> Nostalgic for her former profession, she had the idea of making for the American public films designed to its taste and performed by American actors . . . On September 7, 1910, the Solax Company was registered: president, Alice Blaché . . . [I]t . . . operated from the Gaumont building in Flushing [New York] . . . With its trademark of a blazing sun, the Solax Company produced some 325 films of assorted lengths and types. At least 35 of them were directed by the company's lady president.

The history of Solax was, from its inception, an almost unbroken line of success. Beginning with one reel a week in October 1910, a second weekly release was able to be afforded by March 1911. The ad proclaimed, "Solax films have been on the market three months and have become so popular that we cannot longer withhold our second release."

In November 1911, Solax enlarged its Flushing studio, and in December moved up to one-reel releases on Mondays, Wednesdays, and Fridays. The studio advertisement fairly shouted, "Learn to swear three-times-a-week 'By the rising sun, I want Solax.' "

Francis Lacassin is correct in stating that "At first Alice Guy tried not to draw attention to her unique position as the world's only woman film director." In fact, early advertising created the impression of a studio with nothing to do with women, as Solax films were trumpeted as "The Best Films Made—Ask the Man Who Has Seen Them," and described on at least one occasion as "Made by Men Long in the Business."

By the end of a year of production, however, with the Solax Company on secure financial grounds and apparently guaranteed of survival, Alice Blaché began to emerge from hiding. She allowed a tour of her enlarging studio in Flushing to a reporter for *Moving Picture World* in November 1911, who stated in print that "While Mme. Blaché does not seek personal publicity, she was not averse to discussing her interest in picture making . . ."

. . . Most interesting in this brief article is a theme that would be reiterated often in subsequent writings about Solax Company: the astonishing amount of participation by Alice Blaché in all phases of filmmaking, no matter how many films were in simultaneous production. Stated the reporter, "All scenarios used by the Solax Company are edited by Mme. Blaché and many of the pictures are personally directed by her. Those not made under her personal direction are viséd by her at some stage . . . so that she practically has a hand in the entire output of the company."

. . . Alice Blaché succeeded remarkably. In September 1912, two years after Solax came into existence, the company moved out of its cramped Flushing headquarters to a newly built studio across the river in Fort Lee, New Jersey. This studio was an extraordinary one. Designed by Alice Guy personally and constructed at a towering cost of $100,000, it lived up to the Solax claim of being "the best equipped moving picture plant in the world." Four stories high and constructed of structural iron and glass, the studio included projection rooms, laboratories, darkrooms, prop rooms, carpenter shops, hotellike dressing rooms (a men's area with cuspidors and pinochle table), and a main floor large enough to accommodate five stage settings. Six thousand feet of film could be dried at one time, and Solax now was capable of turning out 12,000 positive feet of film in a day.

Film reporter Hugh Hoffman visited the new plant soon after its opening and was most impressed by Alice Blaché's total contribution. "The entire studio and factory were planned by Madame Alice Blaché, the presiding genius of the Solax Company. She is a remarkable personality, combining a true artistic temperament with executive ability and business acumen. Every detail of the making of a Solax picture comes directly under her personal supervision." Hoffman describes the projection room as the place ". . . where the finished product must meet its final test, which is the all-seeing eye of Madame Blaché."

She obviously was proud of her achievements in bringing Solax to an estimable position at the top of the film companies. For the first time she allowed her own name to be used in Solax ads. A movie she directed in October 1912, called *Flesh and Blood,* was advertised as "Staged by Madame Blaché, the producer of *Fra Diavolo.*" . . .

II

What kind of movies did Alice Blaché produce under the Solax banner? The safe answer, of course, is "all kinds," generally half comedies and half dramas. There was a period of several months in 1911 when all of the dramas were of a military nature (filmed on location at a government post at Fort Myer, Virginia), but generally the types of film were diversified. Although there are indications that Alice Blaché took more care than most producers in directing her films, it is romanticism to see Solax Company as separate from the other companies in the choice of cinematic subject matter. The plots of most Solax movies were clichéd and melodramatic and familiar, typical of the hundreds of movies cranked out monthly at all the studios.

In a 1912 guideline sheet for potential "photoplaywrights," Solax made the most modest demands on the material: "One or two original ideas or situations in a complete photoplay makes the photoplay satisfactory to us." The other considerations were all of a technical rather than thematic nature: ". . . every scene has to be posed before the camera . . . each and every set must be built by stagehands, and that train wrecks, explosions, or shipwrecks are rather expensive, not to say impractical . . . [A] photoplay has more chance to land if its production does not require an outlay of several thousand dollars or require the engagement of a large cast." This statement offers little about the content of Solax movies, and nothing to answer probably the basic question confronting anyone researching Solax: what difference is discernible in movies under the control of a woman from the normal male-dominated studio product?

Obviously such a loaded inquiry places incredible expectations on Alice Blaché to represent a unique point of view. If Solax seems not very unusual in its subject matter or thematic perspectives, and if Alice Blaché's view of the "nature" of woman is much closer to a Victorian male's conception (see "Woman's Place in Photoplay Production," pp. 337–340) than to an advocate of feminism, these discoveries cannot help but be a bit disappointing.

If Alice Blaché were ignorant of the utilization of film as a political tool, that would be one thing. But discovered among Solax products are a handful of movies dealing with labor-management factory struggles in very directly political terms.[1] And women's rights also were no stranger to Alice Blaché, for Solax Company existed during a time of high levels of feminist activism, organized around the question of universal suffrage.

On the second point: although almost every studio produced vehemently antisuffragette movies in the years 1912 and 1913 (at least twenty-five such tracts), Alice Blaché took no stand at all, boycotting the whole question by staying away from topical movies on the subject. Reporter Louis Reeves Harrison claimed in 1912 that

[1] More correctly, *reactionary* political terms. Her labor movies are stringently antistrike, promanagement, and deal typically with a worker protagonist forced to strike against his will who discovers proof of the "goodness" of the boss and leads the men back to work, and away from their "unreasonable" demands.

"She only favors universal suffrage when satisfied that women are ready for it," a comment unsubstantiated by any direct statements from Alice Blaché. But a more likely explanation for her silence is that she felt that she should stay away from editorializing about something so close to her own situation. . . .

Actually, Alice Blaché is slightly misrepresented if she is seen as totally avoiding women's issues, for there are a few Solax movies that, although not blatantly political, do offer some rather strange perspectives. For instance, these four movies among a hundred Solax releases in 1912, with plot descriptions paraphrased from *The Motion Picture World*.

The Call of the Rose. Grace Moore, a professional opera singer, marries a young miner, who takes her West and sets her up in a little cottage. For a time, Grace is happy watching her devoted husband dig for gold. But then "the emptiness of her inactive existence" leads her to leave her husband and go East to resume her career . . . And yet, she still is not completely happy. Her husband comes East and they are reunited. (But does Grace keep her career? The plot outline doesn't say.)

Winsome But Wise. An "impecunious" young lady "full of energy and pluck" goes West. She gets an idea that she can catch a notorious bandit who has eluded posse after posse. The cowboys laugh. The young lady sets out by herself, captures the bandit through trickery when she gets him to try on handcuffs, then takes him in and gets the reward.

The Two Little Rangers. "Wild Bill" Grey, wife-beater and villain, is chased to a shack by two young sisters, Mary and Gladys. "The girls are determined to get him and, after seeing their volley of bullets have no effect, discharge a firebrand from a bow. The firebrand sets the shack on fire and Grey perishes in his own tomb."

Making an American Citizen. "A husband and wife, belonging to the most ignorant and lowest classes of peasantry, emigrate to the United States. On landing in New York, the husband loads a huge bundle on back of his wife, and . . . starts to pass through the Battery . . . Soon a crowd gathers around them, some laughing, jeering, others indignant and threatening, until a huge American pushes his way through the crowd . . . takes the bundle off her back, lays . . . the bundle . . . on his back, and orders him to march on.

"This is the husband's first lesson in Americanism. Other lessons follow . . . until after he has been arrested and sent to jail for beating his wife, he becomes thoroughly convinced that old world methods will not do in this strange new world . . ."

It is tempting to dismiss the feminist urges in the first three movies as accidental or subconscious, especially when placed next to the several hundred traditional love intrigues produced by Solax, and to view the last movie, *Making an American Citizen*, as a truer indicator of the actual "sexual politics" of Alice Blaché. This film about the mistreatment of women in the marriage relationship becomes, in reality, a plea for the worth of all kinds of chauvinism, from patriotic zeal to male chivalry—a key to the contradictions implied in Alice Blaché's essay on woman's "place" in the cinema.

The Years Have Not Been Kind to Lois Weber[*]

Richard Koszarski

INTRODUCTION

Lois Weber, the most respected woman director of the whole silent era, made her last Hollywood movies in 1927, the year in which female directors, with the exception of newcomer Dorothy Arzner, were phased out of the industry. Weber was only forty-five at the time, at the height of her creative powers. She might have helped along her own fall by a brave act of defiance toward the end, captured forever in a Variety *tidbit: proclaiming absolute autonomy over her filmmaking, Lois Weber refused to direct* Topsy and Eva *because United Artists assigned "gagmen" to the project. UA was forced to recall director Sam Taylor, on loan to M-G-M, so that the Duncan Sisters vehicle could go through.*

Richard Koszarski's article is the first modern critical appreciation of this almost forgotten filmmaker. The Library of Congress discovered a print of her 1921 feature film, The Blot, *and it is at last available for showing from The Museum of Modern Art. Perhaps the interest and research will continue and the future will be more kind to Lois Weber than the four decades of neglect.*

146

Among the rank of great women directors the names of Leni Riefenstahl and Dorothy Arzner come to mind immediately. The name of Lois Weber doesn't, although sixty years ago she won wide acclaim for her thoughtful handling of "women's issues" like child labor, divorce, birth control, and abortion. Some of the top-grossing films of the early years were her productions, and when Anna Pavlova made her only dramatic feature, it was Lois Weber who directed it. With such credentials it seems strange that Weber's name doesn't immediately spring to the fore in any discussion of prominent women directors. But this once widely applauded figure has been forgotten with a vengeance.

Born in Allegheny City, Pennsylvania, in 1882, Weber's early training was as a pianist. As a concert prodigy she toured widely before the turn of the century. This career abruptly ended during one southern junket when a piano key broke off in her hand, an incident that, as she later remembered, "broke my nerve." Her background was zealously religious, and so she joined a Salvation Army-style organization upon returning home; as a Church Home Missionary she sang hymns on street corners and worked in the industrial slums of Pittsburgh. But the experience was not a pleasant one. "It gave life a bitter taste," she recalled later. Forced to earn her own living, Weber went against her better judgment and followed the advice of an uncle in Chicago to try the stage. "As I was convinced the theatrical profession needed a missionary, he suggested that the best way to reach them was to become one of them, so I went on the stage filled with a great desire to convert my fellowman."

One of her first positions was as a soubrette in the touring *Zig Zag* company, but her intentions were more serious and she quickly moved over to melodrama, joining in 1905 a road company of *Why Girls Leave Home*. Here she met and married the company's actor-manager, Phillips Smalley, after a week's whirlwind courtship. They continued their careers separately, but conflicting tour schedules kept Smalley and her apart for increasing periods of time, and in 1906 Weber quit the stage to set up a permanent home in New York. Giving up her career at this point could not have been an easy decision, since she had just achieved a certain success at New York's giant Hippodrome; it's entirely possible that Smalley's ego had something to do with it.

But life as a homemaker had little appeal; and one day in 1908, while Smalley was on the road, she went to work for the Gaumont Studios. Legitimate actors despised the movies in those days and only appeared in them under duress, often hiding behind tricky aliases or crepe paper beards. So something special pushed Weber into films, something more than boredom and perhaps even more than money, which was D. W. Griffith's excuse. Lois Weber sensed early the emotional power of the cinema, its unique ability to dramatize an issue and drive home a moral. She had never forgotten her early days of street-corner evangelism, her desire to "convert my fellowman," and right from the start saw the cinema as a tool for moral betterment, perhaps the first to do so and put the idea into practice. "I find at once the outlet for my emotions and my ideals, I can preach to my heart's content; and with the opportunity to write the play, act the leading role, and direct the entire production, if my message fails to reach someone I can blame only myself," she wrote a few years later.

Smalley returned to join her in a writing-directing-acting partnership, and the pair moved on to Reliance and later to Rex, Edwin S. Porter's company. They served here as the studio's dramatic leads, wrote a lot of scripts, and worked as second-string directors under Porter, famous for *The Great Train Robbery* (1902). After 1912, Porter left to direct feature films for Adolph Zukor, and the Smalleys (as they were known in the trade) took charge of Rex, now an important member of the conglomerate of independents that made up Universal. In the early part of their career the creative chores had been split between the two, but by 1914 Weber seems to emerge as the dominant partner. Like all filmmakers in this period, she churned out footage at a feverish rate: between two hundred and four hundred titles according to her own estimates, although less than fifty have been positively identified today.

By 1915, she had become a popular celebrity whose work was as characteristic to audiences as that of Griffith or De Mille. A Weber film could be expected to tell a story with a moral, and often in these years to swing from documentarylike realism to dream-induced allegory. Her films took themselves very seriously indeed, but Weber did not lack the showmanship to bring in the audience. *Hypocrites!* (1914) was a thinly disguised sermon on the corruption of modern society, but the film's copious frontal nudity brought rioting crowds to New York's Strand Theatre. Of its follow-up success, *Scandal* (1918), Weber modestly hoped "that this play will act as a most powerful sermon and will accomplish much lasting good wherever shown."

As the most important director on the Universal lot, she now claimed a salary of $5,000 a week and was given the plum of handling Anna Pavlova and the Ballet Russe in the spectacular film version of their success, *The Dumb Girl of Portici* (1915–1916). But there was little to interest her in this elaborate production, and neither critics nor audiences was satisfied. Weber quickly returned to her overriding passion, reform. *The People vs. John Doe* (1916) pleaded for the abolition of capital punishment. *Shoes* (1916) investigated poverty and child labor, and *Hop, the Devil's Brew* (1916), carried an antisaloon message. But the most famous of all was *Where Are My Children?* (1916), "a five-part argument advocating birth control and against race suicide." This sensational melodrama earned Universal some $3,000,000 and raised storms of controversy and censorship. But while arguing "that birth control might be advantageously applied among the needy," most of the film dealt with the issue of "race suicide"—abortion on demand as practiced by a group of vapid social butterflies. Weber made clear distinctions between charitable humanitarian issues and what she saw as slackening moral standards, and to the end of her career championed the ideals of Christian fundamentalism. The 1920s would destroy her as they whittled down these attitudes, but in 1916 she was at the peak of her popularity. The studio stopped listing her films as "Smalley Productions"; now they were "Weber Productions." That year she told one reporter, "I like to direct because I believe that a woman more or less intuitively brings out many of the emotions that are rarely expressed on the screen. I may miss what some of the male directors get, but I will get other effects that they will miss."

Universal now financed a private studio for her at 4634 Sunset, far from the factorylike atmosphere of Universal City. Visitors were greeted by landscaped gardens, giant pepper trees, and "dancing flames in the fireplace." She had designed the "inspiring and delightful environment" of the studio to fit her own ideas of creativity, and was able to supervise closely all aspects of her productions. Now she spent extra care on scripts and worked more closely with the actors, building up a stock company of players and shooting her pictures in sequence in an effort to make their performances more natural. Most importantly, she broke with her earlier dramatic style and abandoned films of direct social criticism.

Where Are My Children? was a "heavy dinner," she wrote, but now she would devote herself to "light afternoon teas." The Weber films of this period were closer to what Hollywood would soon label "women's pictures," soap operas with saccharine morals, the old Weber sermonizing now buried within a sugar pill. Yet they were still profitable; her new contract emphasized fewer and better pictures, with Weber earning $2,500 a week plus one third of the profits of her films, the most important of which were sold as "Universal Special Jewels." Over the next few years she devoted herself to turning out a smaller number of higher quality pictures. She no longer had the time for acting, since managing the studio took up so much of her attention. The success of these films must have been considerable, because in 1920 she signed a fabulous contract with Famous Players-Lasky (the parent organization of Paramount) calling for $50,000 a picture and half the profits. Not only was her new distributor the most prestigious in Hollywood, but, unlike Universal, they had solid theatre connections in metropolitan areas and so would be better able to exploit her generally thoughtful productions. Reorganizing as "Lois Weber Productions," she turned out five features in 1920 and 1921, all of which survive at least in part (her earlier work is quite rare today). These films bear the indelible stamp of their maker's personality, but that personality was suddenly out of phase with public demands. There was an obsession with the details of middle-class life, with proper form and correct behavior. Poverty is dramatized in *The Blot* (1921) by a family's inability to set a proper tea for prospective suitors. These conven-

The tormented Claire Windsor sees her reflected image in this modern scene from Lois Weber's *The Blot* (1921). (Courtesy The Museum of Modern Art/Film Stills Archive)

tions are sometimes questioned but they are always dominant; they shape the lives of the films' women. Interestingly enough, men count for little here; they are scarcely capable of any deep emotion or thought and are morally neutral figures. They play the interchangeable and generally passive role of "the man," whereas the female characters are cast in a variety of active roles—all, of course, well within the allowable stereotypes of turn-of-the-century melodrama: a good and loyal wife, an unfaithful butterfly, a selfless mother, an immoral vamp, or some other easily identified type. . . . Weber's attention to the details of such roles gives the films their major interest, and loving portraits are created of an invariable small town and the types who populate it. But attention to commonplace details was no longer fashionable on postwar screens, and Weber's types suddenly seemed very out of date, especially to sophisticated urban audiences. The first of this series was a "trite homiletic story of small-town virtue and corrupting vampires" according to *The New York Times,* and most everyone agreed. Sermonettes that frowned on female smokers and [thought well of] stuffy small-town ministers were not palatable to the new audience —an audience that found itself increasingly under the criticism of Weber's films. Unable or unwilling to be flexible on such issues, Weber found her pictures dying at the box office. . . . Famous

Players dropped Weber after only three titles had been released, and the remaining two completed features were handled by a small independent outfit.

After this everything unraveled at once: the loss of her company, divorce from Smalley, complete nervous collapse. For some years Weber was out of sight, then returned to directing in the late 1920s. These last films express even more strongly a scarcely veiled contempt for jazz-age moral standards. "It is disconcerting to watch the young girl of today grow into manhood," says the hero of *The Sensation Seekers* (1927), while in *The Angel of Broadway* (1927) a cabaret dancer burlesques the innocence of a Salvation Army girl—an oblique but bitter allusion to Weber's own early days in Pittsburgh. It was her last major film. Unable to find work as a director, she free-lanced for a while as a script doctor, then was given a charity job at Universal interviewing and screen-testing potential starlets. Finally, in 1934, she contracted with a poverty row outfit to direct *White Heat,* an exploitation film. Shot on location in Hawaii, it was quickly dismissed as "a humorless account of the amorous difficulties of a young sugar planter." In the mid-1930s she tried to promote an ambitious scheme for using film as an audio-visual aid in schools, but no one was interested in the scripts she had prepared. On her death in 1939 burial expenses were paid by friends who remembered her as Hollywood's great woman director. . . .

Interview with Dorothy Arzner[*]

Karyn Kay and Gerald Peary

The following interview was conducted over several months by mail between Wisconsin and California. Questions were posed, answers supplied; then more questions surfaced from the previous answers. Dorothy Arzner personally read over the final print and made corrections and additional comments; so, in the best sense of the term, this ends as an "authorized interview."

Because Ms. Arzner was busily at work writing an ambitious historical novel based on the early settling of Los Angeles, she found it impossible to detail her complete film career. Very generously she allowed a personal visit to her California desert home for additional information. The addendum to the interview is based upon conversations during that meeting (with thanks to Joseph McBride for his questions on that occasion).

Q: How did you decide on a film career?

A: I had been around the theatre and actors all my life. My father, Louis Arzner, owned a famous Hollywood restaurant next to a theatre. I saw most of the fine plays that came there—with Maude Adams, Sarah Bernhardt, David Warfield, et cetera, et cetera, ad

* Reprinted from *Cinema,* no. 34 (1974).

infinitum. D. W. Griffith, Mary Pickford, Douglas Fairbanks, Mack Sennett, and all of the early movie and stage actors came to my dad's restaurant for dinner. I had no personal interest in actors because they were too familiar to me.

I went to the University of Southern California and focused on the idea of becoming a doctor. But with a few summer months in the office of a fine surgeon and meeting with the sick, I decided that was not what I wanted. I wanted to be like Jesus—"Heal the sick and raise the dead," instantly, without surgery, pills, et cetera.

All thoughts of university and degrees in medicine were abandoned. Even though I was an A student and had a fairly extensive education—I had taken courses in history of art and architecture—I became a so-called dropout. Since I was not continuing in my chosen career, I only thought of work to do and independence from taking money from my dad.

This was after World War I and everything was starting to bounce—even the infant picture studios. An appointment was made for me to meet William DeMille. He was told I was an intelligent girl. There had been a serious flu epidemic, so workers were needed. It was possible for even inexperienced people to have an opportunity if they showed signs of ability or knowledge.

Q: Could you describe this meeting?

A: There I was standing before William DeMille, saying: "I think I'd like a job in the movies." William DeMille: "Where do you think you'd like to start?" Answer: "I might be able to dress sets." Question: "What is the period of this furniture?"—meaning his office furniture. I did not know the answer, but I'll never forget it—"Francescan." He continued: "Maybe you'd better look around for a week and talk to my secretary. She'll show you around the different departments."

That sounded interesting enough to me. I watched the four companies that were working, particularly that of Cecil DeMille. And I remember making the observation, "If one was going to be in this movie business, one should be a director because he was the one who told everyone else what to do. In fact, he was the 'whole works.'"

However, after I finished a week of observation, William De-

Mille's secretary told me that typing scripts would enlighten me to what the film to be was all about. It was the blueprint for the picture. All the departments, including the director's, were grounded in the script. So I turned up at the end of the week in William DeMille's office. He asked, "Now where do you think you'd like to start?" I answered, "At the bottom." He looked penetratingly serious as a schoolteacher might, then barked, "Where do you think the bottom is??"I meekly answered, "Typing scripts." "For that, I'll give you a job."

I was introduced to the head of the typing department. I was told I'd be given the first opening, but I had my doubts. Weeks went by. I took a job in a wholesale coffeehouse, filing orders and working the switchboard. It was through that switchboard that the call came from Ruby Miller, the typing department head. I was making $12.00 a week. I said, "What's the salary?" "Fifteen dollars a week for three months, then $16.50." So for $3.00 dollars more a week I accepted the movie job. And that is how I started at Paramount, then called the Famous Players-Lasky Corporation.

Q: How did you become a cutter and editor?

A: At the end of six months I went from holding script to cutter, and a good cutter is also an editor, working in conjunction with the director and producer, noting the audience reaction when preview time comes. I was assigned to Realart Studio, a subsidiary of Paramount. I cut and edited fifty-two pictures while chief editor there. I also supervised and trained negative cutters and splicers.

Q: Did Realart have its own stages and crews independent of Paramount? What kinds of films were made there?

A: Realart Studio was equipped fully—cameramen, set designers, writers, and I was the only editor. It was a small studio with four companies and four stars: Bebe Daniels, Marguerite Clark, Wanda Hamely, and Mary Miles Minter. One picture a week was started there and finished in four weeks. It would be eight reels when finished, and called a "program picture." In those days pictures played for a week in theatres, and the cost of the ticket was thirty to fifty cents. At the end of the week there was another picture.

So much for Realart Studio. I was recalled to the parent company, Paramount, to cut and edit *Blood and Sand* [1922] with

Valentino as star, with Lila Lee and Nita Naldi. Fred Niblo was the director, June Mathis was the writer, having gained much fame and authority from guiding and writing *The Four Horsemen of the Apocalypse* [1921] to enormous success. It was a Big Picture—hundreds of thousands of feet of film, twenty-three reels in the first tight cut, finally brought down to twelve.

Q: What were the physical circumstances in editing at this time?

A: There were no Moviolas or machinery. Everything was done by hand. The film was read and cut over an eight-inch by ten-inch box set in the table, covered with frosted glass and a light bulb underneath. The film pieces were placed over a small sprocketed plate, overlapped, and scraped about one-sixteenth of an inch, snipped with glue, and pressed by hand.

Q: Were scenes shot simultaneously from several angles to help your editing?

A: No, films were shot normally with one camera, except for large spectacular scenes.

Q: Do you feel that editors were paid decent wages before unionization?

A: For the time, I was paid very well. I never had any complaints. If you were a good editor, you asked a reasonable rate.

Q: Had you done any shooting on *Blood and Sand?*

A: Yes, I filmed some shots for the bullfights.

Q: Were there special instructions in editing Valentino's scenes so as to preserve the glamour?

A: There were no special instructions. The glamour was all on the film, put there by the writer and director, both of superior experience.

Q: What other movies were made with James Cruze?

A: Then came *The Covered Wagon* [1923], another "supercolossal" picture made eighty-five miles from a railroad in the "wilds of Utah." We used five tribes of Indians, and oxen were broken to the yoke. I stayed with Cruze through several pictures (*Ruggles of Red Gap* [1923], with Eddy Horton, *Merton of the Movies* [1924], and a number of others), until I left to write scripts for independent companies, like Harry Cohn's Columbia. Then Cruze asked me to work on *Old Ironsides* [1926], another Big Picture. He wanted me to write the shooting script, stay on the deck of the ship with him, keep the script, cut, and edit—all of which I did for more salary.

Q: Could you talk a little about Cruze, a director known today almost only by name?

A: It would take too long to tell you about James Cruze. He was one of the "big directors," but he didn't exploit himself. He saved Paramount from bankruptcy, and he was one of the finest, most generous men I knew in the motion-picture business. He had no prejudices. He valued my ability and told people I was his right arm.

Q: Were you about to walk out on Paramount to direct pictures at a minor studio when given your directorial chance in 1927?

A: Yes. I was going to leave Paramount after *Ironsides.* I had been writing scripts for Columbia, then considered a "poverty row" company. Harry Cohn made pictures for $8,000 to $10,000 and I was writing scripts for $500 apiece. But I had told Jack Bachman, Cohn's production man, that the next script I wanted to direct or "no deal." When I finished *Ironsides,* I had an offer to write and direct a film for Columbia.

It was then I closed out my salary at Paramount and was about to leave for Columbia. It was late in the afternoon. I decided I should say "good-bye" to someone after seven years and much work: B. P. Schulberg. (I had previously written a shooting script for Ben Schulberg when he had a small independent company. He had been short of cash and couldn't pay, so I told him to take it and pay me when he could, which he did later. It was "bread on the waters" because soon after he was made Production Head of Paramount when we were about to start *Ironsides.*)

But Mr. Schulberg's secretary told me he was in conference. So I went out to my car in the parking lot, had my hand on the door latch, when I decided after so many years I was going to say "good-bye" to *someone* important and not just leave unnoticed and forgotten. The ego took over. I had a feeling of high good humor.

So I returned and asked the secretary if she minded if I waited for the conference to be over. She did mind. Mr. Schulberg would not see anyone. It was late then, and he had told her not to make any more appointments. Just about then Walter Wanger passed in the hall. He was head of Paramount's New York studio on Long Island. And, as he passed, I called out, "Oh, you'll do!" He responded, "What's that?" And I told him, I was leaving Paramount after seven years, and I wanted to say good-bye to someone *important*.

"Come into my office, Dorothy." I followed him, and when he sat down behind his desk, I put out my hand and said, "Really, I didn't want a thing, just wanted to say good-bye to someone important. I'm leaving to direct." He turned and picked up the intercom and said, "Ben—Dorothy's in my office and says she's leaving." I heard Ben Schulberg say, "Tell her I'll be right in." Which he was—in about three minutes.

"What do you mean you're leaving?" "I've finished *Ironsides*. I've closed out my salary, and I'm leaving." "We don't want you to leave. There's always a place in the scenario department for you." "I don't want to go into the scenario department. I'm going to direct for a small company." "What company?," he asked. "I won't tell you because you'd probably spoil it for me." "Now Dorothy, you go into our scenario department and later we'll think about directing." "No, I know I'd never get out of there." "What would you say if I told you that you could direct here?" "Please don't fool me, just let me go. I'm going to direct at Columbia." "You're going to direct here at Paramount." "*Not unless* I can be on a set in two weeks with an A picture. I'd rather do a picture for a small company and have my own way than a B picture for Paramount."

With that he left, saying, "Wait here." He was back in a few minutes with a play in his hand. "Here. It's a French farce called *The Best Dressed Woman in Paris*. Start writing the script and get yourself on the set in two weeks. New York is sending Esther Ralston out to be starred. She has made such a hit in *Peter Pan* [1924], and it will be up to you."

So, there I was a writer-director. It was announced in the papers the following day or so: "Lasky Names Woman Director."

Q: What was your directing training prior to *Fashions for Women* [1927]?

A: I had not directed anything before. In fact I hadn't told anyone to do anything before. I had observed several directors on the set in the three years that I held script and edited: Donald Crisp, Jim Cruze, Cecil DeMille, Fred Niblo, Herbert Blaché, and Nazimova. I kept script on one Nazimova picture, *The Secret Doctor of Gaya*,[1] directed by the husband of the "directress" Madame Blaché. But I don't recall meeting her.

Q: Who championed your cause at Paramount? Adolph Zukor? Were you given trouble because you were a woman?

A: Ben Schulberg, Jim Cruze, Walter Wanger. Adolph Zukor was in New York where the pictures were distributed and had little to do with the making of movies. No one gave me trouble because I was a woman. Men were more helpful than women.

Q: Could you talk about Esther Ralston, star of *Fashions for Women*, but a forgotten star today? Was she the same type as Clara Bow, another of your leads?

A: Esther Ralston was not the same type as Clara Bow—just the

[1] Arzner's title is not listed in any of the standard texts. Herbert Blaché directed two films starring Alla Nazimova, *The Brat* (1919) and *Stronger Than Death* (1920). Perhaps Arzner means one of these.—Eds.

Dorothy Arzner on the set of M-G-M's *The Bride Wore Red* (1937) with star Joan Crawford. (Courtesy Dorothy Arzner)

opposite. She was blonde, tall, and more of a showgirl type—very beautiful. Clara was a redheaded gamine, full of life and vitality, with the heart of a child.

Q: The aggressive character that Ralston played in *Fashions for Women*, Lola, seems like the kind of character of many of your women. Do you agree?

A: No, I do not think Esther as Lola was like other women in my pictures. You would have to see Nancy Carroll, Clara Bow, Katharine Hepburn, Ruth Chatterton, Anna Sten in *Nana* [1934], Merle Oberon in *First Comes Courage* [1943].

Q: You made the first movies with Ruth Chatterton. Wasn't she an unlikely movie star—a bit older and more mature than most leading ladies?

A: Ruth Chatterton was a star in the theatre. When talkies came to Paramount, they signed the stage actresses as many of the silent stars fell by the wayside. She was a good actress.

Q: Did you affect her career?

A: Yes, I certainly affected it. When I made Ruth Chatterton's first motion picture at Paramount, *Sarah and Son* [1930], it broke all box-office records at the Paramount Theatre in New York. Chatterton became known to the press as "The First Lady of the Screen."

Q: Why did Ruth Chatterton move over to Warner Brothers?

A: Warners offered her everything an actress could desire—choice of story, director, cameraman, et cetera, including a salary greater than Paramount.

Q: You made a series of Paramount pictures with Fredric March. Was this coincidence or did you ask to work together again and again?

A: I took Fredric March from the stage in *The Royal Family* [1927] and cast him in *The Wild Party* [1929]. I guess my pictures gave him a good start, and I liked his work, so I cast him as the lead in *Sarah and Son, Merrily We Go to Hell* [1932], and *Honor Among Lovers* [1931].

Q: In 1930 you began making movies with Robert Milton. Could you explain the nature of your collaboration?

A: Robert Milton was a fine stage director, but he didn't know the camera's limitations or its expansions. Because I did know the technique so well, I was asked to help him. I codirected *Behind the Makeup* [1930] and I was called in to complete *The Constant Wife* [*Charming Sinners*, 1929—Eds.], which he had started with Ruth Chatterton. I don't believe I took screen credit on it. I merely helped with technical work. He directed the performances. I blocked the scenes for camera and editing.

Q: Didn't you direct one part of *Paramount on Parade* [1930]? What was the idea behind this extravaganza?

A: "The Vagabond King" ["The Gallows Song"— Eds.] was the part I directed. *Paramount on Parade* was an innovative type picture, made mainly to exploit Paramount and its directors and stars and to show off the studio.

Paramount was the greatest studio, with more theatres and more big pictures than any others until the Depression. Its Hollywood plant was one block square, on Sunset Boulevard and Vine.

Q: Were you given a choice of technical crew when directing at Paramount?

A: Yes, I had the cameramen, assistants, costume and set designers I liked best. A director had his, or her, crew that stayed from one picture to another. I made my assistant cameraman, Charles Lang, my first cameraman. Adrian and Howard Greer did clothes for me.

Q: *Honor Among Lovers* was one of the first Ginger Rogers films. Did you discover her? Was her famous "stage mother" found on the set during shooting?

A: Ginger Rogers was a star in *Girl Crazy* in the theatre. I saw her and liked her and requested her for a small part in *Honor Among Lovers*. Paramount gave me about everything I wanted after *Sarah and Son* and *Anybody's Woman* [1930], so I imagine they offered her much money. She could also continue playing in *Girl Crazy* at the same time. I never saw her mother.

Q: *Honor Among Lovers* ends with Julia, the married woman, going on an ocean voyage with a man not her husband. Was this unorthodox ending your choice? Was there pressure to have Julia finish the movie in the arms of her husband?

A: I collaborated in the writing of *Honor Among Lovers,* which I made for Paramount in New York. As audiences were ready for more sophistication, it was considered the smartest high comedy at the time.

No, there was no pressure regarding the script, I had very little interference with my pictures. Sometimes there were differences in casting, sets, or costumes, but usually I had my way. You see, I was not dependent on the movies for my living, so I was always ready to give the picture over to some other director if I couldn't make it the way I saw it. Right or wrong, I believe this was why I sustained so long—twenty years.

Q: Why the title *Merrily We Go to Hell?*

A: The movie was made during the overboard drinking era during Prohibition. Freddy March played a drunken reporter with whom a socialite, Sylvia Sidney, fell in love. He made Sylvia laugh when she was bored with the social life of her class. You would have to know the times to judge, "Why the title?"

Q: You were at Paramount at the same time as Marlene Dietrich and Mae West. Did you ever wish to make a movie with either of them?

A: Yes, I always wanted to make a picture with Marlene. There was a wonderful script called *Stepdaughters of War.* I'd worked on it for months for Chatterton, but when she signed with Warners it had to be called off. Much later, we were planning it again with Dietrich. It was to be a big antiwar picture showing the tragedies of war and how war makes women hard and masculine. When World War II broke out with Nazi Germany, it was called off again.

Q: Could you describe your contract at Paramount? Did you have special clauses giving you control over certain phases of production?

A: I was under contract to Paramount for three years at a time, paid by the week. I ended with a two-year contract, including choice of story. I never had to worry about control over phases of the production. The departments were geared to give a director what he wanted, if he knew exactly what he wanted.

Q: Why then did you leave Paramount?

A: Paramount changed by 1932. When I left, there was a complete change of executives. In fact, they were so fearful of the success of *Merrily We Go to Hell* that they spoke of shelving it. I begged them to release it. I was so sure of its success. A year later they were asking me, "Make another *Merrily We Go to Hell*," but by that time I wanted to free-lance.

Q: You were working already on *Christopher Strong* [1933]?

A: Yes, David Selznick asked me to do a film at RKO, which he headed at the time. It was to be an Ann Harding picture, but she was taken out due to contractual difficulties. So I chose to have Katharine Hepburn from seeing her about the studio. She had given a good performance in *Bill of Divorcement* [1932], but now she was about to be relegated to a Tarzan-type picture. I walked over to the set. She was up a tree with a leopard skin on! She had a marvelous figure; and talking to her, I felt she was the very modern type I wanted for *Christopher Strong*.

Q: Did you pay special attention to directing Billie Burke in this movie? It seems the best acting performance of her career. In fact you seem more interested in all the women characters than in Christopher Strong. Is this true?

A: Yes, I did pay special attention to getting a performance from Billie Burke. But I was more interested in Christopher Strong, played by Colin Clive, than in any of the women characters. He was a man "on the cross." He loved his wife, and he fell in love with the aviatrix. He was on a rack. I was really more sympathetic with him, but no one seemed to pick that up. Of course, not too many women are sympathetic about the torture the situation might give to a man of upright character.

Q: What was your relationship with *Christopher Strong*'s scriptwriter, Zoe Akins, who had also written *Sarah and Son, Anybody's Woman,* and *Working Girls* for you at Paramount in 1931? What did Slavko Vorkapich contribute to the movie?

A: My collaboration with Zoe Akins was very close. I thought her a fine writer. Vorkapich did the montage of the around-the-world flight, when Cynthia (Katharine Hepburn) was met by Chris in San Francisco and their affair was consummated. Incidentally, *Christopher Strong*'s story was not based on Amelia Earhart. It came from an English novel based upon the life of Amy Lowell, who did make the around-the-world flight and also broke the altitude record in her time.

Q: Why do you think Cynthia killed herself? Did you consider other endings?

A: No, there was no other ending. Cynthia killed herself because she was about to have an illegitimate child. The picture was set in England. We had not accepted so easily the idea of an illegitimate child. In the boat scene, she asked, "Do you love me, Chris?" His answer: "Call it love, if you like." This was from a tortured man who deeply loved his wife and child, but fell in love with the vital, young, and daring aviatrix.

Q: Wasn't there a moment when Cynthia tried to save her own life by putting the oxygen mask back on her face after she had ripped it off?

A: No, Cynthia did not try to save her life. If you remember, she looked back over the whole affair seen through superimpositions as she flew to break the altitude record. Suicide was a definite decision.

Q: How would you evaluate this movie?

A: *Christopher Strong* was one of the favorite of my pictures at the time, although I was always so critical of my own works that I could hardly consider any one a favorite. I always saw too many flaws. I was grateful, however, when they were considered so successful.

Q: Some sources have credited you with making an RKO film, *The Lost Squadron* [1932], usually listed as directed by George Archainbaud. Did you work on this film?

A: No, I had nothing to do with George Archainbaud or *The Lost Squadron.*

Q: All articles about your career say that you were the only woman director in Hollywood at this time. But another woman, Wanda Tuchock, codirected a movie called *Finishing School,* at RKO in 1933. Were you aware of this? Did you know her?

A: I vaguely remember Wanda Tuchock was publicized as a woman director, but I paid so little attention to what anyone else was doing. I never was interested in anyone else's personal life. I was focused on my own work, and my own life.

Q: How did you become involved with *Nana* at the Goldwyn Studio? How was Anna Sten picked to play the lead? Were you satisfied with the completed film?

A: Goldwyn chose me to do *Nana* because, when he returned from a trip to Europe, he saw *Christopher Strong* and thought it the best picture of the year. He picked Anna Sten, wanting a star to vie with Dietrich and Garbo. It wasn't that I would like to have shot *Nana* differently, I wanted a more important script. But Goldwyn wouldn't accept any script at all until he finally handed me about the fiftieth attempt.

Q: Why did you choose Rosalind Russell for the lead in *Craig's Wife* [1936]?

A: I did not want an actress the audience loved. They would hate me for making her Mrs. Craig. Rosalind Russell was a bit player at M-G-M, brilliant, clipped, and unknown to movie audiences. She was what I wanted.

Q: Was *Craig's Wife* an expensive picture to produce? Was it profitable for Columbia?

A. No, *Craig's Wife* was not a high-budget picture to make. I told Harry Cohn I would give him an A picture for B picture money. He fell for that. It was not one of the biggest successes when it was released. But it got such fine press that, over the long run, it was released several times and stood high on Columbia's box-office list.

Q: Were you also producer of *Craig's Wife?*

A: I was not the producer, although the whole production was designed by me. Outside of the development of the script, enormously protected from Harry Cohn's interference, Eddie Chodorov was the supervising producer.

Q: Did the playwright, George Kelly, involve himself in the production? Didn't you differ with him on interpretation?

A: George Kelly had nothing to do with making the picture. I did try to be as faithful to his play as possible, except that I made it from a different point of view. I imagined Mr. Craig was dominated somewhat by his mother and therefore fell in love with a woman stronger than he. I thought Mr. Craig should be down on his knees with gratitude because Mrs. Craig made a man of him.

When I told Kelly this, he rose to his six-foot height, and said, "That is *not my* play. Walter Craig was a sweet guy and Mrs. Craig was an SOB." He left. That was the only contact I had with Kelly.

Dorothy Arzner journeyed to M-G-M after *Craig's Wife*, excited about making a film from an unpublished Ferenc Molnar play called *The Girl from Trieste*. It was about a former prostitute—a victim of "economic exploitation," to quote Arzner—trying to go straight. The movie was to star Luise Rainer. M-G-M, however, replaced Rainer with Joan Crawford, and *The Girl from Trieste* was rewritten as the lighter, frothier *The Bride Wore Red* [1937]. (It seems possible that Crawford had requested M-G-M to put her into the Arzner picture at this time. She admired *Craig's Wife* enormously, so much so that she starred in *Harriet Craig*, another remake of the project, at Columbia in 1950.) Despite making a lifetime friend of Joan Crawford, Arzner was disappointed by the rewrite and uncomfortable working in the M-G-M factory. Mammoth sets were constructed for *The Bride Wore Red*, which Arzner was ordered to use. She remembers Joan Crawford decked out in a lavish red gown, even though the picture was shot in black and white. Altogether, Arzner considers *The Bride Wore Red* rather synthetic, not a favorite of her movies.

Arzner was nowhere in sight when *Dance, Girl, Dance* [1940] was begun by another RKO director. This was a personal project of Eric Pommer, the former head of Germany's famed UFA Studio, then in exile in Hollywood. As producer, Pommer had conceived, cast, and started shooting of *Dance, Girl, Dance*, but everyone involved was unhappy and confused. After a week Pommer removed the original director and brought in Dorothy Arzner to take charge. She reworked the script and sharply defined the central conflict as a clash between the artistic, spiritual aspirations of Maureen O'Hara and the commercial, huckster, gold-digging of Lucille Ball. She decided to base Ball's character of Bubbles on the real-life "Texas" Guinan, whom Arzner had spotted waving out of her taxi window to everyone in New York, "Hi, I'm 'Texas' Guinan!"

Dorothy Arzner's contributions to the war effort were a series of

Dorothy Arzner directs Merle Oberon in *First Comes Courage* (1943), Arzner's last Hollywood film. (Courtesy Dorothy Arzner)

short films for the WAC's, and also the training of four women to cut and edit these movies. Arzner had great fun making these shorts, for her actors were the Samuel Goldwyn stock company, including some of her old *Nana* cast. These documentaries were never shown in theatres or in general release, but were restricted to WAC training situations—How to Groom Oneself, etc. Apparently they were successful, for the government offered Dorothy Arzner an appointment as a major. She turned it down, because, as she says, "I never wanted to be in the Army."

She returned to Columbia after seven years' absence for *First Comes Courage,* the story of anti-Nazi resistance and the Norwegian underground. The screenplay was based on *The Commandos* by Elliott Arnold, and, unlike many directors, Arzner read the novel before beginning the movie. She employed a favorite editor on the project, Viola Lawrence, who was also responsible for *Craig's Wife,* and she cast several German expatriates in the major roles. Reinhold Schunzel was reunited with Carl Esmond nine years after they had made a movie together in prewar Germany, *English Wedding*, with Esmond as star and Schunzel as director. There was no second unit work on *First Comes Courage*, or on any movie that Arzner can remember except in a bit of *Sarah and Son*. Arzner herself directed all the location photography, the army maneuvers, the scene inside a submarine, the frightening fistfight in which the battling actors fall between a terrified horse and a potentially lethal pitchfork. (She still shudders to remember the danger in shooting this last sequence.) The final scenes of the movie were filmed by another director when Arzner contracted pneumonia with a week to go, and remained terribly sick for almost a year. Upon recovery, Arzner made a brave decision; one that she has stuck out for thirty years. She told herself that she had had it directing movies, and she left Hollywood forever in 1943.

Occasionally, in the ensuing years, Arzner has become involved in some kind of project. She began the first filmmaking course at the Pasadena Playhouse on a nonexistent budget, instructing her students with a single camera and tape recorder. She made over fifty Pepsi-Cola commercials for her old friend Joan Crawford; and she taught filmmaking at UCLA for four years in the 1960s.

The few movies that Dorothy Arzner sees today are old pictures on television or at the College of the Desert in Palm Desert, California, near her home. Her ties with the industry are absolutely cut. When she shows old photographs of her swank Hollywood estate, sold long ago, she laughs to herself about her youthful affectations. "I was a famous Hollywood director then." There is no doubt that she is totally content with her desert anonymity, the fresh air, and her fifty beautiful rosebushes, in place of the subterranean growth of Los Angeles living.

Interview with Ida Lupino

Debra Weiner

INTRODUCTION

Ida Lupino, the plucky star of such movie classics as They Drive By
Night (*1940*), High Sierra (*1941*), *and* The Sea Wolf (*1941*), *the
tiny Cockney with the heart-shaped face and the chestnut hair, has
served also in her forty-plus years in America as screenwriter, playwright, lyricist, composer (the Los Angeles Philharmonic performed
her composition,* The Aladdin Suite), *producer, director, filmmaker. She once called herself "a terror—slaving long and hard to
make things happen." Film director Raoul Walsh nicknamed her
"Mad Idesy" and recently recalled of his favorite star that "She'd get
so excited and irritable that it would damn near put her in the
bughouse."*

   *Today she is still among the tiny crop of female directors to find
steady work in Hollywood, since she is ever busy turning out television adventure series—"The Fugitive," "Thriller," "Manhunt." In
1949 she was the only woman member of the Screen Directors
Guild, or so she says, when she cut her directing teeth assisting
Elmer Clifton on* Not Wanted (*1949*), *about an unwed mother
forced to relinquish her child. The eight features she directed, produced, or scripted between 1949 and 1954 for her independent company, Filmmakers, dealt with bold, candid themes—rape, bigamy,*

unwanted pregnancy. Except for The Hitchhiker (1953), with its all-male cast, women were the axis of her films. Yet, before feminists get too excited, it must be noted that the solutions to women's problems within the films are often conventional, even conservative, more reinforcing of 1950s ideology than undercutting it. A terse summation of Lupino might be to say that she dealt with feminist questions from an antifeminist perspective. (Not that this summation necessarily would bear up under close scrutiny.)

When I visited her ranch home in a fashionable canyon on the outskirts of Los Angeles, Lupino pointedly explained, "Look. A man is a man and a woman is a woman, and I believe that. All right, so you probably might consider directing a man's job. Well it is. Physically, directing is extremely rough." Yet, a contradiction? On the bookshelves in her dining room was a copy of Marjorie Rosen's Popcorn Venus (1974), a feminist study of the movies.

Had she seen Dorothy Arzner's films? "No, but I had the pleasure of meeting her," she said. Elaine May's work? "I like it very much. I think it is excellent." And Nelly Kaplan's A Very Curious Girl (1969), the French film about an unorthodox prostitute? "Is it in release? I must look that up and see it as soon as I can. I think it is very wonderful that there are more women going into the field." Ida Lupino—of a generation taught that to be aggressive is unladylike, that strength in a woman is out of whack—is trying, despite her sexist posturing.

We talked a while that blistering summer day (I thank Patrick McGilligan for his assistance), and again a few months later on the telephone. Even though she had pulled several chest muscles and had been ordered to take it easy, "Mad Idesy" chatted for several hours. Ever gracious and cordial, apologizing for shouting—she was merely catching her breath—she recounted the skeletal facts of her still-undocumented directing career in Hollywood and television.

D. W.

Q: Why did you start your own independent film company, Film-makers?

A: I'd known Collier Young, a literary agent who had been an assistant to Jack Warner and also to Harry Cohn at Columbia. [Young was her husband at the time.—Eds.] He and I wrote a story, and he said, "What the hell, why don't we get together and form our own company and discover new people and new kids?" I agreed, "Absolutely, that is what I would love." We did it.

Q: What prompted Filmmakers to make *Not Wanted* [1949]?

A: It was a darned good idea—the story of the unwed mother— that we thought should be presented. The girl should be able to get sympathy from the family. Without being too messagey we were trying to say, "Don't treat her like she has some terrible disease. So she made a mistake."

Q: Was the story your idea?

A: No. Another writer thought of it, but we only used about four of his pages. I did most of the screenplay.

Q: How did you break into directing?

A: I did not set out to be a director. I was only supposed to coproduce *Not Wanted* since we had this wonderful old-time director, Elmer Clifton, to make the picture. About three days into the shooting he got heart trouble. Since we were using my version of the script, I had to take over. My name was not on the directorial credits, however, and rightly so. This gentleman, as sick as he was, sat throughout the making of the film. I'd say, "Elmer, is it all right with you if I move the camera, if I do this, and so forth and so on?"

Our editor on this picture happened to be Alfred Hitchcock's editor for *Rope* [1948] and *Spellbound* [1945], William Ziegler. I would run to the phone every five minutes and say, "Bill, listen, I want to dolly in and I think I'm reversing myself." On the first picture he helped me out. He would come down to the set.

On the second film we got Bill again. The picture, *The Young Lovers* [1950], was based on my original story about a young woman dancer who contracts polio, and I co-wrote the screenplay. I'd run to the phone again, but this time he'd say, "Uh-uh, you're on your own. I'm cutting right behind you. You can't afford for me to come down on the set." So that is how I became a director.

Q: You acted with many fine directors. Did any of them influence your directing?

A: Not in style. I had to find my own style, my own way of doing things. I wasn't going to try to copy anybody. But certain directors, like Wellman, Charles Vidor, Walsh, or Michael Curtiz, couldn't help but rub off. And Robert Aldrich, God knows it was a delight to work for him in *The Big Knife* [1955]. He's not only a fine technician, but he certainly knows the actor. He digs down into your role and pulls things out you weren't aware were there.

Q: Did Raoul Walsh ever instruct you in editing?

A: He used to let me watch him in the cutting room. I wouldn't bother him, but I'd ask him certain things, you know, about "lefts-to-rights" and "rights-to-lefts" and "over-the-shoulders." As for splicing the thing, I didn't go into that.

Ann Walton (Mala Powers) recovers from a rape in the sympathetic hands of Ferguson (Tod Andrews), a country minister, in Ida Lupino's *Outrage* (1950). (Courtesy Wisconsin Center for Film and Theater Research)

Q: Most of Filmmakers' pictures were made for under $160,000. How did you manage?

A: Our scripts couldn't call for floods, tremendous fire scenes. We never compromised, but we also always made sure that we were going to bring the picture in for our budgeted price.

As a matter of fact, we used to sell our pictures personally whenever possible—going out on the road, hitting towns and cities, getting magazine coverage while we were shooting. Still, we were lucky that we got backed for our first and second pictures. And when Howard Hughes, then head of RKO, became interested in the company, we received RKO financing, production facilities, and distribution in exchange for half of our profits. It was rather rough on independents that way. We did not become millionaires. We were lucky to get out.

Q: Why did you decide to make *Outrage* [1950], the story of a rape victim?

A: Actually, I just felt it was a good thing to do at that time, without being too preachy. After all, it was not the girl's fault. I just thought that so many times the effect rape can have on a girl isn't easily brought out. The girl won't talk about it or tell the police. She is afraid she won't be believed.

I didn't think it was one of my better directorial efforts. There were certain things in it that I thought were rather touching and really true to life, but we tried to get artsy in places.

Q: The subject material in many of your films was fairly unconventional for the time.

A: Yes, I suppose we were the New Wave at that time. We went along the line of doing films that had social significance and yet were entertainment. The pictures were based on true stories, things the public could understand because they had happened or had been of news value. Our little company became known for that type of production, and for using unknown talent. Filmmakers was an outlet specially for new people—actors, writers, young directors.

I thought Mala Powers's performance in *Outrage* was exceedingly good, considering this was her first film and she was only seventeen. She still had to have a schoolteacher on the set. We discovered Sally Forrest and Hugh O'Brian in the second one; Keefe Brasselle in the first. We never had the opportunity to screen-test them because we were too poor.

Q: Who else directed for Filmmakers?

A: A lovely man, Harry Horner, who was one of the industry's finest set designers was made the director for *Day Without End* [*Beware My Lovely*, 1952—Eds.]. Although we were practically autonomous, from RKO, when it came to introducing new directors, Mr. Hughes was a little leery. Don Weis, for instance, was our script consultant, and we had a script all prepared for him to direct. But it took weeks trying to find Howard Hughes. We had put out quite a bit of publicity about Don, and there was a short at Metro he had a chance to direct, and so we lost him.

Q: Why did you decide to make *Hard, Fast and Beautiful* [1951], about a tennis-player daughter pushed into competition by her aspiring mother?

A: These things happen—the ambitious mother and her daughter and the not sticking to the rules of the game as far as playing it straight is concerned. Again, this picture was based on a true case slightly altered—to this day I will not say which case. Actually, no good came of it for the mother. The gal bowed out of the tennis business.

Q: You are known for playing spirited, tough, offbeat roles. Is this the kind of woman character you like to work with as a director, or write about?

A: I never wrote just straight women's roles. I liked the strong characters. I don't mean women who have masculine qualities about them, but something that has some intestinal fortitude, some guts to it. Just a straight role drives me up the wall. Playing a nice woman who just sits there, that's my greatest limitation.

Q: Many of Filmmakers' pictures focused on women's issues.

A: Not all of them. I directed *The Hitchhiker*, which was a true story, the William Cook story about a hitchhiker murder, and that certainly was not a woman's story at all. And I made *The Bigamist* [1953] and this definitely was the man's story.

Q: Did you write the screenplay for *The Bigamist?*

A: No, I believe it was Melvin Wald, but it struck me as very well written. The challenge to make Lucille, the first wife, completely

Milly Farley (Claire Trevor) pushes a tennis trophy at daughter Florence (Sally Forrest) while the alienated boyfriend, Gordon McKay (Robert Clarke), looks on in Ida Lupino's *Hard, Fast and Beautiful* (1951). (Courtesy Wisconsin Center for Film and Theater Research)

understanding towards her husband interested me very much.

Q: Why did you act in as well as direct *The Bigamist?*

A: I was forced to do that. Joan Fontaine wanted me as the director but said I must also play the other woman because having another name added value.

Q: Was it difficult both to direct and to act?

A: I'm not mad about combining the two. It takes me morning, noon, and night to pull the thing through just as a director, and then to get in front of a camera and not be able to watch myself . . . Unfortunately, I was in all the scenes with the people who could watch me. Joan couldn't watch me because we had to hurry her back to Paramount. And Eddy O'Brien couldn't because I was in every scene with him. I had to have my cameraman tell me when I was overdoing it. When I was acting, I still had to say, "Cut, print, cut, print." I think I needed a separate director.

Q: When you both directed and produced a picture, was that difficult?

A: No, it was an ideal way, but that was because it was all done together. Filmmakers was a family group. We all contributed ideas, we threw them into the pot. Four years, and I never had a happier period in my entire life. I'm very sorry that my partners chose to go into film distribution. If they hadn't, I think we still would be going today. We should have stayed an independent company, with distribution coming from whichever high-level outfit gave us the best break. I thought it was very wrong, but I was outvoted. And sure enough the Filmmakers didn't make it distributing their own pictures. We didn't get the right playing dates in the right houses. We weren't very wise to step into a field which we didn't know too much about.

Q: How did you become a director for television after Filmmakers went out of business?

A: I was asked to direct Joseph Cotten in "On Trial," a series presentation on the trial of Mary Seurat who was hanged as a suspect in the Lincoln trial. It was shot in three days, with three or four days to prepare. I sat up day and night doing all the reseach I could on the assassination of Lincoln. Television—there's nothing rougher, nothing rougher. And from then on it became like a snowball. They'd book me in advance because they had to have answers in advance and I couldn't direct movies again until 1966, with *The Trouble with Angels*.

Q: What are your favorite directorial efforts?

A: Well, I don't think I did a bad job on *The Bigamist*. I like *The Hitchhiker*. I think they were really good. There's been some television shows I've done that I like.

Q: Which television shows?

A: There's been so many, it's a little difficult at the moment to pick out which, but there have been one or two from "Mr. Novak" that I like my work on. There is one "Hong Kong" I like very much. A few on "Thriller" I think are pretty good.

Q: What makes a picture you direct turn out well?

A: It's a matter of chemistry. A combination of a good script that is possible to shoot in the time allotted, a producer I am completely simpatico with, good actors and my cameraman. The night before shooting and during that very first shot I always have butterflies in my stomach. But once I get the first few shots in the camera, well then, the stomach starts to settle down.

Communication with my actors is also very important. Being close to them. I understand their problems. I'm not saying I do awfully good work, but I've done some pretty good stuff.

Q: What genre have you been channeled into in television?

A: The producer who started me began me in Westerns. He had seen *The Hitchhiker* and the next thing I knew I was directing "Have Gun Will Travel" with Richard Boone, "Hong Kong" with Bob Taylor, "The Fugitive" with David Janssen, "Manhunt," "The Untouchables." Who me? I thought. Here I'd always done women's stories and now I couldn't get a woman's story to direct.

Q: In what type of picture do you think you do your best work?

A: I would not be good at *Doctor Zhivago* [1965], *The Longest Day* [1962], the tremendous plains of war. I don't believe that is my channel. I mean if I were going to decide whom we should have as a director, I would not choose me. Suspense pictures, yes. Robert Aldrich things, yes. *Whatever Happened to Baby Jane* [1962], yes. That I would say is my slot. Suspense.

Q: Not women's pictures?

A: I think I fit into the women's pictures category too, but I don't consider myself only a women's director.

Q: You were among the few woman directors in Hollywood. Were there any problems?

A: I guess I was a novelty at the time and it would have been difficult to become a director then if we hadn't had our own company. But as a matter of fact, most everyone went out of their way to treat me like a buddy. After all, I'd worked with practically every crew in town since 1934. And because, well, I don't act like a man. My way of asking a man to do something on a set is not to boss him around. That isn't in me to do that. I say, "I've got an idea, and why don't you see if it feels comfortable because I think it would be effective."

Listen, if a woman came to you and said, "Honey, gee, I don't know what to do. We've finished this and I'm not quite sure whether we should send it down or what grain I should use. I'd like to do this, but, well, what do you think?" You'd want to help me, wouldn't you? Well, all right.

Q: What would you like to be doing?

A: Really, my dream is that some dear old man would see my old movies on television and leave me an oil well in his will. Then I could do good things for the people I like. And I'd want to live on a ranch. I'm definitely small town, the country type.

Q: Would you want to direct more films?

A: It would be lovely as a hobby, wouldn't it? Like Liz Taylor and Richard Burton. They can act whenever they want to because they are so damn rich.

I will have to get going again myself. I've been in front of the camera for so long. I've had offers to direct but they would have taken me out of the country, which would have meant leaving my home, my daughter, being away from here months and months on end. It's a rough setup.

That's where being a man makes a great deal of difference. I don't suppose the men particularly care about leaving their wives and children. During the vacation period the wife can always fly over and be with him. It's difficult for a wife to say to her husband, come sit on the set and watch.

Stephanie Rothman:
R-Rated Feminist

Dannis Peary

INTRODUCTION

It is unfortunate that few feminist cinema researchers are familiar with the series of recent feature films (1966–1974) made in Holly- wood by Stephanie Rothman. Elaine May excepted, she is the only woman active in the industry today as a director of theatrical re- leases. Yet Rothman has seen her pictures pass quickly into relative obscurity. Their distribution so far has been erratic, with many potential markets, including the art-house circuit, bypassed and un- explored; only 35mm prints are available for her later films, so cinema societies can't show them and libraries don't stock them. None of her major films has been bought by television stations, although with a little editing most could be switched from a R rating to the necessary G P.

Again, this is lamentable. Rothman's pictures are all centrally about interesting contemporary women, exploring new occupations, relationships, and living situations, and confronting the ever- changing values of the 1970s. If these films are more personal than strictly feminist in perspective, they are far different from anything male directors have produced.

D. P.

179

The five movies writer-director Stephanie Rothman has made since 1970—*The Student Nurses, The Velvet Vampire, Group Marriage, Terminal Island,* and *The Working Girls*—fall into that critically scorned (and feminist-avoided) category of "exploitation films." However, Rothman's works haven't the unsavory excesses that characterize the genre. There is action—but little of the expected violence; there is ample nudity—but little lurid sex. Rothman has made a series of entertainments that are occasionally exciting, more often amusing, hardly ever offensive. While commercially successful among mass audiences, the movies are really "idea dramas," offering Rothman's unique approaches to modern relationships. The humor, rapid pacing, novel story lines, and interesting characterizations keep even Rothman's tamest films from growing dull.

She is an extremely optimistic filmmaker: instead of showing her women in conflict with a male-dominated world, she likes to place them in cinematic situations in which they are already men's equals. Similarly, Rothman women rarely voice disapproval of demeaning female roles because Rothman has not placed them in such roles. Her heroines are independent young women, aggressive, healthy, and open in their sexual attitudes. They get along fine with their women associates; and their relationships with men are mutually supportive. (There are strong exceptions to these generalizations—but these are meant to stand out by their abnormality or the strange perspective offered by Rothman. For instance, when the female attempts to prove herself competitively against the male in *It's a Bikini World,* the intention is not to increase her worth in his eyes but to deflate *his* worth in *his* eyes.)

There is nudity in all Rothman films, and it is there to arouse and amuse. Rothman isn't embarrassed by the nudity. She desires its presence and wants her R-rating audience to be comfortable also, even considering her divergence from the rules of exploitation films: she has many scenes in which the women are fully clothed and the *men* are nude. As Rothman explained to this writer:

> There is more male nudity in my films than you find in films of most male directors. Eroticism in films has been traditionally concerned with the erotic interests of men while women's interests have usually

been ignored. Women have as much interest in men's bodies as men do in women's. As a woman, I naturally take woman's erotic interests into account. Therefore I have male nudity when it seems appropriate.

Rothman's cinematic preoccupation with contemporary relationships and living situations can be traced back to the mid-1950s when she studied sociology at Berkeley. "I decided to become a filmmaker when I saw *The Seventh Seal*" [1956], she recalls. "I think it's fair to say Bergman inspired me to become a writer-director." The fact that Rothman spent 1960 to 1963 enrolled in cinema at the University of Southern California makes her a contemporary of the original—but infinitely more publicized—film school alumni who direct features, Francis Ford Coppola (University of California at Los Angeles) and Jim McBride (New York University).

Rothman left USC after winning the first Director's Guild Fellowship ever awarded to a woman. She took a path toward a feature-directing assignment—"I didn't have a rough time."—that many aspiring filmmakers have followed: doing pickup shots, assisting Roger Corman, filming second-unit action sequences, and by shooting American-version scenes for a cheapie foreign horror film. In 1966 Rothman got to direct her first feature film: AIP's G-rated *It's a Bikini World*. She told me: "This was one of the last beach pictures made, possibly the last. I doubt that anyone ever chose to make a beach picture because they were attracted to the genre. I certainly didn't. It was simply my first chance to make a feature film."

Rothman doesn't really consider *It's a Bikini World* indicative of her work, and, in fact, almost has to be reminded that she made it: "I thnk that it had pretty interesting photography for the time." Still the film has a fairly amusing script, doesn't star Annette Funicello and Frankie Avalon, and possesses thematic insight into the later Rothman.

Mark Samson is a cocky, female-collecting, peerlessly athletic lad who finds he cannot win Delilah Dawes by merely flexing his muscles. Since she prefers timid boys with brains, Samson dons glasses and becomes "Herbie," his unathletic but scholarly brother. (In Rothman's version of "Samson and Delilah," the male deceives the female.)

While Delilah's affair with "Herbie" flourishes, she strains to give Samson his comeuppance in a series of athletic contests. Of course, Delilah discovers that "Herbie" is a fake, but instead of paying Samson back through a deception of her own—a course taken by most female participants in American comedies—she becomes doubly determined to beat him at sport. She battles Samson through an intricate obstacle race, in which the various contestants must ride skate boards, motorcycles, cars, speedboats, and camels, and demonstrate swimming and running skills. (On the highway, Delilah thumbs a ride, becoming the first of the many Rothman women who hitchhike to get around.) Although Delilah has no trouble defeating the other men, she only beats Samson when he feigns a leg injury inches from the finish line. Samson thinks she will appreciate his gallantry, but Delilah is not one to be patronized. She kicks him mightily, making him really lame.

At the end, Delilah and the hobbling Samson are united, with Samson willing to change into a person more like "Herbie." Delilah gets what she wants, for, even in this earliest film, Rothman won't allow her heroine to end up with a "macho" hero.

The Student Nurses (1970) is perhaps Rothman's most solid film, effectively combining comedy and drama and boasting her best casting. Karen Carlson (Phred), Elaine Griftos (Sharon), Barbara Leigh (Priscilla), and Brioni Farrell (Lynn) are all convincing as third-year nursing students and roommates who have chaotic experiences during the hectic weeks before their nursing-certification day. These women set the pattern for the future Rothman females: they help and root for each other, without petty rivalries over men or career..

Rothman always opens her films with a rousing song over the titles. As the four women hitch to the hospital, the sound track sings out, "We Can Make It If We Try!" Rothman sets up personal and professional roadblocks for each woman throughout the film, making it clear that, for her women to triumph, they must emerge at the end with their occupational goals fulfilled, with nursing diplomas in their hands.

Phred, the least sympathetic of the roommates, is happy to be assigned to obstetrics and gynecology. "It's a clean area of medicine," she says. "Very few people die of female diseases." Her relationship with young gynecologist Jim Casper starts out well but soon begins to disintegrate. That she will only make love with the light on is symptomatic of her inability to face up to the unclean, "darker" side of life; so when Casper tries to tell Phred about a tragedy in the hospital that has depressed him, she stops him, insisting, "I don't like to hear about people dying. I don't want it brought into my private life. Especially my sex life." When Casper gives Priscilla an abortion, Phred breaks off with him and flees to his roommate. Furthermore, she decides to get out of gynecology and become a *receptionist* for a psychiatrist upon graduation. She claims, "Psychiatry is a clean area of medicine," but we know differently after having seen Priscilla interrogated by a heartless psychiatrist during her unsuccessful attempt to get her abortion through legal channels.

Phred often acts unreasonably and is childishly stubborn; she takes advantage of her good looks and is very manipulative. Yet we feel sorry for her. She has missed out on a good relationship and is about to throw away the better career. Asked her opinion of Phred, Rothman replies, "I may not personally approve of what a character represents, but to present them credibly, I must be able to empathize with them."

In what is the most touching relationship in the Rothman films, the second nurse, Sharon, becomes involved with Greg, who has spent his entire life in the hospital waiting to die. When Greg trusts Sharon completely, he asks her a favor, but it is not to be his first lover. Instead he wants her to run around the hospital grounds while he watches from his wheelchair. They are spiritually united, as she becomes *his* legs. When Sharon does make love to Greg, it is because she wants to do so, not because a dying patient asked.

When Greg succumbs (off camera), Sharon can't cope with the knowledge that she can no longer doctor him. Consequently, Sharon decides to transport her nursing to the battlefields of Vietnam. She is the opposite of Phred in that she chases after death, but we feel sad for her as well because she will be futilely searching for her "missing" lover among the dying in the world.

Priscilla pretends to be the sophisticated "love child" as she travels around town in skimpy outfits and goes braless (so she brags) under her nurse's uniform. She is the perfect prey for the biker who picks her up, convinces her to share his spiked orange juice, and makes love to her while they "trip." Priscilla awakes alone and pregnant, but she does not go after the man who has left her that way. The choice to have the abortion is her own.

The abortion sequence is terrifying as Priscilla relives the worst moments of her acid trip and hears the psychiatrist's prying questions being thrown at her. Although the abortion itself is successful, this scene, in truth, could give a woman second thoughts about having one. "The only thing I consider dated about the abortion sequence," says Rothman, "is the fact that the law has changed. Priscilla's attitude would be no different if I made the film today."

Lynn Verdugo's transformation is the most dramatic of the four women. On her way to her job in public health, she stops to watch a Chicano street gathering. (There are Chicanos in almost all of Rothman's movies. "Mexican Americans constitute a sizable portion of the Southern California population, but are rarely shown in film. I grew up with them, and I don't want to ignore a group of people whom I deeply admire and respect.") Lynn soon finds herself witness to a rumble. She walks away rather than get involved. Chicano activist Victor Charlie (Reni Santoni) chastises her, "Your last name is Verdugo and you don't know how to speak Spanish? You ought to be ashamed!" It is only a matter of time before she becomes totally committed to helping indigent Chicanos, even joining Victor Charlie in a shoot-out with the police.

It is significant that Lynn's last scene—her climactic scene—is not when she tells Victor Charlie that she will be his woman but when she goes after her nursing diploma. She realizes that the most essential thing is helping *her* people through medicine. Lynn is the only one of the four women whose love affair survives, but, more important, she is the only one lucky enough to have found a direction in life to make the best use of her potential.

In *The Student Nurses* Rothman's four women make *all* their own decisions, right and wrong. It is true that some of the men they deal with are honorable, helpful people, but the women know they can't trust their futures to them. The male authority figures in the film are discouraging and unhelpful: the cynical doctor who contends that women get their RNs to fall back on in case they lose their husbands; the psychiatrist who refuses to recommend a legal abortion for Priscilla; and the hospital's all-male board that ultimately turns down Priscilla's abortion request. In a rare moment of female hostility toward men in the Rothman films, Lynn sums it up: "Give men a chance to play inquisitor, and its thumbs down on women every time." So the women guide their own lives, and, at the very least, succeed in achieving their basic goal: in the finale, the four women walk side by side into the hospital to get their nursing diplomas. (Phred, Sharon, and Priscilla wear their graduation outfits, and Lynn a pair of old jeans.) It has been tough but they have all "made it."

The Velvet Vampire (1971) is the most fascinating of the Rothman films, a truly offbeat vampire movie. Although it must be classified as a horror film and does in fact contain much in the classic horror tradition, it is basically concerned with an unconventional love triangle in which one of the two women just happens to be a vampire. There is not much bloodletting, but there is plenty of nudity and racy dialogue. "I wanted to make a vampire film," says Rothman, "that dealt explicitly with the sexuality implicit in the vampire legend." The few critics who saw this odd little film had trouble with it: they guessed that they were laughing at lines and situations so outrageous that they couldn't conceive of anyone planning them that way. Rothman says, *"The Velvet Vampire* was obviously intended to be a funny film."

The trip through the desert for Lee (Michael Blodgett) and

Susan (Sherry Miles) is similar to Jonathan Harker's Transylvanian excursion. Naturally the car breaks down, but "velvet vampire" Diane (Celeste Yarnell) appears out of nowhere, driving up in the daylight in her yellow dune buggy. She takes them to her modern, neat, plant-filled house that sits alone in the desert. As she explains, she would move out of this sun-soaked land if it weren't that her husband is buried there.

At first Susan doesn't enjoy her visit at Diane's. She does not like raw meat for dinner, and she does not like her husband's shameless flirting. (The dialogue exchanges seem trite and overloaded with double entendres, but they are strangely funny considering that a vampire is taking part.) Husband and wife begin squabbling like a typical vacationing couple. Stubborn Susan drives Lee crazy by insisting that they cut short their stay. Lee wants to stick around long enough, however, to make love to his seductive hostess, so he tells Susan not to be suspicious of Diane's strange actions and that she is "only imagining" that someone is watching them make love from the other side of the bedroom mirror. When the bloodcurdling scream of Diane's latest male victim sounds through the night, Lee shrugs it off, telling Susan, "It's only a coyote." (Men scream often and loudly in the Rothman films. "When I was a little girl, I was very stoical," she remembers. "And I could not understand why women in films screamed so much while men rarely did.")

It is a matter of time before Diane and Lee are alone. Rothman makes nifty cuts between Diane about to make love to Lee and a snake about to strike the sleeping, unsuspecting Susan. Diane and Lee halt their stripping when they hear Susan's scream and run to her aid. Diane saves Susan's life (a rare feat for a cinema vampire) by sucking the poison from her bloody leg. Susan's attitude toward Diane changes: "I'm beginning to like it here."

That night Susan finds Lee and Diane clutching each other on the living room floor. Lee doesn't see Susan, but the undisturbed Diane smiles invitingly. Susan's reaction is even more surprising: she watches what is happening with complete fascination. Like Diane, Susan is a voyeur. (Later the two women will argue over which of the two is the greater voyeur!) In the morning, Susan is not really furious at what went on the previous night. If she feels jealous, it is only because Lee got to sleep with Diane and she didn't. Afterward, neither Diane nor Susan pays much attention to Lee: the two women are attracted to each other. Now Lee wants to go home.

The film builds toward a sexual encounter between Diane and Susan, but at the exact moment Diane coaxes the willing Susan into her bed, Lee's corpse drops out of Diane's closet. Unfortunately, what follows is not the appropriate lesbian scene but a long sequence in which Diane menacingly chases Susan through the streets of Los Angeles, only to die in a disappointing climax. The time would have been better spent if Susan ignored her husband's body and pulled the covers around her and Diane. Rothman is sympathetic to homosexuality in her works, and it seems likely that she could have provided us with one of the few properly handled love scenes between women in film.

Following *The Velvet Vampire*, Rothman made two ambitious, but lesser films that, utilizing two entirely different settings, placed

(Left to right) Victoria Vetri, Solomon Sturges, Aimee Eccles, and Jeffrey Pomerantz pass an uneasy night together in Stephanie Rothman's *Group Marriage* (1972). (Courtesy Dimension Pictures)

women in analogous situations: *Group Marriage* (1972) and *Terminal Island* (1973). In these works, Rothman sets guidelines for women and men living together in harmony.

"I like comedy best of all," states Rothman, "and *Group Marriage* was the first chance I had to do an outright comedy. Unlike *The Velvet Vampire*, it didn't go under the guise of being something else." *Group Marriage* is perhaps Rothman's most representative film, in that she deals with her primary concerns: alternative life-styles and people involved in open, honest relationships.

The film deals with six people—three young men (a bumper-sticker designer, a social worker, and a lifeguard) and three young women (a rent-a-car countergirl, a former stewardess, and a lawyer)—who live together, sharing responsibilities, work, problems, decision making, and each other. Although there is strong external pressure put on the group and its individual members, as well as moments of internal dissension, the group survives because the six people love and trust each other and don't compete for each other's affections.

If *Group Marriage* has a real weakness, it is that it tries to be daringly topical, even though the subject of "group marriage" seems more unusual than shocking. The violence that ensues when the angry public hears about their living arrangement is a little absurd. If the film has a real strength, it is that all the protagonists are as gentle as they are. It is certainly not typical of movie romances to have so many characters liking each other for an entire film when things are going on that would make everyday people despise one another.

Rothman told this writer:

> *Terminal Island* was the first opportunity I had to deal with major action sequences and a large cast of characters. The majority of the production was shot in the rain, which made production more difficult than normal. But it gave the land a verdant look that is uncharacteristic of Southern California where it was shot. We were intending to make a "Devil's Island" picture.

Terminal Island is a prison island—without guards or confinement—where in the not-too-distant future California will send its murderers on a one-way trip. The film deals with a guerrilla war between a small band of renegades and a larger group of oppressive settlement dwellers for supremacy of the island. Although *Terminal Island* contains the action necessary to carry a film of this type, it is essentially, once again, about life-styles and relationships.

The four women on the island (a revolutionary who blew up a bank and its clerks, a black who killed a cellmate, a mute named Bunny who used an ice pick on the parents who gave her that name, and a sexually promiscuous woman who got rid of her husband) decide to fight alongside the renegades because these men allow them equal status. The women are no longer forced to provide the sexual services that the settlers had demanded. The women give of themselves sexually, willingly—but when they want to and with whom they choose. "My intention," says Rothman, "was to tell

Women as cattle in the settlement camp of Stephanie Rothman's *Terminal Island* (1973). (Left to right) Ena Hartman, Marta Kristen, and Phyllis Davis. (Courtesy Dimension Pictures)

a story in which a group of men and women needed each other for survival, and therefore could not afford the luxury of stereotyped sex-role behavior."

As with *Group Marriage*, the success of the living experiment in *Terminal Island* depends on everybody cooperating instead of competing for affections or power. It is the most democratic—and "unisexual"—movie in memory: the women and men renegades are interchangeable, sharing in all the action, the danger, the plotting of war strategy. When a woman is making love or conversing with one man, it could just as easily be with another. There are no distinct couples formed in the film.

The renegades win the war and control the island. They do not kill the surviving antagonists; they invite them to join in a new society. "I don't believe in writing off human beings, no matter how worthless or dislikable they may seem," Rothman explains. On this island of murderers, a utopian society has a chance to emerge: there is peace; what material wealth there is is shared equally; power is shared equally; the men and women are sexually equal.

The Working Girls (1974) returns Rothman to the familiar milieu: sunny, sandy, washed-out, wacky, decadent Los Angeles. (Rothman is known as a "L.A. filmmaker" because that setting is a dominant factor in her work.) The picture is similar to *The Student Nurses* in being concerned with several women in problematic situations, but this film is almost entirely comic in tone. Once again, Rothman presents roommates: Honey, who is looking for work; Denise, a striving artist who survives by painting billboards; and Jill, a law student who pays for her education by working in a nightclub as a waitress, then as a stripper, and finally as the manager. All three are at a pivotal point in their lives and are searching for the right path to follow.

The Working Girls is the only one of Rothman's films that she scripted alone, and the material seems totally wedded to her interests. The movie is full of characters she likes, and their everyday problems are ones she can relate to. "I am particularly drawn to the

Denise (Laurie Rose) paints her boyfriend (Ken Del Conte) in *The Working Girls* (1973), an example of Stephanie Rothman's use of male nudity. (Courtesy Stephanie Rothman)

problem that the three main characters face, a problem shared by most young people: how to find work that will support them and provide satisfaction at the same time."

The Working Girls is a breezy film that—despite adherence to a tight script—seems free form in style, with the characters delivering their lines so naturally that the actors seem to be improvising. Sarah Kennedy, who plays Honey, is a truly gifted comedienne. She returns the much-chastised "dumb blonde" to the screen, but she is so funny, so brainy, and resourceful that everybody should be comfortable with the characterization. Honey is an unusual lead for an exploitation film: she snores; she is never seen nude; her most important relationship with a male is not in the slightest way sexual; she is a truly intelligent female. Honey's self-advertisement in a newspaper: "I will do *anything* for money. Have a M.A. in math."

There is one scene in *The Working Girls* that deserves mention because it seems to be Rothman's only direct filmic comment about those people who attend her movies only for the female nudity. Ironically, the scene contains the only lengthy nudity in the film: Jill dances out onto a stage but freezes when it comes time for her to do her strip. The lecherous men in the audience howl for her to go on with her act.[1] Jill remembers "the secret" a veteran stripper has just confided to her, and she almost bursts out laughing as she resumes her dance. While Jill strips to some zany Herb Alpert-like music, the now-subjective camera shows us her thought: the bare-bodied audience who don't know that they are the ones putting on the show.

Stephanie Rothman is important because she is that rare commercial filmmaker who has consistently shown a concern for women in her work, who clearly *likes* women. It is not by accident that Rothman's heroines are not violated, that all rapes fail; that all lovemaking is tender, even when the male involved is a scoundrel; that the only woman hit by her lover—Jill in *The Working Girls*—walks out on him *after* hitting him back. Rothman not only respects her women, but she sets her standards high for the men she will allow them to wind up with: a macho man is either converted or deserted.

---

[1] For an extraordinary analogy, see how Dorothy Arzner made a similar attack on voyeurism, explained in the essay on *"Dance, Girl, Dance,"* pp. 24–25. A comparison of the scenes in the two films may give some ideas of what is a "feminist perspective" in the movies. To carry the analogy further, Dorothy Arzner *also* made a film called *Working Girls* (1930).—Eds.

Working with Hawks*

Leigh Brackett

INTRODUCTION

Leigh Brackett, long one of America's most distinguished science-fiction writers, got her big movie break when Hollywood director Howard Hawks read a hard-boiled novel she wrote and wanted her to collaborate with William Faulkner on the script of Raymond Chandler's The Big Sleep *(1946). The name "Leigh" fooled Hawks as it has countless readers. As he told Richard Schickel, "Leigh, I thought, was a man's name, and in walked this fresh-looking girl who wrote like a man" [sic].*

The collaboration was so successful—an eight-day classic Bogart-Bacall script—that Hawks periodically called Brackett back to Hollywood to work on his projects. She wrote the screenplays for Hawks's three greatest films of the last decades, Rio Bravo *(1959),* Hatari! *(1962), and* El Dorado *(1967), plus the less accomplished* Rio Lobo *(1970), Hawks's final film after forty-five years of directing. All these are outdoor adventure pictures, genre films, and they all star "The Duke," John Wayne.*

Of interest is what happens when a woman screenwriter takes on traditional "male" genres. What kind of transformation occurs? And

* Reprinted from *Take One*, 3, no. 6 (October 1972). By permission of the author.

when the screenwriter is an unorthodox woman named Leigh Brackett and the director is an unclassifiable talent named Howard Hawks?

I've been working with Howard Hawks, off and on, since 1944, but I never really stopped to think what exactly he was doing with his women. I only knew that I liked them and was comfortable with them. . . . I learned some things very quickly when I first began to work for Hawks. Conventional heroines bore him; he can't "have fun" with them, and if a character or situation develops that Hawks

Philip Marlowe (Humphrey Bogart) talks to Vivian Sternwood (Lauren Bacall) about her doped-up sister Carmen (Martha Vickers) in Howard Hawks's *The Big Sleep* (1946), coscripted by Leigh Brackett. (Courtesy Wisconsin Center for Film and Theater Research)

can't have fun with, it gets lost, pronto. His heroines must never become shrill, or bitchy, or coy, or cute. They must be honest, and they must have a sense of humor. He likes them with long handsome legs, not too much bosom, and hair that looks well no matter how hard the wind blows. They dress with style, but simply, and wear very little makeup—the natural, straightforward look, without fussy frills and hairdos. As Naomi Wise points out,[1] they often take over and push the whole plot. More than once I've argued with Hawks that the girl was getting too pushy, and couldn't we let the poor boob of a hero make just one decision all by himself? I was always overruled, and I guess Hawks knew what he was doing, because it came out right in the end.

There are some other Hawksian conventions about men/women. The word *love* is not heard, and there is no scene where hero and heroine declare their tender feelings for each other. It's done obliquely. Usually the hero's friend comes to the girl and says, "I think he likes you." Marriage is not mentioned; it's "Are you going to ask her to stay?" Hawks people are not domestic types; nobody ever talks about getting that little spread and settling down to raise a family.

Generally, far in the background, there is the girl who wasn't any good ("I tried to tell him she wasn't any good but he wouldn't listen.") (As though anyone ever did!), or the woman who hated whatever it was the hero was doing and tried to make him stop it; that is, attempted to destroy his individuality and make him over into something he didn't want to be. The hero is woman-shy, living in a male world where he is comfortable with his relationships. When the new girl arrives, he tries at first to get rid of her. She insists on staying, and now she has to win her place in this closed group *as a man* (or asexual human being, if you prefer), proving that she is as honest and courageous and loyal as any of them. Somewhere along the line she is likely to say to the hero, "Any time you want me to go, just tell me, and I'll go." In other words, no strings. When the hero can accept her as he would another man, with the masculine virtues he values, then he can start thinking

[1] Naomi Wise, "The Hawksian Woman," *Take One,* 3, no. 3 (1972), pp. 17–20.

about her as a woman; that is, lose his fear of falling in love again, because he knows she is not going to be like those others. In the meantime, as Naomi Wise says, the woman herself emerges as a whole and complete human being in her own right, and minus the hero's hang-ups.

This brings up a couple of questions. Why should Howard Hawks, almost alone among producers, have this attitude toward the women in his pictures? He is an intensely masculine person, with an intensely masculine outlook on life. He has done most of the things he makes pictures about—driven racing cars, piloted planes, ridden motorcycles. He doesn't like losers, or antiheroes. He values bravery, strength, expertise, loyalty, all the "masculine" virtues (though Lord knows I've known women who had a damned sight more of them than some of the men I've known; it isn't the sex, it's the individual). So why should he give his women a position of equality—often, indeed, dominance—in a genre that usually relegates them either to being decorative in the hero's relaxed moments, or to looking doleful as the hero goes off about his business?

I suspect that it's because Hawks doesn't like women in their *negative* aspect, and until he can accept a female character, as the hero must, as another man, or an asexual *human being* with the attributes he respects, he can't like her. And if he didn't like her, he wouldn't know what to do with her. Hawks has to like all his people (the villains are kept down to a minimum) and this is why such a deal of affectionate good humor comes through in films like *Rio Bravo* (1959) and *Hatari!* (1962).

All right for Howard Hawks, he's a man, he's supposed to value the masculine virtues. What about me?

Well, there's a curious parallel there. A friend who reads my science fiction once asked me, "Why do your heroines always come down out of the hills swinging their swords like Genghis Khan?" And I said, "I suppose it's because conventional heroines bore me." Actually, only a small number of my sci-fi heroines swing swords. But they are all, by God, *people,* with independent lives and thoughts of their own, capable of being comrades and mates but always of their own free choice and always as equals. (*Earned* equality. Men have to earn it. So do they.) So the Hawksian woman fitted my typewriter very well.

How come?

Partly, I suppose, I was just born hatefully independent. Partly, it was because my father died when I was a baby and I was womaned to death by my mother, grandmother, and a great-aunt. They were very high on femininity and the segregation of the sexes, and they had an attitude that I find most interesting now, in the light of women's lib. Far from feeling in the slightest degree inferior to men, they believed that Woman was a sacred and special creation, infinitely superior to the lower orders, such as males, who were put here simply to serve them, support them, protect them, and take their orders. Any attempt to make women equal with men was not to elevate them, but to degrade them. They were proud of their physi-

The cast of Howard Hawks's *Hatari!* (1962), with a script by Leigh Brackett. (Left to right) John Wayne, Elsa Martinelli, Red Buttons, Michele Girardon, Hardy Kruger, Valentin de Vargas, and Bruce Cabot. (Courtesy Films, Inc.)

cal frailty, which was prodigious. They were constantly lecturing me on what little girls/young ladies could/couldn't (mostly couldn't) do, and the core of it all was that one *never* did anything for oneself.

I couldn't relate to any of this even as a small child. I took my values from the boys' books I read, which taught the sterling virtues of self-reliance and good sportsmanship. And I realized, from observation, that no other human being, in this uncertain world of death and taxes, can ever be a permanent possession. Your own self is the only person you can always be certain of having around.

I think Howard Hawks knows this, too, and that is why there is so little of the living-happily-ever-after in his films. His heroes and heroines are what he calls "grown up." They don't expect the moon with a string around it, they do not expect or desire to own each other. They are content with what they have, for as long as they have it, and this is possible because the Hawksian woman is not husband-hunting or looking for "security." She is secure in herself, and she is giving her love as a free person, with open hands.

It has often been said that Hawks's films, in recent years, are concerned chiefly with friendship and its obligations. And in this context, the Hawksian woman has first to become a friend, before she can become a lover.

Which isn't at all a bad idea.

Dede Allen*

Patrick McGilligan

The most democratic of the motion-picture crafts, at least in America, may be editing. None of the other film crafts except costumery has been so comparatively open to Hollywood's women. Although nobody has reasonably explained this phenomenon, it may be enough to remember that editing descended from continuity, and evolved originally as a kind of visual secretarial skill; doors bolted to female directors and photographers opened magically for script girls and cutters. And thus women were among editing's pioneers in Hollywood during the silent and early sound years— women such as Margaret Booth, Dorothy Arzner, and Dorothy Spenser contributed handsomely to the rules and artistic intelligence of film cutting. Today, their legacy continues unabatedly strong; women such as Verna Fields (editor of *American Graffiti*, 1973, winner of an Oscar for *Jaws*, 1975; so revered at Universal that she has been promoted to an executive and is slated for a directing position) and Dede Allen stand out in the field. Dede Allen, especially, has carved her niche in film history; perhaps no other film editor has achieved such overwhelming cult status and loyal critical following.

The Dede Allen story is not a typical Hollywood success story, far

* The author is indebted to Debra Weiner, who interviewed Dede Allen on the set of *Slap Shot* in 1976 and graciously donated material for this article.

199

from it. Indeed, she worked almost fifteen years in the industry before editing her first feature, and she worked another decade and a half before actually editing a feature in Hollywood itself. By 1967, she had amassed three impressive credits, Robert Wise's *Odds Against Tomorrow* (1959), Robert Rossen's *The Hustler* (1961), and Elia Kazan's *America, America* (1963). Then she edited *Bonnie and Clyde* (1967), possibly the most stylistically audacious and thematically provocative American film of the 1960s, accounting for much of what director Arthur Penn has described as its "nervous montage." Pauline Kael called it "the best editing in an American movie in a long time"; Judith Crist began to review Dede Allen's editing (a rare enough compliment) as "infallible" and "incomparable." Shortly, she became a pivotal figure among the East Coast school of directors—Paul Newman, George Roy Hill (before he relocated on the West Coast), Sidney Lumet, and especially Penn— all vaguely improvisatory and socially conscious filmmakers. She accumulated credits on some of the more inventive films of the next ten years—*Rachel, Rachel* (1968), *Alice's Restaurant* (1969), *Little Big Man* (1970), *Slaughterhouse Five* (1972), *Serpico* (1973), *Night Moves* (1974), *Dog Day Afternoon* (1975), *The Missouri Breaks* (1976), and *Slap Shot* (1977). And the editors she trained —Aram Avakian, Jerry Greenberg, and Norman Gay, among them— swelled and invigorated the industry. Among movie buffs she has emerged as something of a saint and, when working with lesser directors, as a virtual savior, an invisible cutting-room redeemer.

"My husband insists he can tell which scenes I have cut," she mused, one afternoon in 1975, when I talked with her. Warm and friendly, she has large, expressive features and a lovely shock of auburn hair; she stretched her legs relaxedly as she talked. Normally, she doesn't extend interviews while working, but editing on Sidney Lumet's *Dog Day Afternoon* was nearly completed, and she was waiting for an "answer print." The telephone rang repeatedly in her small cutting room in the former Warner Brothers building in midtown Manhattan, and she was interrupted by two calls—she recommended an editor for Elia Kazan's then in-progress version of F. Scott Fitzgerald's *The Last Tycoon* (1976), and she discussed possible title changes for the Lumet movie (some concern there about how *Dog Day* would translate for foreign markets). "He says there is an offbeat style to my scenes," she continued, about her husband.

> I don't know. I can't tell. It's certainly not a contradiction to the director, because the final cut is in his hands. Obviously, I have a sense of timing and rhythm that may be different from other editors. But as far as I'm concerned, editing is totally a matter of communication, and trying to interpret what a director is trying to put on the screen. Ultimately, it has to be a style that is right for both of you.

A bit of background. Fresh from college, Dede Allen joined Columbia Pictures in 1943, and became a messenger for the studio; ten months later, she wormed her way into the cutting room. Like many women then, she wanted to become a director and, like most women, she found the obstacles fierce. Instead she became an assistant editor, and worked nights on a "left-wing" documentary on the first interracial housing project in Los Angeles. Then she met her future husband, and they were married shortly thereafter. Her career was interrupted, and she moved to New York City in the early 1950s, raising two children and supporting her husband's freelance efforts. She toiled at bread-and-butter jobs, became a script clerk (thus learning film continuity), cut commercials, industrials, and documentaries; she learned the ropes and bided her time.

"I worked for fifteen years before I got a chance to do a feature," she told me,

> and I worked hard at anything I did. I was always proud of it, even if it was a commercial spot. At that time, my husband was a freelance writer, and I was helping earn a living. We were raising children. I never, never looked down on what I did, no matter what it was, even if I was getting tired of it. There were times I never dreamed that I'd get back into features because I was working in spots, and there were only two or three features that were coming from New York. But one of the most important things about editing is that I learned from everything that I did. Sometimes I was stuck in areas too long, yes, and I got a chance to edit ten years later than I might have, yes. But I learned . . .
>
> When I started out, it was very tough, because I came out of the Depression, and into the Second World War, when women really

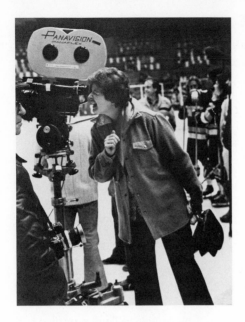

Dede Allen on the set of George Roy Hill's *Slap Shot* (1977), which she is editing. (Courtesy Pamela Redmond)

couldn't take the jobs. If there was a man in the family, out of work with children to support, it was immoral for women to work unless they were widows. And I wasn't. I was a college girl. So I always felt overly grateful for any chance I had . . . I had to work twice as hard and I had to be twice as good as any man, but that wasn't necessarily a bad thing. That gave me a tremendous amount of motivation. There were a lot of doors closed to me and a lot of obstacles. I was told over and over again, "No, you can't; no, you can't." It was always no, no, no. So you had to make it happen. The hardest thing to learn, in my generation, was not to get irritated at being a woman, because you sometimes have a lot of gaffe that goes with it . . . When my children got sick, for instance, I would never go home; my husband was always the one to go home because I figured that if I went home from work, it was always a case of, well, that's a woman . . . We definitely had that problem. I hope today's women won't have to be as hard on themselves as women in my generation had to be. It can be a wonderful motivational thing, if you don't get crushed.

Then in 1959 fortune intervened. At the age of thirty-four, she was contacted by Robert Wise and asked to edit his *Odds Against Tomorrow.* Wise, himself a prolific former film editor at RKO, responsible for cutting Orson Welles's *Citizen Kane* (1941) as well as assembling the studio version of *The Magnificent Ambersons* (1942), gave her encouragement as well as employment. "He was marvelous," she recalled. "He was the first person who said, 'No matter how many directions I give you, if it doesn't play, don't show it to me.' He was excited as hell if I came up with something. He had a great influence on me because he was a tremendous editor in his own time. So he knew." Rarely seen today, the movie is a taut and chilling little heist story that owes much of its compact suspense to Dede Allen's seamlessly crisp editing.

Two years later, she was tapped by Robert Rossen to cut *The Hustler;* and already she was beginning to flex her vigorous editing style. "Rossen was a very careful director," she remembered.

> If a scene played well, he'd say, "Don't water the mustard, leave it alone." I had a crisp way of editing, even then. I was already beginning to cut in a certain way. I remember cutting from something like a wallet to a car. Bang. It was unusual then, everybody does it today. Rossen was very fond of that style. When it was later referred to in *Time* magazine, he took credit for it. I think he thought he invented the style. I definitely think I had an influence on him as a director.

The Hustler was one of the most talked about films of the year, a commercial and critical success, and it established her reputation.

America, America followed in 1963. Kazan had contemplated hiring Dede Allen to edit *Splendor in the Grass* (1961) but, after preliminary discussions, he settled for his customary editor, Gene Milford. Then *America, America* came along, the semiautobiographical account of an immigrant to America, based on his own novelette, and Kazan turned to Dede Allen. Working with Kazan was a seminal experience, intense and instructive; it called for many hours of conversations and notes and letters, producing "a level of communication that became shorthand: which character to play, why, what look, what moment. I never feared suggesting a way different from what his coverage indicated was the direction he intended. By then, I'd learned the most important key to our work relationship. Say what's on your mind—follow your instincts." During the year and a half spent working on *America, America,* "my knowledge and understanding of character, of people and of myself grew geometrically" (*Working with Kazan,* ed. Jeanine Basinger [Middletown, Conn.: Wesleyan University Press, 1973]). A moving example of personal cinema, *America, America* strengthened her credentials and brought her to the threshold of a new security in the industry; Arthur Penn signed her to edit his movie about two Depression era bank robbers, Bonnie Parker and Clyde Barrow.

After *Bonnie and Clyde* (1967), Dede Allen's career is well known. Penn never used another editor for the next decade; something was so compatible about their temperaments, editor and director. "With Arthur," she likes to say, "I just fool around and get familiar with what he's doing. He doesn't impose himself much on you." She worked so often and well with director Penn that, in some circles, she became erroneously known as "Arthur Penn's editor," although, in fact, she edited as many movies without Penn as with him. And it is no accident that these movies were often the undebated masterworks of otherwise erratically brilliant directors: movies such as George Roy Hill's elegaic picture (his best), *Slaughterhouse Five,* based on Kurt Vonnegut's best-selling novel ("I think George was very surprised at things I had done," she explained, "because he was sure he had shot things a certain way. I put things together my way, and he was just very surprised. Of course, too, sometimes I'd go too far, and he'd pull me back."), and movies like Sidney Lumet's *Serpico* and *Dog Day Afternoon.* Box-office blockbusters and winners of countless awards (Dede Allen was herself nominated for an Oscar for *Dog Day*), these are movies with a dramatic cohesion that other Lumet movies often lack.

Of course, editing is an intricate and demanding process that is virtually imperceptible to moviegoers; a good editor must have a mind with locomotive precision, and the visual knack to sort, discard, juxtapose, and assemble myriad snips and trims into the smooth movie mosaic. There are several steps. The initial step is the "first rough cut," according to Dede Allen, which is always excessive, "with too much in it." Often, as with *Serpico,* produced on a rushed schedule, the rough cut is edited nightly while the film is being shot. During these early stages Dede Allen customarily toys with music and sound effects in the rough cut, a quirk that led to an Erik Satie scoring for *Rachel, Rachel* ("I had a feeling that Satie might be right"), for example, and the Mikos Theodorakis sound track for *America, America*. The editor must nurse the picture through its many post-production stages—second rough cut, negative print, sound mix, looping, color processing, and finally, "answer print." Naturally, a good deal depends on the director and the raw footage during these steps; no editor, however resourceful, can pull a rabbit out of a hat or produce a classic film from dreary outtakes.

Thus it is difficult to pinpoint an editor's style, even when the editor is Dede Allen, and she is generally acknowledged to be an energizing influence on her movies. But one thing is certain, she can be reflective or dynamic with equal ease. You can spot her characteristic punctuation in *Bonnie and Clyde* in "the quick panic of Bonnie and Clyde looking at each other's face for the last time," which, as Pauline Kael wrote in *Kiss Kiss, Bang Bang* (Boston: Little, Brown, 1968), "is a stunning example of the art of editing." These are the tiny exclamations—parenthetical visual asides that comment on the larger action—that she specializes in and that make *Slaughterhouse Five*, for example, such a pleasantly surprising movie. Her contribution to the movie's eerie resonance is considerable: witness how she cuts fleetingly to the haunting faces of the peasant citizenry as Billy Pilgrim (Michael Sack) and his fellow prisoners of war enter war-torn Dresden; or witness her crosscutting between Edgar Derby's nomination as German liaison and Billy Pilgrim's nomination as Lion's Club president; she evokes an ingenious aural analogy between solitary (Pilgrim alone claps for Derby's nomination) and tumultuous (the Lions are unanimous) applause. (Of course, these are only the small touches in a movie with a uniquely bizarre continuity structure that must itself have been an awesome editing challenge, because, as Billy Pilgrim becomes "unstuck in time," the movie lurches unpredictably between the past, the present, and the future.) And these small moments are nearly overshadowed by the unforgettable Dede Allen climaxes—the "ragdoll dance of death" in *Bonnie and Clyde;* the breathtaking multisuccession of shots triggered by cops assaulting the back door in

Dog Day Afternoon; or the spectacularly swift carnage of boat and airplane and bloodied victims in *Night Moves.*

"Scenes just have to play," she explained to me,

> and, again, if you ask me what I do when I do what I do, I can't always answer. I don't intellectualize. I'm not that kind of an editor. There are editors who sit and figure out everything they are going to do before they do it, very rigidly. I work totally the opposite. I'm very intuitive. Obviously, I have a very definite reason for doing things; I'm very disciplined. And I'm sure that I have as much of a line of direction. I just don't like talking a cut. There's an awful lot of that in this business, and I don't do that well . . .
>
> As an editor, you must relate very strongly to the characters. You have to. The question of who do you cut to, when, why, and how, is not a technical question. It's really a matter of taste and making the scene play. Again, the mechanics of making a scene play is very technical in my area, but the interpretation, the manner in how you do it, is highly personal . . . [What] makes for good editing, besides understanding what the scene is, is how you are communicating with the director about what the director wants to say. It's not a competitive thing, although it gets to be a hard-nosed competitive thing sometimes. If you get rigid in the cutting room, though, you are obviously of no use to a director. Because there are thousands and thousands of options and decisions to be made every second.

Ironically, as late as 1975, Dede Allen was still involved in a minor struggle for industry recognition. Because of her long period of inactivity in California during the 1950s, her West Coast union card had lapsed and she spent months finagling through official labor channels for reinstatement—although this absurd battle to legitimate one of the leading editors in motion pictures was due primarily to California's own depressed labor situation. In fact, her initial West Coast-cut film (although she worked on Mike Nichols's and Neil Simon's *Bogart Slept Here* before that picture folded) will be George Roy Hill's *Slap Shot,* one of Hollywood's few movies about the hockey world. ("I knew nothing about hockey when we started," Dede Allen told interviewer Debra Weiner on-location, "but when I worked on *The Hustler,* I remember worrying because I knew nothing about pool. Robert Rossen told me, 'Kid, pool is the dullest game on earth. If I were shooting a movie about pool, I'd give up. I'm not shooting a film about pool, I'm shooting a film about people.' Anybody can learn the moves of the game—you can buy a book on ice hockey—but the atmosphere, the world of hockey, is what you come down to . . .")

Would Dede Allen, after all these years of struggle and accomplishment, still like to direct? After all, that was her original ambition. The question didn't faze her as we talked in 1975, waiting for *Dog Day* to arrive from the California laboratories; she had been asked the question many times before and she had thought about it often herself. She sighed wearily. "I've been asked to direct a couple of times," she said, "but when push comes to shove, I've always had the feeling that it wouldn't happen. There are a couple of discussions about directing, but I keep laughing and saying it's not very practical. Studios won't put up money for a new director or, if they do, it would be for the wrong reason, such as a 'woman's film,' and that's a silly kind of reasoning. If I was ten years younger, I don't think there'd be any question I would go in that direction." She smiled inwardly, perhaps thinking of what she might have done as a director. "But I really like what I do," she added. "I consider myself lucky."

Bibliography

Allen, Dede. "On Editing *America, America.*" *Working With Kazan.* Middletown, Conn.: Wesleyan University Film Press, 1973.

Brackett, Leigh. "From *The Big Sleep* to *The Long Goodbye* and More or Less How We Got There." *Take One*, 4, no. 1 (1974).

————; Faulkner, William; and Furthman, Jules. *The Big Sleep.* In *Film Scripts One.* Edited by George P. Garrett, O. B. Hardison, Jr., and Jane R. Gelfman. New York: Appleton-Century-Crofts, 1971.

Cook, Pam. "'Exploitation' Films and Feminism." *Screen* (Summer 1976). [Stephanie Rothman]

Denison, Arthur. "A Dream in Realization—Interview with Lois Weber." *The Moving Picture World*, July 21, 1917. Reprinted in Koszarski, Richard, ed. *Hollywood Directors 1914–1940.* New York: Oxford University Press, 1976.

Ford, Charles. "The First Female Producer." *Films in Review* (March 1964). [Alice Guy Blaché]

Fox, Terry Curtis. "Stephanie Rothman: Feminist on Poverty Row." *Film Comment*, 12, no. 6 (November–December 1976).

Guy, Alice. *Autobiographie d'une pionière du cinema.* Paris: Denoël/Gonthier, 1976.

Harrison, Louis Reeves. "Studio Saunterings." *The Moving Picture World*, June 15, 1912. [Alice Guy Blaché]

Hill, Gladwin. "Hollywood's Beautiful Bulldozer." *Colliers*, May 12, 1951. [Ida Lupino]

Hoffman, Hugh. "New Solax Plant at Fort Lee." *The Moving Picture World*, September 14, 1912. [Alice Guy Blaché]

Johnson, L. H. "A Lady General of the Picture Army." *Photoplay* (June 1915). [Lois Weber]

Lacassin, Francis. "Out of Oblivion: Alice Guy Blaché." *Sight and Sound* (Summer 1971).

Lupino, Ida. "Me, Mother Directress." *Action* (May–June 1967).

———. "New Faces in New Places." *Films in Review* (December 1950).

Olshan, Mike. "Dede Allen, Feature Editor." *Millimeter* (February 1974).

Parker, Francine. "Approaching the Art of Arzner." *Action* (July–August 1973).

———. "Discovering Ida Lupino." *Action* (July–August 1973).

Peary, Gerald. "Dorothy Arzner." *Cinema* (California), no. 34 (1974).

Pelfret, Elizabeth. "On the Lot with Lois Weber." *Photoplay* (October 1917).

Swires, Steve. "Conversation with Leigh Brackett." *Films in Review* (August–September 1976).

Vermilye, Jerry. "Ida Lupino." *Films in Review* (May 1959).

IV
Experimentalists and Independents

Germaine Dulac: First Feminist Filmmaker*

William Van Wert

Puis l'essentiel n'est-il pas que nous soyons nos maîtres, et les maîtres des femmes, de l'amour, aussi?

What is most important, is it not that we be our own masters and the masters of women and also of love?

—André Breton, *Manifestes du surréalisme*, 1924.

In the ten years between 1920 and 1930 French film established itself as the equal of the American, Russian, and German cinemas; more importantly, it showed a skeptical world that film was indeed a serious and formidable art form. Freed from its false reputation as a subgenre of theatre or photography, French film in this decade began to command respect and appreciation from artists and audiences alike for its potential both as product (document) and as performance (fiction). It attracted painters (Duchamp, Picabia, Léger, Dali) and poets (Breton, Desnos). They foresaw very clearly that film would become an immensely popular art, a means of reaching audiences beyond the bookstores and museums, beyond national boundaries of territory and language. They believed that the cinema had almost messianic powers, that through film the postwar audience could be restored to a lost innocence, away from

* Reprinted from *Women and Film*, nos. 5 and 6 (1974).

rationalism, determinism, and naturalism, toward the ancient art of pure sensation and environment.

By far the most important and the most prolific filmmaker of the decade was Germaine Dulac, whose film style proceeded from psychological realism and symbolism through Surrealism to documentaries and formal attempts at transposing musical structures to film; her ultimate goal was that film at its highest level of achievement should become a visual symphony. Yet Germaine Dulac has been largely overlooked or else slandered by most film historians. One reason might be that Dulac cannot be put into categories: for example, she was making films before the abovementioned Surrealists, and she was still making films in the 1930s when most of the Surrealists had stopped. Another reason might be that Dulac's films have never received wide distribution, either in France or elsewhere.

This second reason is linked with a third, perhaps the most important reason of all: Germaine Dulac was intensely interested in the image of women in film. An analysis of both an early film and a later film of Dulac demonstrates that she was the first feminist filmmaker.

Her 1922 film *The Smiling Madame Beudet* could really be retitled "The Original Diary of a Mad Housewife." It is one of the few experimental films of the decade in which women are not fragmented, shown as sexual freaks, stripped in close-ups or through editing to reveal a bleeding mouth, bared breasts, or buttocks. It is one of the few films of the decade in which a woman is main character.

The film is heavily influenced by French Symbolism (especially Baudelaire) in content, by the theatre in its use of type-casting for everyone but Madame Beudet, and by D. W. Griffith in its form: the use of sentence fragments in the titles to convey pieces of dialogue, the use of shadows to separate the mundane from the mysterious, and the use of highlighting on the heroine. In later Dulac films, narration and theatrical acting and sets will disappear. . . . But here we must remember that her main character is a housewife. Dulac was more concerned here with psychic sex and violence

Germaine Dermoz as Madame Beudet in Germaine Dulac's *Smiling Madame Beudet* (1922). (Courtesy The Museum of Modern Art/Film Stills Archive)

than with the fragmented physical sex and violence of the later Surrealists.

Action begins in the film when the maid brings in the mail. Mr. Beudet (played by Arquillière) accepts his mail gruffly, because he thinks it contains more bills to pay. His gruff treatment of the maid extends to all women, including his wife. By contrast, Madame Beudet (played by Germaine Dermoz) accepts her mail gratefully, even greedily, because the mail offers her a temporary escape from her boredom. In one of Mr. Beudet's letters is an invitation from his friend Mr. Labas (played by Jean D'Yd) to a presentation of *Faust* at the opera that evening. Beudet excitedly shows the letter and the opera tickets to Madame Beudet. Confronted with her indifference, he asks her angrily: "How is it that you don't want to understand *Faust?*" Dulac inserts two subjective point-of-view shots to show that Madame Beudet clearly understands the Faust story (male fantasy, female victim) all too well. Mr. Beudet's reactions, when he cannot comprehend his wife's indifference or lethargy, are always violent reactions, like pounding his fists on his desk. Dulac can deftly show in one such shot of pounding fists that Mr. Beudet demands attention both through pouting and brute force.

Madame Beudet's reactions to such situations are always symbolic, that is, to be understood on at least two levels. Outwardly, she maintains the docile posture of a subdued housewife, but inwardly, through Dulac's use of point-of-view shots, she shows herself to be capable of many imaginative fantasies. Such point-of-view shots are clearly recognizable in Dulac's films, since they involve the use of slow motion, or wide-angle lens distortion, or some means of trick photography. For example, Madame Beudet looks at a picture of a male tennis player in a book. The tennis player becomes her symbolic lover, her agent of revenge upon her stupid husband. Against a completely black background, the tennis player swings his racket in slow motion. In Madame Beudet's fantasy the tennis player enters the room; we know that he is part of her fantasy since we can see through his body to the walls behind. While the real Mr. Beudet continues to sit at his desk, an imaginary Beudet is picked up and choked by the tennis player. The usually unsmiling Madame Beudet smiles and even laughs heartily. The real Beudet, meanwhile, thinking that his wife is making fun of him, pulls a gun out of his desk drawer and puts it to his head. A title: 'Parody of suicide. A joke often perpetrated on dear Mrs. Beudet." But since Madame Beudet does not look, he puts the gun down.

When Mr. Beudet leaves for the opera, Madame Beudet is left alone in the unlighted room. At times like this, when she is left alone, we are given glimpses of the depth of her personality, of all the suppressed life forces within her. She picks up Baudelaire's *Flowers of Evil,* and turns to "The Death of the Lovers." For each line that she reads, a corresponding shot of objects in the room both reinforces the verbal line and undermines it by the inherent banality of the objects. She reads: "Our beds are filled with soft smells," and we see a shot of the Beudets' unused bed. She reads: "And pillows deep as graves," and we see two stacked but again unused pillows. She reads: "And strange flowers on the shelves," and we see the flowers that Mr. Beudet always arranges in the center of the table, but that Madame Beudet always rearranges off to one side. Her reading epitomizes the whole film, epitomizes the agonizing differences between imagination/potential (poetry) and her own frustrated existence. She walks to the window. A title tells us: "Always the same horizons." The next shot we see is that of the jail, both in her mind and also physically across the street.

At this point, blocked by the walls that surround her, she returns to her fantasy of the "lover" coming to save her. As the blurred image steps through the closed door, the face slowly comes into focus: it is the smiling, mocking, demonic face of Mr. Beudet. Her enslavement is so total that her husband dominates even her fantasies. His face is especially grotesque, because Dulac uses a wide-angle lens both to flatten and to enlarge the facial features. Madame Beudet takes the real gun out of the drawer and loads it. Then she goes to bed.

The final sequence of the film is a return to the opening tableaux shots. Mr. Beudet is again at his books, this time looking at all the household expenses. He has the maid call his wife in to account for all the expenses. He cannot, however, begin to approach a rational conversation. He begins pounding his fists again, then pulls the gun out and puts it to his head. Madame Beudet, who knows that the gun is loaded, jumps back in fright. He says: "It's you who deserves it more than me." He shoots the gun into the room, and there is a quick cut to the cat running downstairs, an incredible insert to convey the shock and sound of the gun going off. Immediately we see a flower vase broken. Mr. Beudet runs over to his wife and hugs her, his back to us, her drained, expressionless face to us. "So you wanted to kill yourself?," he says. "But how could I possibly live without you?," he says, squeezing her stiff body. Behind them in a picture frame, a drama finishes with a storybook ending. There are puppets in the mirror. A man and woman hug, then a curtain comes down. Then the word *"Theatre."* This excellent *mise-en-abîme* metaphor, like that of the poetry, is typical of Germaine Dulac's amazing ability to capsulize whole worlds of feeling in brief, static shots, and to use the symbolic possibilities of the camera, animating the inanimate (the tennis player, the imaginary "lover," the mirror) or conferring special importance on objects, while making into statues people whose existence contains little hope of true feeling.

Dulac gives us one last title: "United by habit." In the last visual of the film, Mr. and Mrs. Beudet are walking down the street. Mr. Beudet tips his hat to a passing priest. His hat tipped, he turns his face briefly to the camera. All we see of the "smiling" Madame Beudet is her back, and we realize with a chill that she is nothing more than a showpiece for her husband on the street, that she is no better off outside of the house or in the provinces than she was inside the house or in the shadows of the city. She is a victim, without future, without escape.

In the years following the release of *The Smiling Madame Beudet* several Dada painters turned to film, trying to write automatic films, films without plots, films that produced visual shocks through innovative close-ups, fragmentation of objects and rapid editing. Francis Picabia collaborated with René Clair to make *Entr'acte* (1924). Fernand Léger made *Le Ballet Mécanique* (1924), and Marcel Duchamp made *Anaemic Cinema* (1926). But the first truly Surrealistic film was Germaine Dulac's *The Seashell and the Clergyman* (1928, script by Antonin Artaud). In this film she exploits the Freudian symbolism of her male colleagues. She makes a film in their style in order, at the end, to expose male fantasies. For this reason, the clear distinction between objective reality and subjective point-of-view shots that exists in *The Smiling Madame Beudet* no longer exists in *The Seashell and the Clergyman*. Before looking at the film, it would perhaps be interesting to note what the Surrealists appreciated in later non-Surrealist films.

Since most of the Surrealists were men (Léonor Fini is an admirable and astonishing exception), they tended to admire certain films for reasons that would be offensive to most women. For instance, they loved *King Kong* (1933), especially the scene in which Kong rips off Fay Wray's clothes. Apropos of this scene, Ado Kyrou, a leading Surrealist critic, said: "Sadism-protest which leads to revolt after passing through love is the only one that has value for man."[1] They loved Josef von Sternberg's *The Blue Angel* (1930) for the many shots of Marlene Dietrich's thighs, as seen by a roving, caressing, fondling camera. They loved Groucho Marx's sadistic handling

[1] All of these examples come from J. H. Matthew, *Surrealism and Film* (Ann Arbor, Mich.: University of Michigan Press, 1971).

of wealthy matrons and Harpo Marx's complete surrender to his own libido. The portrayal of women in all of these examples is never as women actually are, but always as men fancy them to be in dream and fantasy.

In the Surrealists' own films the same male fantasies and stereotypes of women prevail. They exalt free sex and violence, yet they do not discard the double standard. They consistently portray women as fetishists and transvestites, phenomena that sexologist John Money says occur mainly in men. Or they portray women as castrating mothers or mindless nymphomaniacs. They portray women as statues, as machines, as half-animals. What films like Man Ray's *L'Etoile de Mer* (1928), Buñuel's *Un Chien Andalou* (1928), and Cocteau's *Le Sang d'un Poète* (1933) propose is that men see women with their eyes openly as they had always seen them with their minds: as sexual objects to be fragmented and possessed. The one exception is Germaine Dulac's *The Seashell and the Clergyman.*

In the opening shots we see the back of a woman, seated at a table. She is pouring liquid into bottles, then throwing them on the floor. The glass breaks and the liquid becomes smoke. A fat man dressed in military uniform walks in in slow motion, his feet high-stepping in a kind of goose step. As he passes through the frame, the camera gets a beautiful close-up of the sword (phallic symbol) trailing behind him. And as the woman continues to break bottles, he levitates behind her, his head sticking to the ceiling. The scene fades.

Enter the clergyman (Alex Allin), a thin, nervous, "effeminate" priest. Like the woman, he is seated and pouring liquids. He is pouring them, however, into a seashell. The colonel comes in and stops him. By the repetition of the opening scene, by substituting the priest for the woman and the seashell for the bottle, it is suggested that the colonel represents a kind of sexual stereotype of aggression for both the priest and the woman, that the priest and the woman are to be compared and contrasted, and that the priest and the colonel are rivals for the woman.

Images and sequences objectifying the sexual overtones of religious confession reveal the prurient and violent nature of religion.

After a long series of shots in which the priest locks doors and twirls keys, first as phallic symbols and then as masturbatory symbols, we see the priest chasing the colonel and the woman. In a beautiful shot Dulac shows the woman, who holds her dress up with one hand, while the colonel holds his sword up with his opposite hand: thus, the dress of the woman becomes visually linked with the sword of the colonel and the metaphor is concretized.

In a later shot, eight maids come into a room and begin dusting. They are dressed in black and white, which links them with the religious life. They begin to dust a huge ball on a pedestal in the center of the room. As they dust, the face of the priest begins to emerge in the ball. From the priest's point of view, the effect is that of a harem masturbating him. The women leave, and the priest comes in with the woman for a mock wedding. The "priest" officiating at the wedding is, of course, the colonel. Then the ball, which has been covered up (representing the priest's sexuality covered up), is unveiled (the priest is "coming out"). The priest picks up the ball, but since he is impotent, he drops it, and it smashes into little pieces on the floor, corresponding to the visual of the woman breaking bottles on the floor in the beginning of the film. The priest's face is seen among the pieces of glass. He picks it up, and it becomes a seashell. The priest sees his face upside down in the seashell. The seashell, thus, is both a religious and a sexual symbol: it is a symbol of suppressed sexuality, of sacrifice. In another scene the priest begins to move toward the woman, and we see that his black cassock is cut in two and that there is a long flowing train to his cassock, a replica in black of the woman's white evening gown. The camera focuses on the train after the priest walks out of the frame, just as it had focused on the sword of the colonel after he had walked out of the frame. In one brilliant shot Dulac shows us that the priest identifies both with the colonel and with the woman. He does not want to possess the woman, the real woman, sexually; rather, he wants to become her, he wants to become his idealized embodiment of her. He wants her to become, like the seashell, a symbol that he can possess without risking himself sexually. Later the priest runs backward into the church, his refuge, his womb, where he backs up to the pedestal with the ball restored. He motions with his finger for someone unseen (presumably the woman) to come in. A close-up of the curling finger, shot in slow motion, is here a tremendously powerful shot.

Up to this point, the film has been typically and faithfully Surrealistic, the dreams and fantasies, the slow motion and dissolves, the split screens and editing upon association rather than upon linear narrative or cause and effect, all representing the inner states of the priest, making his interior world the only world, the outer world, equating religion and violence and sex. But here, for the final shots of the film, Germaine Dulac chillingly breaks away from Surrealism toward realism, in order to expose the priest's fantasies for what they pathetically are. For a moment, we are no longer inside the priest's disoriented mind, but rather outside, watching the real priest. Contrary to the usual Surrealist method in film, Dulac moves from the subjective point-of-view shot here to the objective, authorial camera shot, for these final shots cannot possibly belong to the priest's fantasy world. In other words, up to this point, the priest that we've seen is the priest within the unseen thinking priest's mind. Now we see the real priest; now we clinically observe his last fantasy from outside.

That we are in the realm of realism is poignantly brought out in this shot of the real priest holding, hugging, squeezing, fondling— empty air. If we were still in his fantasy world, we could of course see the priest fondling the woman. But we are not. The woman, who has only been there in the mind of the priest, is now absent, as in reality she has always been absent. After squeezing empty air, the priest begins to choke the air. His hands close up, as if he were squeezing the woman into a little ball and trapping her within his fists. His hands still closed, he walks over to the ball, which seems more like a vault or prison or tabernacle now, given his actions. We see her face, a captive inside the ball. This shot identifies even further his sexuality with hers, since his face had been a captive in the ball earlier. The film ends with this shot of her face in the ball, and we are left wondering whether this final shot is Surrealism or realism, a twist of the unreal (or the more than real), or whether it is rather a turn of the everyday world, women as sex objects trapped inside the crystal-ball prisons that are the minds of such men.

The film created a great deal of controversy when it first came out, since Artaud, who had written the script, publicly claimed that Dulac had betrayed his scripts, had destroyed his original idea of what the film should be. Indeed, at the first showing of the film, Artaud and Desnos disrupted the whole audience by screaming from the first row. Desnos: "What is Madame Dulac?" Artaud: "She is a cow." Artaud enlisted the help of the other Surrealists in denouncing Germaine Dulac for having, as critic Alain Virmaux says, "feminized" the script! The priest was supposed to have been played by Artaud himself, according to Artaud. As such, the priest was to have been much more masculine, and his fantasies were to have been filled with masculine rage and fury, not revealed as the pathetic fantasies of a hung-up priest. Regarding the film, Ado Kyrou, filled with self-righteous indignance, reported: "The script is very beautiful; filled with eroticism and fury, it could have been a film in the same class as Buñuel's *L'Age d'Or* [1930], but Germaine Dulac betrayed the spirit of Artaud and made a FEMININE film. Artaud, who wished to play the role of the clergyman and participate in the shooting and editing, could do nothing about it, since Germaine Dulac had delayed the original shooting date, knowing that Artaud would then be taken up with other obligations."[2] Bettina Knapp also recognizes this cry of indignance as a masked cry against feminism, but even she refuses to see the extent of Dulac's feminism in the film; her interpretation of the film remains couched in Jungian terms of *animus* and *anima*.[3] Only Alain Virmaux, of all the French critics, recognizes that *The Seashell and the Clergyman* was not only the first Surrealist film, but that it was also the greatest film of the decade.[4]

---

[2] Ado Kyrou, Le Surréalisme au Cinéma (Paris: Editions Arcanes, 1953), p. 186.

[3] Bettina L. Knapp, *Antonin Artaud: Man of Vision* (New York: Avon Books, 1969), pp. 91–96.

[4] Alain Virmaux, "Une promesse mal tenue: le film surréaliste," *Etudes Cinematographiques,* nos. 38–41 (1965), pp. 103–105.

After *The Seashell and the Clergyman* Germaine Dulac evolved beyond Surrealism and returned in earnest to her ideas of transposing musical structures to film. She tried to replace theatrical drama and narration in film with recurrent themes and leitmotifs, using them as they are used in music. She extended her psychological or symbolic use of the camera to include treating movement within the frame and editing as one would treat rhythm or tempo in music. The result of her research was *Theme and Variations* (1930), which was perhaps the closest the French have ever gotten to making film a visual symphony. After this film she became head of production at Gaumont studios and began to supervise the films of others.

Approximately forty-five years later, we can only stand in wonder and awe of Germaine Dulac; we are just beginning to appreciate her flexibility and her wide repertoire of film styles; we are just beginning to understand the full extent of her originality and her courage in the face of so many entrenched critics.

A Letter to James Card[*]

Maya Deren

INTRODUCTION

Born in Russia in 1917, Maya Deren studied French Symbolist poetry at Smith College and voodoo in Haiti. She was also a film-maker—a pioneering American experimentalist from 1943 until her death in 1961 at the age of forty-four. Deren lectured and wrote extensively on the "personal film"—in which the artist "crosses the threshold from that which already exists into the void where . . . she creates . . . highways through the once empty spaces over the abyss." A somewhat frustrated poet, Deren transformed words into visuals with the help of a camera. Light, sound, body movement, and time abstracted through montage became her means of rhyming.

Personal filmmaking meant personal film distribution for Deren. She rented space at the Provincetown Playhouse in Greenwich Village to screen her movies and later helped found the Creative Film Foundation and Cinema Sixteen to support the cinematic endeavors of other avant-gardists. She won prizes at Cannes, as well as the first Guggenheim Fellowship for film work.

Deren wrote a significant book on aesthetics, An Anagram of Ideas on Art, Form, and Film *(1946). Film historian Georges*

[*] Reprinted from *Film Culture*, no. 39 (Winter 1965). Reprinted by permission of Jonas Mekas.

Sadoul called her, "Perhaps the most important figure in the post-war development of the personal, independent film in the U.S.A."

April 19, 1955

Dear Jim:

. . . I know that *Meshes of the Afternoon* [1943] seems to be a favorite of yours (as, indeed, it is a number of people) and, since I am both pleased that you should have remembered it so vividly and honored that you should have ordered it [for the George Eastman House collection—Eds.], it is not very discreet of me to look a gift horse in the mouth, as it were. But I must tell you that, if I were confronted with the selection, among my own films, of the one which is most representative—to date—I would select *Ritual in Transfigured Time* [1946], along with *A Study in Choreography for Camera* [1945].

Meshes of the Afternoon is my point of departure. I am not ashamed of it; for I think that, as a film, it stands up very well. From the point of view of my own development, I cannot help but be gently proud that that first film—that point of departure—had such relatively solid footing. This is due to two major facts: first, to the faςt that I had been a poet up until then, and the reason that I had not been a very good poet was because actually my mind worked in images which I had been trying to translate or describe in words; therefore, when I undertook cinema, I was relieved of the false step of translating images into words, and could work directly so that it was not like discovering a new medium so much as finally coming home into a world whose vocabulary, syntax, grammar, was my mother tongue; which I understood, and thought in, but, like a mute, had never spoken. The first speech of a mute is hoarse, ugly, virtually unintelligible. If *Meshes* is not that, it is because of the second fact, namely, that Sasha Hammid contributed the mechanics (and I use this in the largest sense) of that speech. It is because of him that *O* sounds like *O*, and not like *A*, that the sibilants hiss when they should, that the word emerges in a single whole and does not stutter. My debt to him for teaching me the mechanics of film expression, and, more than that, the principle of infinite pains, is enormous. I wish that all these young filmmakers would have the luck for a similar apprenticeship. As it is, when they revolt against the meaningless rhetoricians of film, they tend to throw out the baby with the bath water. They don't bother to shape the lips and mouth carefully before letting the sound out, and ignore the fact that a good idea merits careful enunciation with the result that a good many of them sound, at best, like Marlon Brando . . . I mean, you just *know* he's feeling things like crazy, but why doesn't he take those marbles out of his mouth!

Anyway, *Meshes* was the point of departure. There is a very, very short sequence in that film—right after the three images of the girl sit around the table and draw the key until it comes up knife—when the girl with the knife rises from the table to go towards the self which is sleeping in the chair. As the girl with the knife rises, there is a close-up of her foot as she begins striding. The first step is in sand (with suggestion of sea behind), the second stride (cut in) is in grass, the third is on pavement, and the fourth is on the rug, and then the camera cuts up to her head with the hand with the knife descending towards the sleeping girl. What I meant when I planned that four-stride sequence was that you have to come a long way— from the very beginning of time—to kill yourself, like the first life emerging from the primeval waters. Those four strides, in my intention, span all time. Now, I don't think it gets all that across—it's a real big idea if you start thinking about it, and it happens so quickly that all you get is a suggestion of a strange kind of distance traversed, which is all right, and as much as the film requires there. But the important thing for me is that, as I used to sit there and watch the film when it was projected for friends in those early days, that one short sequence always rang a bell or buzzed a buzzer in my head. It was like a crack letting the light of another world gleam through. I kept saying to myself: "The walls of this room are solid except right there. That leads to something. There's a door there leading to something. I've got to get it open because through there I can go through to someplace instead of leaving here by the same way that I came in."

And so I did, prying at it until my fingers were bleeding. And so came to the world where the identity of movement spans and transcends all time and space and that becomes the central theme of *At*

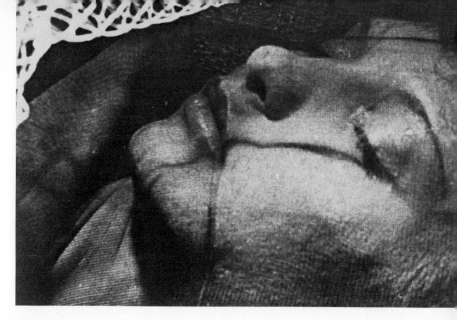

Maya Deren, dead at the end of her film, *Meshes of the Afternoon* (1943). (Courtesy The Museum of Modern Art/Film Stills Archive)

Land [1944], which was the film after *Meshes*. In *At Land* the identity which is continuous even transcends the other identities (as in the scene along the road). So here is continuity, as it were, holding its own in a volatile universe.

This principle—that the dynamic of movement in film is stronger than anything else—than any changes of matter . . . I mean that movement, or energy, is more important, or powerful, than space or matter—that, in fact, it creates matter—seemed to me to be marvelous, like an illumination, that I wanted to just stop and celebrate that wonder, just by itself, which I did in *A Study in Choreography for Camera*. The movement of the dancer creates a geography, in the film, that never was. With a turn of the foot, he makes neighbors of distant places.

And now, again, looking at the last films, there were short sequences which buzzed and rang when they went by on the screen. Like where the girl (in *At Land*) is looking for a way to come down the rock and—by filming a rapid swing of the head from side to side in extreme slow motion—looks from side to side at a normal rate of curiosity *but,* her hair travels horizontally (which belongs to a rapid tempo of movement). Or in *Choreography,* where, by accelerating the camera, the dancer is made to pirouette at an impossible (humanly) speed. In these moments the dynamic element was not even the movement of the protagonist—transcending space and time and matter—but it was the camera which created even the movement of the protagonist.

And so comes *Ritual in Transfigured Time,* in which the camera (and by this is included editing, lab work, motor, everything) is total master, as it were. There is a death by time, for example, in the first sequence . . . the girl getting slower and slower until she isn't (instead of thinner and thinner); the party scene, in which, by reprinting informal movements, dance is conferred upon nondancers; and finally, film itself, changes the widow into bride.

I believe that *Ritual* contains everything that *Meshes* had, but has more, and, of course, differently.

I have described all this development in terms of a technical progression because it's easier to talk in these terms. I have a reticence about the more profound significance which is hard for me to explain except, perhaps, by analogy—the way a woman will look up and say to a man "That suit looks very well on you" instead of "I love you. I am happy that you are here to look at." The trouble is that people often think that technique is my primary consideration when I speak of techniques—just as if that man would begin discussing wholesale prices and yard goods, which would make the woman feel peculiar. The fact is, of course, that each time one of those technical sequences buzzed in my head, like a beacon signaling "This way, this way," it was because I was tuned to that frequency. I was not simply trying to get out of that room and go somewhere, anywhere, I was heading in a certain direction, and no matter how minute the crack that gave upon it, it was to pass through there that I labored. There may have been wide doors to both sides. I did not even try them for they did not give in my direction. And, looking back, it is clear that the direction was away from a concern with the way things *feel,* and towards a concern with the way things *are;* away from personal psychology towards nerveless metaphysics. I mean metaphysics in the large sense, not as mysticism but beyond the physical in the way that a principle is an abstraction, beyond any of the particulars in which it is manifest. *Meshes* is, one might say, almost expressionist; it externalizes an inner world to the point where it is confounded with the external world. *At Land* has little to do with the inner world of the protagonist; it externalizes the hidden dynamic of the external world, and here the drama results from the activity of the external world. It is as if I had moved from a concern with the life of a fish, to a concern with the sea which accounts for the character of the fish and its life. And *Ritual* pulls back even further, to a point of view from which the external world itself is but an element in the entire structure and scheme of metamorphosis: the sea itself changes because of the larger changes of the earth. *Ritual* is about the nature and process of change. And just as *Choreography* was an effort to isolate and celebrate the principle of the power of movement, which was contained in *At Land,* so I made, after *Ritual,* the film, *Meditation on Violence* [1948], which tried to abstract the principle of ongoing metamorphosis and change which was in *Ritual. Meditation on Violence* was not as successful in this effort to summarize the essence, as *Choreography* had been. But I am getting a real strong itch to re-edit it (*Meditation*), shortening it, and this will improve it, I think.

I think the reason this has become such a wildly long letter, which it was never meant to be when I sat down at the typewriter, is because I have recently finished my last film, *The Very Eye of Night* [not released until 1959—Eds.], and I think it's taken me out in space about as far as I can go. I ran it for George Amberg during that convention week, and what especially interested me in his comments (he apparently liked it very, very much, which, of course, pleased me) was his remark that he had been wondering, really, where I could go from *Ritual,* and now, of course, he saw that it had to be this, but that there truly seems no place to go from here, at least in the same direction. It's the kind of point, where, before you can go any further, you've got to swing around and take stock and get your bearings. I guess I've been doing this in my mind for some time now, and the thing sort of came to a head by accident today, as I started to write this letter. Not by accident, perhaps. I think it was crystallized by my desire to explain to you what I felt about *Meshes* as being a point of departure. Each film was built as a chamber and became a corridor, like a chain reaction.

You know those puzzle games where, if you draw a continuous line from one point to another, consecutively numbered, you end up with a picture? Well, in this letter, I finally drew those points and got a picture.

Last May I had an emergency operation; it was touch and go for a few hours there, and I came out of it with a rapidity that dazzled: one month from the date of that operation (I had to be slit from side to side) I was dancing! Then I actually realized that I was overwhelmed with the most wondrous gratitude for the marvelous persistence of the life force. In the transported exaltation of this moment, I wanted to run out into the streets and shout out to everyone that death was not true! that they must not listen to the doom singers and the bell ringers! that life was more true! I had always believed and felt this, but never had I known how right I was. And I asked myself, why, then, did I not celebrate it in my art. And then I had a sudden image: a dog lying somewhere very still, and a child, first looking at it, and then, compulsively, nudging it. Why? to see whether it was alive; because if it moves, if it can move, it lives. This most primitive, this most instinctive of all gestures: to make it move to make it live. So I had always been doing with my camera, nudging an ever-increasing area of the world, making it move, animating it, making it live. This is part of the picture. *Meshes* is the warmest of my films; *The Very Eye of Night* is the coolest, the most classicist. Or so it seems, on an emotional, intimate, level. But the love of life itself, in *The Very Eye of Night*, seems to me larger than the loving attention to *a* life. But, of course, each contains the other, and, perhaps, I have not so much traveled off in a direction, as moved in a slow spiral around some central essence, seeing it first from below and now, finally, from above.

Anyway, this is one way to look at that reel of films. You can't say you haven't been briefed! . . .

My very best wishes,
Maya Deren

A Conversation*

Storm De Hirsch and Shirley Clarke

INTRODUCTION

The eye of the women's movement has yet to notice talented Storm De Hirsch, veteran experimentalist. A typical concoction from her repertoire is Shaman, a Tapestry for Sorcerers (1966), *described fancifully by the filmmaker:* "For the magic makers of the world, those who enter the atlas of the soul and rummage through the refuse and flowers of time to weave a talisman for man's rebirth in his house of breath." *Her little-known narrative work,* Goodbye in the Mirror (1964), *is perhaps the first full-length American independent film of directly feminist interest. De Hirsch tells the story of three single women who share a Rome apartment. According to Jeanne Betancourt in* Women in Focus, *"It sets forth Maria's conflicts with her roommates, her hunt for a man, and her ultimate decision to refuse her knight in shining armor."* Goodbye in the Mirror *is ripe for revival. Since 1974 Storm De Hirsch has been experimenting with super 8, creating ciné-sonnets from her own poetry.*

Shirley Clarke became a cause célèbre with The Connection, *her 1960 screen version of Jack Gelber's junkie play. In 1963 she made*

* Abridged from *Film Culture,* no. 46 (Autumn 1967) (published October 1968). Reprinted by permission of Jonas Mekas.

the even more successful The Cool World, *shot on the streets of Harlem. In 1967 she released her third and last feature,* Portrait of Jason. *For years, Shirley Clarke was looked to as the woman who would crack Hollywood. However her Chelsea Hotel nonconformity never quite led her onto the industry payroll. Her one artist's sojourn to Los Angeles was to star as herself in Agnes Varda's raggedy ann and anti-Hollywood* Lion's Love *(1969). In recent years Shirley Clarke has moved from film to video, where she can be a true independent.*

Note that this conversation, mostly about women filmmakers, occurred ten years ago. Clarke and De Hirsch were typically ahead of their time.

STORM DE HIRSCH: What about lady taxi drivers?

SHIRLEY CLARKE: When I see them I still smile and say, what's going on, what is this chick up to? There's something to me strange about her. Now my conditioning—and, of course, it must seem awfully silly to hear me say that—I think this is silly when I work in a so-called masculine field, but it never occurred to me that I worked in a masculine field because of how I got in, in that I was a dancer and started making dance films on a very personal basis. It never occurred to me that masculinity and femininity and being in a field called filmmaking was not what I thought I was doing. I was making dance films. Only as it progressed, I started to become aware that I was a woman doing something that most other women weren't doing or in a field, rather, that had very few women.

SDH: Maybe it's better that it took that natural sequence . . .

SC: Well, in your case it's true also. In other words, you started as a poet and a painter and you extended your work into film.

SDH: Yes. But to me, making poems and making films are one, and neither activity excludes the other. My way of getting into films was simply by association, by knowing so many filmmakers, sitting and discussing with them and wondering what in hell they were making such a big fuss about. I found myself walking around and observing things and I found myself writing a script, and I also found that I was being very secretive about it because there was a kind of embarrassment about it. The following year when I went to Rome, I completed the script and I kept hiding it, but several people eventually saw it and that was the way I made the film. But it was sort of ridiculous in a way, because to make a feature film as my first film [*Goodbye in the Mirror*, 1964] is the most idiotic and foolish thing anybody would ever conceive of, except that it was in sheer ignorance.

SC: . . . I know that I had decided to make dance films because I had seen a bunch of dance films and I thought they were just awful, and it occurred to me that really you had to be an idiot not to be able to make a good dance film—what was so tough about it? And I went into it thinking, really, this is going to be quite a simple thing to do and that it was just the fact that the wrong people had been doing it—people who didn't know anything really about dance and that, since I knew about dance, I would learn about this rather simple thing called film and do it. I must say that certain successes I had and certain failures were very basic flaws in a lot of thinking that's been done and that I was doing, and that it wasn't that easy. The fact that I never realized was that one art destroyed another.

SDH: Well, do you really think so?

SC: Well, I think that if you're going to think of doing a dance film and taking already existing dance and transferring it onto film—you will destroy that dance. That does not mean though that you cannot make a dance for film and it was this that I finally learned and that this was the mistake that had been made until then.

SDH: But then you did feel—it did evolve to a point where you didn't feel it necessary to do just dance film.

SC: No. Well, that's because the medium of film became much more intriguing and exciting than just dance, in terms of action and passivity. Dance for me started to be too limited. There were too many other things that danced.

SDH: But you know, Shirley, . . . here we are, two "quote-unquote" lady filmmakers. We're talking, I assume, objectively—like any filmmaker. I mean, what is the distinction here? We both operate differently. We have a different approach to our work. We have different concepts or goals, what we want to attain visually. What is it, then, that would make this distinction in terms of are-you-a-lady-filmmaker-or-are-you-an-artist?

SC: Well, now, let's ask another question. Is there a difference, let's say, in lady and men writers?—these days? Let's not talk about the past, because that's another time and another world. But in our world today, if people didn't sign their names to things they wrote, would you be able to say this was written by a man, this was written by a woman?

SDH: Well, I tell you, I'm in a peculiar position. I'd like to get a little personal about it. That is, because my name is Storm.

SC: That's right—everybody thinks you're a man.

SDH: I don't know, maybe this is all a myth that has to be broken at some time, because I have had the experience of sending manuscripts to magazine editors and gotten back—usually rejections—but with a note enclosed saying, "Dear Mr. Storm (De Hirsch) we are sorry . . ." but going into a very respectful kind of analysis of what it is they want, if I would revise it thus and so, et cetera, because fundamentally, they like the idea or they like the images or something. When they accept me, sometimes I've been very suspicious that I have been accepted sheerly as a Mr. (outside of the fact that I may think they have good taste)—that same good taste somehow evaporates when it is Miss Storm.

SC: Right on this issue of whether you know if it's a man or a woman—because there are attitudes—chauvinism exists—we're just kidding ourselves if we think it doesn't. . . . One of the things that exists about the difference of reading a woman writer and a man writer, if you didn't know, would be in terms of subjectivity. In other words, if one's writing is extremely subjective writing, certainly it would be noticeable if someone was a man or a woman. Do you think that women tend to be more subjective than men anyway? In other words, this whole problem that I think De Beauvoir brought up as clearly and as well as anybody—the need for men to be transcendental because they do not have within them the reproductive capacity in the same way that women do.

SDH: I think it's questionable as to whether the biological structure makes that much difference in terms of art. I have my own little theories about this, and I feel that when it comes to art, there's a question of soul, of the inner world, that's a universal thing; and I feel that the soul is neither male nor female. When I work and get involved with filmmaking, especially in my animation, I become both man and woman or either one. It isn't a sexlessness, but rather an awareness of the sexuality involved.

SC: But isn't that inner world Storm De Hirsch's soul, which has been influenced by having been a woman?—All your life? Now we're all everything. To begin with, none of us is only masculine or only feminine. This we have finally learned. But I'm thinking now in terms of looking at your work or my work—now I don't know why I knew that you were a woman right from the beginning. Somehow I did.

SDH: That's interesting—because generally, the reaction is just the opposite.

SC: Well, for some reason, either I had already been told—but the thing that struck me is that you can take your work, you can take mine, and in many cases the subjects are neither-sexed. Certainly in animation, it's not sexed per se. A film like *The Cool World* [1962] is not masculine or feminine. Yet, I would bet my bottom dollar a man doing any of these films would have done it differently.

SDH: Well, he may have done it differently—but I think . . .

SC: But maybe it's only because he's a different person.

SDH: Both films—I think both *The Connection* [1960] and *The Cool World* are very powerful films and they have a sense of violence and they have a large sense of strength which, if one didn't know, they would unquestionably be identified by most people as the work of a man.

SC: And yet to me, it's an endless giveaway in both those films and in the one I'm just doing, that is, what I would consider a feminine way of looking at something. In other words, one of the fights that I've always battled against—and this is very interesting that you brought up the very crux of it, which is violence—in other words, violence personally, to me, is extremely repugnant. It's something I'm terribly afraid of. And yet, I'm obviously very attracted to it, because I am always doing it and I'm always making films that seem outwardly to have nothing to do with me, me as (let's say) anyone who knows me in my own personal life. They have to do with me because they attract me, and what is it about them that's attracting me and making me want to get involved in these kinds of things? Isn't it in an odd way my very femininity making this attractive to me? Why do I like violence?

SDH: In this case, we're similar, because my writing has always had a sense of violence about it, and what I've done so far in film has a related sense of violence.

SC: But don't you think that in a strange way, this is stronger? In other words, the way we react to violence is quite different from a man. For instance, you and I are not used to being hit and we don't hit people physically. Women don't do this.

SDH: No, I find this very repugnant also.

SC: As far as I know, punching someone back and forth is not a female way of reacting to a fight. We might scream and yell.

SDH: Just as I do agree that all or most women are antiwar.

SC: There is just something in it, that violence is repugnant, and it's also obviously attractive to us. Now maybe this is a sexual thing that makes it attractive. Whatever reason it is, when we deal with violence, we are certainly going to do it differently from a man who is not afraid. Most men have had experiences in their life of being knocked down. I've never been knocked out by anybody in my life—I never expect to be, except under some really weird fluke. And I'm sure that the same thing is true with you, so that the whole way we would deal with violence would definitely have to be different, because it would come through a very different sensitivity that we have. All I'm really trying to say is that women really do have certain sensitivities that are different and this is not the soul that's different. Even with the admitting that the human being's soul is neither masculine nor feminine, you go to the next layer and then you have to say, but there is something that's different between men and women that is psychobiological . . .

SDH: It depends on what level you're working on . . .

SC: And that it shows up. Now, for instance, just offhand—and I'm not even talking about whether I like or don't like other women filmmakers' films—but offhand, thinking of Mai Zetterling's films and Varda's films, one of the things that I particularly noticed in them is again violence, and a kind of concern with sexual violence.

Jason Holliday, the voluble star of Shirley Clarke's *A Portrait of Jason* (1967). (Courtesy Film-Makers Distribution Center)

SDH: But you also understand that a man—I'm sure you've seen films, even commercial Hollywood films, where there's a male director who handles situations with tremendous sensitivity. I remember, for some reason it comes to mind, about *East of Eden* [1955] that was directed by Kazan, I thought there were sequences there with Jimmy Dean that were some of the most beautiful structures of sensitivity that I have ever experienced in my life. I must say like a woman, if one puts it in those terms, I just sat there and cried. There was a lyrical quality there which . . .

SC: But he was still dealing with a man, and I have a feeling that up to this point the only person so far who's done a real woman's film has been your *Goodbye in the Mirror*. In other words, for some reason, even so far, women filmmakers have yet to deal with the subject of women. That usually, for instance, Varda's heroes are men. Her women may or may not be what brings them to their salvation, or whatever. In Zetterling's film, the women may be the enemy or the devil or the one who gets everything going. But so far in film, we have yet to have treated, on the most basic level, very personal reactions of women. Because so far, we've had mostly men directors who, whether they've been very sensitive or not, have not really been able to deal with women this way. Just like when they write about women, they're writing from a certain separateness. *Goodbye in the Mirror* is dealing with women. And women's reactions to a series of events. That has not been true of *The Cool World* or *The Connection* or—and it's something I must say, that I not only admire you for, but I'm jealous that you have been able to do it because I wish I had been able to do it.

SDH: Well, you probably will at some time. If you already have that kind of motivation. Of course, I've been accused of being very unkind to women—this attitude of, well, you are a woman, you must hate women to have made the heroine so ugly, which I didn't think she was—I thought she had a bold and sensual kind of beauty.

SC: But who's talking to you? Are women telling you this, or are men telling you?

SDH: I don't remember, but one of them was a man . . .

SC: If we're going to use you and I as examples, and one or two other women filmmakers, I don't think we can point our finger and say, yes, women are making films that are different—because I don't think we are. But I have a sort of feeling that maybe we should be and that maybe we will as we get more secure in the medium. All I mean is that it takes a lot of musicians to make Beethoven, and it's going to take a lot of filmmakers to make great films, and we are merely part of something that ten years from now, twenty years, fifty years from now, won't even be discussed anymore. It will be actually a ridiculous discussion to discuss men and women filmmakers in the future, because it will be just such a common thing. At this point, it's still not common.

SDH: You do feel that the time will come when there will not be the labeling?

SC: Yes. I don't think there will be labeling. I don't think anybody's going to be concerned. I think you're more bothered by that. To me, it would be very nice if there would be something called femininity, although I'm not quite sure what the hell that is, but I know there's a difference between men and women and this is going to be revealed in our work as artists, filmmakers, and that this is going to be good. This is going to be a contribution of sensitivity and perception that is beyond what we've got right now. Now I have read your poems and I have seen your films and I've seen some of your paintings and to me, you are always exploring your femininity. I mean, I think that's very much what they are about.

SDH: I regard this as a compliment.

SC: I mean it as one. To me, this is a goal, and if I could articulate what I would like for myself in the future, it would be to find that in me that is feminine. I have found that in me that is like everyone else or that is even the masculine part of myself, but I've had a much more difficult time finding the feminine part. . . .

SC: You must have had the experience that I had, with this festival-going. My film may be discussed, but invariably I am described physically in the review. Now, what in the world my looks have got to do with a review of the film—and yet . . .

SDH: Well, that's the journalistic approach.

SC: Invariably this is true when it's a woman film director. And it's never discussed—I've no idea what most men filmmakers look like from reading reviews. If I've met them, fine, otherwise I really wouldn't know. Yet I can tell you what every woman who's making films looks like—size, shape, her coloring. They are described that way. . . . You know what I've gotten that's always somewhat puzzled me—let's say I'm brought in and introduced to someone who has seen my work and has heard about me, but has never met me, and I will often get a comment like, "Oh, I didn't expect you to look like you do—you're so little." What do they expect, some amazon? That's exactly what they expect. They expect some gal about eight feet tall with big husky muscles who obviously is going to be able to cart a lot of things around, and they're immediately shocked by how small I am; and it's an endless comment that I've gotten and that level of patronage I've had.

SDH: We are both little women . . .

SC: Right. So it's always, I guess, something of a surprise in terms of, let's say, discussing my work. I've always felt this and maybe this is my own problem—but that my work has never been taken as seriously as it might have been had I been a man. But I feel this on a very broad basis; I feel this almost totally. I really mean this. I feel this from the most commercial levels to the most artistic level. That

I am not dealt with as seriously as I'd like to be, and I question whether it's my work or whether it's my sex that has produced this kind of reaction. . . . I remember the first day I was on the set of *The Connection*, which was a union-made film with an all-man union crew, and basically a male cast. The script girl, the wardrobe mistress was a girl, and outside of that, that was the end of the female part of it. I know that the first couple of days there was a self-consciousness on everyone's part.

SDH: Do you feel the self-consciousness was due to the fact that you were a woman?

SC: Well, there were two reasons. One, that I was unknown. In other words, who was this person? let alone who was this crazy girl that had the nerve to want to direct a feature film? It was eliminated in two ways. One, as soon as I revealed that my language was as foul as everyone else's . . .

SDH: You mean it was "un-ladylike."

SC: Yes. Apparently, we didn't have to worry about the words that were going to be said on the set. And secondly, when they realized I knew what I was doing. And it took a few days for everyone to say, it's just Shirley and it couldn't be anyone else. You know, the night before I went on the set, as I went to bed that night, I said to myself, you have to be out of your mind to think that you're going to show up tomorrow and sit and direct a film. You must be crazy. That's some nerve getting all these people involved.

SDH: Well, you weren't the only one that thought that way. I did, too. I'd sit there and say, who the hell talked me into this?

SC: Yes, right. And here are all these people and you know film-making does involve lots of people sitting and waiting—all right now, you're supposed to say something and you know—go—and there you are kind of with your tongue hanging out. I'm sure you did exactly what I did, which was I just went. And after going, we all learned that we could go, that you could walk and it wasn't all that horrible, and after the first week it was fun. The first week was not fun.

SDH: Well, my experience was similar and, although I was accepted in a position of authority, I noticed that the second day on location the three girls in the cast had gotten into a huddle, looking at me and whispering. I knew two of the British girls were curious about something. They told me later they had found it strange that I was wearing a dress. The first day I had worn slacks and this they took to because it was in character for them. I guess that was it—the male identification. But whenever I wore a dress, I noticed that there was a kind of change in the weather. . . .

SDH: The thought just occurred to me that since we're talking about females and femininity—I wondered what advantages there are to being feminine in terms of, let's say, producers, getting money for film: do you think this is utilized . . .

SC: Well, I must be honest—I never have been successful that way. This has always bothered me. I've always thought that one should use the feminine wiles to con people out of money. Frankly, I've never found that being very successful. Usually, I make people more secure by behaving more abstractly than if I try to come on cute and so forth. On the other hand, there are certain things I've gotten as a result of being a woman and using the feminine wiles— physical things, like people helping me, which—let's say, I'm going to lift something heavy and there's a man around, he'll help me and obviously, with a man they wouldn't get that sort of thing. Also, people being a little bit more generous in terms of lending things to me, or making it possible for me to do a certain kind of work and in an odd way, partly because they don't take me quite seriously. Oddly enough, I'm not competitive with them. In other words, they don't think of me as a competitor, which can be very helpful.

SDH: You mean for the moment, you don't mind that; in other circumstances, you might.

SC: If someone will help me because they don't take me that seriously, I'll let them flounder around if I get something I need and want.

SDH: I've sometimes gotten things done as a result of making my needs known. But getting myself to ask for assistance is something I find difficult to do.

SC: Have you gotten money from people because you were a woman?

SDH: That's hard to say. I think, in certain instances, yes. I like to think that. But I don't know, because it doesn't happen all the time. If it happened all the time, then I would have the statistical guarantee that this works to advantage in that sense. But I was thinking also of the role of the male director who becomes a heroic figure, and thinking of what you said about women filmmakers not being taken that seriously. I mean, to be a male director—even on a small scale—becomes a very glamorous kind of occupation; but with the woman, oddly enough, being an actress holds a great deal more glamour, even though she may have a very small part, than the position of being a female director. On the other hand, there's an indulgence toward the female which sometimes works to a very great advantage in terms of getting things done.

SC: Do you think it's slightly a disgrace to be a woman film director?

SDH: This depends on the eyes of the beholder.

SC: Haven't you noticed that labs, for instance, are very friendly with you—they immediately call you by your first name. I mean, I'm always "Shirley" to everybody.

SDH: I haven't had quite that experience; but that might have been because of my own attitude in coming in.

SC: I pick up the phone and I say, this is Shirley Clarke and I'd like to know how much it costs to print such-and-such. "Well, Shirley, it's . . ." I mean, immediately. Now, I'm pretty sure that this is not what is done with the average man. Since it happens to be an attitude that they have, then women should use it, because actually, it's better if people don't take you completely seriously. Strangely enough, they are more agreeable and more willing to do things for you than if they are afraid of you. And if they're not afraid of you because they don't take you seriously, you know what you're doing yourself—that's still your business. If your goal is a certain goal, you go right ahead getting it, and let them think whatever they want.

On Yoko Ono*

Yoko Ono

October 1968

on *Film No. 4, 1967* (in taking the bottoms of 365 saints of our time)

I wonder why men can get serious at all. They have this delicate long thing hanging outside their bodies, which goes up and down by its own will. First of all having it outside your body is terribly dangerous. If I were a man, I would have a fantastic castration complex to the point that I wouldn't be able to do a thing. Second, the inconsistency of it, like carrying a chance time alarm or something. If I were a man, I would always be laughing at myself. Humor is probably something the male of the species discovered through their own anatomy. But men are so serious. Why? Why violence? Why hatred? Why war? If people want to make war, they should make a color war, and paint each other's city up during the night in pinks and greens. Men have an unusual talent for making a bore out of everything they touch. Art, painting, sculpture, like who wants a cast-iron woman, for instance.

The film world is becoming terribly aristocratic, too. It's professionalism all the way down the line. In any other field: painting,

* Reprinted from *Film Culture*, nos. 48–49 (Winter/Spring 1970), pp. 32–33. Reprinted by permission of Jonas Mekas.

music, etc., people are starting to become iconoclastic. But in the film world—that's where nobody touches it except the director. The director carries the old mystery of the artist. He is creating a universe, a mood, he is unique, etc., etc. This film proves that anybody can be a director. A filmmaker in San Francisco wrote to me and asked if he could make the San Francisco version of *No. 4*. That's OK with me. Somebody else wrote from New York, she wants to make a slow-motion version with her own behind. That's OK, too. I'm hoping that after seeing this film people will start to make their own home movies like crazy.

In fifty years or so, which is like ten centuries from now, people will look at the film of the 1960s. They will probably comment on Ingmar Bergman as a meaningfully meaningful filmmaker, Jean-Luc Godard as the meaningfully meaningless, Antonioni as meaninglessly meaningful, etc., etc. Then they would come to the *No. 4* film and see a sudden swarm of exposed bottoms, that these bottoms, in fact, belonged to people who represented the London scene. And I hope that they would see that the 1960s was not only the age of achievements, but of laughter. This film, in fact, is like an aimless petition signed by people with their anuses. Next time we wish to make an appeal, we should send this film as the signature list.

My ultimate goal in filmmaking is to make a film that includes a smiling face snap of every single human being in the world. Of course, I cannot go around the whole world and take the shots myself. I need cooperation from something like the post offices of the world. If everybody would drop a snapshot of themselves and their families to the post office of their town, or allow themselves to be photographed by the nearest photographic studio, this would be soon accomplished. Of course, this film would need constant adding of footage. Probably nobody would like to see the whole film at once, so you can keep it in a library or something, and when you want to see some particular town's people's smiling faces you can go and check that section of film. We can also arrange it with a television network so that whenever you want to see faces of a particular location in the world, all you have to do is to press a button and there it is. This way, if Johnson wants to see what sort of people he killed in Vietnam that day, he only has to turn the channel.

April 1969

on *Rape II* (a film)

Violence is a sad wind that, if channeled carefully, could bring seeds, chairs, and all things pleasant to us.

We are all would-be Presidents of the World, and kids kicking the sky that doesn't listen.

What would you do if you had only one penis and a one-way tube ticket when you want to fuck the whole nation in one come?

I know a professor of philosophy whose hobby is to quietly crush biscuit boxes in a supermarket.

Maybe you can send signed plastic lighters to people in place of your penis. But then some people might take your lighter as a piece of sculpture and keep it up in their living room shelf.

So we go on eating and feeding frustration every day, lick lollipops and stay being peeping toms dreaming of becoming Jack the Ripper.

This film was shot by our camerman, Nick, while we were in a hospital. Nick is a gentle-man, who prefers eating clouds and floating pies to shooting *Rape*. Nevertheless it was shot.

Interview with Joyce Wieland*

Kay Armatage

This interview was taped and transcribed early in October 1971. Since then, Joyce Wieland has rewritten some parts of the interview, and has added some explanatory material. —K.A.

KAY ARMATAGE: Can you tell me about *Hand Tinting* [1967–1968] and about the . . . was it a school or a retraining center?

JOYCE WIELAND: It was a retraining center in West Virginia run by Xerox and we made a documentary—

KA: Who's we?

JW: Another Canadian, Sylvia Davern, who was working in animation at the time and two American girls, one doing sound and another shooting. The job came through Sylvia's company.

KA: Were you commissioned to do it?

JW: Yes.

KA: And where was it to be shown?

JW: TV. Anyway I took some of my own outs from the film— some of which were genuine old-fashioned cutaways, and which I felt very strongly about, and began to make *Hand Tinting*.

KA: It's a lovely film.

JW: I think it has more to do with what was going on at the center than the commissioned film.

* Reprinted from *Take One*, 3, no. 2 (February 1972). Additional material supplied by author.

KA: Some of the images that are repeated . . . I began to feel very warm, for instance, toward that girl with the bathing cap.

JW: Yes, there's a lot of repetition in a small space.

KA: How do you feel about the subjects that you're working with?

JW: I hardly know whether to laugh or cry about those girls. The center was about eighty percent black kids who had come from everywhere. They were lonely, rebellious, funny, restless, and hopelessly poor. What they were offered in the way of education was humiliating to me—some rooms with typewriters, and a machine that spoke to them as they typed. Most of them wanted to make movies when they met us. It was a corporate pacification program. I wanted to do my own film about them. I was sorry—so was Sylvia —to see all their swearing and astounding wit cut out of the final version.

KA: In a film like *Hand Tinting,* how much of your concern is just working with form, or how important is your subject? I'm trying to think of showing this film to my class of women, and to think of the way that they as women would understand that film, women who aren't interested in art or film.

JW: It could be interesting to them to know that I dyed the film with cloth dyes and punctured it with my sewing needles.

KA: The images that you used as well . . .

JW: When I first did it, I thought it might not be useful to anyone. It was a poem. There's nothing out of the way in it, it has mystery and rhythm and some repetitive portraits of some beautiful faces. The editing and the girls are the subject of *Hand Tinting.* The editing and the so-called subject matter are equal. You can look at the editing or you can look at the girls. Just as in *Reason Over Passion* [1967–1969], you can look at the permutations, the images, listen to the beeps, or count on the flag inserts—or, just let it happen.

KA: Well, the feeling I got at the beginning of *Reason Over Passion*—I went through a gradual transition from the feeling that was there when everyone in the room spoke at once and a friend of mine said this is my hometown. We felt very strongly that we were watching Canada. Then gradually all the elements of the film come together more. But at first it's a very strong surge of feelings for what you're looking at.

JW: Yes, it starts off much more stridently and clearer than the passages of the second half, where it gets into an episodic long white fade.

KA: There's a credit at the end for Computer Photographic Planning. What was that?

JW: Hollis Frampton, who is a wonderful filmmaker, devised a simple and inexpensive method of photographing all 537 permutations of *Reason Over Passion*. I couldn't afford to use an animation stand. And so he invented a machinelike masking device, whereby each permutation was photographed very rapidly on a setup in his darkroom . . . perfect and simple.

KA: How often has *Reason Over Passion* been shown and reviewed?

JW: It was premiered in Canada at the National Arts Centre in 1969 and in New York at Jonas Mekas's Christmas Festival in 1969. Then I showed it at The Museum of Modern Art. After that it was taken to Cannes for the Directors Fortnight. Then it sat in New York. It had a few write-ups in Italy and Holland. It's been shown at universities in the United States. It had a good response in Canada; there have been quite a few pieces written on it and in the last few months it's been written about in the U.S. and France. The CBC and BBC wanted to show parts of it, but after projecting it, found that the four-times-removed printings in it were too difficult to transmit. They are afraid people will blame them for the grain— grain is dirt in their eyes.

KA: You're very important as a woman artist because you take what women do and make your art out of that. Is that a conscious thing, or have you just eventually come to it?

JW: It has become more of a conscious thing over the years. As I started being an artist I was influenced by many things, artists, et cetera, and by my husband, who influenced me not so much in style as in having my own well-developed outlook, philosophy, and so on. I was on my way in a sense to becoming an artist's-wife-type artist until I got into looking around in history for female lines of influence. I read the lives and works of many many women, salonists, diarists, revolutionaries, et cetera. I started to invent myself as an artist. I saw only gradually that my husband's artistic concerns were not mine, although I loved Cézanne, Vermeer, et cetera. I still had to look into the lives of women who had made independent statements in their lives. In a sense my husband's great individuality and talents were a catalyst to my development. Eventually women's concerns and my own femininity became my artist's territory.

KA: And you've got this double-barreled thing, being a woman and a Canadian—the underdog in nationality and in sex.

JW: I think of Canada as female. All the art I've been doing or will be doing is about Canada. I may tend to overly identify with Canada.

KA: Do you see this artist's territory that you've staked out opening out to other women besides you?

JW: Sure, why not. I would like to see them in that space, just as much as I would like to see us gain control of our government from the U.S.—or the Canadian Film Development Corporation.

KA: In the past you have involved other people in your artworks, women embroidering, knitting, for you, et cetera.

JW: Yes, in my recent exhibition at the National Gallery—"True Patriot Love"—fulfilled a lot of plans that I've had in my last few years for having other people work on parts of the artworks.

KA: Does that sort of participatory art carry over to the films?

JW: Not very much in my past personal films. But in my future film, *True Patriot Love,* there will be people working on costumes, music, et cetera.

KA: Do the women who worked on your recent work, do they do anything themselves in art, or did you find them because they were good craftswomen?

JW: They were craftswomen who were doing good work, who have won many prizes in their fields.

KA: Did working on your things inspire them to do more themselves?

JW: Yes, it got a couple of women going on to working more original pieces. Less to do with traditional patterns. And on Canadian themes, too!

KA: Are there any women, living or dead, that you've been able to find sources from, or is it more of a general source?

JW: There are quite a few, generally and especially women from different periods in France, Pompadour, Colette, Madame Roland, the diarists, salonists, mistresses, et cetera. English writers—Austen, the Brontë's, Beatrix Potter. Fictional women like Stendhal's heroines. These people all have had a sustaining influence on me. And also Adelle Davis . . . and my mother-in-law, Marie Antoinette Levesque, who is French Canadian and after whom the character Eulalie de Chicoutimi is drawn in my projected feature film, *True Patriot Love.*

KA: How about the gerbils? I'm trying to find out more and more how the question of women's art affects your work. Is *Rat Life and Diet in North America* [1968] a generally political film, or do you see this as having any connection with women?

JW: It has to do with women in a way. It was a domestic epic made on my kitchen table with my pets, who were gerbils, and my cats too. It's also a political film. But it all came about from reading an article in *Scientific American* about rat behavior under crowded conditions, simulating New York conditions. The film has very little to do with that, however.

KA: You mentioned before that the gerbils were family animals.

JW: Yes. Well, I had lived with them for a long time and found their little family structure very interesting. These little creatures whose lives were lived inside the glass container. One of the many interesting things about them was their acute reaction to sound—their lives were literally ruled by sounds. They were haunted little characters, little prisoners, little victims no matter how nicely they were treated. They were wild creatures, and after photographing them for several months, I started to see what the film was about: their escape to freedom.

KA: How do these concerns—women, Canada—work in *Reason Over Passion?*

JW: *Reason Over Passion* is part three in a series of artworks. The first two were a pair of bilingual quilted wall hangings. The words *Reason Over Passion* and *La Raison Avant La Passion* attached in big stuffed letters. But in the film *Reason Over Passion,* in making this film and particularly while editing I had the fantasy that I was a government propagandist, churning out the government line. I thought I was Leni Riefenstahl, you know *The Triumph of the Will*

[1936] and *Reason Over Passion*. But I put Trudeau in the middle of my film almost as an exercise, similar in a way to male artists always having had their odalisque, throughout the history of art and in their films, as stars.

KA: Do you think of it as a process of objectification of Trudeau, in the way that women have always been objectified in movies?

JW: You mean like what they did to Marilyn Monroe? No. I guess what I'm doing to Trudeau is putting him on for his statement "Reason over passion—that is the theme of all my writings." Taking the words *Reason Over Passion* in the beginning of the film, treating them as a propaganda slogan, and through permutation, turning them into visual poetry, into a new language.

KA: If you were doing that to Trudeau, how do you feel about that sequence where you photograph yourself singing "O Canada"? Didn't you do that in *Water Sark* [1964–1965] also?

JW: Yes, I used the same idea in *Water Sark* as in *Reason Over Passion* of photographing myself—talking, making faces, et cetera. This idea makes the audience aware of the filmmaker and especially in *Water Sark*, where the whole film is about me making the film. In *Reason*, the self-portrait says I predict, I make the film, I am a character in the film. The whole film is a bit of a primer on Canada and my singing lends a quality of dutiful schoolchild flogging the anthem. And as I carefully sing the words, my camera is beneath my chin photographing, mostly the lower part of my face, and especially the lips. This soundless singing is the overture to the film. Almost announcing the death of the country, which is what this film is partly about—a last look at Canada.

KA: What are the films correctives to?

JW: That's the title of my film company. It was very funny to me when I thought of it seven years ago. Since then we put the Corrective Film logo on all of my films. A lot of people have wondered what a corrective film would be.

KA: Are you involved with this group of women filmmakers in New York?

JW: No, I didn't know they existed until there was something about it in *The Village Voice*, and it said there was going to be a Feminist Film Festival.

KA: Yes, that's all I know about it too so far. Have you worked with other women filmmakers?

JW: I worked with Shirley Clarke a couple of times. Once she was doing a film which dealt with Tim Leary. It was fun to do. And I don't know what became of it. I did photography for it. Then I worked on her film about André Vosnesensky, who seemed a bit of a jerk. Then later Mary Mitchell, the Canadian playwright, and myself decided to do a film on Norman Mailer. We have lots of footage of that boring neurotic existentialist. The best part is a conversation Mary has with Mailer. We got Normie pounding Freedman's head in Brooklyn Heights in front of his house—it looks like a typical vignette of U.S. social problems. Then Jane Bryant and I did a half-hour film on Ed Blair, the New York poet—it's not finished. Ed died three weeks after we did the final shooting of the film. He was such a wonderful poet, and would open his poetry readings with a singsong, choosing songs like "After the Ball Is Over." In the four years since we did the shooting I haven't had a minute even to think of finishing it. In 1965 Betty Ferguson and I made a collage film called *Barbara's Blindness*. It's very funny, and is distributed through the New York Film-Makers Co-Op. Wendy Michener and I started a film about each other's lives about eight months before she died. I hope to finish this film somehow.

A lot of women have had problems in film. It hasn't been easy for Shirley Clarke either. She should have had a few of the things that Agnes Varda got, or Chytilova for that matter. She should have gotten something out of Hollywood. She's equal to Varda and Chytilova. But what an absolutely brutal scene to try and raise money from.

KA: Have you gone through the same sort of struggles?

JW: No, not the same in the U.S. But after I made *Reason Over Passion*, my first long film, I was made to feel in no uncertain terms by a few male filmmakers that I had overstepped my place, that in New York my place was making little films.

KA: Do you think it's a different problem in underground films, or do they parallel the problems of women making ordinary feature films?

JW: I don't know. I guess it's just a general problem.

KA: Have you had trouble raising money for your films?

JW: I have only raised money for one film. The rest I paid for myself, by sales of my artworks. And I had a grant to do one film.

KA: I think that Sylvia Spring talks about her problems in raising money; that seemed to have a lot to do with the fact that she is a woman.

JW: Well everyone knows what she went through, but it's amazing that she finally got the money. I guess only two or three women have ever made a feature film in Canada, and up until the last few years, men have successfully kept women out of filmmaking at the National Film Board.

KA: Do you have any hope for women artists getting together, like at the Whitney last year?

JW: Well I don't know about last year. I heard they threw their Tampax around the Whitney and that they wanted Nancy Graves's sculpture removed because they thought a man had done it. But they were right too in some ways. Books dealing with women's problems like *Sisterhood Is Powerful* [1970] are the most unifying of all. They just turn your head right around overnight. You feel differently, you just aren't the same after those books.

KA: Do you feel that coming back to Canada will ease problems or create new ones?

JW: Well you see in New York I've become part of a movement called Structural Films. This movement involves seven people and has evolved over the last four years. I've given a lot, and learned a lot from these filmmakers, and I don't like to leave that scene but I have to, to go on with what I'm about. My subject matter has been bringing me back to Canada for a long time. I've been thinking and working and researching for the feature film I want to do.

KA: What's it about?

JW: It's a film about Tom Thomson, the Canadian landscape painter. It involves Quebec and Ontario, and his fictional lover Eulalie de Chicoutimi. It deals with the French and English language and is a play on subtitles. It's about the last days of a great country and is placed around 1919, the days before Canada lost control of its destiny. Dennis Reid, a curator of the National Gallery, has done extensive research on Tom Thomson, and has been able to give me much more understanding of this great artist who is so much the spirit of Canada, as she was. His information has enabled me to go on with scripting this film.

KA: Do you think there will be any change in the way you'll treat Canada now that you are here?

JW: No, because I've been on this path a long time. I wrote the outline for this film two years ago in New York.

KA: Will *True Patriot Love* be an avant-garde film?

JW: That's complicated. I have made nine short films in the last seven years, all of which could be termed avant-garde, and three of which are considered to be Structural Cinema. These personal films mean more to me than any of the documentaries I've worked on. Films like *Catfood* [1968], *1933* [1967–1968], *Sailboat* [1967–1968] are all working in new areas of seeing and thinking. But *Rat Life and Diet in North America* contains the seed of something else. It had a message and a very accessible story. It was bought by German and Netherlands television, and was shown on the Canadian network. After it was shown on Canadian TV people I know or didn't know told me how much they liked it, including a man who drove a truck for Pepsi-Cola, whom I met at the Pilot Tavern. He offered to invest $100.00 in my next film. I was so knocked out! After making *Reason Over Passion*, I wrote the outline for *True Patriot Love*, which is a traditional narrative film. It will be a well-researched, tragicomic historical love story.

What follows has been edited from a long conversation, so that parts of it have been rearranged and parts left out. This 1976 interview was done four nights after *The Far Shore*, the release title of *True Patriot Love*, premiered in Toronto.

KA: When we did that interview in *Take One* that ends where this one begins, you were describing *The Far Shore* [1976] as the next film you would make. You wanted to make a narrative film that would tell a story that would be important to Canadians and to tell it in a way that would be accessible to Canadians.

JW: Yes, in a traditional narrative form.

KA: But then after that you made *Pierre Vallieres* [1972] and *Solidarity* [1973]. What was happening there? Was this film kind of developing in the background while you were still going on?

JW: It was developing in the background but both of those films were from my immediate response to coming back to Canada. You know, the revolutionary in Quebec being Pierre Vallieres and then just the women's problems at the Dare cookie factory.

KA: In the films you did before, you weren't dealing with narrative, except in *Rat Life and Diet in North America.*

JW: And that was an awakening too, the sudden joyful thought that this was not barred from me. Even though I was part of the underground that didn't like to tell too many stories because it was involved with opening up our vision. I thought, Jesus Christ, I could make this into a little story you know—it wouldn't have to be just an incredible image that would burn itself on your mind.

KA: How did you find the task of working with narrative?

JW: Well it's very difficult. I mean I would have made a much different film had it just been in 16mm and all my own dialogue.

KA: How would it have been different? Actually this is leading to another question. Ian Christie and I talked about the film, and he mentioned scenes from *The Far Shore* that seemed to have more to do with your other films than with traditional narrative films. The picnic scene, for example, where all of the crucial stuff happens out of the frame—the very way that *Solidarity* works, focusing on the feet when you knew that everything was going on outside the frame.

JW: Yes it's very much like my other work I think.

KA: That scene or the whole film?

JW: I think the whole film because I really love those camera movements. I really like the color, I really like what's in the frame, the kind of texture, the kind of lighting—what I feel is just a continuation of my own development.

KA: You said before that with the editor you fought to leave the frame empty, not cut on action. Why?

JW: I wanted you to be able to feel their absence for a few seconds rather than use another device to get from one scene to another. To empty the frame and hear the footsteps disappear or something like that, and then make the direct cut to the next scene. It's nice to have this moment; it's sort of a pulse in the film.

KA: Do you have any philosophical rationale for things like that? Do you think that has any special effect on the viewer?

JW: I think there's always a question. It brings something up in the viewers' minds for a moment. It's on the viewers for a few seconds and it makes them pause and wait for the next thing. They're brief pauses but they're used quite a few times. It throws the spectators back on themselves. And the film does that many ways because there's an aspect of tragic comedy within the film and that leaves the audience on their own. You're standing outside it but everything is going on in it in a very intense way. But the audience is left—they have to find their own way through this film. And they're not getting what Richard Foreman calls instant gratification. They're just being asked to float with it or relax. Just saying come along if you want to. But it has some kind of a pull in it because people have talked about it—that there is a pull like a current and it gets stronger as it goes along.

KA: But that seems to me to have everything to do with the rhythm of the film. It moves, as you say, like a current in a river, goes along quite slowly with a kind of heartbeat.

JW: It's a tide. It has a lot to do with water. Many of my films have a lot to do with water, and this is a real Pisces film and the motif of the fish is throughout the film.

KA: What about the magnifying-glass scene?

JW: In the silent scene when they speak through their magnifying glass, her text is from Madame Roland who is a French revolutionary. It simply says something like when the people have had enough, they will make revolution and they will turn on the government or something like that. But it's really what Eulalie is saying about herself: I am in the state of revolution because of what I feel. . . . He says as an answer to her a poem from Wilfred Campbell, who's one of the great Canadian poets that we all read in school. It's about a drowning in a lake up north, so his reply is that it can only end in a drowning, it can only end in death, what you feel.

KA: But this is never in the film. You never know what they're saying.

JW: No. That scene is a secret between the two of them. That's what makes the audience start to—they get very restless in that scene because you know why? Because it's not for the audience, it's for those two people in the film. But it doesn't matter that we don't know what they say because it's their unspoken love. And I feel that the film has a lot of mystery in it. It doesn't come out and give you everything in the stupidest possible manner. And all the films that I've admired have so much mystery in them . . . That's what cinema once was: it was concerned with magic and shamanism and the evocation of spirits you know.

KA: I was interested in what you said on Saturday about your film being slow and women responding to that—the film allowing you to breathe. And the film breathes.

JW: And that's the comment that nearly every woman at the opening said. Did I tell you that? The most amazing thing. One after the other said I like the pauses, I like the chance to look and think about what's happening.

KA: I think more and more that a lot of that is going on in films that women are making. It's speaking from and speaking to a totally different sensibility—and particularly in the sense of time.

JW: It's as though the masculine world in a way—the perception now is changing and the world has to change too. So it's almost as though we're saying, wait a minute, we're calling a halt to the whole thing. By being slow. Contemplative.

KA: Do you see a connection between that whole movement and that sensibility and the romantic nature of your film?

JW: Yes. I think that for me anyway the romantic nature of the film reflects my own nature, that I'm romantic. But the main thing is that I want to go back in time. If I make another film of my own, it will go back further in time. This is also very necessary for Canada because none of the stories has been told about the English Canadian past in features, not to my satisfaction. So in going back, things change, and I imagine the period 1919 in a kind of romantic setting. But the reality lies within it—of the capitalist, the wealthy husband. Nothing has changed but their postures are different. They walk differently, they talk differently, they have a different code of morals. . . . So I guess I've always just liked the past. And I don't

like too much dialogue. I like the feeling to get across you know—
like when they part in the cabin.

KA: It's such a beautiful scene isn't it?

JW: I remember you liked it. It takes a long time but the intensity of feeling is there—and his inability to speak because he knows
there's no answer.

KA: And the restraint. They're very close together, and the back
of the chair is separating them and his arms are on the back of the
chair and her hands are there, but they never touch each other
and . . .

JW: And he looks at her hand. And you know what's going on.
He's a totally introverted Canadian artist—not completely introverted but you know that kind of loner that goes to the woods. And
he knows the dangers of Ross. She doesn't know how dangerous her
husband is. So that takes a long time but I mean it's a very compel-
ling scene . . . So I wanted to show that. But I also wanted to
show what it was like for a woman who was an artist. And her
situation is almost—well his situation is almost as hopeless as hers,
living in Canada which has never been into the appreciation of the
arts. And the fact that as a woman she came from Quebec and she
came from the upper class, and was hidden from society literally
until she was brought out to have one of those things that you have,
you know a party when you're twenty-one and all that. . . . But I
know for truth that that's what a woman went through at that time.
I know because my mother-in-law (whom the character is based
on) told me. But Eulalie shapes up—she has some of myself in her
because I know what it is to be an artist, too—but she shapes up in
a way that is a bit like a Stendhal heroine. I like his women because
they're so courageous and they're so intelligent and they're so individual. . . . I worked with a writer whom I've known for many
years, and he likes the same kinds of films I do, so we didn't have
trouble communicating. You know he may shout once in a while
and I may have been amazed at the way he wanted to portray
Eulalie but we certainly ironed that out in a hurry.

KA: How did he want to do it?

JW: Well here's an example. When she goes to Tom's shack, I
had all these scenes that I wanted to see which are all there anyway
because they're silent—they're mood scenes. He wanted her to clean

it up—to take a broom. And I said listen, this is no groupie coming over to visit a pop star, you know. This is a woman who is all together; she just got the wrong companion in marriage because she had to get out of her situation. It was very common in those days to just go off if you got a rich person to take you out of your village if you're disappointed by another suitor. So he said, well tell me more, what is she like? I said no, she's never been seen before—this woman—on film. Never.

KA: And then how did you find directing the film?

JW: It was a great pleasure. It was terrifying at first, completely terrifying.

KA: And then?

JW: And then, well the first week was the most difficult but even after the third day I was beginning to feel that it was all right and everybody was great. Richard Leiterman [the cinematographer] was really kind.

KA: What do you mean, "kind"?

JW: Well, like we spent a few weeks before going over the storyboards which were all prepared with the camera movements and the color and everything and the kind of paintings that I was interested in showing the lighting from. And he had been very absorbed in this idea and really intrigued and found that here at last was a chance to really use his talent. So on the set he was very nice. There were a lot of women on that set, and they were very supportive too. But the underlying terror was that I knew that the people in that industry for example despised the kinds of films that I had made.

KA: So then how was the reception at the Edinburgh Film Festival?

JW: I think it was good. Except that there were a lot of the avant-garde people there from all over the world, and I think they were absolutely disgusted that I would do a film like that.

KA: Rather than continuing in the structuralist non-narrative tradition?

JW: Not even that, but there are a lot of women in the avant-garde who are making films about feminist things and politics. I don't really know much about what they're doing, but there's something depressing to me about it from what I know. . . . It's so masochistic. We have souls and spirits and we have the job of shamans, not the job of reiterating the misery that's been done to us . . . It's so neurotic, that stuff. What do those things do? You come out feeling even worse—it takes your energy away from you. But we have to transmit our spirits to each other. That's what lives. . . . But in Edinburgh not one woman came to me. Not one woman. I was there for two days after and not one woman—and I know them all—and not one woman writer except a New York critic who had to come over to talk to Mike [Snow, Joyce's husband]. And I've known her for seven years and I said, well what do you think? She wasn't even going to talk about it, she was so embarrassed. She said, well it was really romantic.

KA: Yes, well I saw her in New York and she told me to ask you about the romanticism and the idealization of the artist and the politics of that. She was concerned about that. The individualism of the whole story.

JW: What do you mean, "the individualism"?

KA: Well, the setting up of the artist as the kind of beleaguered soul in a group of crass nonpeople and what seemed a tremendous sentimentalization of the artist and the artist's role in society.

JW: Well why don't they talk about Eulalie?

KA: But there again, she's a truncated artist, an artist who's cut off.

JW: That's right. It's the truth. It's not like a flat-footed feminist movie. And the main idea is—well, I'm not interested in making depressing movies about social problems. And I see that being done over and over again and I can't bear it. I can't bear any more misery. God damn it, I will not go along with it. I want to talk about something that goes on inside us—I mean, Jesus Christ, the worker. I'm a member of CAR [Canadian Artists Representation] where we're working with each other for the betterment of our role in society and our relationship to society. I've been in on all those film briefs, I'm involved in the whole social thing about—we actually work as artists joining with the farmers' union and stuff like that. . . . But I cannot bear any more misery. And my greatest dream is that I would be able to make great comedies. It's a miserable world. And I don't want to make people escape into bourgeois artists' lives or anything like that, artists who suck around collectors, but I mean I'm telling the truth about what went on here.

KA: What's all this about shamans? Have you done a lot of work on that?

JW: I've read a lot about them and I couldn't really tell you what they are, but I think that art is a religious practice and I think it's an offshoot of the religious thing. And many women were shamans. In another interview I told the story of an Eskimo woman who happened to go out one night to urinate and as she pulled down her drawers, at that moment a meteor came from the sky and entered into her and from that moment on she was given her song. She was given the power to tell the truth to her people and I made a great quilt from that song. It's called The Great Sea: "The great sea has set me adrift/set me in motion./It moves as a weed in a great river. /Earth and the great sky move my inward parts with joy." Something like that. I mean if we're not concerned with that, then screw it. It's a religious practice. And I don't know what I mean by religion even, but I know that there were men and women shamans, and especially in the Arctic, who spoke in tongues and who were in touch with something that we're no longer in touch with. . . . And there's a few visionaries around who aren't afraid to have visions about this.

KA: What are you going to do next?

JW: It's more about that. But I have to go through something to get there. I know it's not going to be given to me. I know I have to go through something.

KA: How is the success of *The Far Shore* going to affect what you do?

JW: Well I want to help produce Margaret Laurence's *The Diviners* with Judy [Steed, coproducer of *The Far Shore*], and she wants to direct it. But what happens to this film will affect that because it's a very large budget film and a very important film. A love story between a woman and an Indian—a Métis. And if this film dies, as they call it, then I don't know how easy it's going to be to do the next one at that scale. But if it's all too impossible, then in a few years I'll do a film. I'll do another feature in 16mm or something like that.

Marilyn Times Five*

Chuck Kleinhans

Marilyn Times Five (1968–1973; known variously as 5 × *Marilyn*, *Five Times Marilyn*, etc.) is a short work by New American Cinema veteran Bruce Conner that uses "found" footage to attempt a discovery of Marilyn Monroe. At the same time, Conner's film explores the question of how a film's form can influence the way an audience receives the content. He takes a little over a minute of material from a film purported to be of young Marilyn Monroe: a girlie film with the actress dressed only in underpants. Conner's intent, he has said, was to take footage with the crudest victimization of a woman, deconstruct it by rearranging the parts, and see if the quintessential "Marilyn" could emerge. The filmmaker admits that the content—sexist images of a female body—is so gross that it was and is questionable in his mind if he succeeded in changing the given footage, in which Marilyn is the victim of our voyeurism, into something else. The film is experimental in the scientific sense: Conner set himself a project to see if he could do it. What he came up with is five different re-editing jobs, using loop repetitions of the original footage, black leader, and Monroe on the sound track singing "I'm Through with Love" (from *Some Like It Hot*, 1959) five times.

Marilyn Times Five forces us to come to terms with the raw

---

* Excerpted from "Seeing Through Cinéma Vérité," *Jump Cut*, no. 1 (1974).

content of the footage, which unmistakably has a sexist voyeurist appeal, by showing the same few hundred frames five, or twelve, or twenty times. Conner isolates through selection and then uses repetition to show the irreducibly human element in the film. A single fleeting gesture becomes the same gesture twenty times, and no longer fleeting and thereby it stands out from the naked body in the image. Thus Conner lets us see those little things that can be read out of context by formal rearrangement: the gesture, the smile, the pout, the way of crossing arms and legs.

Is Conner's new version sexist or not? That depends on the context of viewing and on the audience's predisposition. As it is, the film does not satisfy as porn, which is some achievement in overcoming the given footage, but it still acts as a voyeuristic film: we can't totally stop watching the body, the torso, the legs, the breasts —they are inescapable. This seems to show that, as Conner says, we can't escape the content through the form, though we can distance it. Conner can indicate certain things: that Marilyn Monroe was a human being, not merely an object, even in a film designed to make her an object. We see Marilyn as a victim of our voyeurism, but through Conner's isolation of and attention to the particularly individual traits of the actress, we also see she is more than a victim. In the end, the Conner version is a homage to Marilyn Monroe as a person, and it is the most respectful homage to her that I know.

Bibliography

Arnheim, Rudolf. "To Maya Deren." *Film Culture* (Spring 1962).

Berg, Gretchen. "Interview with Shirley Clarke." *Film Culture* (Spring 1967).

Brown, Robert K. "Interview with Bruce Conner." *Film Culture*, no. 33 (1964).

Cornwall, Regina. "Activists of the Avant-Garde." *Film Library Quarterly* (Winter 1971–1972). [Maya Deren, Germaine Dulac]

———. "*True Patriot Love:* The Films of Joyce Wieland." *Artforum*, 10, no. 1 (September 1971).

De Hirsch, Storm. "Astral Daguerreotype." *Film Culture*, no. 33 (1964).

———. "Roman Notebook." *Film Culture* (Summer 1962).

Deren, Maya. "Notes, Essays, Letters." *Film Culture*, no. 39 (Winter 1965).

———. "A Statement of Principles." *Film Culture*, nos. 22 and 23 (1961).

Farber, Manny. "Maya Deren's Films." *The New Republic*, October 28, 1946.

Flitterman, Sandy. "Heart of the Avant-Garde: Some Biographical Notes on Germaine Dulac." *Women and Film*, 1, no. 4 (1974).

Lennon, John, and Ono, Yoko. "Our Films." *Filmmakers Newsletter* (June 1973).

Markopoulos, Gregory. "Three Filmmakers." *Film Culture* (Winter 1964–1965). [Storm De Hirsch]

Polt, Harriet. "Interview with Shirley Clarke." *Film Comment* (Spring 1964).

Rice, Susan. "Shirley Clarke: Image and Images." *Take One*, 3, no. 2 (1970).

Soltero, Jose. "Shirley Clarke on *Jason*." *Medium* (Winter 1967–1968).

V
Women
and Political Films

Women at Work: Warners in the 1930s*

[Susan] Elizabeth Dalton

When the harsh years of the Depression hit America, the predominant female image in film was affected by the grim economic reality. The carefree, dance-mad flapper of the 1920s suddenly had to go to work. When she did, she found a long and difficult fight for survival in a cynical, male-dominated world. Since it was Warner Brothers, "the workingman's studio," which specialized in topical films that reflected the contemporary scene, it was there that the woman at work was most often depicted; it was there that her image was most fully defined. These films were remarkable in analyzing the dynamics of male-female relationships; and they exposed the struggle and prejudice that women really faced. But in the conceptions of women that they put forth, and in the plot resolutions they offered, they revealed a traditional male bias: a woman is made for love, not work.

The primary Depression heroine at Warners was the gold digger. As counterpart of the tough, snarling gangsters of Cagney and Robinson and the cynical shysters of Warren William, she had guts and the ability to fend for herself. Popularized in *Gold Diggers of 1933* and innumerable other musicals with backstage plots and vast, phantasmagoric displays of female flesh, the gold digger was also a

* Reprinted from *The Velvet Light Trap*, no. 6 (Fall 1972).

staple in lesser, nonmusical productions. Her philosophy was simple: "It's one of two things. Either you work the men or the men work you." Joan Blondell and Glenda Farrell personified the type in film after film: *We're in the Money* (1935) demonstrates their usual modus operandi. As two process servers working for a shyster (who handles breach-of-promise suits for gold diggers), they feign sweet, suggestive smiles in order to get close to men, who suddenly find themselves holding a subpoena. Their justification? "For a thousand dollars we'd make a sap out of any man."

Gold Diggers of 1937 is a typical case. Blondell and Farrell, two chorus girls, are stranded with their comrades-in-arms when the show flops. (And, naturally, the manager has run off with the money.) Happily, there is an insurance convention in town, and the chorines can dig into the salesmen. When Blondell, however, meets Dick Powell, a musically minded salesman, she opts for a job with his company. ("I want a job. One where they hand you a pay envelope every Saturday night.") Farrell, meanwhile, meets the partners of J. J. Hobart (Victor Moore), a hypochondriacal theatrical producer. Since the partners have squandered Hobart's money, they conspire with Farrell to have him take out a $1,000,000 policy with Powell. Naturally, Farrell and the partners are the beneficiaries (they need the money for a new show), and, with characteristic cynicism, they scheme to move up Hobart's "expiration" date. ("Hobart? Why, he's got two feet in the grave already." "Yeah, now all we have to do is make him lie down in it.") But Powell is trying to keep him alive—he needs the commission checks so he can marry Blondell. Needless to say, someone must give up the struggle. It is Farrell who finally has a change of heart and falls in love with Hobart. ("J. J. is one of the finest men I've ever known, and I wouldn't do the least little bit to hurt him.") Her "feminine instincts" have triumphed. The film's final production number, "Love Is Just Like War," is a literal battle of the sexes. The men shoot cannons to protect "No-Woman's-Land," but the women use "feminine" weapons. They charge with perfume atomizers and win. A woman's objective in life is to capture a man, and "All is fair in love and war."

Theatrical producer J. J. Hobart (Victor Moore) is surrounded by dames on the take in Lloyd Bacon's *Gold Diggers of 1937*. (Courtesy Wisconsin Center for Film and Theater Research)

The gold-digger comedies were not the only films in which a woman used her "natural resources" to get ahead. *Baby Face* (1933), far blacker in mood, is a truer reflection of the condition real women faced. Lily (Barbara Stanwyck) has grown up in her father's speakeasy. "A swell start you gave me," she berates him. "Nothin' but men, dirty, rotten men . . ." When her father's still blows up, he is killed; Lily is left with her only asset—her body—and accepts a job as a stripper. A male friend, dismayed at her lack of vision, gives her some cynical advice. "A woman, young, beautiful like you, can get anything she wants in the world." Lily rides a freight to New York and sleeps her way to the top of the financial world, eventually marrying the head of an international bank. (Unlike the gold digger, she "puts across," but only after she has what she wants—in this case his "name.") When the bank folds and her husband is held responsible, Lily, at first, refuses to help him. "I have to think of myself . . . My life has been bitter and hard. I'm not like other women." But Lily soon finds that she is, and turns over her bonds and securities to save him. Her reason? "I love you. I've never said that to any man. I never knew what it meant. Oh, darling, you can have anything I've got. I'll do anything for you. Anything!" Love has taught her what a woman should be.

Although the Depression meant hard times for everyone, it was especially tough on women unwilling to trade on their sex. *Blondie Johnson* (1933) reveals how few options there were. The film opens with a shot of Blondie's tattered stockings. The camera rises and pans across the desperate faces of the men, women, and children in the welfare and relief office. Blondie (Joan Blondell) is looking for work, any kind of work—almost. She had a job but quit ("I had to. The boss wouldn't let me alone. He . . ."), which makes her ineligible for welfare. Her mother sickens and dies when the landlord evicts them into the rain, but when Blondie tries to sue him, the lawyer is snide: "Why, it takes money to go into court with a thing like this." Blondie: "Money. That's all I've ever heard. Money . . . I'm going to get money and I'm going to get plenty of it." Minister: "Just a moment, my dear. There are two ways of getting money." Blondie: "Yeah, I know. The hard way and the easy way."

Since she refuses to become a prostitute, Blondie turns to crime instead. As the leader of a clever extortion racket, she fights her way to the top of the underworld. But unlike Little Caesar, who avoids love because it weakens a man, makes him vulnerable, Blondie falls for one of her henchmen. Little Caesar falls prey to his own ego; Blondie is captured because she refuses to abandon her wounded lover. Ego and the quest for power are still the exclusive domain of men. For a woman, those she loves must always come first.

Because it is "unnatural" for her, a woman, much more than a man, must be pushed into crime. Blondie Johnson was destitute; Margaret Lindsay, in *The Law in Her Hands* (1936), is stymied by prejudice and corruption. Lindsay, an idealistic lawyer fresh from her bar exams, cannot get clients because of her sex. Her boyfriend, the assistant DA, wants her to give up and become his wife. After all, "The legal profession is full of tricks and technicalities. It's not for a woman." But Lindsay doesn't want to give up; she asks for a year to prove she can make good. When she finally gets a case, however, she loses it; her client is convicted on evidence forged by the other (male) attorney. Double-dealing might be expected of an opponent, but even her boyfriend is trying to stack the cards against her. He assigns her a client from whom he has just gotten a confession. For Lindsay, it is the last straw. "If it's tricks he wants, we'll show him a few." She photographs her client in ketchup and bandages to "prove" his confession was forced, and the jury acquits him. It is only too obvious that these "masculine" tactics work.

A notorious racketeer, capitalizing on Lindsay's disillusionment, offers her a retainer. She accepts and becomes his influential, but crooked, mouthpiece. But the seriousness of her futile rebellion is brought home when seven children die because the gangster had poisoned the milk of a distributor who refused "protection." Lindsay has failed to beat the system. She risks her life to testify against her client, and he is convicted. Then, taking full responsibility for her previous actions, she indicts herself for malpractice and is disbarred. As a woman, she cannot make it in a man's world. She is now ready to become "one of those 'woman's place is in the home types.' "

A woman might sometimes compete with a man on his own terms and win; but her motivations must always be unselfish. In *Traveling Saleslady* (1935) Joan Blondell plays the daughter of an old-fashioned toothpaste manufacturer who refuses to give her a job because women are "unstable, unreliable, and know nothing about business." To prove him wrong, she buys the rights to Cocktail Toothpaste and, as his competitor, she is enormously successful. On one of her sales trips she meets, and falls in love with, a salesman from her father's company. Characteristically, her boyfriend, dismayed at the thought of a female competitor, plots to ruin her business. Blondell, however, meets him trick for trick, outdoing his double-crossing schemes with numerous ploys (e.g. putting a quarantine sign on his showroom door at a druggists' convention). When he finally relents and admits she has what it takes, she gives it all up to marry him. After all, she was only trying to prove a point. Besides, she had already planned to give Cocktail Toothpaste, Inc., to her father. Clearly, a woman's responsibility is to the men in her life, not to herself.

The woman who competed most frequently, directly, and successfully against men was the "sob sister,"[1] the "intrepid girl reporter" who battled crooks, patronizing policemen, and hard-boiled editors in countless films. Although she constantly proved herself the equal of any man, she, too, would "find love" in the end. *Mystery of the Wax Museum* (1933) is a classic example. Glenda Farrell is a self-sufficient and fun-loving newshound who would "rather die with an athletic heart from shaking cocktails and bankers than expire in a pan of dirty dishwater." When she takes New Year's Eve off to "do experiments with Scotch and soda," her editor threatens to fire her. ("There's no room on this rag for the purely ornamental.") Washed up unless she turns in a story for the next edition, she discovers that the suicide of a young girl is really a murder. Despite the paper's policy to pin the guilt on a rich young dandy, Farrell believes he is innocent. She investigates and uncovers the grisly scheme of a mad sculptor who covers corpses with wax, but the editor razzes her theory. ("Work that up into a comic strip and we'll syndicate it.") She meets the challenge ("I'm going to make you eat dirt, you soap bubble. I'm going to make you beg for somebody to help you let go!") and scoops every paper in town when she exposes the sculptor. In the last sixty seconds of the film the editor gets romantic: "Cut out this crazy business. Act like a lady. Marry me." Her reply: "I'm going to get even with you, you dirty stiff. I'll do it."

Farrell's surprise capitulation is typical. A woman could be resourceful, intelligent, even cynical, for fifty-nine minutes, but in the last two she would realize that it was love and marriage that she really wanted. As Rosalind Russell (who played at least twenty "career women" at various studios) put it:

> Except for different leading men and a switch in title and pompadour, they were all stamped out of the same Alice in Careerland. The script always called for a leading lady somewhere in the thirties, tall, brittle, not too sexy. My wardrobe had a set pattern: a tan suit, a gray suit, a beige suit, and then a negligee for the seventh reel, near

[1] The term *sob sister*, which was originally coined to refer to writers of lonely hearts columns, was eventually derogatorily applied only to female reporters, who had to fight constantly to prove themselves the equal of men.

the end, when I would admit to my best friend that what I really wanted was to become a dear little housewife.[2]

Even when a woman did not openly compete with men, her struggle for self-recognition was equally hopeless. Loretta Young (who, because she was a young divorcée, "had to be very carefully cast to avoid offending cinemagoers"[3]) often played the Innocent who fought to maintain herself, and her purity, in dire circumstances. In *She Had to Say Yes* (1933) Young is a secretary in a large garment firm that is losing accounts because out-of-town buyers "who get hot flashes every night about nine" are tired of the hard, gold-digging "customer girls" that the firm provides for their entertainment. Young's fiancé, a salesman who wants to get ahead, suggests that the firm's own stenographers might be a pleasant change of pace for the buyers. He refuses, however, to let Young join the "entertainment committee." ("If there's any manhandling going to be done, I'm the guy that's going to do it.") But when it becomes a question of his commission or her virtue, he changes his mind.

On her "date" with the prospective customer (Lyle Talbot) Young is ruthlessly pawed ("Yours is the penalty for being so lovely"). When she repulses him, Talbot finally realizes that her "innocent line" is not "part of the racket" and instantly falls in love. Her fiancé, who is himself seeing another woman, accuses her of "going the limit." Understandably annoyed, Young continues as a "customer girl" just to spite him. Soon, Talbot also begins to feel possessive and suspicious of her morality. In the last few minutes of the film Young is nearly raped by Talbot ("I was a sap to fall for that untouched line of yours . . . From now on you and I are playing for keeps."); rejected by her fiancé ("He's used you, paid you off . . ."); and then fought over when both realize that she is still "innocent." Realizing that she can expect no better from men ("You treat us just like the dirt under your feet."), she consents to

---

[2] David Shipman, *The Great Movie Stars* (New York: Crown Publishers, 1971), p. 483.
[3] *Ibid.*, p. 563.

marry Talbot "as the lesser of two evils." Better to be the possession of one man, she feels, than the possession of all.

Bette Davis meets a similar fate in *Ex-Lady* (1933), a surprisingly frank revelation of how "unattached" women are treated. Davis is a career girl with modern ideas. She doesn't want to get married and be a "yes-woman" for some man. When she does give in to her suitor's incessant pleading, she discovers she was right all along—marriage is boring, and her husband is jealous of her successful career. Davis moves out, and on her first date with another man, she is almost raped. ("I'm not going to let you bluff me tonight, Helen. Not tonight. You'd better start screaming.") When she complains to her husband about the brutal aggressiveness of men, he replies: "But that's how it always will be when a wife leaves her husband—for any reason." Davis has learned her lesson; she returns to her husband. Again, better the property of one man than many.

Helen (Bette Davis) and her husband (Gene Raymond) share a pre–Production Code bed in Robert Florey's *Ex-Lady* (1933). (Courtesy Wisconsin Center for Film and Theater Research)

Woman as Object. No matter where she went, no matter what she did, a woman was bound to encounter this definition. In *Big Business Girl* (1931) Loretta Young plays an ambitious college graduate who tries to make it in the business world. She is hired into a large advertising firm by Ricardo Cortez, a lecherous playboy with an eye for legs. But Young is not satisfied with being "a slave to a typewriter," and hoping for a promotion, she turns in some sample copy to Cortez. He tells her her writing is "awful, rather childish," but when she is out of the room, he admits that her copy is terrific; he "can use every line of it without changing a word." More important, however, is her body. Young overhears Cortez remark that "a girl with a chassis like that can be a half-wit and get by." She realizes that intelligence and capability mean nothing; it is sex appeal, and only that, which will help her career. Accordingly, she begins to "charm" contracts out of clients and is a smashing success.

The denial of her talents is not Young's only problem. She is married but keeps it a secret because, "When a girl is just starting out in business, if she's married and everybody knows it, they're afraid to give her a responsible job . . . afraid she's going to quit—keep house for her husband—start a family and all that." Cortez, thinking her single, makes advances that she must constantly put off. When he finally discovers that she is married, he apologizes *to the husband* by saying: "It could have happened to any man."

Like it or not, Young is married to a real loser, a simpering and totally irresponsible boy. He flunks out of school, and although finally persuaded to take his college band to Paris, he walks out on a year's contract because "he needs to be with her." When she accuses him of throwing away chance after chance, his only reply is "Puppies and babies take to me." She still loves him, however, and secretly convinces an advertiser to sponsor her husband's band on a radio show. Hubby skyrockets to fame, never realizing how he got there; and Young, of course, never tells him. It is her duty to help her mate, but she must never weaken his ego by letting him know.

The woman who did the most for a man was his secretary. After all, if she was good, the boss might marry her. *The Office Wife*

(1930) is a typical secretary story. Lewis Stone is a "strictly business" businessman, and Dorothy Mackaill, the "office wife," knows what the "business game is for a girl. It's about as fair as the marriage game. Catch-as-catch-can and anything goes." Since Stone is married, Mackaill must be really clever to win him. By lighting his cigarettes, watching his health, doing his work, and being sexually attractive, she is able slowly to wear him down. Still, Stone is a busy man, almost too busy to notice. When his real wife (who is so neglected that she must find another man) asks for a divorce, it is she who must help Stone recognize his hidden emotions. ("Larry, don't you realize that you're in love with your Miss Murdock?") And Miss Murdock? She has found happiness in serving her man; but when Stone proposes, she has a simple request: "Let me pick your new secretary." She knows that all men are vulnerable to an "office wife."

"The secretary finds her man" fantasy occurs in film after film after film. Joan Blondell captures William Powell in *Lawyer Man* (1932) and Warren William in *Goodbye Again* (1933). Bette Davis wins over William in *The Dark Horse* (1932) and Powell in *Fashions of 1934*. Marian Marsh gets yet another chance at William in *Beauty and the Boss* (1932), while Laura La Plante conquers Ian Hunter in a remake, *The Church Mouse* (1935). Aline MacMahon follows after Edward G. Robinson in *Five Star Final* (1931), and so on. Even if in most of these films the secretary was only a secondary character, she always played a variety of roles. She was a slave who did a man's work; a conscience who watched a man's soul; a mother who guarded a man's health; and, at the end of the last reel, a lover when she was "discovered" by her boss. The secretary was always a model woman, and so naturally a frequent image in films.

As opposed to the secretary, there were many images of really successful business and professional women, able to be so because they were smart enough not to compete directly for a "man's job." These women were: fashion illustrators and designers (Bette Davis in *Ex-Lady*, Kay Francis in *Street of Women*, 1932, and *Stolen Holiday*, 1936); advertising copywriters who handled the "woman's angle" (Lorretta Young in *Big Business Girl*, Bette Davis in *Housewife*, 1934, Priscilla Lane in *Men Are Such Fools*, 1938); nurses

(Barbara Stanwyck in *Night Nurse,* 1931, Kay Francis in *The White Angel,* 1936, Bebe Daniels in *Registered Nurse,* 1934); airline hostesses (Virginia Bruce in *Flight Angels,* 1940); and "maternal" doctors (Kay Francis as obstetrician in *Dr. Monica,* 1934, and as pediatrician in *Mary Stevens, M.D.,* 1933). Women lawyers were either failures (Margaret Lindsay in *The Law in Her Hands*), or secretaries for their husbands (Eve Arden in *She Couldn't Say No,* 1941).

If a woman worked in a traditionally male occupation, it was because of necessity, or family ties. When the right man came along, she was quite willing to surrender her difficult tasks to his capable hands. Kay Francis, who "came from a long line of magazine editors" in *Man Wanted* (1932), finds a male partner to take on the harder parts of the job. Beverly Roberts in *God's Country and the Woman* (1936) is stuck with a lumber camp when her father dies; she turns it over to George Brent. In *Daredevil Drivers* (1938), she is stuck once again, this time with her father's trucking business, but Barton MacLane is there to save her from gangsters.

Some women, however, did not instinctively recognize a male's "supremacy"; they had to be taught. In *Female* (1933) Ruth Chatterton inherits the Drake Motor Company upon the death of her father, and for five years runs it with an iron hand. She is imperative, decisive, efficient—but just a little too bitchy, and somehow unsatisfied. That she is searching for something is evidenced by the way she invites attractive male employees to her home "to discuss business" and then seduces them. When they fall in love with her, she is disgusted and transfers them to another city.

It is not until George Brent arrives on the scene that Chatterton discovers what she is lacking: *love.* Brent is a *real* man and rejects her aggressive attentions. ("I was hired as an engineer, not as a gigolo.") In order to win him, Chatterton must learn to act like a woman, a woman who will look up to him, "gentle, feminine, someone he can protect." It works; but once she has what she wants, she is still unwilling to marry. Brent becomes furious: "I suppose you think you're too superior for marriage and love and children. The things women are born for . . . Say, who do you think you are? . . . The great superwoman. Cracking your whip and making these poor fools jump around. You and your new freedom. Why, if you weren't so pathetic you'd be funny!" At first, Chatterton rejects his "masculine" onslaught; but when she bursts into tears at the next board meeting, she discovers that she *is really* a woman, and so marries Brent. And the business? "You're going to run it from now on," she says. "I never want to see that factory again."

Still, women did not always have to make the choice between love and career; nor were they always objects misused and mistreated by cads. Kay Francis, Warners' "sophisticated" star ("Superb actress—superbly gowned—creates a new screen sensation that would startle even Paris!"), usually played an educated, strong, professional woman. She never "copped out" the way other women did, and her men never wanted her to; but her films were pulsating romances that defined her image as woman in other, and more subtle, ways. In *Street of Women*, for example, she is a famous fashion designer in love with a married man. ("Ravishing Kay Francis as the woman who gives all and asks nothing," said the ads.) Her lover adores her, for she has inspired him to become a brilliant architect ("Everything that I've done, everything that I've accomplished in the past few years, I owe to her"). Thus, the title's "Street of Women" refers not to prostitution row, but to the fact that "Behind every skyscraper is a woman. You dress 'em up and make 'em beautiful—then some poor fellow comes along and puts up a skyscraper to lay at their feet." Woman as the Ideal, immortalized in song, poetry, and skyscrapers; and Francis accepts this role—it is even more important than love. She has put her brother through school in Paris, and when he is about to come home, she tells her lover that they must dissolve their illicit affair. ("You see, he isn't just like a brother. I brought him up. He thinks I'm perfect. To him, I'm his ideal and . . .")

Francis's choice, then, is not between love and career but between love and a duty to remain as the Ideal. Even though she fulfills this obligation, she suffers horribly. Her brother finds out about the affair and rejects her ("And who do I thank for my Paris education? The lady who gave her services—the gentleman who paid for them?"); she is separated from the man she loves; and she can find no solace in having her sketches accepted by *Vanity Fair*. Her sorrowful face, throbbing with emotion, fills the screen. But finally, the architect's shrewish wife gives him up; Francis is able to marry him, her brother forgives her, and she can be happy once more. At no point is her career more than a secondary factor. It is only what she does, not, in any sense, what she *is*. As a woman she is defined only through her relationships with others—through her men.

Francis was again involved in an unholy affair in *Mary Stevens, M.D.*, a film that explicitly pointed out the difficulties that a woman in the medical profession had to face. In the opening scene Francis arrives to deliver the baby of an Italian immigrant's wife and her life is threatened if the baby should die. ("The lady doctor no save bambino, Tony's a going to kill!") This is just the beginning. She loses patient after patient when they realize that she isn't the nurse, but the doctor. ("A woman doctor, huh? No thanks.") Finally, Francis is successful as a pediatrician. A woman, after all, ought to know something about children. She becomes very famous as the head of the Mary Stevens Clinic, and the reason she is able to do this is simple: When she reminds her lover that he told her a woman couldn't do it, his reply is "A woman couldn't. But you, well, you're a superwoman."

She is not really quite as super as the film would have us believe; she again accepts the definitions of a woman. As she is returning from Europe in order to get married, her illegitimate child dies. She has a breakdown and refuses to eat, sleep, or continue her practice. ("My life stopped when my baby died.") But this neglect of *duty* is suddenly over when she must save a baby's life; even her grief is too selfish. As a woman she must think of others first.

In her next portrayal of a doctor, Francis had to deliver her husband's illegitimate offspring. As *Dr. Monica* she is an obstetrician, but is herself unable to have children. ("You women who know the triumph of motherhood, bring all your pity—all your tears—when you see this drama of a woman denied life's greatest ecstasy"—advertisement.) Monica and her author-husband John have an ideal relationship. They are both successful, involved in important work, and they are in love. The perfect couple with the perfect marriage. But not quite.

John loved Mary before he met Monica, and although he doesn't know it, Mary is pregnant. It is Monica who takes care of Mary in her "difficulty"; it is not until a few moments before she is to deliver the child that she discovers that her husband is "the man." She is about to find a doctor for Mary ("the little tramp"), but she is slapped by a friend who reminds her of the duties of a physician; Monica stoically delivers the baby. Monica now realizes that she must leave her husband, even though she loves him, and knows that he loves her in return. "The existence of that child can't be ignored," and she herself can never provide him with children. Mary, however, is even more sacrificial: she commits suicide. Monica and John adopt the baby, but John never knows he is really its father. The guilty one, Mary, has paid for her sin; and John, as a man, must be protected. He must not ever know.

Dr. Monica does have another female image, though, one truly amazing for its own, or any, time. This is Anna, the friend who slaps Monica; and who also urges Monica to level with John about the child. Anna, too, is beautiful, sophisticated, and successful—an architect important enough to win a national competition. . . . Although the film never shows her with a particular man, she has an active social life with many friends; but more incredible, she is not *looking* for a man, being happy and satisfied without one. A far cry from the bitter, unsexed career woman that Eve Arden played in so many films. . . .

➤ The message, then, in all of these films is clear: Sure, a woman may not *really* be a passive, exploitable, "feminine" creature, but she damn well had better be if she expects to be happy. Although a woman may be ambitious, talented, may strive for a career, without love she is nothing—a mockery, a vestige of womanhood. It is through love, and only through love, that she will find her true meaning. The Depression films, by "exposing" the struggle of women, demonstrate that she had more to offer than sex; but only sex was acceptable. . . .

The results of this constant reiteration of the definition of Woman are exactly what one might expect. Toward the end of the decade, a woman no longer struggled for a self-defined image; no longer tried to find a "place" in the world. Just as films reflected the chaos and social upheaval of the Depression, so they reflected the changing outlook as conditions got better; the urgent examination of the contemporary social scene was exchanged for a reaffirmation of old values, values held in the time "before." The doomed, defiant heroes of *Little Caesar* (1931) and *Public Enemy* (1931) metamorphosed into the dashing adventurers of *Captain Blood* (1935) and *The Sea Hawk* (1940). And the heroines? They, too, accepted the old values. The "predicament" of Woman as Object was no longer a problem; in *Ever Since Eve* (1938) it is the subject of comedy. That Marion Davies must dress up in an ugly disguise because she is tired of being chased around office desks by leering businessmen is funny. The ambition of the "big business girl" has turned sour; in *Women in the Wind* (1939) the members of "the Dawn Patrol of women that no man dares to love" although they "do things that other women dream of" must themselves only "dream of the love that other women have." The best summation of this transformation is, perhaps, shown in the comparison of two films.

Loretta Young opted for marriage in *She Had to Say Yes* because it was the only refuge in a barbarous world; in *She Couldn't Say No* Eve Arden becomes a wife because she realizes that is the "natural" role of a woman. Arden, a lawyer, is content to work as her fiancé's secretary because he doesn't want "two careers in the family." When she finally does take a case, it is only to help him out of a jam; but he, misinterpreting her intentions as defiance, takes the opposite side in the case (sixty-five-year-old Pansy Hawkins's breach-of-promise suit against seventy-nine-year-old Eli Potter). At the trial, Arden makes the following plea to the jury:

> What if I were in love with a man who neglected me? Who regarded me merely as a piece of furniture . . . I might willingly do office drudgery for the man I love, leaving him free for the more exciting angles of his business . . . even do his washing for him for fifteen years if necessary, and love every minute of it . . . I might do all these things merely hoping that someday he might marry me . . . Would I be justified in suing him if he didn't? . . . No woman has

the right to do that. It isn't womanly; it isn't feminine. Gentlemen, if a woman loves a man, she must be willing to love him, and love him, and love him . . .

Here is the ultimate female—a helpmate, a nurse, a mother, a lover—all wrapped up in one woman. Naturally, Arden's fiancé is willing to get married immediately.

Notes on Women's Liberation Cinema*

Ruth McCormick

INTRODUCTION

In 1972 Ruth McCormick first surveyed short films coming from the women's movement for Cinéaste. In 1977 she has added to her original article by choosing from the recent works shown at the Second New York International Women's Film Festival. This piece, although expanded, remains by choice a modest survey, an indication of the type of filmmaking.that has been done, without trying to fill in the gap between 1971 and 1975, a time of enormous productivity in which women filmmakers became dominant in the independent field.

Among the first women's liberation films receiving general attention in the United States was Newsreel's *The Women's Film* (1971), which managed to take a class perspective. An interwoven series of interviews with middle- and working-class women, black, Latin, and white, it covers in less than an hour the various problems that confront us—sexism, poverty, raising children, job discrimination— in a warm, down-to-earth, appealing way.

* Revised from *Cinéaste*, 5, no. 2 (Spring 1972). Additional material supplied by author.

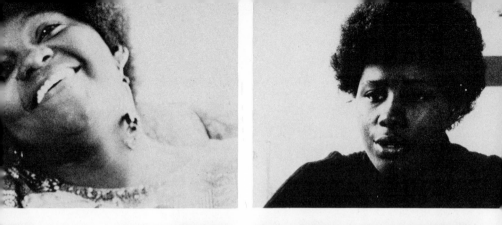

Shots from *The Women's Film* (1971). (Courtesy Newsreel)

Another of Newsreel's women's films, *Janie's Janie* (1971), with direction by Geri Ashur, is an extended interview with a young, white, working-class mother of five who has recently left her husband. She is developing both a feminist and a class consciousness. From her earliest childhood, Janie tells us, she has been bossed around by men, first by her father, and then, when she married to escape home, by her husband. She talks about her day-to-day problems: a tiring and badly paid job at a five-and-dime store; a horrendous but hardly surprising battle with Con Edison; inability to afford a lawyer; attempts to put a good meal together.

"Being poor makes you humble," Janie says, and then suddenly wonders how the rich have the nerve to look down on poor people. She has gotten involved in day-care struggles and is angry at the indifference of people in power to women like herself. "After all," she says, "I'm raising kids for the country." "Maybe our parents weren't really fighters," she reflects, and adds that she *will* fight for her kids, and if the fight has to get drastic and violent, then "We'll do it and tell people why." Despite technical flaws and a certain political naïveté, *Janie's Janie* remains one of the few women's films to deal with the politically problematic American white working class. Janie discusses her former racism, and her new consciousness. When she says, "I've got a right to be happy," she is telling why revolutions are made.

Probably the most widely distributed of the early women's films is the Kate Millet–produced *Three Lives* (1970), named for Gertrude Stein's very dissimilar novella. It is a work that disappointed militant feminists, who hoped that Millet would articulate her developing political theory within its context. The camera concentrates on three women, all likable, intelligent, and sensitive, talking about their lives. The first is Kate's sister, Mallory, a woman in her early thirties who has left her husband (an American businessman living a life of imperialist luxury in the Philippines) and she is now on her own with a small daughter. She reminisces about a father whom she both hated and adored, and a mother whose life of hand-wringing and quiet desperation she desperately wants to avoid. Bored by the menial jobs that she is deemed qualified for without higher education, unconditioned to fend for herself, she is just beginning to reconstruct her life. The second woman, Lillian, is an attractive middle-aged housewife, raised in a paternalistic Italian family, who gave up a successful career as a chemist for marriage and motherhood. The third, Robin, is twenty-one, a veteran of the "hippie" movement, and a lesbian. Highly individualistic and inclined toward mysticism, she philosophizes about her distrust of causes, about freedom, fear, and people's messed-up heads.

Three Lives succeeds in its simple, limited intent. Millet says she was more interested in women as "human beings" than "as the proponents of some theory or political movement." But, of course, why can't a woman be shown both as a "human" and a political being?

There have been fine films on specific issues. One example is black documentarist Madeline Anderson's *I Am Somebody* (1971), an account of a militant and successful struggle by Charleston, South Carolina, hospital workers—black women—against miserable working conditions and low pay and for representation by District 1199 of the National Union of Hospital and Health Care Employees. The women show how they fought the neanderthal hospital administrators and got the majority of the Charleston black community to support their cause through marches, demonstrations, and boycotts of white-owned businesses. Made for public television, *I Am Somebody* is superbly executed and shows the kind of gusto and working-class solidarity rare in films since the 1930s.

It Happens to Us (1971) by Amalie Rothschild is a half-hour color film on abortion, loosely divided into three parts. The first segment consists of interviews: a woman still cries when she talks of the trauma of having undergone an illegal abortion; an obviously affluent middle-aged mother of four describes how she and her husband together decided to have her fifth pregnancy terminated; a young black woman tells how her mother threw her out of the house when she was found to be pregnant. The second segment presents statistics, health facts, and an abortion counselor discusses the need for legalization. The third segment returns to interviews, the most memorable of which is with a woman whose father arranged for an

illegal abortion in a nearby ghetto. When she returned home, terrified, bleeding, and in pain, he gloated over her being "punished" for
her "sin." *It Happens to Us* is an effective educational film, showing
a cross section of women and proving that abortion is the concern of
all women. Its weakness, from a political point of view, is that although a strong case is made for legalization, no demand is made
for free abortion.

The social conditioning of women is the subject of Julia Reichert
and Jim Klein's *Growing Up Female* (1971), perhaps the best and
most comprehensive of the early independent women's films. Beginning with scenes in a kindergarten where girls and boys are already
being conditioned to different roles, the film moves on to eleven-
year-old Ginelle, still a tomboy; sixteen-year-old Terry, who sets
great store by her looks, is studying to be a cosmetologist, has a
steady boyfriend, and hopes to be married by the time she's twenty;
Tammy, a white, middle-class secretary, and Jessica, a black factory
worker, both twenty-one—the former is into pop culture, travel, and
making a career for herself, the latter is already divorced with a
child and plans to marry a much older man because he offers security; finally, a thirty-four-year-old housewife who has all the things
the other women in the film are told they should want—a husband
with a good job, a nice home, three attractive children, a place in
the sun. Her generation was marriage-oriented, she says, and although she's "happy," feels that perhaps if she had her life to live
over, she might very well have acted differently. *Growing Up
Female* raises important questions: if the woman who "has everything" feels unfulfilled, if the college graduate encounters difficulty
rising above the level of secretary, what about the majority of
women who don't ever get that far? And what happens to a carefree eleven-year-old that can make her, ten years later, obsessed
with makeup and diets, a slave to mass-media advertising?

What of more recent "women's liberation cinema"? There have
been several unusual films about jailed women. Suzanne Jasper's
Being a Prisoner (1975) explores the plight of several inmates in a
"model prison," focusing especially on mothers separated from their
children and, very interestingly, on women who have either injured

or killed men in self-defense and believe their sentences are unjust. *Like a Rose* (1975), by Sally Barrett-Page, concentrates on two no-longer-young women serving twenty-five-year sentences for heroin abuse. Both are highly intelligent, and, except for addiction, they were productive people on the outside. Now they feel isolated from society and useless. Cutbacks have taken away even the educational programs that were their salvation in jail. They only have each other and ironically, if paroled, they will not be allowed to associate. *Paul* (1972), made by a group of women from the New York University Film Department, is a brief, moving study of a young, black, gay woman who was arrested after having been accused by a family friend of stealing ten dollars' worth of groceries. Although a "first offender," she sat in the Manhattan Women's House of Detention for three months because she did not have one hundred dollars bail money, until a woman's group heard about her case and bailed her out. She talks, with considerable good humor, about her life in the street and in jail.

Several of the recent women's films fall into a category of what we might call "informal documentary." Nancy W. Porter and Micky Lemle's *A Woman's Place Is in the House* (1975) visits Elaine Noble, radical lesbian elected to the Massachusetts State Legislature two years ago. We follow her daily routine, meet her constituents, hear her tell about the difficulties of her work, the harassment to which she is subjected, the people who seek her help, and we meet her lover, feminist author Rita Mae Brown. Radicals may well question how effective Noble can be, working within the present system to improve the lot of women, gays, or oppressed people in general, but the facts that it is such a rarity for such a person to be elected to public office and that Elaine Noble is so capable and articulate are enough to make the film worth our while.

Chris and Bernie (1975), by Bonnie Friedman and Deborah Shaffer, concerns two divorced women, a nurse and a carpenter, one with a young daughter, the other, a son, who attempt to build a life outside the traditional family structure. We see the difficulties and occasional joys of their day-to-day life, their pride in their work, their frustrations and hopes. As an interesting afternote, we learn that Chris has since married, whereas Bernie has joined a communal group. In a similar vein Joyce Chopra's *Clorae and Albie* (1975) follows the lives of two friends, young black women, one of whom is a working mother, the other, once a dropout, back in college. Both are determined to make their lives work. The strength of these two films is the women themselves, dealing courageously with moving forward while also making ends meet. Neither film analyzes why they are up against such difficulties in the first place, and in that sense, they are not "political" films.

Union Maids (1976), by Julia Reichert and James Klein, is unique both in its concern with American labor history and with the specific role of women within the 1930s workers' movement. Interviewed are three delightful and still militant former labor organizers. They are Kate, who came from the farm to Chicago to work in an underwear factory; Sylvia, a black woman employed in a

Bernie and son in *Chris and Bernie* (1975) by Bonnie Friedman and Deborah Shaffer. (Courtesy New Day Films)

laundry; and Stella, a Polish-American assigned to the stockyards, who tell us about their lives as radicals and union leaders. They recall sit-downs and stoppages, scabs and goon squads, demonstrations and Red-baiting, the birth of the CIO and fighting sexism in the unions, all with enthusiasm and pride that accounts for the fact that, although they are disappointed with the conservatism of the present-day union bureaucracy, they have lost none of their revolutionary fervor. *Union Maids* is a rousing film, complete with fascinating footage from the struggles of the 1930s and authentic labor music. Inspirational rather than theoretical, *Union Maids* serves to remind us of the revolutionary potential of the American worker and of the central role of women in the class struggle. These women have not lost faith in that revolutionary potential and they welcome the women's movement as "long overdue." As Stella points out, she may have had some trouble with the younger, middle-class women, who don't seem to be aware enough of the problems of working women, but she is very happy that the new feminism is coming up with important questions and ideas. . . .

We have been talking here not about "commercial" films but about films made expressly to educate, to raise consciousness, to help create the forces for change. Every year, since its humble beginnings in 1969/70, women's liberation cinema can boast more, and better films. We learn by doing. The possibilities are endless for militant women's cinema: we could hope for films about working women, about black, Puerto Rican, Chicano, and Indian women, about women in the military, women in jail, in old-age homes, in factories and in ghettos. How about a film showing how difficult it is for a poor woman to obtain an abortion? Or a truthful, sensitive film about gay women? Or about women who hustle to· get money for their children, or for drugs, or for an education or, like the prostitutes who so shocked a group of feminists recently, who have so few options to make enough money for a really decent life that they see prostitution as a "better job than most I could get." We have no really comprehensive films about welfare mothers, or miners' wives, or, for that matter, athletes, ballet dancers or models, those disciplined, highly specialized creatures whose lives are hardly as glamorous or well paid, except at the very "top," as most people imagine. We need films about day care and hospitals and food prices, films about very young women and aging women, about women on strike and women in school. We need women making films about themselves, and about the men and children in their lives. These films should have a lot of anger in them, and as much humor as possible. The films we've talked about are a start.

Interview with Jane Fonda*

Dan Georgakas and Lenny Rubenstein

In 1974, with Haskell Wexler and two Vietnamese assistants, Fonda and Tom Hayden made Introduction to the Enemy, *a documentary film about Vietnam.* Cinéaste *editors Dan Georgakas and Lenny Rubenstein interviewed Fonda on the occasion of the film's New York opening. The discussion focused, among other things, on the possibilities for making progressive films in the Hollywood context, on the political problems posed for a radical actress.*

Q: What kind of problems has becoming a political activist created for you as a performer?

A: One of the first things was to resolve certain contradictions that were posed in my life, if I should continue acting or not, and if I continued, in what way? Should I continue in Hollywood films or should I join a group like Newsreel? I almost decided that it would be better to totally disappear into the faceless crowd of organizers (I thought then there were crowds) in the GI coffeehouses. The people who dissuaded me were John Watson and Ken Cockrel.[1]

* Abridged from "I Prefer Films That Strengthen People," *Cinéaste*, 4, no. 4 (1975).

[1] At that time, Watson and Cockrel were members of the executive board of Revolutionary Black Workers.

Yves Montand and Jane Fonda in Jean-Luc Godard and Jean-Pierre Gorin's *Tout Va Bien* (1972). (Courtesy New Yorker Films)

That must have been 1970 or 1971. They sat me down and said: "We've seen too many people with very important middle-class skills—doctors, lawyers, and others—who have rejected their class, and with it their talents. There's a need for doctors and lawyers, and there's a need for people who can reach mass audiences. You must continue." That was a very important statement for me to consider.

Q: What about the kind of roles you decided to play?

A: Well, I had always been the kind of actress who waited for people to come to me with scripts and ideas. The performers in Hollywood who are active producers are almost all men. Producing was an area that had been mystified. I found myself not working very much because I didn't like the roles coming my way. I think the problem with Hollywood is that the directors, and the writers even more so, don't view things historically and don't view things socially. Stories are unraveled in the context of an individual's particular personality and psyche and in the events of one life, never against a social background. You never see things dialectically, which means they are lying to people. They lead people down blind alleys.

I started to realize that if I was going to work, and if there were going to be movies made that I thought were important, and if I wanted to remain in the context of the mass media, I was going to have to produce them myself.

Q: Is it feasible to expect roles with ideas in them that are in any way compatible with your political views if you are not producing?

A: It's not impossible. I'm doing a film . . . based on a story by Lillian Hellman called "Julia." It's a true short story from a book of hers called *Pentimento* [1973]. It's the story of Lillian Hellman and a woman she knew who became a socialist. Well, you don't know for sure. All you know is that the woman becomes a committed activist who joins the French antifascist underground and gets killed by the Nazis. It's a very beautiful story about two women. It's about why people change and about the relationship of women with strong social commitments. I think it could be a very exciting film.

Q: There have been suggestions that you should play famous revolutionaries like Rosa Luxemburg and Emma Goldman.

A: I'm very wary of playing any role which makes me look like I view myself as La Pasionaria. I would rather play a fascist, if that exposed something about racism and power, than to play a famous revolutionary. Someone wanted me to play one of the Weather-women killed in the town house explosion. A rumor has me playing Patty Hearst. Those kinds of roles are the last thing I would think of doing. There is one revolutionary woman I would like to play though, but only when I'm old and shriveled. That's Mother Jones. That would be a great joy to do.

Actually, the kind of parts that I think are the most exciting to play and the most viable in terms of communication are characters that are complex; that is, characters that are full of contradictions that can be shown, that are in motion, that are trying to deal with problems that are real to people. I prefer films or any kind of cultural expression that strengthens rather than weakens people. That's why I would rather not play a villain's role or, if I did, I would want her to be at least moving in an upward direction. I think all of us are trying to figure out—what is a progressive movie, what is a revolutionary movie? Is it really possible to make a movie that is a weapon for political change? I don't know. I honest-to-God don't know. I do have the feeling that, at this stage, in this country anyway, it wouldn't necessarily be a film that offers a solution. I have a feeling that there is a kind of frustration that may be progressive at this point. Perhaps the best we can do now is create in the audience a sense of hopeful frustration. Perhaps they should leave the theatre with a sense of wanting to move and a feeling that there is good reason to move.

Q: Most of the films made by Americans who consider themselves leftists are documentaries. Why are there so few fiction films that are radical and that appeal to masses of people?

A: There's *Billy Jack* [1972]. Maybe you don't share my view of it. I think it was an extremely progressive film. You're not going to make a mass movie that is revolutionary. You're not going to make a *Battle of Algiers* [1967] that is a mass movie. I think it's important to do a picture that is going to be seen by a lot of people. *Billy Jack* takes the American superman as its main image, and that has to be improved on, but here you have a Vietnam veteran who comes to the aid of a minority people and you have a real debate about pacificism versus armed resistance. . . .

Q: You've expressed interest in doing a movie based on Harriet Arnow's *The Dollmaker*. Would such a film be more like *Grapes of Wrath* [1940] in terms of themes and characters? Is it likely we'll see such films if the recession should deepen into a major depression?

A: I think so, but we must always remember that it's not 1929 and nothing repeats itself. I wouldn't want *The Dollmaker* to be a downer the way a lot of the Depression films were. I think it can be hopeful. I met with Harriet Arnow and we both share the sense that it can be a positive movie. I disagree with the thinking in Hollywood on the part of producers that people don't want to think, that they only want to be entertained. People want to be led out of the morass or at least to have a little help in clearing away the confusion. The problem is what we said earlier. People who have a social vision haven't found a way to express it in a mass language. There's so much rhetoric and so much sectarianism. It gets manifested in the cultural field and I think that's why culture gets left in the hands of the entertainers.

Q: How would you rate your own film, *They Shoot Horses, Don't They?* [1969].

A: I think that was a movie a lot of people related to on a political level. The author of the book was definitely drawing an analogy with American society: the tragedy of all those people killing each other for a prize that doesn't exist at the behest of one man who they could replace if they were conscious of what was being done to them. I realize the shortcomings of the movie. The woman who does realize what is going on commits suicide. No, really something worse: she has a man kill her. I think for what is possible, however, it was a good movie. It would be wonderful if someone could go around with the movie and, after it was over, have a discussion with the audience about what it means. It's too bad that movies are sort of thrown out and left that way.

Q: You improvised the scene in the analyst's office in *Klute* [1971]. What does that mean exactly? Did you have any script to begin with, or what?

A: That was the last scene we shot, and by that time I knew the character very well. You find areas in yourself that relate to the character and then learn how those things are expressed differently than you would express them. By that time, I knew Bree well enough to improvise the scene. I think it worked real well. I didn't have to think about it too much, but I set myself certain tasks. Bree was the kind of woman who at a crucial point in her analysis would find an excuse, like it was costing too much or that it wasn't doing her any good, to keep from revealing another layer of herself. She would create barriers and conflicts. It was wonderful fun to do that scene. We did it real quick. We didn't do anything twice.

Q: That seems an example where the performer gets rid of the director and writer at least in one scene and sort of takes charge.

A: Not really. We all worked closely. The director and I had a lot of discussion beforehand about how the scene was going to be used and what we wanted to convey. It was his idea that the analyst be a woman and that was an important decision. Bree would not have talked the same way if it had been a male analyst. Someone else decided where the camera should be and that was important. What's so wonderful about movies and so frustrating if you're working in Hollywood is that filmmaking really is a collective effort even though the director has the final control. That's what seems exciting about filmmaking in a socialist country. Filmmaking is a socialized process. When it is working right, everyone is participating. The cameraman is doing the lighting and setting the angles in conjunction with what is being attempted in the overall effort. Everyone has thoroughly discussed and understood what is being undertaken.

I was very interested to talk to the film people in Vietnam. They described how everyone worked together. The performers, the directors, the technicians would discuss a story and carefully work out what was to be conveyed and how to tell a story. It would all be

Jane Fonda in still another prostitute role in Alan Myerson's *Steelyard Blues* (1972). (Courtesy Warner Communications)

done very collectively. The writers would then write and there would be more discussion. They all said this, laughing about the fact that everything takes so long.

Q: Sometimes in discussing the films you made before you became politically involved you seem defensive, especially about the subjects of nudity and sex. Nowadays the left is generally puritanical about sex, but this wasn't always so. At the turn of the century, leftists were attacked as often for their sexual beliefs as for their political beliefs.

A: I don't object to the movies I made because of the nudity in them. I don't think that nudity is the problem. It's how it's used. The problem is that movies that are made with sex and nudity, including some of the films I participated in, were exploitive of sex. *Barbarella* [1968] is a film that's always brought up, but as a matter of fact, I was hardly ever nude. Most of the pictures where I was dressed to the teeth and played a cute little ingenue were more exploitive than the ones with nudity because they portrayed women as silly, as mindless, as motivated purely by sex in relation to men. The simplest way to explain why women do that in this country is because there are limited avenues open to women to gain some power. One of the avenues is to marry a powerful man; another is to become a sex symbol. Things are changing slowly, but it used to be if a woman got offered one of those avenues, she didn't generally turn it down.

I don't think I'm particularly sexy. I don't know why I should be made a symbol of anything. At that time, it didn't occur to me to say, wait a minute, this isn't what I am. I never felt like Barbarella. I never felt like the American Brigitte Bardot. I always felt slightly out of focus. There was Jane and there was this public figure. It was extremely alienating. I never liked it. I never felt comfortable with it. I'm not defensive about it anymore. I think it's important to try to understand why women do that and how it is possible to change. It's hard to tell what a revolutionary future might bring. Some people think marriage should be abolished. Who knows? I believe that you can't build a mass movement around the questions of sex and marriage. I've been in a revolutionary society where marriage is very much an institution. It did not appear to be particularly oppressive for women because the power distribution within the institution is different than here. We would call Vietnam extremely puritanical. I think the importance that is placed on sex is a cultural thing. I don't think that in a healthy society there would be all the importance put on sex that we do. I don't think that in a healthy society you would have to show anybody naked on the screen. I don't think it would be an issue.

Q: You were in France in May of 1968. How did those events affect you?

A: . . . It didn't happen as dramatically for me as perhaps for Godard who looked out the window and there were his people in the streets. I looked at television and saw my people, where I came from, and I suddenly felt I was in the wrong place. I was extremely pregnant at the time. I lived in the country and my husband wouldn't let me go into Paris because I was about to give birth. I wanted to do something, yet I knew that wasn't my place. I subscribed to *Ramparts* and *The Village Voice* at the time and I read everything I could get my hands on. I identified with Joan Baez. It was new. It was like rumblings going on inside all the time. . . .

What was important about being in France was that for the first time I realized that it really could all come down. There were days there when we thought it was going to stop. Who would have thought that students and maybe workers were going to bring France to a halt. No gas. No food. No nothing. We were beginning to stockpile basic provisions. People were leaving Paris to come stay with us because we had a vegetable garden. Many of the people I knew were "at the barricades." It so happened that at that time my husband, Vadim, had just been made head of the union of cinema workers. So he was having to drive to Paris all the time for these mass meetings of all the movie people, including technicians and other workers, to decide if the studios were going to close down, or what. I just felt—let's get this baby out, I want to pack it up and go home, I want to get involved. And that's what I did.

Coup pour coup:
Radical French Cinema*

Julia Lesage

In France, the largest and strongest left-wing organization is the Communist Party. It controls the largest labor union (the CGT, Confédération Générale du Travail), has a whole mechanism for diffusing its ideas, and controls a certain stable percentage of the vote in each election. Yet in France, the CP seems conservative to many radicals, its goals of material progress being those of the middle class.

The maker of *Coup pour coup* (1972), Marin Karmitz, believes that the CGT is dominated by revisionist ideology. He sees the union as pushing for higher salaries but as having abandoned all politically and socially revolutionary goals.

Unlike that of Godard and Gorin, Marin Karmitz's commitment to make proletarian cinema is also a commitment to teach workers how to make their own films about their own struggles. His film *Camarades* [see "Towards a Proletarian Cinema," *Cinéaste*, 4, no. 3—Ed.] was the first in France after the uprisings in 1968 to have workers present their own image of themselves in a commercial 35mm film. Karmitz submitted *Camarades* (1970) to many intensive critiques by working-class audiences who told him all the ways in which they found the film inaccurate. In general, they judged this

* Reprinted from *Cinéaste*, 5, no. 3 (Summer 1972).

treatment of a young worker's coming to political awareness as the work of an "outsider," traditional in form and not a complete and just representation of themselves. However, as one young worker said in an interview in *Jeune Cinema* (February 1972), "We were really very happy that such a film just existed."

Karmitz's next film, *Coup pour coup* (*Blow for Blow*), is one of the few political films dealing with a French topic to have commercial success in France. It is the fictional reconstruction of various real strikes that occurred in 1968, here represented by women workers occupying a mill and garment factory where they sequester the boss. The protagonists are women workers, some of them young, some old, and there are no stars. It's rare to have women, especially in France, as heroines in films on some other basis than sophistication and sex. In this case the women workers *are* the film. A few professional actors play the "heavy" roles, such as factory director, union boss, floor manager, etc. Before shooting started, the workers criticized Karmitz's script and after their first revision it was revised again on location. The cast improvised their own dialogue when they thought the script sounded unnatural. Some of the scenes were shot with video tape and replayed so the workers could judge whether the desired naturalness had been achieved.

The women in the cast had participated in various similar real strikes and they knew the problems working women would face in the long-term occupation of a factory. The mothers all had to face the problem of who would care for their children. The unions made no demand for child care and never fought to get women's wages equal to men's. *Coup pour coup* shows the CGT as having no room at all for any feminist leadership, the one woman union representative being a well-dressed, pretty person in high heels who does nothing but echo the male head of the union local. Unsatisfactory as they are over a long term, wildcat strikes seem to be the only answer for women, and *Coup pour coup* prefigured the long Thionville strike in France, where the women had to conduct the strike on their own.

Coup pour coup opens on women sewing in an assembly line in a garment factory. The camera picks out faces of women on the line and then shows the ever-present efficiency expert checking how fast they work. The knowledge that these women are not actresses but really working women makes these early close-ups—of young and old faces alike—of special interest to the audience. One knows that theatrical films have not presented this image before. These women look beautiful precisely in their uniqueness, presented as themselves.

In the other section of the plant looms clack harshly with a noise that follows the women even as they go home. The sound track reintroduces this noise at various times, sometimes to show the intense mental fatigue workers on an assembly line suffer, later as an audio motif to show the insistence of the women on strike.

The clack of the mills changes to the chatter of the women in the locker room on payday, changing to go home and in a rush to get to the supermarket. From early in the film, there is an insistence that these women do double work—an eight-hour day as factory worker and then all the late afternoon and evening and early morning, too, as "homemaker." As the shift goes off and they are paid, one woman rushes to the bus stop, having no time to converse a few minutes with her friends. She explains in voice-over that she has to catch the early bus so she can make it to the supermarket and then home. In the supermarket she shops with one baby in the shopping cart and another toddler holding onto her hand. The loud clack of the looms continues on the sound track. This mother is too tired and too rushed to get her shopping done to even hear the conversation of her child, laughing and talking as he walks by her side. The scene changes to the back of an old flat where she is hauling now three children, one crying, and all her groceries up a flight of rickety stairs. Then she has dinner to prepare. Only after supper is there quiet, as she stands ironing baby clothes on the kitchen table, with the kids playing quietly near her on the kitchen floor. Suddenly the scene switches abruptly back to the factory, with the assembly line and all its noise. This whole sequence, set near the opening of the film, shows the daily routine of working mothers, and indicates why the occupation of a factory will be more difficult for them than it would be for men.

The image of children becomes a leitmotif for the film. After the women have started their strike and are occupying the factory, a sympathetic man—a fellow worker—comes to the gate to see what he can do to help. The woman who'd been shown earlier with her children in the supermarket gives the man her keys and asks him to take care of her children. As the women occupy the factory the first night, they build up a strike organization and also share a great deal of camaraderie. But they worry about their homes. The next day, they again gather by the gates under the sign defying the management and announcing to the world, "Factory occupied. The occupants are angry. SECOND DAY." Coming up to the gates, hauling a baby buggy and two toddlers, is the young man who'd offered to baby-sit. He says he just couldn't manage it. All the women on strike hoot and call him a coward. The babies are brought into the occupied mill and their mother takes them back into a floor manager's office as she tries to find a place for them to stay. Later on, the women turn this office into a nursery as more children are brought in. Humorously, the children are shown typically drawing on walls, making a mess, and needing baths and their diapers changed. In a scene critical of the union, the local union representative, a woman dressed up in a suit and high heels, comes in to complain about the mess; the women on shift in the nursery ask her to help but she refuses to do anything at all. Other scenes show children at strategy meetings, and finally the older ones taking their places outside with strikers.

The issue of children in working mothers' lives is not the main point of the film—women's ability to conduct a strike, even to the point of imprisoning their boss, is. All these scenes with children, however, show in a cumulative way how the economic system fragments working mothers' lives. The capitalist system makes child care somehow different and separate from working in a factory. The reason corporations do not want to bring a woman's two labors together is that they would then have to admit that child care is part of a woman's real work and that mothers should have both facilities and equal pay for this labor that they now do for free.

Child care as unpaid labor is specifically a woman's problem, not a man's, and *Coup pour coup* shows very clearly that working women get no help from unions in this regard. The women are not only oppressed by factory bosses but must also reject the union since it refuses to recognize their needs. And even on the level of comradeship, a fellow male worker wouldn't handle the same burden of child care that was standard for the women. The male head of the union local, dressed nicely in a suit and tie, comes out to talk to these women, to call them his "comrades," and to try to get them to accept a settlement that would let the factory fire the militants. We see him on the telephone talking to a higher union official—also male. This one then phones what must be a high-ranking official of the Communist Party—all three looking very comfortably middle class and handsomely masculine. "Keep on negotiating," the top official says to the union boss. "How would it look in your union to have a factory occupied by women? Negotiate. Later on you can start separating the healthy elements from the sick."

Needless to say, *Coup pour coup* was offensive to the unions. It does not present all the oppressors as men, however, for the time-and-motion controller is a woman, as is one of the local union heads. In the main body of the film, however, women, portrayed by real workers, find themselves capable of carrying on their own strike. The camera style and the sound track, as well as the incident itself, dignify the role of the working woman, who is usually most under-paid and least respected by management and union alike. These women's faces are seen as beautiful. Their dialogue is caught naturally; their voices are never ponderous but laughing and joking, even during tense moments of the strike.

At the end of the film, the names of everyone who worked on the film appear in alphabetical order, their task on the film following their name. The credits last about ten minutes and labels like "worker," "*cinéaste*," "painter," "musician," "student," "teacher," and "high school student" are used. But most of the names are followed by the label "*ouvrière*"—"woman worker." The audience sometimes find this list of participants as moving as the film itself and stay through to the end to applaud even though they don't know the individual participants.

On *Sambizanga**

Sarah Maldoror

Introduction

Black feminist and revolutionist Sarah Maldoror, real name Sarah Ducados, was born in France of parents who emigrated from Guadeloupe in the French West Indies. She founded a Paris theatrical group, Les Griotes, in 1956 and adapted works of Jean-Paul Sartre and Aimé Césaire to the stage. Following the path of Senegalese filmmaker Sembene Ousmane, she studied at the Moscow Film Academy under Mark Donskoi. She was an assistant director for the Algerian Ahmed Lallem and then made her first short, Monangambéee (1969). It was based on a short story by white Angolan writer-activist, Luandino Vieira, who was deported to a Portuguese concentration camp in 1961. The title, Monangambéee, was the call used by the anticolonialist forces in Angola to signal a village meeting.

In this seventeen-minute film, shot with amateur actors in Algeria, Maldoror told of an impoverished black woman who visits her husband, wrongly imprisoned, in the miserable jails of Luanda, Angola's capital city. Maldoror has explained her strategy, "I wanted people to get a feeling of how the prisons are in the Portuguese colonies. When the woman visits . . ., she winds up in a hermeti-

* Excerpted from *Women and Film*, 1, nos. 5 and 6 (1974).

305

cally sealed cellar atmosphere in which the men, all pushed to-gether, are just waiting. What are they waiting for? They're waiting to be sent away—to anywhere, nobody knows."

In 1970 Maldoror acted in a fiction feature about the liberation movement in Guinea-Bissau, the Algerian-made Des Fusils pour Banta (Guns for Banta). *In 1971 she directed* The Future of St. Denis, *a documentary on the Commune, and she worked on a collective film project,* Louise Michel, La Commune et Nous, *about the most renowned woman of the Paris Commune, who supported a new type of school in which girls would have equal rights to educa-tion. Both projects were sponsored by the French Communist Party.*

In 1972 Sarah Maldoror made her ambitious, 103-minute revolu-tionary feature Sambizanga *in the People's Republic of the Congo. The film was released prior to the expulsion of the Portuguese from Angola, and the gradual internal victory there of the MPLA—the Marxist-oriented Popular Movement for the Liberation of Angola.*

In 1974 Maldoror was living in St. Denis, a suburb outside Paris, trying to obtain funding for the project described below, a film based on King Christopher, *the play by black poet Aimé Césaire. Maldoror has two children and is married to Mario de Andrade, Angolan writer and leader in the liberation struggles.*

These notes on Sarah Maldoror are based on material that origi-nally appeared in Women and Film *magazine. The following essay combines a short explanatory piece by Maldoror on* Sambizanga *along with her answers to questions on other facets of her career in an interview by Elin Clason in Sweden. The Maldoror material appeared originally in* Film & TV *(Stockholm), and was translated for* Women and Film.

I am one of those modern women who try to combine work and family life, and just like it is for all the others, it's a problem for me. Children need a home and a mother. That's why I try to prepare and edit my films in Paris during the long summer vacation when the children are free and can come along. . . .

My situation is a very difficult one. I make films about liberation movements. But, the money for such film production is to be found

not in Africa, but in Europe. For that reason, I have to live where
the money is to be raised, and then do my work in Africa.

To begin, *Sambizanga* is a story taken from reality: a liberation
fighter, one of the many, dies from severe torture. But my chief
concern with this film was to make Europeans, who hardly know
anything about Africa, conscious of the forgotten war in Angola,
Mozambique, and Guinea-Bissau. And when I address myself to
Europeans that is because it is the French distribution companies
who determine whether the people in Africa will get to see a certain
film or not. After twelve years of independence, it is your companies
—UGC, Nef, Claude Nedjar, and Vincent Malle—who hold in their
hands the fate of a possible African distribution for *Sambizanga.*

At any rate, I don't want to make a "good little Negro" film.
People often reproach me for that. They also blame me for making a
technically perfect film like any European could do. But, technology
belongs to everyone. "A talented Negro . . ." you can relegate that
concept to my French past.

In this film I tell the story of a woman. It could be any woman, in
any country, who takes off to find her husband. The year is 1961.
The political consciousness of the people has not yet matured. I'm
sorry if this situation is not seen as a "good one," and if this doesn't
lead to a heightened consciousness among the audience as to what
the struggle in Africa is all about. I have no time for films filled with
political rhetoric.

In the village where Maria lives, the people have no idea at all
what "independence" means. The Portuguese prevent the spread of
any information and a debate on the subject is impossible. They
even prevent the people from living according to their own traditional culture.

If you feel that this film can be interpreted as being "negative,"
then you're falling into the same trap that many of my Arab
brothers did when they reproached me for not showing any Portuguese bombs or helicopters in the film. However, the bombs only
began to rain on us when we became conscious; the helicopters
have only recently appeared—you sell them to the Portuguese and

they buy them precisely because of our consciousness. For, not too long ago, people here believed that all that was happening in Angola was a minor tribal war. They didn't reckon with our will to become an independent nation: could it be true that we Angolese were like them, the Portuguese? . . . no, that wouldn't be possible! . . .

I'm against all forms of nationalism. What does it in fact mean to be French, Swedish, Senegalese, or Guadeloupian? Nationalities and borders between countries have to disappear. Besides this, the color of a person's skin is of no interest to me. What's important is what the person is doing. . . .

I'm no adherent of the concept of the "Third World." I make films so that people—no matter what race or color they are—can understand them. For me there are only exploiters and the exploited, that's all. To make a film means to take a position, and when I take a position, I am *educating* people. The audience has a need to know that there's a war going on in Angola, and I address myself to those among them who want to know more about it. In my films, I show them a people who are busy preparing themselves for a fight and all that that entails in Africa: that continent where everything is extreme—the distances, nature, etc. Liberation fighters are, for example, forced to wait until the elephants have passed them by. Only then can they cross the countryside and transport their arms and ammunition. Here, in the West, the Resistance used to wait until dark. We wait for the elephants. You have radios, information—we have nothing.

Some say that they don't see any oppression in the film. If I wanted to film the brutality of the Portuguese, then I'd shoot my films in the bush. What I wanted to show in *Sambizanga* is the aloneness of a woman and the time it takes to march. . . .

I'm only interested in women who struggle. These are the women I want to have in my films, not the others. I also offer work to as many women as possible during the time I'm shooting my films. You have to support those women who want to work with film. Up until now, we are still few in number, but if you support those women in film who are around, then slowly our numbers will grow. That's the way the men do it, as we all know. Women can work in whatever field they want. That means in film, too. The main thing is that they themselves want to do it. Men aren't likely to help women do that. Both in Africa and in Europe woman remains the slave of man. That's why she has to liberate herself. . . .

People know nothing about Africa. That's why I want to make my next film about King Christopher, a Haitian slave who led a rebellion that ended in a defeat for Napoleon, and then named himself king.

In this film I want to show that Africa also has a history, that Africans are not historyless savages, but that there have been many outstanding people coming out of the culture of Africa. Aimé Césaire has given me all the liberty I want to rework the script. The film won't only concern itself with events that took place more than one hundred years ago, but will also deal with the Africa of today and will include documentary material on Malcolm X, George Jackson, Amilcar Cabral, Schou Touré of Guinea, and others. The film will offer an answer as to why African countries which got their "independence" in the 1950s failed to keep it in the true sense of the word. By using King Christopher as an example, I'll try to compare his failure with the failure of these "independent" African states.

King Christopher will be shot in Cuba. The Cubans have already promised all the help they can give as far as food and lodging and transportation are concerned. What still remains though is the raising of the necessary money for all the rest: actors and actresses, costumes, raw stock, etc. . . .

No African country, with the exception of Algeria, has its own distribution company. In the French-speaking areas of Africa, distribution is handled by a monopoly that is in French hands. There is not one *cinemathèque* nor even a so-called art cinema . . . All too often, you hear that there is no African film, or that if there is, it's just Jean Rouch. That's to make it easy for those who say such things. One day, we'll come to France and shoot a film, then we'll show the African people our view of France—that'll be an entertaining film . . .

The Swedish, the Italian films and the films of other countries did not sprout up like mushrooms from the earth. In Africa there are several young people who are really talented filmmakers. We have to put an end to the lack of knowledge and the utter ignorance that people have about the special problem of Africa.

Personally, I feel that Sembene Ousmane is the most talented of our directors. He's often reproached for financing his films with French capital. So what! The most important thing is that we have to develop a cultural policy that can help us. Show to the world that such a thing as African film does exist. We have to teach ourselves to sell our films ourselves and then get them distributed. Today we are like small sardines surrounded by sharks. But, the sardines will grow up. They'll learn how to resist the sharks . . .

Part-Time Work of a Domestic Slave, or Putting the Screws to Screwball Comedy*

Karyn Kay

Part-Time Work of a Domestic Slave, the third feature[1] of West German director Alexander Kluge, revolves around six months in the life of one Rosewitha Bronski—at twenty-nine, wife, mother, abortionist, and growing political activist. Rosewitha is a part-time personality; partly in the home, functioning as wife and mother; partly in the factory, organizing workers; partly working as an abortionist. (Like Mother Courage, the Brecht protagonist who feeds off the Thirty Years War to keep her family and finances intact, Rosewitha absurdly performs abortions to afford more children of her own.) Rosewitha's life is anarchic—in bits and pieces of half-shaped ideas and unresolved actions against the disorder and injustices surrounding her: doctors who don't pay fees, factories plotting relocation, husband and children screaming for attention.

Kluge likewise disjoints his narrative with basic Brechtian alienating devices, interjecting voice-over and filmic inserts as comments on Rosewitha's domestic and political activities. Her story is told in Epic/episodic fashion, with the film divided into two major segments: the first half focusing on her family life and abortion prac-

* Reprinted, with additional material, from *Film Quarterly,* 24, no. 1 (Fall 1975) and 29, no. 4 (Summer 1976).

[1] Alexander Kluge's two previous films are *Yesterday Girl* (1967) and *Artists Under the Big Top* (1968). Alexandra Kluge, the director's sister, played Rosewitha Bronski in *Part-Time Work of a Domestic Slave* and Anita G., the heroine of *Yesterday Girl.*

tice, while the second half follows Rosewitha outside the home and into political organizing. The parts are bridged by discussions and debates between Rosewitha and a female comrade about "what to do politically."

Rosewitha is married to Franz, a gloomy, unemployed chemist. He piles books across the floors, walls, windows, and cracked crevices of their pinhole apartment. He hates their life, is ill-tempered, and bickers about Rosewitha's friends, the children, baby-sitting, her sloppiness, laziness, tardiness, et cetera and et cetera. He admonishes Rosewitha, "Why isn't dinner ready? Can't you keep the children quiet? Don't you know I'm studying?," and secretly dreams of foreign employment, release from domestic ties.

Rosewitha met Franz in school, where she was a chemistry student too. Now, between family and abortions, she possesses neither time nor energy for intellectual pursuits. Rosewitha borrows books from the local library, hoping to keep up with Franz's cerebral activities. But the demands of her small child interrupt her studies, and piles of unread volumes collect upside down on her desk. The texts are digested by Franz, who afterward lectures Rosewitha on their contents.

Pathetic Rosewitha—the situation is stultifying. Yet it gets worse. When a police investigation forces her to abandon her lucrative abortion business, Rosewitha is confined to home. While Franz takes a dreaded factory job, Rosewitha is the domestic slave in the truest sense, no longer fulfilling any function beyond the boundaries of her family. And she hates this life as surely as Franz loathed their prior existence. Satisfaction can be reached only through some meaningful, but as yet undefined, cause. Rosewitha takes to political activity.

Rosewitha and Sylvia, her ex-partner in the abortion business, begin a process of radical education. They read: newspapers, pamphlets, political tracts—anything. They listen to and try memorizing words from Brecht's *Threepenny Opera*. They partake of investigative excursions through West German tenements and demand that the city newspaper print atrocity stories about the local factory and slum conditions. But the women are too disorganized to know what they want the stories to say.

Rosewitha and Sylvia finally find a concrete political issue. They discover the factory's secret plans to relocate—an illegal act that would leave nearly all the workers, including Franz, unemployed. The women get jobs in the factory, join the union, intent upon mobilizing a workers' force against management. They distribute leaflets among the employees, paint slogans on the factory walls, rifle confidential files searching for proof of the pending move (with Rosewitha nearly getting shot in one such midnight raid). But they never find the evidence and they fail to motivate—and even alienate—the factory workers.

Sylvia returns home, and Rosewitha continues alone, traveling to a distant city where she uncovers material proof that a new factory is being built. But, in her fervor, Rosewitha neglects to bring a camera to record the evidence, and the trip is wasted. She returns home to discover that Franz has lost his job due to her agitation, and the factory has publicly announced its decision *not* to move. It seems Rosewitha has made a mess out of everything.

Yet, even after her setbacks, Rosewitha continues to challenge the economic and social morass around her. She is last observed selling sausages in a kiosk located outside the factory gates. And "the troublemaker Bronski" wraps her goods in precious political leaflets.

At times it appears that director Kluge is making a mockery of Rosewitha as he comments on her political methodology—individualized struggle, initiated as much out of fear of domestic servitude as out of true political commitment. One minute Rosewitha is portrayed as a loon, barely capable of functioning, driving her automobile into other parked cars. Yet the next instant she is seen capably hammering out the dented fender so she can drive home and—good citizen—leaving a note of explanation to the smashed auto's owner. She appears a proficient abortionist (with graphic, if not necessarily accurate, details of her work shown on the screen). She is confident enough to call the needed help for dangerously ill clients, including those carelessly treated by other abortionists. But when she is angered by a doctor who mistreats her, calls her "lowlife," and refuses to pay her referral fee, Rosewitha demolishes his car with a hammer. (Interestingly, it is the same tool she used to mend the other car.)

The terrific gut satisfaction of her action swiftly disappears with knowledge that she has lost her referral fee and, for related reasons, her abortion practice as well. As noted earlier, Rosewitha travels far investigating the factory but is too addled to bring a camera to record her findings, also too flustered to report conditions for the local newspaper. She prowls the factory at midnight, risking her life from a management assassin's bullet, but she fails to organize the workers.

If Rosewitha and Sylvia are to sit home memorizing Brecht, they would do well minding the solid advice Mother Courage offers a young soldier in the scene of "The Great Capitulation." Her words seem a reference to Rosewitha's hammer-wielding method of fighting social injustice, as she distinguishes between what Eric Bentley calls "the anger of a sudden fit, which boils up and over and is gone," and the anger which "informs . . . of long years of change."[2] Mother Courage preaches: "How long won't you stand for injustice? One hour? Or two? . . . I only say your rage won't last. You'll get nowhere with it, it's a pity. If your rage was a long one, I'd urge you on. Slice him up, I'd advise. But what's the use if you don't slice him up? . . . They know us through and through . . ."

Rosewitha must prepare for the long haul; the struggle that doesn't quit quickly; the anger that transcends the smashing of a car. Rosewitha is a dynamo, but she is flaying futilely in the context of undisciplined political consciousness, removed from ideology. Like Vera Chytilova's crazy nihilists, Mary I and Mary II of *Daisies* (1966), who decide that "since everything is rotten in this world, we too shall be rotten," Rosewitha must learn that there is more to righting the rotten world than tearing about outrageously.

The narrative of *Part-Time Work of a Domestic Slave* is intercut by Kluge with clips from the 1934 Soviet film *Chapayev*. As these segments are shown, a narrator comments, "Rosewitha knows the power of ideas . . . She has seen it proven in films." From *Cha-*

---

[2] Eric Bentley, ed., *Mother Courage* (New York: Grove Press, 1963).

payev, Kluge suggests, Rosewitha can gain her most significant political lesson. (Is Kluge taking a seemingly Stalinist[3] position in advocating that Rosewitha learn from this particular Russian movie?) *Chapayev* concerns the famous peasant general who fought with the Leninists against the White Russians. Chapayev (a Stalin surrogate?) was an enthusiast, a talented amateur tactician, who acted impulsively and emotionally rather than theoretically. In the film, an educated, urban Leninist teaches Chapayev temperance and ideology, and when he leaves, Chapayev hugs him. He loves this man who has educated him to become "a great leader" at last. Because so many of Rosewitha's mistakes stem from tempestuous political behavior, her solution, like the Chapayev in the movie, is to develop temperance, ideology, and a sound political program.

To begin: instead of pushing off into factory organizing, perhaps the women should start with issues of greatest relevance and immediacy to their own lives. One problem is that Rosewitha and Sylvia never direct their political activity inward, to analyzing their family situations. Quotations from Engels on the obsolescence of the family flash across the screen, yet Sylvia and Rosewitha are loath to challenge this basic institution that truly oppresses them. The women are so consumed by their families that even when they discover outside causes to promote, they fret and worry over their unattended households. Finally, Sylvia drops out, feeling the political work interferes too seriously with her domestic obligations. Unfortunately there is no wise theoretician around to explain that political work begins at home. Rosewitha and Sylvia need to integrate radical feminism into their political theory. As wives and mothers and childbearers, their workplace is primarily in the home and secondarily in the factory.

---

[3] It should be noted that *Chapayev* was used as a tool against Eisenstein and other innovative Soviet filmmakers by Stalinist theoreticians. *Chapayev* is a nonmontage, psychological drama about the personal relationships between elite heroes—the differences from early Eisenstein are obvious. The film was made by Sergei and Georgi Vasiliev, based on the memoirs of Dimitri Fumonov, the real Chapayev's political commissar. It was released in 1934 in honor of the fifteenth anniversary of Soviet cinema. It was just subsequently that Eisenstein received his most searing public rebuke when he was by-passed for the Order of Lenin.

Perhaps Rosewitha and Sylvia should be agitating toward legalized abortion. As Kluge pointed out in a recent interview,[4] women, like the working class, should demand control over the means of production—or, in this case, the processes of reproduction. But instead of politicizing toward change in the abortion laws—an issue hotly debated in West German courts around the time Kluge's film was in production—the women give abortions on the sly and seem to accept the establishment's estimation of themselves as "lowlife." They possess no apparent awareness of the intrinsically subversive nature of their abortions because they have no analysis of their role as women within the workers' revolution. For instance, Rosewitha confronts a former abortion client whose life she once saved. The woman now works for the bosses and is embarrassed by their encounter. Both women fail to recognize the feminist bonds that unite them.

Furthermore, Kluge seems to believe that Rosewitha acts alone too much of the time. Without a support group, allies in the workplace, Rosewitha remains vulnerable to the factory management. Perhaps subconsciously, Rosewitha understands the need for organized, collective action. When the police begin their investigation of her abortion business, she, Franz, and Sylvia avoid prosecution by working together. Franz goes to jail for Rosewitha while she and Sylvia clean out the office, even using a watchdog in their trickster plot to outwit the cops. The three function cooperatively and, through their mutual efforts, avoid catastrophe.

For all her mistakes, Rosewitha is not, after all, a hopeless fool. She is learning by trial and error how to use her anger constructively, and she IS unstoppable. As Kluge comments about her, "Rosewitha, whose path in my opinion is closer to the right one—because it is more effective, more practical—has more opportunities for making mistakes. The only possible way to avoid making mistakes is to do nothing."[5]

In the last shots of the film, Rosewitha sells sausages and passes out propaganda in her little station-on-wheels, strategically located

---

[4] Jan Dawson, "The Invisible, Indivisible Man: An Interview with Alexander Kluge," *Film Comment*, 10, no. 6 (November–December 1974).

[5] *Ibid.*

just beyond the factory portals. She is spied upon by the fearful management lackeys, and viewed by the bosses as a dangerous, inimical force. She is a volatile revolutionary whose efforts cannot be dampened even by the firing of her husband or threats against her life.

Most significant: because vending profits are presumably the Bronskis' sole means of support, Rosewitha's responsibilities to her family are soundly united for the first time with her political activities. Mother Courage's wagon is turned toward the revolution.

The most striking and perhaps most radical feature of *Part-Time Work of a Domestic Slave* is its structure, for the Kluge film is a farce that subverts the essential form and theme of "screwball comedy." Surprisingly, the dramatic beginnings of this genre can be traced back beyond Shakespeare's *Taming of the Shrew*, all the way to the obscure "Noah" plays of the medieval cycles. In the locking of horns of Noah and the aggressive, crazy Mrs. Noah, the threat to marriage, and the correct world order of male domination of the family, screwball comedy takes root.

The typical plot of these Noah farces, found in every mystery play cycle, is something of this sort: God tells Noah of the torrential rain to come as punishment against earthly sinners and advises Noah to build an ark and to take aboard his wife, three sons, and their spouses. But when Noah orders his wife aboard, she refuses to budge at all. In *The Wakefield Noah*[6] she refuses because she is weaving and can't be bothered to leave home. Besides she resents men bossing their wives around. In *The Chester Noah*[7] the wife refuses to board the boat unless her friends, The Gossips, can accompany her; and similarly, in *The York Noah*,[8] Mrs. Noah won't go unless she can bring her relatives aboard to safety. Anyway, she thinks Noah is insane.

Mrs. Noah acts perversely, proudly exhibiting behavior that

[6] Robert B. Heilman, ed., *An Anthology of English Drama Before Shakespeare* (New York: Holt, Rinehart & Winston, 1967), pp. 23–43.

[7] Alexander Franklin, *Seven Miracle Plays* (London: Oxford University Press, 1963), pp. 38–52.

[8] J. S. Purvis, *The York Cycle of Mystery Plays* (London: Society for Promoting Christian Knowledge, 1957), pp. 45–58.

feminist scholar Rosemary Woolf terms "irrational obduracy."[9] Mrs. Noah hangs about drinking and risking her life—anything at all but obey her husband. She is in league with all the cantankerous wives and lovers "common to . . . misogynistic literature, Latin satire, sermons, comic poems, and fabliaux." These women are seen by their male creators as Eves and Pandoras, hazarding everything, including death, for the pure pleasure of contradicting their husbands. (In *The Art of Courtly Love*, Andreas Capellanus cites approvingly the case of the clever man who killed his bellicose wife simply by cautioning her *not* to drink poisoned liquor.) In her excellent feminist volume, *The English Mystery Plays*, Woolf warns the reader that in the Chester deluge ". . . the attachment of Noah's wife to her friends might be taken as a sympathetic sign of human feeling, which the authors manifestly do not intend."

V. A. Kolve, in the authoritative critical work, *The Play Called Corpus Christi*, contends that Noah's wife is treated with genuine empathy by the Chester author. Yet however understandable her motives, Mrs. Noah's Falstaffian desire to remain drinking with her friends still can not be allowed any more than merrymaker Falstaff could be carried over by Shakespeare into *Henry V*.[10] The wellmeaning Mrs. Noah (the Chester playwright according to Kolve) performs the same ill functions as the troublemaking Mrs. Noah (the Chester playwright according to Woolf). She jeopardizes the lives of her family who wait for her—and they are the very lifeline of the human race if it is to survive the flood. She disobeys her husband. She disobeys God.

The Noah plays remind and reaffirm for the medieval audience the rightful order of the universe as God ordained in Genesis: "Unto the woman He said: '. . . thy desire shall be to thy husband, and *he shall rule over thee.'* "

This command established the proper world order. God rules the universe, master of all creation. But man rules woman. Eve is taught the lesson for all her future sisters to follow.

<hr>

[9] Rosemary Woolf, *The English Mystery Plays* (Berkeley: University of California Press, 1972).

[10] V. A. Kolve, *The Play Called Corpus Christi* (Stanford, Calif.: Stanford University Press, 1966).

In refusing to enter the ark, the reckless, insubordinate Mrs. Noah blasphemes outrageously. She essentially re-creates the conditions of the first Fall, the original sin (even to the literal inclusion of the devil as her adviser in the Newcastle play of Noah). Mrs. Noah—"off-spring of that initial mistake in marital 'maistrye'" (Kolve)— must relearn Eve's lesson. Salvation depends on obedience to one's husband as much as to God. Kolve continues:

> . . . "maistrye" . . . serves as a major principle . . . in the cycles . . . it is the notion that all things exist in their proper degree . . . the lower shall be subject to the higher. God is greater, stronger, more worshipful than the angels, the angels are above man, man is above woman . . . So the progression goes, with obedience as its binding force and stability the proper condition within it. The alternative was . . . chaos and sin.

Mrs. Noah's comic disobedience leads to cosmic disorder. The world flung awry. In the typical middle section of the plays, Noah and his wife accuse, scream at, and clout each other, with the sons and daughters-in-law joining in the tumult, urging Mrs. Noah to board the ship before the floods come. At last Mrs. Noah gives in and enters the ark. Mr. Noah is victorious in the battle of wills and even the physical struggle with his obstinate wife.

Northrop Frye has written: "The theme of the comic is the integration of society, which usually takes the form of incorporating a central character into it . . . in Christian literature it is the theme of salvation" ("The Mythos of Spring: Comedy," *The Anatomy of Criticism*).

As a comic rebel, Mrs. Noah sits on the periphery of society when she drinks with her gossips, the sinners about to die. She is reintegrated into the familial community when she enters the ark— dragged bodily toward salvation. The conclusion of the Noah play marks the beginning of the new world. God ends the destruction, and the Noah family quarrels cease—Mrs. Noah is docile now. With the final sending off of the raven and the dove, salvation is assured. And the proper, heavenly ordained, man-above-woman world order is reaffirmed.[11]

[11] The idea of looking to medieval drama was suggested to me by Gerald Peary.

Back to the movies! In modern screwball comedies the narrative inevitably unwinds to a reiteration of this man-above-woman world order. In his autobiography Frank Capra refers to *It Happened One Night* (1934), the paradigmatic screwball tale, as a sort of contemporary *Taming of the Shrew* (whose character, as Kolve notes, finds a "root-form" in Mrs. Noah). Capra's "shrew" is Ellie (Claudette Colbert)—the bored and bratty heiress. When Ellie dives off her father's yacht, she plunges into the flood waters, the deep blue sea of the "real world." She's never been on her own before, and she can't get along alone. Ellie is a baby—throwing food at her father in a temper tantrum, losing her bus ticket, and finally wanting to spend her last pennies on candy. She needs guidance, someone to protect and amuse her and, yes, hold her in line during Daddy's absence. That man is reporter Peter Warne (Clark Gable)—the real "King" (as his newsroom comrades call him). Ellie's fiancé, literally named King Westly, is just a pretender to Ellie's throne, a weak-willed buffoon who wants to skydive into his wedding.

Peter is of the practical world, not from outer space. If Ellie is a brat, he is punk enough to put her in place. Peter functions as a patriarchal surrogate. He carries Ellie across the creek (she doesn't swim anymore). And when she tells him she hasn't ridden piggyback since childhood, he spanks her—both cute acts Daddy used to perform. Peter also protects her from a potential seducer and shelters her from a storm. Mr. Andrews happily gives Ellie away to Peter—a younger, more virile version of himself—for Peter knows *how* to tame this shrew. He tells Ellie's father—who agrees heartily—she needs to be spanked once a day, whether she deserves it or not. Mr. Andrews not only approves marriage between Ellie and Peter but, in fact, aggressively conspires to unite them. He even plants a getaway car with Peter in it for Ellie's quick escape from the wedding ceremony to King.

The father's final role in this marriage plot—a bizarre part—is to send off the message allowing Ellie and Peter to "drop the walls of Jericho"—a motel blanket that has stood between them in their battle of the sexes. Like the "Captain of the Lord's Host" who ad-

vised Joshua in battling Jericho and felling those infamous walls,
Mr. Andrews takes over as heavenly messenger, signaling his children to consummate their wedding vows. Marital sex is OK in a
world restored to its proper man-above-woman order. Gable dominates Colbert with her father's (God the Father!) complete approval. Ellie's short-lived revolt is over, just as quickly as Mrs.
Noah's. She has gained neither true independence from her father
nor a marriage of equals. She has simply learned—as all spoiled
female adolescents must—to listen to her father and to her man
and not to be a runaway. Like God in the Noah plays, her father
turns out to be infinitely wise, knowing from the start that King
Westly is the wrong guy, but that Peter is perfect for his daughter.
Ellie is back on the ark.

In *Woman of the Year* (George Stevens, 1942) Katharine Hepburn and Spencer Tracy reverse traditional family roles and
menace the male-dominated world structure. She is the important
news reporter, he, the simple sports writer. He mopes when she
ignores his new hat or forgets a dinner appointment. He wants children; she doesn't. He cooks; she can't. In a rage at her familial in-
sensitivity, Tracy walks out the night she is named Woman of the
Year. Wanting to make amends, Hepburn sneaks into his now
bachelor flat to cook a surprise breakfast, which she completely
messes up. But Tracy forgives her. She is the wife, and he is the
boss, as he takes control by shoving her male secretary out the
kitchen door and down a flight of stairs to end the movie.

In Lewis Milestone's 1931 production of *The Front Page*, Adolph
Menjou, as editor, becomes a boss/God figure to Pat O'Brien's
Noah/reporter, Hildy, with the female fiancée placed in her structurally correct, secondary position. And even Hawks's seemingly
unorthodox *His Girl Friday* ends by reaffirming the Noah form.
Rosalind Russell as Hildy discards proper marriage to Ralph Bellamy for work on the newspaper and remarriage to the nasty editor,
Cary Grant. The essential power pattern reasserts itself: woman
reporter gives in to her bullying husband/editor. Hildy climbs
aboard the ark when she resumes her position behind the reporter's desk and throws Ralph Bellamy back into the sea.

In *Part-Time Work of a Domestic Slave,* Kluge, whether consciously or unconsciously, sabotages the basic Noah screwball mold, and breaks with its ancient and conventional conclusion of reasserting the male-dominated family order. As self-involved as Mrs. Noah, Rosewitha does do a series of crazy stunts that jeopardize her family and threaten her relationship with Franz. She performs abortions, which land him in jail, and also forces him from unemployment to the factory job he's resisted. And later her agitation in the factory causes Franz to be thrown out of work all over again.

Yet Rosewitha never reforms and never again functions as Franz's humbled, dutiful wife. In the film's last frame she is outside her home selling sausages, continuing to disrupt the society (epitomized by the factory) in which she exists. The bosses, the gods of this farce, carry no influence over Rosewitha, even when they use bullets. Neither does Franz—she shrugs when she finds out her husband has been fired. In refusing to enter the ark, Rosewitha remains a threat to the male-dominated, family oriented, capitalist power structure. Nothing runs smoothly or complacently while Rosewitha is around to cause trouble, not even the ordained world order.

Perhaps I lay my claims to the relationship between screwball comedy and the medieval Noah plays a bit too stiffly. Although I do perceive an affinity between the two forms, it is not my intention to posit an intractable or reductive formula upon which to hang all comedy (marriage=screwball comedy=oppression).

To know a structure is not to know a film. This is only the most primary step—the beginning of analysis. Do structures "mean"?—as Frye would suggest of the comic structure's essential conservatism? Perhaps. Then to see how, in individual cases, an innate structure and its "meaning" is manipulated, transformed, commented upon, reaffirmed, or subverted is to understand the strategies of artistic works, to understand the shaping effects of social-historical forces, to detect the differences between one director's work and that of another.

Yet screwball comedies do seem to obey the form of the medieval Noah plays, the battles of husband and wife that I have tried to show end up as homiletics about the need for wives to obey husbands. Some screwball comedies not only go along with the form of the medieval dramas but the conservative theme also—*It Happened One Night*. Other films borrow the form, but gloriously subvert the theme: my choice, *Part-Time Work of a Domestic Slave*.

Interview with Lina Wertmuller

Peter Biskind

INTRODUCTION

Lina Wertmuller is the latest victim of the American critical wars, blown to pieces as she picks her way across the difficult terrain of film and feminism, stumbling over buried mines, booby traps, and unexploded shells. Everyone takes sides, stakes out and defends extreme positions, for or against: Seven Beauties (1975) *is the best film since* Citizen Kane (1941); Seven Beauties *is fascist trash. In the inflationary climate of film reviewing, in this atmosphere of escalating rhetoric, only the wildest claims purchase our attention.*

Wertmuller's first film in American release, The Lizards (1963), *grew moldy from a decade of disuse, sitting on the 16mm shelves of a distributor in Tulsa, Oklahoma. Her first picture shown here theatrically,* Love and Anarchy (1973), *was received with coterie respect but passed almost unnoticed among the populace. Its mixture of comedy and politics confused audiences more used to Mary Tyler Moore than to Malatesta, and certainly unaccustomed to a mixture of the two. But the wolfish farcing of Giancarlo Giannini seduced a mass audience to* The Seduction of Mimi (1972), *and* Swept Away (1974) *brought throngs of young lovers, budding intellects, feminists, and antifeminists back into the art houses. Her last,* Seven Beauties, *was hailed as almost everyone's personally*

324

*discovered masterpiece, each twitch of her camera likened to a
brushstroke of Leonardo, a flourish of Botticelli.*

*For a time, a blizzard of interviews and television appearances
made Wertmuller's tiny figure, white glasses, red tent dress, and riot
of rings, beads, and bracelets, as familiar as Barbara Walters. Interviewers reported her opinions on everything from Marx to Mary
Hartman, downplaying, of course, and sometimes drowning out
what Wertmuller, director, had to say of her pictures. Although her
opinions and intentions are not privileged discourse, they add a
dialectic dimension to the films.*

P. B.

Q: Many feminists were shocked and offended by *Swept Away*
(1974), in which Giancarlo Giannini beats and rapes Mariangela
Melato, and she seems to like it. Do you consider yourself a
feminist?

A: Very much. But when I hear people asking why women are hit
in *Swept Away*, I see that this way of looking at the film is very
superficial. It is clear to me that *Swept Away* is a juxtaposition of two
social classes, in the sense of who stays above, and who stays below,
who gains power, and who loses it. Giancarlo always plays Sicilians
in my films, which for me is a symbol of the south of all the world,
the subproletarians, the women, the people below. I use very easy
symbols. I know symbols are supposed to be mysterious, but I'm
looking for a direct language for a popular cinema.

The scene where he hits her is clearly a certain type of revolution,
and the love that happens between the two of them is a love which
the intellectual bourgeoisie always has for the Third World. It
would have been the same had they both been men, or both been
women. I realize that the appearance of the female body, and the
male body, creates misunderstandings in the interpretation of my
meaning by feminists. And this really makes me sad. I've absolutely
been a feminist all my life. I've always worked for civil rights, but I
would like the word *feminist* to have a social significance. That
seems to me most important.

The feminists who have mistaken my films are conservative, bourgeois feminists. They would be happy if a woman were president of

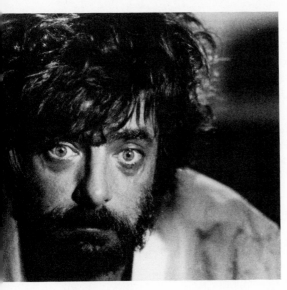

Lina Wertmuller's perennial leading man, Giancarlo Giannini, in *Swept Away* (1974). (Courtesy Cinema 5)

General Motors, or if Nixon were a woman. In the end, I'm happy they don't like my films. I would be worried if they did. Last year, Molly Haskell wrote an article in *The Village Voice* comparing me to Liliana Cavani who directed *The Night Porter* [1973]. This is the worst insult, for feminists. Although Cavani and I are very different, the only thing that interested Molly Haskell was that we are both women. This is a true complex that she has. [See "Are Women Directors Different?," pp. 429–435.—Eds.]

Q: But on the island, in *Swept Away*, when Mariangela Melato says, "Give a proletarian a little power and he becomes a tyrant," she seems to be right.

A: In reality, he is not so terrible with her. Clearly, he has so many centuries of hatred for what he was forced to submit to that he's looking for revenge. It would be unthinkable that the subproletarians would not look for revenge against the bourgeoisie. But in reality, in the course of the relationship, all this anger melts, and at the end of the story, the person who has been violated, the wounded person, is he, and not she. And he always represents women. And she represents men. And this is the concept of who's above and who's below.

Q: I noticed that she's never bruised. You never show her black and blue, or covered with welts. Does this mean that the beatings are symbolic and not "real"?

A: No, not particularly, but these are not really strong blows. He altogether slaps her five times. That's all. Only five slaps.

Q: One of the things that I liked about the film is that it critiques the bourgeois happily-ever-after myth of romantic love across class lines.

A: Nothing overcomes class.

Q: So if nothing overcomes class—

A: But the love is not less authentic, for all that. You always have to remember that the intellectuals, all over the world, love the concept of the *people,* the oppressed. Because the intellectuals are all leftists. It is a genuine love. But it remains theoretical. It always ends up badly for the Third World, because we don't really do shit for them. They should not believe in us too much. They have to work it out by themselves, and not rely on the bourgeoisie.

Q: This idea reappears in *All Screwed Up* [1974], when the working-class hero repeatedly catches fleeting glimpses of a beautiful, unattainable woman.

A: Yes, the boy sees this girl, mysterious, very beautiful, very elegant, with a smile like Gioconda, and he looks at her. Maybe she's a friend. He always finds her close to him in a moment of revolution. But afterwards, he sees her again, and she's distant, inaccessible. She and all the symbols of her class are closed, like a queen, like the enemy. They are the enemy.

Q: You were assistant director on Fellini's *8½* [1963], and this motif in *All Screwed Up* reminds me of those moments in *8½* in which Marcello Mastroianni has a vision of Claudia Cardinale. That's what I like about your films. You bring Fellini back to earth. You give him a class base.

A: I love Fellini. Fellini comprehends all these social struggles, doubts, and fears within himself. He cannot do anything but tell about himself. Even *Satyricon* [1969] and *Casanova* [1976] are about himself.

Q: I know. It's boring. So, to get back to what we were talking about, if love is only theoretical, and in *Mimi* and *Seven Beauties,* the old codes, honor and so forth, are bankrupt, what's the alternative? Humanism? A Communist morality?

A: A new man has to be born, who has the right values.

Q: Where do these values come from? Class struggle?

A: I call it harmony. It comes from disorder, from conflict, from the competition of many political parties and ideas. This compels people to think, not to have faith. People should not have faith in anybody. You always have to think with your own brains. Man in disorder has to think. Man in order does not have to think.

Q: That's what the anarchist says in *Seven Beauties*. Are you more an anarchist or a Marxist?

A: I'm a socialist. I love anarchists very much, even though I know very well that anarchism is a total utopia, and that it can have horrendous faces. But in the utopian ideology of anarchism is the key to the human being, which means the desire of man to become a free and civilized being. The freedom of each of us must end where the other person's freedom begins. This is wonderful, even if anarchy is utopian. An ideal society should be democratic, and socialist, with many parties, and with an anarchic spirit. We will get there.

Q: But in *Seven Beauties,* it seems as if all the alternatives are closed off. Even the anarchist ends up dead in a pool of shit.

A: The action of the anarchist who decides to throw himself in the shit is an extremely positive action, free and vital. The action of the socialist who thinks in the moment in which Mussolini doesn't want him to think is an extremely positive action. The problem is that he's the only one who does it.

Q: Does Pasqualino learn anything?

A: In fact, he doesn't understand anything that's happened to him, as often men do not understand what is going on. Instead of understanding the right problems, he understands that all he has to do is to live at any cost, that he has to make 200,000 children, that he has to attack to defend, that he has to accept money from everywhere it comes. He is poisoned as a man. He says that he is alive, but he is dead. And his death is the logical consequence of a very long series of wrong choices.

Q: The conclusions of all your films are very bleak and pessimistic. People make wrong choices, they're victims of cultural roles, they split off from the people, and they're destroyed. Do you see any possibility of change?

A: It is absolutely necessary to make the right choices, because if we don't, the world will end very soon, from overpopulation, famine, the destruction of nature. I see the necessity of change, especially individual change. My movies are about moments of choice, not about revolution. There must be revolution inside, before there can be revolution outside. I start from the concept that each one of us is society. When we detach our responsibility and delegate it to others, or the government, we will feel fine, but we're not fine.

Let's not think that society is a monster that is outside us, that we have to fight from a distance. The truth is that society is born because so many people believe that this is the right one. We are society, and we are the only ones who can change it. Only when we have the strength to say no to those things we should say no to, and only if this happens quickly, will we have any hope for the future. My movies are not pessimistic movies. But they are alarms.

Q: Is there any immediate relevance of *Seven Beauties* to the political situation in Italy at the moment? Was it intended as a warning against a resurgence of fascism?

A: Not much. At this moment there isn't a particular fear of fascism, as there was three years ago. Right now in Italy, it's a very fertile moment. Italy used to be a rural country, and in fifteen years it became an industrial country. There was an economic boom that transformed the industrial structure of Italy. It was completely turned upside down. For thirty years we have had a government that has been very static, completely blind to the need for social reforms that are very important. In America people are afraid of a Communist take-over in Italy, but in Italy the situation is very different. Certainly, there is an opening to the left, but it is a time of great vitality. *Seven Beauties* was not born out of fears of fascism, but in relation to other fears concerning our society.

Q: What fears were those?

A: Nazism, fascism, the Mafia, they're not something which stays outside us. They're inside us as well. It's a way of thinking that can attack each one of us. It's always alive. For God's sake, let's not be quiet, let's not think the enemy is Hitler or Mussolini, and they're dead. Each one of us has Mussolini inside of us. Each one can become Mussolini. Each one can become Mafioso. Without knowing it.

Q: Speaking of Mussolini, both *Love and Anarchy* and *Seven Beauties* begin with stills of Mussolini. His face seems to have a powerful resonance for you. It becomes almost an icon, expressive of the essence of masculine authoritarianism. It draws together the personal and the political.

A: Yes, because I work in the grotesque. There are few things more grotesque than a dictator. Mussolini and Hitler were ideal protagonists for the grotesque.

Q: But it often seems in your films that myth is the possession of the rulers, the fascists, and the Mafiosi, whereas the leftists are flat, almost comic figures.

A: No, I would like to take myth away from authority. Comedy is the enemy of myth. It frightens me when the face of power is presented with seriousness. As for the leftists, it is very important that people preserve the ability to laugh at themselves. We must laugh about ourselves, and other people too, all the time, knowing that other people are also ourselves. It is a sign of great civilization, because it is a sign of self-criticism. Those who take themselves too seriously, who feel charismatic, are cut off from criticism, from discussion, from polemic, from the vitality that these bring to our search for a new society.

Q: Do you see the grotesque as a political category?

A: Grotesque is a political means like any other. I'm against those who think that the face of politics must have a serious expression. Seriousness separates people from politics, makes politics something for experts. In reality, politics is for all of us.

I used to make serious "art" films. My first film, *The Lizards*, was very well liked by the critics. It won a lot of prizes, but only the intellectuals went to see it. I took this to heart. I understood that I couldn't work that way, that it was impossible for a temperament like mine. I have an earthy, popular nature. I was born a bourgeois, but I know where my work goes, my interest, my affections, my emotions—to the people. So I embraced the popular cinema. *The*

Lizards was a form of ego. Maybe I could have made a little monument to Lina Wertmuller, Engaged Artist, but this didn't give me any pleasure. It gives me more pleasure to entertain, to make movies that everybody sees, not just the intellectuals. I couldn't give a shit about the intellectuals.

Q: What do you think of the attack from the left which argues against using popular forms like farce, or even narrative, because it becomes appropriated by bourgeois culture? Godard says that revolutionary content demands revolutionary form.

A: Godard caressed revolutionary content with revolutionary form. There is only one element that for me is not Marxist in his work—the communication with the masses. How many people do you think saw his movies? Very few. Who are they? Intellectuals or the people? The intellectuals. That's the answer.

Of course, you have to be very careful. The ruling class sucks up dissidence like a sponge. It is very annoying for me, for example, to go into a room of the children of a rich bourgeois family and find the portrait of Che Guevara everywhere. The bourgeoisie saps our strength. Certain political ideas become fashionable. When fashion is not followed by real consciousness and real action, it becomes a way of escape. Our civilization buries the passions of the young.

It's like when the feminists think that equality is born from talk about the erogenous zones. Equality between the sexes can't be achieved if we don't resolve the contradictions within the social nucleus at the base of society, which is the family. If the family stays the way it is, the woman is thrown into a trap of love, in relation to the children and the husband, from which she can't escape. A woman thinks she frees herself when she starts fucking, or she finds a solution with the clitoris. This has nothing to do with the real problems of social organization. And in the end, the causes are always economic.

Another example is the equation between freedom and drugs. It is not true. During the '68 movements, look how much strength was lost on the road to drugs. Look at the hippies. The possibility of communication between labor, or subproletarians, and students was immediately sabotaged by drugs and what you call here the counterculture. One escaped from reality, and the other stayed in reality.

This division was a device that broke the strength of each. This is a powerful society. We have to do better.

Q: Given the potential for co-optation, do you feel your own films escape consumerism, escape being commodities? Perhaps people just go, laugh, and forget about them. Do you think your films make any lasting impression, that people think about the issues they raise?

A: Yes. The problems remain. Very often, people stay outside the movie theatres and discuss them.

Q: Don't you think that by working within the commercial system, you're asking to be co-opted? In New York the long lines for your films are at the expensive theatres on the Upper East Side.

A: Listen, there are two ways to make revolutionary films. One, you can put yourself on an island or lock yourself up in a room. And study around the problems, rejecting society as it is. Or, you can work in the industrial jungle, following its laws and using the means at hand, even if you soil your fingers in the process. This society, which is based upon mass communications, contains within itself something that can change it. We can all take the road of mass communications. We must take this road. I've succeeded in reaching people all over the world (except in the Soviet Union where they don't want my films), and I hope to do the same in America. Without using sharks or earthquakes, although if I find I need these, I'll use them too.

In the end it all reduces itself to economics. When I have five films playing in New York at the same time, the industrialists will think that maybe they can make money with political comedies. This is important. It creates space, enables others to do as I have done, enables us to agitate, to move the ideas. They have the illusion that laughter takes the ideas away. It's not true. I have a great faith in laughter, and I'm not afraid to be obvious. People go to see my films, and laugh at them, even if there are alarms and pessimistic talk along the way. For me, laughter is the Vaseline that makes the ideas penetrate better. Not in the ass, but in the brain. In the heart.

Bibliography

Baxandall, Rosalyn Fraad. "A Union Man Leads a Happy Life . . ." *Seven Days,* 1, no. 3 (1977). [*Union Maids*]

Biberman, Herbert. *Salt of the Earth: The Story and Script of the Film.* Boston: The Beacon Press, 1965.

Biskind, Peter. *"Lucia." Jump Cut,* no. 2 (July–August 1974).

Brom, Tom. *"Angela: Portrait of a Revolutionary." Cinéaste,* 5, no. 2 (1972).

Campbell, Marilyn. "RKO's Fallen Women, 1930–1933." *The Velvet Light Trap,* no. 10 (Fall 1973).

Eckert, Charles W. "The Anatomy of a Proletarian Film: Warner's *Marked Woman." Film Quarterly* (Winter 1973–1974).

————. "Shirley Temple and the House of Rockefeller." *Jump Cut,* no. 2 (July–August 1974).

Haskell, Molly. "Introduction to Jane and the Enemy." *The Village Voice,* November 7, 1974.

Kaplan, E. Ann. " 'Women's Happytime Commune': New Departures in Women's Films." *Jump Cut,* no. 9 (October–December 1975).

Kay, Karyn. *"Sisters of the Night." The Velvet Light Trap,* no. 6 (Fall 1972).

————. "The Revenge of Pirate Jenny: *A Very Curious Girl." The Velvet Light Trap,* no. 9 (Summer 1973).

Kleinhans, Chuck. *"Chris and Bernie:* The Virtues of Modesty." *Jump Cut,* no. 8 (August–September 1975).

————; Lesage, Julia; and Martineau, Barbara Halpern. "New Day's Way: Julia Reichert and Jim Klein Interviewed." *Jump Cut,* no. 9 (October–December 1975).

Lesage, Julia. "Filming for the City: An Interview with the Kartemquin Collective." *Cinéaste*, 7, no. 1 (Fall 1975).

———. "*Memories of Underdevelopment*." *Jump Cut*, no. 1 (May–June 1974).

McCormick, Ruth. "*Salt of the Earth*." *Cinéaste*, 5, no. 4 (1972).

Nelson, Joyce. "Warner Brothers Deviants: 1931–1933." *The Velvet Light Trap*, no. 15 (Fall 1975).

Peary, Gerald. "Jane Fonda on Tour: Answering *Letter to Jane*." *Take One*, 4, no. 1 (1974).

Roth, Mark. "Some Warners Musicals and the Spirit of the New Deal." *The Velvet Light Trap*, no. 1 (June 1971).

Waldman, Diane. "The Eternal Return of Circe: *A Very Curious Girl*." *The Velvet Light Trap*, no. 9 (Summer 1973).

Wikarska, Carol. "*Attica*." *Women and Film*, 2, no. 7 (Summer 1975).

———. "An Interview with Tra Giang at the Moscow Film Festival." *Women and Film*, 1, nos. 5 and 6 (1974).

VI
Polemics

Woman's Place in Photoplay Production*

Alice Guy Blaché

INTRODUCTION

The following essay appeared July 11, 1914, many years into Madame Blaché's film career, during which time she had not only directed hundreds of pictures on two continents, but also owned her own studio, the Solax Company. Alice Blaché was alone among women in 1914 for either accomplishment.

Needless to say, most of Madame Blaché's arguments for women in film strike one today as hopelessly arcane, growing directly out of Victorian conceptions of the nature of the female—emotional, religious, sensitive, superior "in matters of the heart." Yet ingenious is the way Alice Blaché takes these traditionalist, often absurd, reasonings and turns them to advantage in her plea for increased participation of women in filmmaking. And no matter the faults in her logic, Alice Blaché deserves praise for recognizing and demonstrating half a century ago that, "There is nothing connected with the staging of a motion picture that a woman cannot do as easily as a man, and there is no reason why she cannot completely master every technicality of the art."

* Reprinted from *Moving Picture World,* July 11, 1914.

It has long been a source of wonder to me that many women have not seized upon the wonderful opportunities offered to them by the motion-picture art to make their way to fame and fortune as producers of photodramas. Of all the arts there is probably none in which they can make such splendid use of talents so much more natural to a woman than to a man and so necessary to its perfection.

There is no doubt in my mind that a woman's success in many lines of endeavor is still made very difficult by a strong prejudice against one of her sex doing work that has been done only by men for hundreds of years. Of course this prejudice is fast disappearing, and there are many vocations in which it has not been present for a long time. In the arts of acting, music, painting, and literature, woman has long held her place among the most successful workers, and when it is considered how vitally all of these arts enter into the production of motion pictures, one wonders why the names of scores of women are not found among the successful creators of photodrama offerings.

Not only is a woman as well fitted to stage a photodrama as a man, but in many ways she has a distinct advantage over him because of her very nature and because much of the knowledge called for in the telling of the story and the creation of the stage setting is absolutely within her province as a member of the gentler sex. She is an authority on the emotions. For centuries she has given them full play while man has carefully trained himself to control them. She has developed her finer feelings for generations, while being protected from the world by her male companions, and she is naturally religious. In matters of the heart her superiority is acknowledged, and her deep insight and sensitiveness in the affairs of Cupid give her a wonderful advantage in developing the thread of love that plays such an all-important part in almost every story that is prepared for the screen. All of the distinctive qualities that she possesses come into direct play during the guiding of the actors in making their character drawings and interpreting the different emotions called for by the story. For to think and to feel the situation demanded by the play is the secret of successful acting, and sensitiveness to those thoughts and feelings is absolutely essential to the success of a stage director.

The qualities of patience and gentleness possessed to such a high degree by womankind are also of inestimable value in the staging of a photodrama. Artistic temperament is a thing to be reckoned with while directing an actor, in spite of the treatment of the subject in the comic papers, and a gentle, soft-voiced director is much more conducive to good work on the part of the performer than the overstern, noisy tyrant of the studio.

Not a small part of the motion-picture director's work, in addition to the preparation of the story for picture-telling and the casting and directing of the actors, is the choice of suitable locations for the staging of the exterior scenes and the supervising of the studio settings, props, costumes, etc. In these matters it seems to me that a woman is especially well qualified to obtain the very best results, for she is dealing with subjects that are almost a second nature to her. She takes the measure of every person, every costume, every house, and every piece of furniture that her eye comes into contact with, and the beauty of a stretch of landscape or a single flower impresses her immediately. All of these things are of the greatest value to the creator of a photodrama, and the knowledge of them must be extensive and exact. A woman's magic touch is immediately recognized in a real home. Is it not just as recognizable in the home of the characters of a photoplay?

That women make the theatre possible from the box-office standpoint is an acknowledged fact. Theatre managers know that their appeal must be to the woman if they would succeed, and all of their efforts are naturally in that direction. This being the case, what a rare opportunity is offered to women to use that inborn knowledge of just what does appeal to them to produce photodramas that will contain that inexplicable something which is necessary to the success of every stage or screen production.

There is nothing connected with the staging of a motion picture that a woman cannot do as easily as a man, and there is no reason why she cannot completely master every technicality of the art. The technique of the drama has been mastered by so many women that it is considered as much her field as a man's and its adaptation to picture work in no way removes it from her sphere. The technique of motion-picture photography, like the technique of the drama, is fitted to a woman's activities.

It is hard for me to imagine how I could have obtained my knowledge of photography, for instance, without the months of study spent in the laboratory of the Gaumont Company in Paris at a time when motion-picture photography was in the experimental stage, and carefully continued since [in] my own laboratory in the Solax Studios in this country. It is also necessary to study stage direction by actual participation in the work, in addition to burning the midnight oil in your library, but both are as suitable, as fascinating, and as remunerative to a woman as to a man.

That's Not Brave, That's Just Stupid*

Barbara Bernstein

Introduction

The male Hollywood director drawing the attention of many feminist film critics is, strangely, the king of adventure movies, of buddy-buddy male love stories, the filmmaker once summed up by a worshipful French film critic with the words, "Above all, this is a Man." The man is Hollywood veteran Howard Hawks, maker of Scarface *(1932),* Bringing Up Baby *(1938),* Only Angels Have Wings *(1939),* His Girl Friday *(1940),* The Big Sleep *(1946),* Gentlemen Prefer Blondes *(1953), among many other films.*

What is the particular appeal of Hawks to feminist thinkers? (See the testimonial of his woman screenwriter Leigh Brackett, pp. 193–198.) There is the excitement that Hawks's women are "doers," involved in the narrative excitement as with no other male director. As Molly Haskell once wrote admiringly of Hawks, "He may not penetrate the secret of a woman's heart . . . But at the same time he never excludes her from the action, never even implicitly suggests that a woman occupies a fixed place—the home, society—or that she is man's subordinate."

At the other end, there are those who see Hawks as an incredible chauvinist, a political irresponsible, a perennial juvenile who ex-

* Reprinted from *Focus!: Chicago's Film Journal*, no. 8 (Autumn 1972).

pands crude traveling salesman jokes into full-length pictures. Giv-ing credence to this position are Hawks's exasperating remarks about "women's lib" in his many interviews, comments such as "I haven't thought too much about the movement, mostly because the people who seem to be doing most of the talking are so unattractive that I don't think its fun" (Take One, *March 1973*).

There is a third position, that offered in the essay below. Barbara Bernstein is an immense fan of Hawks, but she admires him because of his moviemaking talents and not because she is beguiled by his problematic sexual politics.

Howard Hawks was our entering wedge into the great neglected world of American movies. The first issue of *Focus!* ran an article by Robin Wood entitled "Who the Hell Is Howard Hawks?," and ex-cept for the editors (who had read it beforehand), none of us knew. But the French adored him, so we read and watched and once we arranged a series of fifteen Hawks films and looked at them all carefully. Since Hitchcock was already a household name, and Ford was respectable with his six Oscars, discovering the underground Hawks meant allowing ourselves to love all that genre "entertain-ment" from the 1930s and 1940s and 1950s. For that alone, we owe Hawks, the French, Robin Wood, and the original editors of *Focus!* a lot.

Now it's many years later, and without even thinking about it, we take American films seriously. Very seriously. In the case of Howard Hawks, at least, too seriously.

Hawks movies do have consistent themes, concerns, characters, and situations. It is important to notice that in order to give Hawks credit for being a personal artist and not just an able technician wandering from studio to studio, shooting scripts written by other people. No argument: "self-respect and responsibility," "the group," "the instinctive consciousness"—these things are all there in abun-dance. But they are not what is most important about Hawks; if they were, he would be a questionable artist indeed. What is lasting about Hawks lies more in the "able technician" direction than in the "consistent themes" direction.

The adventure dramas show the Hawks problem most clearly. A Hawks movie creates its own universe, with its own rules and codes. Hawks is so good, so seductive, at creating a setting in which his moral code seems noble, even inevitable, that one hates to say, "Yes, but . . ." for fear of sounding, God forbid, like one of those *women* who just don't understand.

But are we really to take that dashing and attractive code of professionalism, loyalty, and stoicism seriously? The repercussions nag more and more with each viewing. Yes, but maybe you shouldn't send boys out on a suicidal mission because this is war and you're the commander and that's your job. Maybe you shouldn't risk your life and the happiness of a woman who loves

Maudie (Charlene Holt, second from left), John Wayne's girl, stands among the opposition MacDonald clan, led by Kevin MacDonald (R. G. Armstrong) and hard-shooting Joey MacDonald (Michele Carey, right) in Howard Hawks's *El Dorado* (1967). (Courtesy Paramount Pictures)

you because you signed a contract to get the mail through and that is your job. Maybe you shouldn't railroad a man to twenty years in prison because you're the DA and that's your job. A fanatical sense of shortsighted responsibility becomes the worst kind of irresponsibility.

The heroes in the adventure films are crippled men using abstract responsibility to avoid real responsibility. Some vague sense of "it's what I've got to do" drives Jimmy Cagney to near-suicide on the racetrack in *The Crowd Roars* (1932) over the protests of his wife. And we're made to feel that she's wrong to ask him to give it up. In *Only Angels Have Wings* (1939), Jeff jumps into an airplane and takes off every time a woman on the ground asks something of him. That famous ending (and it is unfailingly moving) is pathetic; after all that, Jeff can't even say, "I'd like you to stay with me." He has his pride, he has to play games with two-headed nickels. It's not hard to get annoyed with his eleven-year-old behavior, and with Hawks for endorsing it.

Similarly, *The Dawn Patrol* (1930) is a preadolescent fantasy of war. Here's a tough job you've got to face like a man, lots of fun in the trenches with the fellows, a best friend you might have to die for, and no girls around to get mushy and spoil things. It's a turgid and heavy movie that comes to life only when the men stop torturing themselves and start flying airplanes. Hawks *is* an action director. Why focus on all that sitting around and agonizing and playing at heroism when Hawks can put together a flying sequence that makes men look like angels? Why pay this inordinate attention to a "morality" that is in itself at best sophomoric?

When the body of an artist's work displays a certain philosophical orientation, one can accept it or reject it and still respect the artist for expressing it well and consistently. The worst reason for disliking a director's work is because you disagree with his view of the world. But Hawks is a special case. His philosophy is the most trivial part of his artistry, and concentrating on it makes his work less, rather than more, great. His movies are masterpieces for reasons other than their specious "moral density," and we are doing him a disservice by insisting upon his weakest aspect.

After all, Hawks wasn't living in total obscurity until Robin Wood came along and demonstrated that it was OK to like him because his films had depth. Back in the 1930s and 1940s Hawks's contemporaries hailed him as a great choreographer of physical spectacle: a battle, an airplane taking off, a cattle drive, a car race, a shoot-out. Any one of these is as great an accomplishment as a film full of "instinctive morality." If we can't see the beauty and profundity in a perfect action sequence, what do we love American movies for?

On top of that, Hawks, is one of the best comedy directors we've ever had. Like George Cukor, he inspires actors to spontaneity, honesty, and infectious delight with each other. Some improvised moments of zany affection (Ann Sheridan breaking up during the wedding in *I Was a Male War Bride,* 1949, the phone call in *The Big Sleep,* 1946, innumerable moments in *His Girl Friday,* 1940, all the songs in every movie) are classic examples of what the medium can inspire and capture for its audience. It's that same kind of inspiration that falls embarrassingly flat when the performers aren't up to it, which none of the new faces in the last four or five Hawks movies has been. But when it worked, not just moments but whole relationships shined and crackled. If we can't delight in that kind of artistry, what do we love American movies for?

On the thematic, "self-respect and responsibility" level, Hawks's films are silly, childish, and morally questionable. His world is like a fourth-grade classroom where the boys wouldn't be caught dead talking to the girls, and the girls keep trying to trick them into it. It's his world and he's welcome to it, but what use is *that* as a reason for Hawks to receive our affection and respect? While the duty/sacrifice/stoicism ethos in *Only Angels Have Wings* grows transparent, the flight sequences, lovely performances, and the sympathy between characters stands out more and more. A movie like *Red Line 7000* (1965) is full of theme but totally without grace, and it is a singularly unpleasant and inept film.

Hawks's movies were made to be "shamefully underrated." He is an action director, a director of actors, not an existentialist philosopher. Searching for profundity (is that the only way we can respect an artist?), we have elevated the most shallow thing about his films. They don't ask to be taken at that level, so this attack, aimed at exposing their weaknesses at that level, is admittedly unfair and irrelevant. But then, so is revering Hawks for his themes, and calling *The Big Sleep* or *Gentlemen Prefer Blondes* (1953) "marginal" because they don't fit it.

What enjoying Howard Hawks movies should have taught us about American films is that profundity isn't the only mark of a fine work of art. There's a difference between great ideas and great experiences, and it's for great experiences that we can go to the movies.

Documenting the Patriarchy: *Chinatown*

Barbara Halpern Martineau

I approach the altar of film worship as a pagan, not even a blasphemer but an other-believer, a witch descended from an older, nonhierarchic tradition. I approach with reluctance—there is little for me there, and the danger is well defined.

As an "alternate" critic, one of the "alternate" sex, I give most of my attention to women's work, work that tries to open consciousness rather than distract and stifle it. I am therefore reluctant to write articles on matters peripheral to my central focus. Yet there is need to clear away false mystery. We are surrounded, daily impinged upon, by the enormous power of the patriarchy. Some attention must be given to unveiling the false idol.

The following letter was my response to two reviews of Roman Polanski's *Chinatown* (1974) that appeared in *Jump Cut* (no. 3, September–October 1974). The letter is specific to those two reviews, but it applies as well to criticism of *Chinatown* in other journals (see also *Film Quarterly*, Winter 1974–1975, and *The Velvet Light Trap*, Fall 1974). I think there is also a wide application to the current state of film criticism, which has all the trappings of a priesthood mystifying the object of its veneration, the Film.

Dear *Jump Cut*,

This is an angry letter about the two reviews of *Chinatown* that appeared in your third issue. I try to avoid writing angry letters because they take so much energy that I would rather spend writing positive constructive criticism, especially of films by women, but I think *Jump Cut* is a good forum in which to express anger transformed into constructive criticism.

The key to my anger about the two *Chinatown* reviews can be seen in two casual phrases: James Kavanagh remarks that "the movie brings us, with Gittes, to the unsettling realization that we can't always tell what's going on, even in our comfortable middle-class womb; it forces us to resign ourselves to our petty insignificance, and follow a strategy for survival which directs that we do 'as little as possible.'" And Murray Sperber makes it perfectly clear: "Polanski gets us to identify with J. J. Gittes." Well just who is that "us" that Kavanagh and Sperber are so relaxed about being? For Sperber, it seems to be anyone who can afford the price of admission, hence a middle- and upper-class us. (And, it would seem, a masochistic us who relish the intricacies of the way "our" hopelessness is depicted.) For Kavanagh, us clearly doesn't include the inhabitants of Chinatown, which he sees as "the *other* place, a place outside the universe of bourgeois discourse." Kavanagh approves of the film's strategy in not pretending to "capture the reality of poverty and oppression," but he doesn't seem aware of the *other* other whose oppression the film does pretend to capture, but only to exploit it, namely that old reliable *other* whose oppression Simone De Beauvoir described in *The Second Sex* (1953), namely us. Meaning us women (*chuckle*), why honey, how do you expect *us* to identify with J. J. Gittes? On the *other* hand, do you expect us to identify with the bloody corpse of Evelyn Mulwray, whose death, according to both reviewers, stands for any number of social horrors *except* the pervasive oppression of women by men?

Of the two reviews I find Kavanagh's (the cover story) more useful and intelligent, and therefore more interesting to attack. Sperber seems lost between his obvious relish of the film's sensationalism and his guilt and subsequent desire to show how politically unacceptable the film is. Although he has minor insights into Gittes's total inability to understand the women he encounters, his stance is made clear to me when he speaks of the "picture of the woman being penetrated from the rear—a sexist image Polanski uses to say, in this world everyone takes it in the ass." Well, maybe, but that just doesn't gloss over the fact that it's a woman taking it in the ass and, as usual, having even her specific oppression denied her by the sexist language that melts her into the everyone she isn't. Enough for Sperber.

Kavanagh is concerned to show the merits of the film as bourgeois art, and then to show the limitations of bourgeois art—a fair enough proposition. But because he doesn't analyze the film's obvious and extremely oppressive depiction of patriarchy to discover whether that depiction is consciously intended by Polanski or simply imbedded in the film as an aspect of Polanski's own patriarchal attitudes, Kavanagh's disscussion simply extends the patriarchy one level further. This is particularly ironic when he introduces the idea of Chinatown as the *other* place, pointing out that Polanski doesn't deal with the concept of the ghetto as such, but uses it as a backdrop for the film's final violence. Throughout this passage, and in the article as a whole, Kavanagh studiously avoids letting us know that the victim of the final violence is a woman. The blood and horror are abstract neutralities—once more the woman is deprived even of the recognition of her specific oppression. And the vision of J. J. Gittes as the helpless but well-meaning petit bourgeois completely overlooks the fact that it was his overweening determination to control the film's denouement, to set himself up as an opponent of Cross, rather than simply to help Evelyn quietly escape, that leads to the spilling of all that female blood. If Gittes's role is studied in terms of his relationship with Evelyn, a relationship in which he refuses to trust her and at the same time demands that she trust him, thereby putting her life on the line, then a strong ambivalence is brought into his role as blundering crusader against evil. He is also, in a very direct way, imitating the very evil he opposes—as in all wars the antagonists resemble each other, and those who suffer most are the noncombatants, the women and children.

If this analysis is brought to bear on the film, its relationship to *The Maltese Falcon* (1941), mentioned as a piece of trivia by Sperber, becomes important, and Huston's treatment of Bogart as he finally betrays Mary Astor, a vision I find ambivalent and distanced, can be compared with Polanski's handling of Gittes as Evelyn Mul-

J. J. Gittes (Jack Nicholson)
in a doomed romance with
Evelyn   Mulwray   (Faye
Dunaway)   in   Roman   Polanski's *Chinatown* (1974).
(Courtesy   Paramount   Pictures)

wray's unwitting destroyer. Then, also, the element of plot that
Sperber sees as evidence of Gittes's "romanticism," the fact that he
tells Evelyn how once, in Chinatown, he ended up by hurting a girl
he was trying to help, becomes part of a pattern that shows Gittes's
relationship to women as constantly destructive. Neither review
even mentions the other death of a woman in the film, but that is
also linked to Gittes, when the woman who posed as Mulwray's
wife is murdered shortly after giving information to Gittes, which
he casually accepts without inquiring about the possible consequences for her. With all this left out of both talkative reviews, it's
not surprising that Polanski's little sexist jokes don't come up for
comment, such as the story Gittes tells in such an out-of-character
fashion just at the moment when he is using the house of a former
client as an escape route. It's then that we see the woman who was
shown in the film's first sequence being fucked in the ass, now she's
been beaten in the face by her husband as punishment for letting
that happen, and so she's settled down to cooking and taking care
of the kids and not asking questions. That's the role Gittes wants to

impose on Evelyn Mulwray, but lacking the straightforwardness of working-class machismo, he fumbles and gets her killed instead.

I agree with Kavanagh when he says that bourgeois art at its best "discerns some of the more complex contradictions in bourgeois social life, realizing that there are 'other' kinds of oppression even more frightening than those suffered by the male middle class, seeing some connection among different kinds of oppression, and putting all this in relation to capitalism in a way that avoids creating illusory heroes, illusory victims, or illusory escapes." But then it is the job of responsible criticism to examine that presentation as fully as possible, which means not ignoring the fact that while the male star gets a slit nose, the female star gets shot through the eye.

Fascinating Fascism[*]

Susan Sontag

The Last of the Nuba, Leni Riefenstahl.

SS *Regalia,* Jack Pia.

I

First Exhibit. Here is a book of 126 splendid color photographs by
Leni Riefenstahl, certainly the most ravishing book of photographs
published anywhere in recent years. In the intractable desert of the
southern Sudan live about eight thousand aloof, godlike Nuba, emblems of physical perfection, with large, well-shaped, partly shaven
heads, expressive faces, and muscular bodies that are depilated and
decorated with scars; smeared with sacred gray-white ash, the men
prance, squat, brood, wrestle in the arid sand. And here is a fascinating layout of twelve black-and-white photographs of Leni
Riefenstahl on the back cover of the book, also ravishing, a chrono-
logical sequence of expressions (from sultry inwardness to the grin
of a Texas matron on safari) vanquishing the intractable march of
aging.

The first photograph was taken in 1927 when she was twenty-five and already a movie star, the most recent are dated 1969 (she is cuddling a naked African baby) and 1972 (she is holding a camera), and each of them shows some version of an ideal presence, a kind of imperishable beauty, like Elisabeth Schwarzkopf's, that only gets gayer and more metallic and healthier-looking with old age. And here is a biographical sketch of Riefenstahl on the dust jacket, and an introduction (unsigned) entitled "How Leni Riefenstahl Came to Study the Mesakin Nuba of Kordofan"—full of disquieting lies.

The introduction, which gives a detailed account of Riefenstahl's pilgrimage to the Sudan (inspired, we are told, by reading Hemingway's *The Green Hills of Africa* "one sleepless night in the mid-1950s"), laconically identifies the photographer as "something of a mythical figure as a filmmaker before the war, half-forgotten by a nation which chose to wipe from its memory an era of its history." Who but Riefenstahl herself could have thought up this fable about what is mistily referred to as "a nation" which for some unnamed reason "chose" to perform the deplorable act of cowardice of forgetting "an era"—tactfully left unspecified—"of its history"? Presumably, at least some readers will be startled by this coy allusion to Germany and to the Third Reich. (It does, however, dare more than the all-concealing brevity of Harper & Row's ads for *The Last of the Nuba*, which identify Riefenstahl simply as "the renowned film maker.")

Compared with the introduction, the jacket of the book is positively expansive on the subject of the photographer's career, parroting the misinformation that Riefenstahl has been dispensing for the last twenty years.

It was during Germany's blighted and momentous 1930s that Leni Riefenstahl sprang to international fame as a film director. She was born in 1902, and her first devotion was to creative dancing. This led to her participation in silent films, and soon she was herself making—and starring in—her own talkies, such as *The Mountain* (1929).

These tensely romantic productions were widely admired, not

least by Adolf Hitler who, having attained power in 1933, commissioned Riefenstahl to make a documentary on the Nuremberg Rally in 1934.

It takes a certain originality to describe the Nazi era as "Germany's blighted and momentous 1930s," to summarize the events of 1933 as Hitler's "having attained power," and to assert that Riefenstahl, most of whose work was in its own decade correctly identified as Nazi propaganda, enjoyed "international fame as a film director," ostensibly like her contemporaries Renoir, Lubitsch, and Flaherty. (Could the publishers have let LR write the jacket copy herself? One hesitates to entertain so unkind a thought, although "her first devotion was to dancing" is a phrase few native speakers of English would be capable of.)

The facts are, of course, inaccurate or invented. For starters, not only did Riefenstahl not make—or star in—a talkie called *The Mountain*. No such film exists. More generally: Riefenstahl did not first simply participate in silent films, then, when sound came in, begin directing her own films, in which she took the starring role. From the first to the last of all nine films she ever acted in, Riefenstahl was the star; and seven of these she did not direct.

These seven films were: *The Holy Mountain* (*Der Heilige Berg*, 1926), *The Big Jump* (*Der Grosse Sprung*, 1927), *Fate of the House of Hapsburg* (*Das Schicksal derer von Hapsburg*, 1929), *The White Hell of Pitz Palü* (*Die Weisse Hölle von Piz Palü*, 1929)—all silents—followed by *Avalanche* (*Sturm über dem Montblanc*, 1930), *White Frenzy* (*Der Weisse Rausch*, 1931), and *SOS Iceberg* (*SOS Eisberg*, 1932–1933). All but one were directed by Dr. Arnold Fanck, auteur of hugely successful Alpine epics since 1919, whose career, after Riefenstahl left him to strike out on her own as director in 1932, petered out with a German-Japanese coproduction, *The Daughter of the Samurai* (*Die Tochter des Samurai*, 1937), and *A Robinson Crusoe* (*Ein Robinson*, 1938), both flops. (The film not directed by Fanck is *Fate of the House of Hapsburg*, a royalist weepie made in Austria in which Riefenstahl played Marie Vetsera, Crown Prince Rudolf's co-suicidee at Mayerling. No print seems to have survived.)

These films were not simply "tensely romantic." Fanck's pop-Wagnerian vehicles for Riefenstahl were no doubt thought of as apolitical when they were made, but they can also be seen in retrospect, as Siegfried Kracauer has argued, as an anthology of proto-Nazi sentiments. The mountain climbing in Fanck's pictures was a visually irresistible metaphor of unlimited aspiration toward the high mystic goal, both beautiful and terrifying, which was later to become concrete in Führer-worship. The character that Riefenstahl generally played was that of a wild girl who dares to scale the peak that others, the "valley pigs," shrink from. Her first role, in the silent *The Holy Mountain,* is that of a young dancer named Diotima being wooed by an ardent climber who converts her to the healthy ecstasies of Alpinism. This character underwent a progressive aggrandizement. In her first talkie, *Avalanche,* Riefenstahl is a mountain-possessed girl in love with a young meteorologist. She saves him when he is stranded on his storm-wrecked observatory on the peak of Mont Blanc.

Riefenstahl herself directed six feature films. Her first, which was released in 1932, was another mountain film—*The Blue Light* (*Das Blaue Licht*). Riefenstahl starred in it as well, playing a role similar to the ones in Fanck's films for which she had been "so widely admired, not least by Adolf Hitler," but allegorizing the dark themes of longing, purity, and death that Fanck had treated rather scoutishly. As usual, the mountain is represented as both supremely beautiful and dangerous, that majestic force which invites the ultimate affirmation of and escape from the self—into the brotherhood of courage and into death. (On nights when the moon is full, a mysterious blue light radiates from the peak of Mount Cristallo, luring the young villagers to try to climb it. Parents try to keep their children home behind closed window shutters, but the young are drawn away like somnambulists and fall to their deaths on the rocks.)

The role Riefenstahl devised for herself is of Junta, a primitive creature who has a unique relation to a destructive power. (Only Junta, a rag-clad outcast girl of the village, is able to reach the blue light safely.) She is brought to her death, not by the impossibility of the goal symbolized by the mountain but by the materialist, prosaic

The outcast mountain girl, Junta (Leni Riefenstahl), in Riefenstahl's *The Blue Light* (1932). (Courtesy The Museum of Modern Art/Film Stills Archive)

spirit of envious villagers and the blind rationalism of a well-meaning visitor from the city. (Junta knows that the blue light is emitted by precious stones; being a creature of pure spirit, she revels in the jewels' beauty, indifferent to their material value. But she falls in love with a vacationing painter and naïvely confides in him the secret. He tells the villagers, who scale the mountain, remove the treasure, and sell it; when Junta starts her ascent at the next full moon, the blue light is no longer there to guide her, and she falls and dies.)

After *The Blue Light,* the next film Riefenstahl directed was not "a documentary on the Nuremberg Rally in 1934," for Riefenstahl made five nonfiction films—not two, as she has claimed since the 1950s and as all current whitewashing accounts of her dutifully repeat. It was *Victory of Faith* (*Sieg des Glaubens,* 1933), celebrating the first National Socialist Party Congress held after Hitler seized power. Her third film, *Day of Freedom: Our Army* (*Tag der Freiheit: Unsere Wehrmacht,* 1933; released in 1935), was made for the army, and depicts the beauty of soldiers and soldiering for the

Führer. Then came the two films that did indeed make her internationally famous—the first of which is *Triumph of the Will* (*Triumph des Willens*, 1935), whose title is never mentioned on the jacket of *The Last of the Nuba*, lest it awaken lingering anti-Teutonic prejudices in the book buyer of the 1970s perhaps.

The jacket copy continues:

> Riefenstahl's refusal to submit to Goebbels' attempt to subject her visualisation to his strictly propagandistic requirements led to a battle of wills which came to a head when Riefenstahl made her film of the 1936 Olympic Games, *Olympia*. This, Goebbels attempted to destroy; and it was only saved by the personal intervention of Hitler.
>
> With two of the most remarkable documentaries of the 1930s to her credit, Riefenstahl continued making films of her devising, unconnected with the rise of Nazi Germany, until 1941, when war conditions made it impossible to continue.
>
> Her acquaintance with the Nazi leadership led to her arrest at the end of the Second World War: she was tried twice, and acquitted twice. Her reputation was in eclipse, and she was half forgotten—although to a whole generation of Germans her name had been a household word.

Except for the bit about her having once been a household word, in Nazi Germany, not one part of the above is true.

To cast Riefenstahl in the familiar role of the individualist-artist, defying philistine bureaucrats and censorship by the patron state, is a bold try. Nevertheless, the idea of her resisting "Goebbels' attempt to subject her visualisation to his strictly propagandistic requirements" should seem like nonsense to anyone who has seen *Triumph of the Will*—the most successfully, most purely propagandistic film ever made, whose very conception negates the possibility of the filmmaker's having an aesthetic or visual conception independent of propaganda.

Besides the evidence of the film itself, the facts (denied by Riefenstahl since the war) tell quite another story. There was never any struggle between the filmmaker and the German minister of propaganda. *Triumph of the Will*, after all her third film for the Nazis, was made with the fullest cooperation any filmmaker has ever had from any government. She had an unlimited budget, a crew of 120, and a huge number of cameras—estimated at between thirty and fifty—at her disposal. Far from being an artist who was conscripted for a political task and later ran into trouble, Riefenstahl was, as she relates in the book she published in 1935 about the making of *Triumph of the Will*,[1] in on the planning of the rally—which was, from the beginning, conceived as the set of a film spectacle.

Olympiad is actually two films, one called *Festival of the People* (*Fest der Völker*) and the other *Festival of Beauty* (*Fest der Schönheit*). Riefenstahl has been maintaining in interviews since the 1950s that both Olympics films were commissioned by the International Olympic Committee, produced by her own company, and made over Goebbels's protests. The truth is that the films were commissioned and entirely financed by the Nazi government (a dummy company was set up in Riefenstahl's name because it was thought "unwise for the government itself to appear as the producer") and facilitated by Goebbels's ministry at every stage of the shooting.[2]

Riefenstahl worked for two years on the editing, finishing in time so that the film could have its world premiere on April 29, 1938, in Berlin, as part of the festivities for Hitler's forty-ninth birthday. And later in the year *Olympiad* was the principal German entry at the 1938 Venice Film Festival, where it was awarded the Gold Medal. (Riefenstahl had already gotten the Gold Medal at the government-sponsored Venice festival in 1932 for *The Blue Light*.) Even the plausible-sounding legend of Goebbels objecting to her footage of the triumphs of the black American track star Jesse Owens is untrue. For this film, like the previous ones, Riefenstahl had Goebbels's full support.

More nonsense: to say that Riefenstahl "continued making films of her devising, unconnected with the rise of Nazi Germany, until

[1] Leni Riefenstahl, *Hinter den Kulissen des Reichsparteitag Films* (Munich, 1935).

[2] See Hans Barkhausen, "Footnote to the History of Riefenstahl's 'Olympia,'" *Film Quarterly* (Fall 1974)—a rare act of informed dissent amid the large number of tributes to Riefenstahl that have appeared in American and Western European film magazines during the last few years.

1941." In 1938, as a present to Hitler, she made *Berchtesgaden über Salzburg,* a fifty-minute lyric portrait of the Führer against the rugged mountain scenery of his new retreat. In 1939, she accompanied the invading Wehrmacht into Poland as a uniformed army war correspondent with her own camera team; but there is no record of any of this material surviving the war. After *Olympiad* Riefenstahl made exactly one more feature film, *Tiefland,* which she began in 1941 and, after an interruption, finished in 1944 (in the Barrandov Film Studios in Nazi-occupied Prague). *Tiefland,* already in preparation in 1934, has echoes of *The Blue Light,* and once again the protagonist (played by Riefenstahl) is a beautiful outcast; it was released in 1954 to resounding indifference. Clearly Riefenstahl would prefer to give the impression that there were only two documentaries in an otherwise long career as a director. The truth is that four of the six feature films she directed are documentaries, made for and financed by the Nazi government.

It is less than accurate to describe Riefenstahl's professional relationship to and intimacy with Hitler and Goebbels as "her acquaintance with the Nazi leadership." Far from being an actress-director whom Hitler happened to fancy and then gave an assignment to, Riefenstahl was a close friend and companion of Hitler's—long before 1932. She was a friend, not just an acquaintance, of Goebbels, too. No evidence supports Riefenstahl's persistent claim since the 1950s that Goebbels hated her. Moreover, any suggestion that Goebbels had the power to interfere with Riefenstahl's work is unrealistic. With her unlimited personal access to Hitler, Riefenstahl was the only German filmmaker who was not responsible to Goebbels. (Normally she would have been under the Short and Propaganda Production section of the Reich Film Chamber of Goebbels's ministry of propaganda.)

Last, it is misleading to say that Riefenstahl was "tried twice, and acquitted twice" after the war. What happened is that she was briefly arrested by the Allies in 1945 and two of her sumptuous houses (in Berlin and Munich) were seized. Examinations and court appearances started in 1948, continuing intermittently until 1952 when she was finally "de-Nazified" with the verdict: "No political activity in support of the Nazi regime which would warrant punishment." Most important: whether or not Riefenstahl deserved punishment at the hands of the law, it was not her "acquaintance" with the Nazi leadership but her activities as a leading propagandist for the Third Reich that were at issue.

The jacket copy of *The Last of the Nuba* summarizes faithfully the main line of the self-vindication that Riefenstahl fabricated in the 1950s and that is most fully spelled out in the interview she gave to the prestigious French magazine *Cahiers du Cinéma* in September 1965. There she denied that any of her work was propaganda, insisting it was *cinéma vérité.* "Not a single scene is staged," Riefenstahl says of *Trumph of the Will.* "Everything is genuine. And there is no tendentious commentary for the simple reason that there is no commentary at all. It is *history—pure history.*"

Although *Triumph of the Will* has no narrative voice, it does open with a written text that heralds the rally as the redemptive culmination of German history. But this opening commentary is the least original of the ways in which the film is tendentious. *Triumph of the Will* represents an already achieved and radical transformation of reality: history become theatre. In her book published in 1935, Riefenstahl had told the truth. The Nuremberg Rally "was planned not only as a spectacular mass meeting—but as a spectacular propaganda film. . . . The ceremonies and precise plans of the parades, marches, processions, the architecture of the halls and stadium were designed for the convenience of the cameras." How the Party convention was staged was determined by the decision to produce *Triumph of the Will.* The event, instead of being an end in itself, served as the set of a film, which was then to assume the character of an authentic documentary. Anyone who defends Riefenstahl's films as documentaries, if documentary is to be distinguished from propaganda, is being ingenuous. In *Triumph of the Will,* the document (the image) is no longer simply the record of reality; "reality" has been constructed to serve the image.

The rehabilitation of proscribed figures in liberal societies does not happen with the sweeping bureaucratic finality of the *Soviet Encyclopedia,* in which each new edition brings forward a dozen hitherto unmentionable figures and lowers an equal or greater number through the trapdoor of nonexistence. Our rehabilitations are softer, more insidious. It is not that Riefenstahl's Nazi past has suddenly become acceptable. It is simply that, with the turn of the cultural wheel, it no longer matters. The purification of Leni Riefenstahl's reputation of its Nazi dross has been gathering momentum for some time; but it reached some kind of climax this past year, with Riefenstahl the guest of honor at a new cinéphile-controlled film festival held in the summer in Colorado and the subject of a two-part interview program on CBS's "Camera, Three," and now with the publication of *The Last of the Nuba.*

Part of the impetus behind Riefenstahl's recent promotion to the status of a cultural monument surely is owing to the fact that she is a woman. In the roll call that runs from Germaine Dulac and Dorothy Arzner to Vera Chytilova, Agnes Varda, Mai Zetterling, Shirley Clarke, *et al.,* Riefenstahl stands out as the only woman director who has done work likely to turn up on lists of the Twenty Greatest Films of All Time. The 1973 New York Film Festival poster, made by a well-known artist who is also a feminist, shows a blonde doll-woman whose right breast is encircled by three names: Agnes Leni Shirley. Feminists would feel a pang at having to sacrifice the one woman who made films that everybody acknowledges to be first rate.

But a stronger reason for the change in attitude toward Riefenstahl lies in a shift in taste that simply makes it impossible to reject art if it is "beautiful." The line taken by Riefenstahl's defenders, who now include the most influential voices in the avant-garde film establishment, is that she was always concerned with beauty. This, of course, has been Riefenstahl's own contention for some years. Thus the *Cahiers du Cinéma* interviewer set Riefenstahl up by observing fatuously that what *Triumph of the Will* and *Olympiad* "have in common is that they both give form to a certain reality, itself based on a certain idea of form. Do you see anything peculiarly German about this concern for form?" To this Riefenstahl answered:

> I can simply say that I feel spontaneously attracted by everything that is beautiful. Yes: beauty, harmony. And perhaps this care for

composition, this aspiration to form is in effect something very German. But I don't know these things myself, exactly. It comes from the unconscious and not from my knowledge. . . . What do you want me to add? Whatever is purely realistic, slice-of-life, what is average, quotidian, doesn't interest me. . . . I am fascinated by what is beautiful, strong, healthy, what is living. I seek harmony. When harmony is produced I am happy. I believe, with this, that I have answered you.

This is why *The Last of the Nuba* is the final, necessary step in Riefenstahl's rehabilitation. It is the final rewrite of the past; or, for her partisans, the definitive confirmation that she was always a beauty-freak rather than a horrid propagandist.[3] Inside the beautifully produced book, photographs of the perfect, noble tribe. And on the jacket, photographs of "my perfect German woman" (as Hitler called Riefenstahl), vanquishing the slights of history, all smiles.

Admittedly, if *The Last of the Nuba* were not signed by Leni Riefenstahl, one would not necessarily suspect that these photographs had been taken by the most interesting, talented, and effective artist of the Nazi regime. Most people who leaf through *The Last of the Nuba* will probably look at the pictures as one more lament for vanishing primitives, of which the greatest example is Lévi-Strauss on the Bororo Indians in Brazil in *Tristes Tropiques* (1970). But if the photographs are examined carefully, in conjunction with the lengthy text written by Riefenstahl, it becomes clear that they are continuous with her Nazi work.

Riefenstahl's choice of photographic subject—this tribe and not another—expresses a very particular slant. She interprets the Nuba as a mystical people with an extraordinarily developed artistic sense (one of the few possessions that everyone owns is a lyre). They are

---

[3] This is how Jonas Mekas (*The Village Voice*, October 31, 1974) salutes the publication of *The Last of the Nuba*. "[Leni Riefenstahl] continues her celebration—or is it a search?—of the classical beauty of the human body, the search which she began in her films. She is interested in the ideal, in the monumental." Mekas in the same paper on November 7, 1974: "And here is my own final statement on Riefenstahl's films: If you are an idealist, you will see idealism; if you are a classicist, you will see in her films an ode to classicism; if you are a Nazi, you will see Nazism."

all beautiful (Nuba men, Riefenstahl notes, "have an athletic build rare in any other African tribe"); although they have to work hard to survive in the unhospitable desert (they are cattle herders and hunters), she insists that their principal activity is ceremonial. *The Last of the Nuba* is about a primitivist ideal: a portrait of a people subsisting untouched by "civilization," in a pure harmony with their environment.

All four of Riefenstahl's commissioned Nazi films—whether about Party congresses, the Wehrmacht, or athletes—celebrate the rebirth of the body and of community, mediated through the worship of an irresistible leader. They follow directly from the films of Fanck in which she acted and from her own *The Blue Light* The fictional mountain films are tales of longing for high places, of the challenge and ordeal of the elemental, the primitive; the Nazi films are epics of achieved community, in which triumph over everyday reality is achieved by ecstatic self-control and submission. *The Last of the Nuba*, an elegy for the soon-to-be-extinguished beauty and mystic powers of primitives, can be seen as the third in Riefenstahl's triptych of fascist visuals.

In the first panel, the mountain films, heavily dressed people strain upward to prove themselves in the purity of the cold; vitality is identified with physical ordeal. Middle panel, the films made for the Nazi government: *Triumph of the Will* uses overpopulated wide shots of massed figures alternating with close-ups that isolate a single passion, a single perfect submission; clean-cut people in uniforms group and regroup, as if seeking the right choreography to express their ecstatic fealty. In *Olympiad*, the richest visually of all her films, one straining scantily clad figure after another seeks the ecstasy of victory, cheered on by ranks of compatriots in the stands, all under the still gaze of the benign Super-Spectator, Hitler, whose presence in the stadium consecrates this effort. (*Olympiad*, which could as well have been entitled *Triumph of the Will*, emphasizes that there are no easy victories.) In the third panel, *The Last of the Nuba*, the stripped-down primitives, awaiting the final ordeal of their proud heroic community, their imminent extinction, frolic and pose in the hot clean desert.

It is Götterdämmerung time. The important events in Nuba society are wrestling matches and funerals: vivid encounters of beautiful male bodies and death. The Nuba, as Riefenstahl interprets them, are a tribe of aesthetes. Like the henna-daubed Masai and the so-called Mudmen of New Guinea, the Nuba paint themselves for all important social and religious occasions, smearing on their bodies a white-gray ash that unmistakably suggests death. Riefenstahl claims to have arrived "just in time," for in the few years since these photographs were taken the glorious Nuba have already started being corrupted by money, jobs, clothes. And, probably, by war—which Riefenstahl never mentions since she cares only about myth, not history. The civil war that has been tearing up that part of Sudan for a dozen years must have brought with it new technology and a lot of detritus.

Although the Nuba are black, not Aryan, Riefenstahl's portrait of them is consistent with some of the larger themes of Nazi ideology: the contrast between the clean and the impure, the incorruptible and the defiled, the physical and the mental, the joyful and the critical. A principal accusation against the Jews within Nazi Germany was that they were urban, intellectual, bearers of a destructive, corrupting "critical spirit." (The book bonfire of May 1933 was launched with Goebbels's cry: "The age of extreme Jewish intellectualism has now ended, and the success of the German revolution has again given the right of way to the German spirit." And when Goebbels officially forbade art criticism in November 1936, it was for having "typically Jewish traits of character": putting the head over the heart, the individual over the community, intellect over feeling.) Now it is "civilization" itself that is the defiler.

What is distinctive about the fascist version of the old idea of the Noble Savage is its contempt for all that is reflective, critical, and pluralistic. In Riefenstahl's casebook of primitive virtue, it is hardly the intricacy and subtlety of primitive myth, social organization, or thinking that are being extolled. She is especially enthusiastic about the ways the Nuba are exalted and unified by the physical ordeals of their wrestling matches, in which the "heaving and straining" Nuba men, "huge muscles bulging," throw one another to the ground—fighting not for material prizes but "for the renewal of sacred vitality of the tribe."

Wrestling and the rituals that go with it, in Riefenstahl's account, bind the Nuba together:

> Wrestling provides, for the Nuba, much of what the search for wealth, power and status does for the individual in the West. Wrestling generates the most passionate loyalty and emotional participation in the team's supporters, who are, in fact, the entire "nonplaying" population of the village. . . .
>
> [Wrestling is] a basic concept in the idea of "Nuba" as a whole. Its importance as the expression of the total outlook of the Mesakin and Korongo cannot be exaggerated; it is the expression in the visible and social world of the invisible world of the mind and of the spirit.

In celebrating a society where the exhibition of physical skill and courage and the victory of the stronger man over the weaker have, at least as she sees it, become the unifying symbol of the communal culture—where success in fighting is the "main aspiration of a man's life"—Riefenstahl seems only to have modified the ideas of her Nazi films. And she seems right on target with her choice, as a photographic subject, of a society whose most enthusiastic and lavish ceremony is the funeral. *Viva la muerte.*

It may seem ungrateful and rancorous to refuse to cut loose *The Last of the Nuba* from Riefenstahl's past, but there are salutary lessons to be learned from the continuity of her work as well as from that curious and implacable recent event—her rehabilitation. Other artists who embraced fascism, such as Céline and Benn and Marinetti and Pound (not to mention those, like Pabst and Pirandello and Hamsun, who became fascists in the decline of their powers), are not instructive in the same way. For Riefenstahl is the only major artist who was completely identified with the Nazi era and whose work—not only during the Third Reich but thirty years after its fall—has consistently illustrated some of the themes of fascist aesthetics.

Fascist aesthetics include but go far beyond the rather special celebration of the primitive to be found in *The Nuba*. They also flow from (and justify) a preoccupation with situations of control, submissive behavior, and extravagant effort; they exalt two seemingly opposite states, egomania and servitude. The relations of domination and enslavement take the form of a characteristic pageantry: the massing of groups of people; the turning of people into things; the multiplication of things and grouping of people/things around an all-powerful, hypnotic leader figure or force. The fascist dramaturgy centers on the orgiastic transactions between mighty forces and their puppets. Its choreography alternates between ceaseless motion and a congealed, static, "virile" posing. Fascist art glorifies surrender; it exalts mindlessness: it glamorizes death.

Such art is hardly confined to works labeled as fascist or produced under fascist governments. (To keep to films only, Walt Disney's *Fantasia*, 1940, Busby Berkeley's *The Gang's All Here*, 1943, and Kubrick's *2001*, 1968, can also be seen as illustrating certain of the formal structures, and the themes, of fascist art.) And, of course, features of fascist art proliferate in the official art of communist countries. The tastes for the monumental and for mass obeisance to the hero are common to both fascist and communist art, reflecting the view of all totalitarian regimes that art has the function of "immortalizing" its leaders and doctrines. The rendering of movement in grandiose and rigid patterns is another element in common, for such choreography rehearses the very unity of the polity. Hence mass athletic demonstrations, a choreography and display of bodies, are a valued activity in all totalitarian countries.

But fascist art has characteristics that show it to be, in part, a special variant of totalitarian art. The official art of countries like the Soviet Union and China is based on a utopian morality. Fascist art displays a utopian aesthetics—that of physical perfection. Painters and sculptors under the Nazis often depicted the nude, but they were forbidden to show any bodily imperfections. Their nudes look like pictures in male health magazines: pinups that are both sanctimoniously asexual and (in a technical sense) pornographic, for they have the perfection of a fantasy.

Riefenstahl's promotion of the beautiful, it must be said, was much more sophisticated. Beauty in Riefenstahl's representations is never witless, as it is in other Nazi visual art. She appreciated a range of body types; in matters of beauty she was not a racist. And she does show what could be considered an imperfection by more naïve Nazi aesthetic standards, genuine effort—as in the straining veined bodies and popping eyes of the athletes in *Olympiad*.

In contrast to the asexual chasteness of official communist art, Nazi art is both prurient and idealizing. A utopian aesthetics (identity as a biological given) implies an ideal eroticism (sexuality converted into the magnetism of leaders and the joy of followers). The fascist ideal is to transform sexual energy into a "spiritual" force for the benefit of the community. The erotic is always present as a temptation, with the most admirable response being a heroic repression of the sexual impulse. Thus Riefenstahl explains why Nuba marriages, in contrast to their splendid funerals, involve no ceremonies or feasts. "A Nuba man's greatest desire is not union with a woman but to be a good wrestler, thereby affirming the principle of abstemiousness. The Nuba dance ceremonies are not sensual occasions but rather 'festivals of chastity'—of containment of the life force."

In the official art of communist countries, there is some democracy of the will: the workers and peasants are sometimes shown doing something on their own. In fascist art, the will always reflects the contact between leaders and followers. In fascist and communist politics, the will is staged publicly, in the drama of the leader and the chorus. What is interesting about the relation between politics and art under National Socialism is not that art was subordinated to political needs, for this is true of all dictatorships, both of the right and the left, but that politics appropriated the rhetoric of art—art in its late romantic phase. Politics is "the highest and most comprehensive art there is," Goebbels said in 1933, "and we who shape modern German policy feel ourselves to be artists . . . the task of art and the artist [being] to form, to give shape, to remove the diseased and create freedom for the healthy."

Nazi art has always been thought of as reactionary, defiantly outside the century's mainstream of achievement in the arts. But just for this reason it has been gaining a place in contemporary taste. The left-wing organizers of a current exhibition of Nazi painting and sculpture (the first since the war) in Frankfurt have found, to their dismay, the attendance excessively large and hardly as serious-minded as they had hoped. Even when flanked with didactic admonitions from Brecht and concentration camp photographs, Nazi art still could remind these crowds of—other art. It looks dated now, and therefore more like other art styles of the 1930s, notably Art Deco. The same aesthetic responsible for the bronze colossi of Arno Breker—Hitler's (and, briefly, Cocteau's) favorite sculptor—and of Joseph Thorak also produced the muscle-bound Atlas in front of Manhattan's Rockefeller Center and the faintly lewd monument to the fallen doughboys of World War I inside Philadelphia's Thirtieth Street railroad station.

To an unsophisticated public in Germany, the appeal of Nazi art may have been that it was simple, figurative, emotional; not intellectual; a relief from the demanding complexities of modernist art. To a more sophisticated public now, the appeal is partly to that avidity which is now bent on retrieving all the styles of the past, especially the most pilloried. But a revival of Nazi art, following the revivals of Art Nouveau, Pre-Raphaelite painting, and Art Deco, is most unlikely. The painting and sculpture are not just sententious; they are astonishingly meager as art. But precisely these qualities invite people to look at Nazi art with knowing and sniggering detachment, as a form of Pop art.

Riefenstahl's work is free of the amateurism and naïveté one finds in other art produced in the Nazi era, but it still promotes many of the same values. And the same very modern sensibility can appreciate her as well. The ironies of pop sophistication make for a way of looking at Riefenstahl's work in which not only its formal beauty but its political fervor are viewed as a form of aesthetic excess. And alongside this detached appreciation of Riefenstahl is a response, whether conscious or unconscious, to the subject itself, which gives her work its power.

Triumph of the Will and *Olympiad* are undoubtedly superb films (they may be the two greatest documentaries ever made), but they are not really important in the history of cinema as an art form. Nobody making films today alludes to Riefenstahl, whereas many filmmakers (including myself) regard the early Soviet director Dziga Vertov as an inexhaustible provocation and source of ideas about film language. Yet it is arguable that Vertov—the most important figure in documentary films—never made a film as purely effective and thrilling as *Triumph of the Will* or *Olympiad*. (Of course Vertov never had the means at his disposal that Riefenstahl had. The Soviet government's budget for propaganda films was less than lavish.) Similarly, *The Last of the Nuba* is a stunning book of photographs, but one can't imagine that it could become important to other photographers, that it could change the way people see and photograph (as has the work of Weston and Walker Evans and Diane Arbus).

In dealing with propagandistic art on the left and on the right, a double standard prevails. Few people would admit that the manipulation of emotions in Vertov's later films and in Riefenstahl's provides similar kinds of exhilaration. When explaining why they are moved, most people are sentimental in the case of Vertov and dishonest in the case of Riefenstahl. Thus Vertov's work evokes a good deal of moral sympathy on the part of his cinéphile audience all over the world; people consent to be moved. With Riefenstahl's work, the trick is to filter out the noxious political ideology of her films, leaving only their "aesthetic" merits.

Thus praise of Vertov's films always presupposes the knowledge that he was an attractive person and an intelligent and original artist-thinker, eventually crushed by the dictatorship that he served. And most of the contemporary audience for Vertov (as for Eisenstein and Pudovkin) assumes that the film propagandists in the early years of the Soviet Union were illustrating a noble ideal, however much it was betrayed in practice. But praise of Riefenstahl has no such recourse, since nobody, not even her rehabilitators, has managed to make Riefenstahl seem even likable; and she is no thinker at all. More important, it is generally thought that National Socialism stands only for brutishness and terror. But this is not true. National Socialism—or, more broadly, fascism—also stands for an ideal, and one that is also persistent today, under other banners: the ideal of life as art, the cult of beauty, the fetishism of courage, the dissolution of alienation in ecstatic feelings of community; the repudiation of the intellect; the family of man (under the parenthood of leaders).

These ideals are vivid and moving to many people, and it is dishonest—and tautological—to say that one is affected by *Triumph of the Will* and *Olympiad* because they were made by a filmmaker of genius. Riefenstahl's films are still effective because, among other reasons, their longings are still felt, because their content is a romantic ideal to which many continue to be attached, and which is expressed in such diverse modes of cultural dissidence and propaganda for new forms of community as the youth/rock culture, primal therapy, Laing's antipsychiatry, Third World camp-following, and belief in gurus and the occult. The exaltation of community does not preclude the search for absolute leadership; on the contrary, it may inevitably lead to it. (Not surprisingly, a fair number of the young people now prostrating themselves before gurus and submitting to the most grotesquely autocratic discipline are former antiauthoritarians and antielitists of the 1960s.) And Riefenstahl's devotion to the Nuba, a tribe not ruled by one supreme chief or shaman, does not mean she has lost her eye for the seducer-performer—even if she has to settle for a nonpolitician. Since she finished her work on the Nuba some years ago, one of her main projects has been photographing Mick Jagger.

Riefenstahl's current de-Nazification and vindication as indomitable priestess of the beautiful—as a filmmaker and, now, as a photographer—do not augur well for the keenness of current abilities to detect the fascist longings in our midst. The force of her work is precisely in the continuity of its political and aesthetic ideas. What is interesting is that this was once seen so much more clearly than it seems to be now.

II

Second Exhibit. Here is a book to be purchased at airport magazine stands and in "adult" bookstores, a relatively cheap paperback, not an expensive coffee-table item appealing to aesthetes and the *bien-pensant* like *The Last of the Nuba*. Yet both books share a certain community of moral origin, a certain root preoccupation. The same preoccupation at different stages of evolution—the ideas that animate *The Last of the Nuba* being less out of the moral closet than the cruder, more efficient idea that lies behind SS *Regalia*. Although SS *Regalia* is a respectable British-made compilation (with a three-page historical preface and detailed notes in the back), one knows that its appeal is not scholarly but sexual. *The Last of the Nuba*, whatever the dubious aesthetic underlying it, is certainly not pornographic: SS *Regalia* is. The cover already makes that clear. Across the large black swastika in the Nazi flag is a diagonal yellow stripe which reads "Over 100 Brilliant Four-Color Photographs" and the price, exactly the way a sticker with the price on it used to be affixed—part tease, part deference to censorship—dead center, covering the model's genitalia, on the covers of pornographic magazines.

Uniforms suggest fantasies of community, order, identity (through ranks, badges, medals that "say" who the wearer is and what he has done: his worth is recognized), competence, legitimate authority, the legitimate exercise of violence. But uniforms are not the same thing as photographs of uniforms. Photographs of uniforms are erotic material, and particularly photographs of SS uniforms. Why the SS? Because the SS seems to be the most perfect incarnation of fascism in its overt assertion of the righteousness of violence, the right to have total power over others and to treat them as absolutely inferior. It was in the SS that this assertion seemed most complete, because they acted it out in a singularly brutal and efficient manner; and because they dramatized it by linking themselves to certain aesthetic standards. The SS was designed as an elite military community that would be not only supremely violent but also supremely beautiful. (One is not likely to come across a book of this sort called "Brownshirt Regalia." The SA, whom the SS replaced, were not known for being any less brutal than their successors, but they have gone down in history as beefy, squat, beerhall types.)

SS uniforms are stylish, well cut, with a touch (but not too much) of eccentricity. Compare the rather boring and not very well cut American army uniform: jacket, shirt, tie, pants, socks, and lace-up shoes, essentially civilian clothes. SS uniforms were tight, heavy, stiff. The boots made legs and feet feel heavy, encased, obliging their wearer to stand up straight. As the jacket of SS *Regalia* explains: "The uniform was black, a color which had important overtones in Germany. On that, the SS wore a vast variety of decorations, symbols, badges to distinguish rank, from the collar runes to the death's-head. The appearance was both dramatic and menacing."

The tone of the cover is an almost wistful come-on, not quite preparing one for the banality of most of the photographs. Besides those celebrated black uniforms, SS troopers were issued almost American-army-looking khaki uniforms and camouflaged ponchos and jackets. And besides uniforms, there are pages of collar patches, cuff bands, chevrons, belt buckles, commemorative badges, regimental standards, trumpet banners, field caps, service medals, shoulder flashes, permits, passes—few of these bearing either the notorious runes or the death's-head; all meticulously identified by rank, unit, and year and season of issue. Precisely the innocuousness of practically all of the photographs testifies to the power of the image. For fantasy to have depth, it needs detail. What was the color of the travel permit an SS sergeant would have needed to get from Trier to Lübeck in the spring of 1944? One needs all the documentary evidence.

If the message of fascism has been neutralized by an aesthetic view of life, its trappings have been sexualized. This erotization of fascism has been remarked, but mostly in connection with its fancier and more publicized manifestations, as in Mishima's *Confessions of a Mask* (1949) and *Sun and Steel* (1970), and in films like Kenneth Anger's *Scorpio Rising* (1963), Visconti's *The Damned* (1969), and Liliana Cavani's *The Night Porter* (1973).

The solemn eroticism of fascism must be distinguished from a sophisticated playing with cultural horror, where there is an element of the put-on. The poster Robert Morris made for his recent show at the Castelli Gallery in April 1974 is a photograph of the artist, naked to the waist, wearing dark glasses, what appears to be a Nazi helmet, and a spiked steel collar, attached to which is a large chain that he holds in his manacled, uplifted hands. Morris is said to have considered this to be the only image that still has any power to shock; a singular virtue to those who take for granted that art is a sequence of ever-fresh gestures of provocation. But the point of the poster is its own negation. Shocking people in this context also means inuring them, as Nazi material enters the vast repertory of popular iconography usable for the ironic commentaries of Pop art.

But the material is intransigent. For one thing, Nazism fascinates in a way other iconography staked out by the pop sensibility (from Mao Tse-tung to Marilyn Monroe) does not. No doubt some part of the general rise of interest in fascism can be set down as a product of curiosity. For those born after the early 1940s, bludgeoned by a lifetime's palaver, pro and con, about Communism, Fascism—the great conversation piece of their parents' generation—represents the exotic, the unknown. Then, there is a general fascination among the young with horror, with the irrational. Courses dealing with the history of fascism are, along with those on the occult (including vampirism), among the best attended these days on college campuses. And beyond this, the definitely sexual lure of fascism, which *SS Regalia* testifies to with unabashed plainness, seems impervious to deflation by irony or overfamiliarity.

In pornographic literature, films, and gadgetry throughout the world, especially in the United States, England, France, Japan, Scandinavia, Holland, and Germany, the SS has become a reference of sexual adventurism. Much of the imagery of far-out sex has been placed under the sign of Nazism. More or less Nazi costumes with boots, leather, chains, Iron Crosses on gleaming torsos, swastikas, have become, along with meat hooks and heavy motorcycles, the secret and most lucrative paraphernalia of eroticism. In the sex shops, the baths, the leather bars, the brothels, people are dragging out their gear. But why? Why has Nazi Germany, which was a sexually repressive society, become erotic? How could a regime that persecuted homosexuals become a gay turn-on?

A clue lies in the predilections of the fascist leaders for highly sexual metaphors. (Like Nietzsche and Wagner, Hitler regarded leadership as sexual mastery of the "feminine" masses, as rape. The expression of the crowds in *Triumph of the Will* is one of ecstasy. The leader makes the crowd come.) Left-wing movements have tended to be unisex, and asexual in their imagery. Extreme right-wing movements, however puritanical and repressive the realities they usher in, have an erotic surface. Certainly Nazism is "sexier" than Communism. (Which is not something to the Nazis' credit, but rather shows something of the nature and limits of the sexual imagination.)

Of course most people who are turned on by SS uniforms are not signifying approval of what the Nazis did, if indeed they have more than the sketchiest idea of what that might be. Nevertheless, there are powerful and growing currents of sexual feeling, those that generally go by the name of sadomasochism, that make playing at Nazism seem erotic. These sadomasochistic fantasies and practices are to be found among heterosexuals as well as homosexuals, although it is among homosexuals that the eroticizing of Nazism is most visible.

"Fascism is theatre," as Genet said.[4] And sadomasochistic sexuality is more theatrical than any other. When sexuality depends so much on its being "staged," sex (like politics) becomes choreog-

---

[4] It was Genet, in his novel *Pompes funèbres* (trans. 1969), who provided one of the first texts that showed the erotic allure fascism exercised on someone who was not a fascist. Another prescient description is by Sartre, an unlikely candidate for these feelings himself and who may have heard about them from Genet. In *La Mort dans l'âme* (1949), the third novel in his four-part *Chemins de la liberté*, Sartre describes one of his protagonists experiencing the entry of the German army into Paris in 1940.

"[Daniel] was not afraid, he yielded trustingly to those thousands of eyes, he thought 'Our conquerors!' and he was supremely happy. He looked them in the eye, he feasted on their fair hair, their sunburned faces with eyes which looked like lakes of ice, their slim bodies, their incredibly long and muscular hips. He murmured: 'How handsome they are!' . . . Something had fallen from the sky: it was the ancient law. The society of judges had collapsed, the sentence had been obliterated; those ghastly little khaki soldiers, the defenders of the rights of man, had been routed. . . . An unbearable, delicious sensation spread through his body; he could hardly see properly; he repeated, gasping, 'As if it were butter—they're entering Paris as if it were butter.' . . . He would like to have been a woman to throw them flowers."

raphy. Regulars of sadomasochistic sex are expert costumers and choreographers; they are performers in the professional sense. And in a drama that is all the more exciting because it is forbidden to ordinary people. "What is purely realistic, slice of life," Leni Riefenstahl said, "what is average, quotidian, doesn't interest me." Crossing over from sadomasochistic fantasies, which are common enough, into action itself carries with it the thrill of transgression, blasphemy, entry into the kind of defiling experience that "nice" and "civilized" people can never have.

Sadomasochism, of course, does not just mean people hurting their sexual partners, which has always occurred—and generally means men beating up women. The perennial drunken Russian peasant thrashing his wife is just doing something he feels like doing (because he is unhappy, oppressed, stupefied; and because women are handy victims). But the Englishman in a brothel being whipped is re-creating his own experience. He is paying a whore to act out a piece of theatre with him, to reenact or reevoke the past— experiences of his school days or nursery that now hold for him a huge reserve of sexual energy. Today it may be the Nazi past that people invoke, in the theatricalization of sexuality, because it is that past (imaginary, for most) from which they hope a reserve of sexual energy can now be tapped. What the French call "the English vice" could, however, be said to be something of an artful affirmation of individuality: the playlet referred, after all, to the subject's own personal case history. The fad for Nazi regalia may indicate something quite different: a response to an oppressive freedom of choice in sex (and, possibly, in other matters), to an unbearable degree of individuality.

The rituals of sadomasochism being more and more practiced, the art that is more and more devoted to rendering its themes, are perhaps only a logical extension of an affluent society's tendency to turn every part of people's lives into a taste, a choice. In all societies up to now, sex has mostly been an activity (something to do, without thinking about it). But once sex becomes defined as a taste, it is perhaps already on its way to becoming a self-conscious form of theatre, which is what sadomasochism—a form of gratification that is both violent and indirect, very mental—is all about.

Sadomasochism has always been an experience in which sex becomes detached from personality, severed from relationships, from love. It should not be surprising that it has become attached to Nazi symbolism in recent years. Never before in history was the relation of masters and slaves realized with so consciously artistic a design. De Sade had to make up his theatre of punishment and delight from scratch, improvising the decor and costumes and blasphemous rites. Now there is a master scenario available to everyone. The color is black, the material is leather, the seduction is beauty, the justification is honesty, the aim is ecstasy, the fantasy is death.

Is Lina Wertmuller
Just One of the Boys?[*]

Ellen Willis

Although it may be wishful thinking—her two latest movies are a huge commercial success and critics have compared her not only to Fellini and Bergman but to Stendhal and Proust—I suspect that Lina Wertmuller is a classic case of this-year's-darling-next-year's-embarrassment. Wertmuller's basic appeal is a clever double-dealing that allows high-minded people to indulge their lowest-minded prejudices. She is not only a female woman hater—a type that has actually surpassed the Jewish anti-Semite in popularity—but a woman hater who pretends to be a feminist. She pities the benighted masses and calls it radicalism, evades responsibility for what she says and calls it comedy. This sort of duplicity requires finesse—if it's too blatant it gives the game away. But subtlety is not Wertmuller's strong point. No doubt swept away by the triumph of *Swept Away* (1974)—which I thought stretched bad faith to its limit—she has, in *Seven Beauties* (1975), stretched it even further. If she continues to overreach herself, it's only a matter of time until everyone knows that everyone knows exactly what's going on. And that, like getting caught masturbating at a porno movie, will be embarrassing.

[*] Reprinted from *Rolling Stone*, March 25, 1976, by permission of International Creative Management and Ellen Willis. Copyright © 1976 by Rolling Stone.

The first Wertmuller movie to receive much attention in this country was *Love and Anarchy* (1973). I liked it, mostly because of its energy—Wertmuller's penchant for excess has its positive side— and Giancarlo Giannini's moving performance. My personal anti-Wertmuller cult began with *The Seduction of Mimi* (1972), the story of a worker who sells out to the bosses. I sat through most of the movie juggling double messages. When Wertmuller made fun of Mimi for his arrogance, his sexual double standard, his sandbox sense of honor, I had the uncomfortable feeling that what she was really ridiculing, under cover of feminism, was her idea of a dumb Sicilian. When she set up Mimi's independent-minded mistress as a "liberated" alternative to his (dumb Sicilian) wife, then played their relationship as celebration of traditional romance (choosy virgin meets love of her life and bears him a son), I was downright confused. Was Wertmuller being ironic—so subtly ironic I was missing it—or what?

But then discomfort turned to rage as I was subjected to one of the most obnoxious scenes I've ever seen on film. To revenge himself on his wife's lover, Mimi plots to seduce the lover's wife, a middle-aged, ugly, hugely fat mother of five. She is made to seem thoroughly ridiculous not only because she is so old, so ugly, so fat, and so prolific, but because she is so gullible: how can she possibly believe Mimi's protestations of love? Doesn't she *know* how repulsive she is? The seduction scene, which depends for its effect on grotesque "comic" shots of gigantic buttocks, wobbly thighs, rolls of stomach blubber, is an exercise in the sadistic humiliation of the character, the actress who plays her, and women in general. As Mimi watches his victim undress, his eyes—those notoriously expressive Giannini eyes—widen with shock. The poor guy, having to get it up for that horror. Serves him right, the dumb Sicilian fucker, but still—! The audience at the show I saw thought it was hilarious. I thought it was as funny as cancer.

Combine the cheap-shot mentality of that scene with the political weaseling of the rest of the movie and you have the winning formula that produced *Swept Away* and *Seven Beauties*. *Swept Away* is by far the more effective—and dangerous—film. The story

—a rich bitch persecutes a communist seaman; they are stranded on an island where she needs him to survive; he beats her into submission; they fall madly in love—is a rehash of *The Taming of the Shrew* in socialist drag. Yet a lot of people who should know better insist that *Swept Away* is a serious (or satiric) comment on class politics or sexual politics or both. That is discouraging. To begin with, an allegory of class struggle that casts the woman as the bourgeoisie and the man as the proletariat is inherently corrupt. In effect, it denies the reality that it is men who exploit women and workers. This distortion is neither accidental nor original. Woman as symbol of capitalism, materialism, puritanism, or whatever repressive force is victimizing the beleaguered male is a basic cliché of our popular culture. Rebels of the 1960s from Mick Jagger to Ken Kesey relied on it; Wertmuller herself based *All Screwed Up* (an earlier 1974 movie recently released here) on the premise that women are tight-assed social climbers obsessed with consumer goods. Behind the cliché are two cherished male myths—that women dominate men and that women are economic parasites—and a volatile store of misdirected hate: not only is the rich bitch a more vulnerable target than her banker husband, but her assertion of even the most limited power and privilege is an affront to the man who soothes his class resentment with the balm of male superiority.

It is this hatred, not just class revenge, that powers Giancarlo Giannini's revolt against Mariangela Melato. For a promising moment the movie seems to be heading toward an examination of that fact. To use the stock rich woman/poor man situation to say something new about the complexities of sex and class oppression would have been a brilliant move. Instead, Wertmuller shifts gears. Suddenly our class allegory becomes a romantic idyll, our antagonists classless Man and Woman. His brutality is no longer revenge or misogyny but the necessary assertion of his manhood—an act of love, really, for now that she has experienced a "real man," she is able to fulfill herself as a "real woman," which is to say as blissful slave. The turning point comes when he is about to rape her. He makes her admit that, yes, she really wants him, whereupon he refuses to do it, unless she falls in love with him and begs him. She does and she does.

I've heard it argued that all this stuff is a parody of romanticism, and Wertmuller does adopt a spoofy tone, throwing in allusions to *Lady Chatterley's Lover* and *From Here to Eternity* to make sure we get it. But this is a transparent attempt to forestall criticism. It's instructive to note just where Wertmuller chooses to use comic exaggeration and where she doesn't. As Molly Haskell pointed out in *The Village Voice,* Melato is a caricature from beginning to end—her bitchiness is as unbelievable as her ecstasy—while Giannini is a real character. It's not just that he is more sympathetic than Melato (though he is), but that he has plausible human motives: we can identify with his outrage and understand his cruelty. Melato's love makes no sense in ordinary human terms; it depends on a stereotype that Wertmuller doesn't even try to make convincing. Instead, begging all the questions (aesthetic as well as political), she flips blithely into the comic mode where they are (she hopes) irrelevant. It doesn't work. Parody implies criticism, but Wertmuller isn't criticizing the *idea* that women want to be conquered; at most she's raising an eyebrow at the supposed *fact* of it, saying in yet another way, aren't women ridiculous? Nor can this be defended as a comment on "female masochism." Personally, I believe that women's so-called masochism is generally an attempt to make the best of a bad situation. But one need not accept that view to find Wertmuller's "parody" outrageously glib; it offers no insight into the woman's behavior, only justifies the man's. The scenes of Melato's violent subjugation, the most vivid in the movie, aren't designed to force the audience to confront its own fantasies; their function is to get people off.

The ending is more complicated. The lovers are rescued; Melato wants to remain on the island, but Giannini insists on subjecting her love to the test of civilization. She fails, shallow materialist that she is, and leaves him. The betrayal is played straight—no parody here—and so is his heartbreak. Although the sexual deck stacking is still irritating, the last scenes make a genuine political point—that the underclass carries on a one-sided love affair with bourgeois values, while the bourgeoisie uses the underclass for temporary, masochistic titillation. This idea, insisted on as more than a partial insight, becomes patronizing, but it does touch on an unpleasant truth. And Wertmuller's version of it contains an interesting ambiguity: although Melato's reluctance to go back and confront the temptations of her class privilege can be construed as escapist cowardice, it also implies a realism that is its own kind of courage. But then something nastier happens. Giannini's wife comes to meet him. She is a working-class woman, ill-dressed, old for her years, fat from childbearing and pasta, hysterical over her husband's disappearance. He looks at her with weary disgust. How can he go from a real woman—slim, sleek, blonde, with an exciting imperiousness only a real man can subdue—back to *this?* That question could be the final expression of Giannini's deluded lust after bourgeois decadence. But it isn't, because the wife is made into a caricature, a joke like Mimi's fat lady. Wertmuller looks at the woman with Giannini's eyes, shares his contempt. Her pity is not just for crushed illusions; she thinks he deserves a better class of cunt. So much for her socialism.

Seven Beauties is much more democratic; almost all the characters are contemptible. The protagonist, a big-headed punk, murders the man who has made his bovine oldest sister into a whore. He is caught, pleads insanity, and is sent to an asylum. He gets out by volunteering for the army, deserts, is captured by the Germans and sent to a concentration camp, where he sucks up to the Nazis to save his hide. The movie is a maniacal assault of images that switch back and forth from slapstick to melodrama, kicking up a cloud of political portentousness. Hero shoots pimp and has trouble cutting up the body. Hero tries to fuck three-hundred-pound Nazi commandant, a monstrous woman who will kill him if he doesn't succeed and may castrate him even if he does. Hero, ordered by the Nazis, shoots his buddy. Fellow prisoner, a sensitive anarchist, commits suicide by diving into a tub of shit. Goose. Slap. Clobber. Although *Seven Beauties* is primarily a purveyor of sensations, it is not devoid of ideas. I count at least four. (1) Life is shit. (2) Some men drown in it; others hold their noses. (3) The men who hold their noses smell bad, but after all they are only human. (4) Women are inhuman. It also boasts a central irony: hero commits a crime of honor because his sister is a whore, but in the camp he becomes a whore, and when he gets home his other sisters and his fiancée have become whores. So add (5) the world is a whorehouse.

Pasqualino (Giannini again), the man who holds his nose, is another dumb Sicilian fucker. Like all Wertmuller's male characters he is a cocky chauvinist. While she clearly disapproves of this (a shameless bid for brownie points), it is not solicitude for women that moves her, but amused contempt for silly, lower-class, culturally deprived behavior. Pasqualino is also hopelessly inept, an ambiguous trait. It is made to seem the essence of his moral failings—if he were ever to run into an ideal, he would probably knock himself cold. But it also serves as a metaphor for his mitigating, muddling-through, only-humanness—especially when he tangles with women.

In *Seven Beauties,* Wertmuller's hang-ups about women really

The Nazi commandant (Shirley Stoller) in Lina Wertmuller's *Seven Beauties* (1975). (Courtesy Cinema 5)

get out of control. Rich bitches do exist but a female Nazi commandant is a fantasy utterly divorced from historical or emotional reality. Her grotesque commandant is a bizarre tribute to her empathy
with male paranoia. Then there is the obligatory rape scene: in the
asylum, overcome by a fit of horniness, Pasqualino attacks a tied-up
psychotic woman, who bites him. It's all great fun, aimed at Pasqualino the bungler; the woman is portrayed as a machine that's
had the wrong button pushed. But when he is caught and tortured
by water hoses and electric shock, the fun stops. The torture is grim,
horrible. It is supervised by an efficient woman doctor.

Wertmuller is not your average woman hater; she has what
amounts to an obsessional conviction that women have no souls. She
sees woman as a symbol of capitalism because she sees capitalism as
a reflection of woman's acquisitive, unfeeling, frivolous nature. The
bleakest expression of that is in *All Screwed Up*. It's another comic
scene. A nice proletarian boy, driven past endurance by his girl
friend, who will neither sleep with him nor marry him (she is waiting till they can afford plastic flowers), decides to rape her. She
fights him off, but at the crucial moment her new television set
starts to topple over. Forced to make a choice, she saves the TV and
loses her virginity. Naturally, it's what she really wanted all along
(rape means never having to say you're sorry). But eventually she
ends the relationship because she is interested in money, not love.

For a woman with such a vision to call herself a feminist is not
only hypocritical but perverse. In several interviews Wertmuller has
answered women's objections to *Swept Away* by explaining that
we've misunderstood: symbolically, the woman in the movie is
really the man, and the man, the woman. I don't want to burden
this sort of sophistry with more seriousness than it deserves, but it
shows how far Wertmuller will go to deny the obvious. My guess is
that she is trying to conceal, even from herself, a dirty little secret—
that the opportunism she projects onto her sex is her own. Lina
Wertmuller wants desperately to play on the boys' team: in the end
it may be as simple as that.

The Ladies' Auxiliary, 1976

Andrew Sarris

Critic Andrew Sarris has always been sensitive to the subtle values of so-called women's genres and has written sympathetically of love stories, melodramas, soap opera, and other denigrated film types. However, he has opted consistently for women's pictures made by male "auteur" directors—Max Ophuls, Douglas Sirk, George Cukor, etc. In his influential book The American Cinema *(1968), Sarris committed the egregious sin of listing only one woman, Ida Lupino, among two hundred American directors under consideration. (He reiterates the details below.)*

In the last years Andrew Sarris's review column in The Village Voice *has shown an increasing concern for feminist issues. But has he widened his respect for the talents of women directors? In an essay solicited especially for this collection, Sarris was offered a forum to reconsider his comments in* The American Cinema *and to amend his "errant ways" for the year 1976.*

The new feminist perspectives on the cinema in the past decade (particularly in Molly Haskell's *From Reverence to Rape,* 1974) have refocused attention on the real and potential roles of woman directors. Back in 1968 (in *The American Cinema*) I tossed off the whole subject with a flippant comment on Ida Lupino's very marginal directorial career: "Ida Lupino's directed films express much of the feeling if little of the skill which she has projected so admirably as an actress." I then lumped together Dorothy Arzner, Jacqueline Audrey, Mrs. Sidney Drew, Lilian Ducey, Julia Crawford Ivers, Frances Marion, Vera McCord, Frances Nordstrom, Mrs. Wallace Reid, Lois Weber, and Margery Wilson as "little more than a ladies' auxiliary." I then cited Leni Riefenstahl (*Olympiad,* 1938, *Triumph of the Will,* 1936) and Alexander Dovjenko's widow, Yulia Solntseva (*Poem of the Sea,* 1958, *The Years of Fire,* 1961), for special mention. I concluded by reserving judgment on Vera Chytilova, Shirley Clarke, Juleen Compton, Joan Littlewood, Nadine Trintignant, Agnes Varda, and Mai Zetterling. Typical of my attitude at the time was the following comment: "Lillian Gish, that actress of actresses, once directed a film (*Remodeling Her Husband,* 1921) and declared afterward that directing was no job for a lady."

Has the situation changed appreciably since 1968? Well, there has been much more research on the careers of Dorothy Arzner (by Karyn Kay and Gerald Peary), Lois Weber (by Richard Koszarski), and Mrs. Wallace Reid. I am prepared to make a much stronger case for Leni Riefenstahl now than I was then. Barbara Loden, Elaine May, and Joan Silver have been added to the roster of American feature-film directors. Liliana Cavani, Claudine Guilmain, Marguerite Duras, Lina Wertmuller, Jeanne Moreau, and Anna Karina have directed films in Europe. Wertmuller, particularly, has become all the rage in 1976, but she seems to me to have been grossly overrated. Indeed, except for segments of *The Seduction of Mimi* (1972) and *Seven Beauties* (1975), her films have struck me as shrill, strident, confused, and strikingly antifeminist.

A great many women have entered the documentary field with the result that feminist biographies and autobiographies now constitute a subgenre of sorts, and one with which I am unfortunately unfamiliar. But even Leni Riefenstahl's reputation has been based more on her documentaries than on her fiction features, although *The Blue Light* (1932) has never been given its proper due by most film historians, including the redoubtable and usually reliable Susan

Sontag. Actually, Riefenstahl's reputation has to be reconstructed from whatever footage we have available. The justifiable passions aroused by her involvement with the Nazi regime have literally blinded most of the civilized world to her artistic contributions. Still, it is unlikely that she will ever be embraced by the women's movement. The moral here is that an increase in the number of woman directors will not in itself guarantee an increase in the number of ideologically correct films from the feminist viewpoint.

There will undoubtedly be more woman directors in the future, partly because of the self-conscious thrust of feminism, and partly because of the ever-increasing glamorization of the role of the director in auteurist criticism. In the future a creative producer-scenarist like Joan Harrison, who was so influential in the careers of Alfred Hitchcock and Robert Siodmak, will turn to direction. But it remains to be seen how many women will ever be able to sustain their careers on a regular basis for as much as a decade. In this respect Dorothy Arzner has stood alone in America as a viable woman director since the sound era. Auteurist analysis, particularly, requires a sizable body of work before any personal style can be discerned. Ida Lupino was easy to do in the days when the very subject of woman directors seemed a frivolous one. Lupino had already established her personality as an actress, and it was not surprising that her protégées—Sally Forrest and Mala Powers—should look like her. Her weepy social consciousness and snarling paranoia were also in accord with her previous Warners image. But in her best films—*Not Wanted* (1949), *Outrage* (1950), *Hard, Fast and Beautiful* (1951), *The Bigamist* (1953)—her woman protagonists were disconcertingly dependent on the supportive love of men. *Hard, Fast and Beautiful* went even further by espousing an anti-careerist, promarriage destiny for women. In fact, it is hard to imagine the role of the bitch-mother (played by Claire Trevor) being directed any more misogynously by a male director. As for the driven daughter (Sally Forrest) with the tennis talent, she seems light-years rather than mere decades away from the aggressive life-styles of Chris Evert and Billie Jean King.

So it is to Dorothy Arzner rather than to Ida Lupino to which the feminist revisionist film historian must turn for sociological sustenance. All sorts of enlightened interpretations can be read into *The Wild Party* (1929, female camaraderie on a sensual level), *Merrily We Go to Hell* (1932, maturing woman redeeming the dissolute man-child), *Christopher Strong* (1933, courageous aviatrix taking her life and death into her own hands to end a messy affair), *Nana* (1934, the temptress made ambiguous), *Craig's Wife* (1936, George Kelly's murderously materialistic wife made so emotionally vulnerable that Kelly himself disowned the movie), *The Bride Wore Red* (1937, a harder edge to the Cinderella story), and *Dance, Girl, Dance* (1940, women learning to define themselves apart from the weak males fluttering like moths around the flames of femaleness). Dorothy Arzner also seemed unique in her graphic mannerisms, her Greek statues, and ornate bric-a-brac, etc. Still, she must be judged in the context of an era (the 1930s and early 1940s) in which women stars, women writers (both in and out of the medium), and women audiences were far more powerful and influential than they were to be in the 1960s and 1970s. It is hard to make too strong a case for Miss Arzner's being more woman-oriented than Ernst Lubitsch, Max Ophuls, Josef von Sternberg, Frank Borzage, Gregory La Cava, Vincente Minnelli, Douglas Sirk, Lowell Sherman, or Joseph L. Mankiewicz. Picture by picture, they are simply too overwhelmingly accomplished for her. And her only ideological edge from a feminist point of view may turn out to be the spectacular spinelessness of her male characters. Her work remains eminently worthy of study and of pleasurable perusal, but it would have been too much to expect that her art could have flowered amid such extraordinarily high occupational odds. From a mere footnote Dorothy Arzner has risen to a chapter heading all her own. It is too early to tell if she will have any American successors of her own sex. Perhaps all the feminist action has shifted irrevocably to television, and it is there and there only that we shall have to look for the emergence of female talent and a feminist viewpoint.

Bibliography

Barkhausen, Hans. "Footnote to the History of Riefenstahl's 'Olympia.'" *Film Quarterly* (Fall 1974).

Barsam, Richard M. *Filmguide to TRIUMPH OF THE WILL.* Bloomington, Ind.: Indiana University Press, 1975.

Biskind, Peter. "Lina Wertmuller: The Politics of Private Life." *Film Quarterly* (Winter 1974–1975).

Blumenfeld, Gina. "The (Next to) Last Word on Lina Wertmuller." *Cinéaste,* 7, no. 2 (1976).

Delahaye, Michael. "Interview with Leni Riefenstahl." *Cahiers du Cinéma* (September 1965). Reprinted in Andrew Sarris, ed., *Interviews with Film Directors.* New York: Avon Books, 1969.

Goodwin, Michael, and Wise, Naomi. "Howard Hawks." *Take One,* 3, no. 8 (1973).

Gregor, Ulrich. "A Comeback for Leni Riefenstahl?" *Film Comment* (Winter 1965).

Haskell, Molly. "Howard Hawks—Masculine Feminine." *Film Comment* (March–April 1974).

Hitchens, Gordon. "An Interview with a Legend." *Film Comment* (Winter 1965). [Leni Riefenstahl]

Jameson, Richard. *"Chinatown." Movietone News* (July 1974).

Kael, Pauline. "Seven Fatties." *The New Yorker,* February 16, 1976. [*Seven Beauties*]

Kavanagh, James. *"Chinatown:* Other Places Other Times." *Jump Cut,* no. 3 (September–October 1974).

Leiser, Erwin. *Nazi Cinema.* Translated by Gertrud Mander and David Wilson. New York: The Macmillan Co., 1975.

Modleski, Tania. "Wertmuller's Women: Swept Away by the Usual Destiny." *Jump Cut*, nos. 10 and 11 (1976).

Peary, Gerald. "Fast Cars and Women." In Joseph McBride, ed., *Focus on Howard Hawks*. Englewood Cliffs, N.J.: Prentice-Hall, Inc., 1972.

Penley, Constance; Salyer, Saunie; and Shedlin, Michael. "Interview with Howard Hawks." *Jump Cut*, no. 5 (January–February 1975).

Quacinella, Lucy. "How Left Is Lina?" *Cinéaste*, 7, no. 3 (1976).

Simon, John. "Wertmuller's *Seven Beauties*—Call It a Masterpiece." *New York*, February 2, 1976.

Sperber, Murray. "*Chinatown:* Polanski's Message and Manipulation." *Jump Cut*, no. 3 (September–October 1974).

Wise, Naomi. "The Hawksian Woman." *Take One*, 3, no. 3 (1971).

Wood, Michael. "All Mixed Up." *The New York Review of Books*, February 16, 1976. [Lina Wertmuller]

VII
Feminist Film Theory

Interview with British Cine-Feminists

E. Ann Kaplan

INTRODUCTION

*The following discussion took place in London in September 1974,
with Laura Mulvey, Claire Johnston, and Pam Cook. Laura Mulvey
had just finished a film,* Penthesilea, *made jointly with Peter Wollen; Claire Johnston was completing a collective film project, referred to here as* The Equal Pay Film *but now called* The Amazing
Equal Pay Show; *Pam Cook was working on feminist film theory
and had written an essay with Claire on "The Place of Women in the
Cinema of Raoul Walsh," subsequently included in an Edinburgh
Film Festival monograph on the American director. Claire had also
edited a British Film Institute Pamphlet,* Notes on Women's
Cinema, *and another,* Dorothy Arzner, *with essays by Pam and
herself.*[1]

*The preliminary discussion transcribed here begins to high-
light some of the basic differences in feminist film criticism and
film practice between England and America. These differences ap-*

[1] Most recently, Claire Johnston has edited, together with Paul Willemen,
another Edinburgh Film Festival monograph, *Jacques Tourneur,* and helped
organize an Edinburgh Film Festival Event, "Psychoanalysis and Cinema," in
the summer of 1976 (along with Peter Wollen and Laura Mulvey). Peter and
Laura recently obtained a British Film Institute grant to make another avant-
garde film.

ply equally to the form and style of the women's movement in the two nations, and are in turn linked with larger matters of intellectual and political traditions. When the discussion occurred, America had produced more feminist film criticism than England. The first issue of the California-based Women in Film *had been published in 1972, and subsequent issues offered a crucial forum for approaches to feminist film criticism. The exchange of ideas stimulated others to connect feminism and filmmaking (cf., for example,* The Velvet Light Trap's *special issue, number 6, on sexual politics). The three books about women in film that came out in 1973 and 1974 (those by Joan Mellen, Marjorie Rosen, and Molly Haskell), limited in theory as they all were, nevertheless opened much ground. Rosen and Haskell dug up forgotten films and prepared the way for more methodical approaches to the history of women in the American film, while Mellen offered an unorthodox critique of women in the contemporary foreign film.*

All of this diverse writing was important in exploring the general idea of women in film, but it is striking (even if characteristic) that most American criticism lacked self-consciousness about methodology and concern with the theory of the cinema. Many critics were writing popular sociology, so little did they deal with the process of cinema itself, with film production, audience/screen relationship, formal and theoretical problems. This nonsystematic approach to criticism can produce occasionally excellent results (writers are not inhibited by awesome notions of what must be achieved before they can contribute anything), but the drawback is that discipline, careful thought, or even the most basic scholarship are often lacking.

The British group are perhaps at the other extreme. Before writing any feminist film criticism, the British women wanted first to develop a viable theoretical position based on a thorough investigation of the nature of the cinema; second, to figure out what a feminist approach to film might be, given that framework; third, to explore the complex relations between culture, ideology, the conscious and the unconscious, the artist and artworks, and how these matters affect the presentation of women in film.

The position of the British women has been developed within a specific, minority intellectual context that has arisen around The

New Left Review, *the British Film Institute Education Department, and the periodical* Screen, *published by the Society for Education in Film and Television. Other influences came from Peter Wollen's* Signs and Meaning in the Cinema *(1973), the writings of Raymond Williams, and* Working Papers in Cultural Studies *out of Birmingham University. The more current influences have arrived from abroad: the difficult Marxist theories of the post-auteur* Cahiers du Cinéma *in France; new ways of reading Brecht; French structuralism, particularly as articulated by Claude Lévi-Strauss and Roland Barthes; Freudian psychoanalysis as interpreted by Jacques Lacan, a French analyst, whose work has been propagated in England through Anthony Wilden's edition,* Language of the Self: The Function of Language in Psychoanalysis *(1973). And Juliet Mitchell, in linking Lévi-Strauss's notion of women as the basis of exchange with the precepts of psychoanalysis, made a central contribution to the thinking of the British feminist film critics (cf. her* Psychoanalysis and Feminism, *1974). In addition, there are the influences of linguistics, the Russian formalists, the writings of Marx, and of Louis Althussers' reinterpretations of Marx (cf. his* For Marx, *1970).*

To the American feminist, the arguments of the British critics may seem rigid, overly scholastic, or simply intimidating. Most of us do not think in terms of "correct" political, aesthetic, or theoretical positions to the exclusion of more flexible and spontaneous approaches to problems. But a certain humility is essential in considering the British work. The virtue of the British approach is that it offers specific frameworks within which to carry on dialogue and develop theories that can be applied to both analyzing and making films. Whatever we may think about the specific resolutions of the British feminists to complex cinematic issues, we probably must agree that the questions asked are the ones that we in America must confront and resolve in our own ways.

E. A. K.

ANN KAPLAN: Perhaps you could begin by talking about what's been happening in England in terms of developing a feminist cinema—what movies women have made, are currently making, film workshops and collectives that exist and how they are functioning.

CLAIRE JOHNSTON: There is only one women's film group— the one that I'm involved with—and we've been going for about two and a half years. It was set up to fill distinct needs that women have. The film industry in this country reflects the American industry: it's extremely hierarchically structured and in a state of tremendous crisis, but with all the prestige and capitalist orientation of the American system. Women obviously have a marginal role. They tend to exist in ghetto jobs—in continuity and, in television, as production assistants. There are no camerawomen and virtually no sound women. Whole areas are closed, so there was, and is, a need for women to actually start making films, acquiring and sharing skills. A number of American documentary films were around, like Midge MacKenzie's film, *Women Talking* [1971], and Kate Millet's *Three Lives* [1970], that were shown at a weekend seminar. Some people were dissatisfied with the films because they reflected the American notion of the women's movement and didn't seem useful here. Other people were dissatisfied with *cinéma vérité* orientations, and likewise wanted to develop some notion of what British feminist films could be.

AK: When did this all start?

CJ: This was in Christmas 1971/72. For the first six months the London Women's Film Group wasn't very active, and then a lot of people started doing things. For instance, Laura Mulvey, myself, and Linda Myles were involved in organizing the first women's film festival in Edinburgh, where we showed about twenty feature films, many that had never been shown in England before. The film group had just started production on the first film that was going to be made collectively, although films by individual members, like Linda Dove's *Miss Missus* [1972], had been shown at Edinburgh. The collective film, *Bettshanger, Kent 72,* was shot in February and March 1972 at the Bettshanger miners' strike. It was a dramatic strike, and we went and interviewed a lot of women (wives who were backing their husbands and organizing behind their husbands) about their position in the mining community. Several other films were made by Esther Ronay, one of the active people in the film union. She was an assistant editor, one of the ghetto jobs that women have in the film industry. The left-wing union decided to make films against the Industrial Relations Act—a bit of Tory legislation designed to curb how workers bargain. One of them was *Women Against the Bill* [1972], and Esther directed it. The film has had a lot of influence, since it's not just about the Industrial Relations Act—that would make it useless now—but also deals with the problem of equal pay, the position of women in terms of the contradiction between home and work, and that kind of thing. Esther made another film, *Women of the Rhondda* [1973], that consists of interviews with women in the Rhondda about the general strike in 1926 and their lives as women in the mining community. But despite her activity in the film group and these films she has made, Esther was refused an interview with the National Film School.

AK: Where are these films shown, outside of festivals?

CJ: We don't distribute the films—we're just not set up for that—so we've given them to The Other Cinema, which is a left-wing distribution company. But we always keep copies ourselves, since we think it's important to go out and talk with the films. We take them to colleges, schools, women's groups, conferences, and a couple of us usually go.

AK: So you are really using the films as stimulants to discussion?

CJ: Yes, although I don't agree with that particular way of using film. I always try to generate discussion about what a feminist cinema would be. I think the attitude that a lot of filmmakers have, that films merely can be used as stimulants in a discussion, is a pernicious one.

AK: I'd like you to explain more about that in a moment, but I wanted first to say that your description fits what women in America have been doing with their films. Women have been making *cinéma vérité* documentary films almost exclusively in America, although there are few about working-class women. Is there still interest in *cinéma vérité* here and why do you object to it?

CJ: I think the influence of American *cinéma vérité* is extremely strong. There are people in the film group still very committed to it; but over the past year or so, as a result of film festivals, some of us have gotten interested in feminist film criticism, and have begun to query the whole idea of political cinema. Some people were also very struck with entertainment movies that were shown, seeing how effective these could be from a feminist standpoint. I'm thinking of a film like Dorothy Arzner's *Dance, Girl, Dance* [1940], for instance. Most people were totally unaware that there were women making big entertainment movies. So there has been this interest in entertainment film, very much linked with Brecht. The whole idea that entertainment and politics don't go together is absurd.

AK: But are you concerned mainly with effective ways of getting a message across, or do you view these as specifically aesthetic questions?

CJ: I have often been very struck by *cinéma vérité* movies and am convinced of their importance to the women's movement. But to people outside, what a lot of *cinéma vérité* movies do—women talking endlessly and telling their experiences—often has no effect at all. It doesn't do any work in terms of presenting ideas or actually engaging the audience at any level. It encourages passivity.

AK: But I do think that the films work in the context for which they were perhaps designed—the classroom or discussion session where the teacher or leader elicits response to the issues raised in the film and gets people to think through for themselves the implications of the women's experiences. I have used the American films numerous times and found that they opened up students to all kinds of awarenesses they didn't have previously. But do you really think that entertainment, comedy or other modes than realism, in fact reach people better, engage, and excite them more?

PAMELA COOK: Obviously it's quite a crucial question for us. It's difficult to know how to put it simply, but I see the whole notion of *cinéma vérité* as being linked to direct speech, the notion of actually being able to apprehend the message, as you call it, in some direct way. This idea is what we're deliberately trying to work against, which is why Claire tried to move us into the notion of entertainment. At least in the entertainment film you are in some sense aware of strategies at work; there is a possibility of standing back from the material.

CJ: We could say that our *Equal Pay Film* [1974] was, in fact, quite a break. A theatre group wrote and performed it first, but our decision to rework and film it is significant. It is based on notions of an epic theatre and is an extraordinarily didactic parody of male chauvinist notions in unions and male chauvinism in the media.

AK: It's not realism at all, then.

CJ: No. Everybody is a woman, for instance. All the men are played by women. It's most unrealistic, based on pleasure, the actual amusement of the situation. Yet it's a politically very well worked out film.

PC: It's the idea of realism which we're trying to question rather than saying that *cinéma vérité* is realist and the entertainment film is nonrealist. We tried to interrogate the notion of realism in the cinema.

AK: It seems to me that there's a difference between working with Brechtian ideas in trying to develop a countercinema in a self-conscious way, and applying Brechtian and Barthesian concepts in a feminist way to Hollywood directors who were obviously working with quite antithetical notions about the cinema. Take, for example, your and Claire's recent collaborative article, "The Place of Women in the Cinema of Raoul Walsh."[2] Your discussion of how women in Walsh's films are exchanged and function merely as signs in the male world is fascinating, but your conclusions come out of a postulated framework of absolutes, none of which Walsh himself was aware of. Brecht, on the other hand, was totally aware of what he was doing.

CJ: In that Marx chose not to study what revolutionary society would be, but rather to concentrate on what capital is, and to give a scientific rationale of what it is, so I think that feminist film criticism can only emerge out of an analysis of the existing cinema. You have to have a correct view of Hollywood, because it is the largest kind of film variable, the most important area; most concepts about film derive from the Hollywood genres. So, we study Walsh, not because we want to make a case for him (we don't want to do this, although Walsh is interesting for all kinds of reasons), but because we think it's absolutely essential to look again at the big Hollywood directors

[2] Phil Hardy, ed., *Raoul Walsh* (London: Vineyard Press, 1974), pp. 93–109.

from a feminist standpoint. We must do this scientifically because only if we can do that will we be able to develop strategies for what feminist cinema could be; the ideas will emerge from that knowledge. What is wrong with so much American film criticism, and most feminist film criticism in fact, is that it actually takes an extraordinarily superficial view of Hollywood. It doesn't in any way account for the film. People like [John] Ford—not that I'm making a case for them in terms of feminism—are extraordinarily interesting—however unconscious artists they are. They are not tied in any simple way to an ideology. There is this simple notion in much feminist film criticism of an ideological message superimposed by the studio, which is always there. But in fact ideology is an extraordinarily complex and contradictory thing.

PC: You can't actually read directly from a film. We reject an ideological or sociological reading. We ought to say that we're very influenced by contemporary European criticism.

CJ: We should really say that both Pam and I, and Laura Mulvey too, have come to feminist film criticism out of an interest in film criticism in general. Our work stems from the theoretical kind of apparatus which has developed over the last few years out of auteur theory and semiology. We see these tools as being absolutely crucial for feminist film—that is, auteurism, structuralism, and psychoanalysis.

AK: Out of all the other possible approaches, why is it that you choose to utilize these specific tools for feminist criticism? Aren't they developed outside of feminist concerns?

CJ: As far as I'm concerned, it's a question of what is theoretically correct; these new theoretical developments cannot be ignored, just as feminists cannot ignore Marx or Freud, because they represent crucial scientific developments. There are aspects of them that show patriarchal ideology at work, but there are also aspects of them that are obviously extremely useful to feminism.

PC: We would never deny the reality of the patriarchal order and we are particularly concerned with delineating women's position within that patriarchal order. In fact, the kind of theoretical approach deriving from Lévi-Strauss is in a direct line with the work that we're talking about.

AK: So what makes your criticism feminist is not the analytical tools but the focus you adopt in using the tools.

PC: Women are fixed in ideology in a particular way which is definable in terms of the patriarchal system. I think we see our first need as primarily to define that place—the place that women are fixed in.

AK: I'd like to move on to a question arising from your introduction to *Notes on Women's Cinema* [1973], Claire. You say there that "we have to make use of the theory of the working of the unconscious as developed by Freud." I wish you would expand on that, particularly in the light of the effect that Juliet Mitchell's book *Psychoanalysis and Feminism* had on American feminists. People are puzzled as to why she wants to defend Freud and to vindicate Freud's concept of the unconscious.

CJ: As far as I'm concerned, Freud is the only psychoanalyst to develop a theory of the unconscious that is viable. Reich actually abandoned the notion of the unconscious and most feminists are Reichian.

AK: Or Laingian.

CJ: Laing certainly rejects the theory of the unconscious completely. The interest in Freud comes out of the centrality that he places on the primary process which is the unconscious. We're also interested in him because of the link that Freud made, but didn't go into in much detail, between the role of language and its relation to the unconscious. Freudian followers like Jacques Lacan (although I'm sure Lacan would not see himself as a follower) have developed this connection in detail. It is clear that film is closely allied to fantasy. The placement of the audience vis-à-vis the film is a voyeuristic one and conjures up a sort of dream situation in which the primary process is very much in operation. There are a lot of analogies between dream and film; the actual mechanisms that take place invite displacement. We talk about woman as being displaced by man; there are close connections between the phenomenon of psychological displacement and how men use women on the screen. We started our film criticism group with a Freudian study group in which we particularly studied the interpretation of dreams and what relation it could have to art.

PC: Freud has situated the unconscious in a quite specific way. It is structured like a language, and that's quite crucial. It's also very difficult to explain, but it's central to what we're trying to say.

AK: Are you saying that the unconscious has laws that are as rigid as the grammar of a spoken language?

PC: In that it is manifested through what one would call conscious discourse, I guess that's right. On the other hand, it's not there for the taking, so to speak. Because of the primary processes involved, which are complex and multilevel, it is something which has to be deciphered. The work that goes into producing any art is similar to the work that goes into dreamwork. The dream doesn't exist except when it's spoken. In that sense, the processes are analogous—not the same, I think, but the same pattern.

CJ: What is one talking about when one mentions the sexism or the patriarchal system in operation in Walsh or Ford? One is talking about a largely totally unconscious structure that's culturally received, and that exists within the language that Walsh and everybody else has inherited. Our interest in Walsh is not that he is sexist or that he is a victim of patriarchal ideology, but in how the ideology of the patriarchal order is mediated through all the other interests that he developed in his films, partly consciously and partly unconsciously. Almost all directors are patriarchal in different ways, and the ways that they differ are extraordinarily interesting. One of the first people to point all this out was a male critic, Peter Wollen, in his *Signs and Meaning in the Cinema* [1969]. His account of Hawks includes the first kernel of a feminist critique. The way these male directors differ is interesting because it lays bare whole areas of how ideology operates within any cultural product. But film is particularly interesting and unique as an art form, as a product, because of its relationship to the audience. It is a total experience shared by a large number of people in the dark, and it plays on various kinds of senses that people like—the voyeuristic desires and things of that kind that are closely related to fetishism. That's why women have probably been fetishized far more within the cinema than, say, they have in the novel, because it is *possible*— the cinema plays on the pleasure of sight.

PC: So films are only analogous to dreams in certain ways. Claire has made some of the differences somewhat clearer now. It's obviously not the same voyeuristic pleasure that comes into play as when you're talking about dreams, but there are analogous processes at work.

AK: I'm interested in how you link ideology—which is really the key thing—with these unconscious processes. You're saying that male directors are not consciously sexist and patriarchal.

CJ: Oh, they could be as well.

AK: But you're saying that we need a theory of the unconscious in order to lead us better into the way ideologies are internalized by men and women, and then reproduced in various artworks. This gives us a method of analyzing that is rather different from the usual political one, or one in terms of sociology and realism. Those other methods try to make a connection between the situation of women in the culture at any one time that a movie is made, and the movie image of women. Marjorie Rosen, for example, in *Popcorn Venus,* makes these kinds of connections.

CJ: I don't think you *can* make any direct link between a sociological kind of analysis of society and the art products involved. Such attempts are extraordinarily misleading, and offer extremely simplistic views of what ideology is.

AK: What about Marx in this context? In your pamphlet in *Notes on Women's Cinema* there seems to be a contradiction in the positions you assign to Marx. At one point you say that both Marx and Lenin pointed to there being no direct connection between the development of art and the material base of society, yet at another point you say that, following Marx, "works of art are products—products of an existing system and the economic relations, in the final analysis." This Marxist concept of the link between the capitalist system and art products seems to contradict what you say earlier.

CJ: There *is* a connection but I said that there was no *direct* connection. Lenin was very interested in art and put Leon Trotsky in charge of education and art. He encouraged all kinds of clearly bourgeois artists to continue. The theory was that actually bourgeois art could be enormously illuminating and useful, and this is what we're saying. A study of Raoul Walsh and of sexist directors could be very useful to us. Jacques Lacan is an extraordinarily brilliant sexist psychoanalyst. Some of his scientific discoveries are very important. It was badly put in the essay, and should have been elaborated, but what I meant was that Marx and Lenin said there was no direct connection between ideology and the material base. That idea of the relative autonomy of ideology is one you find in Althusser and people like that.[3]

PC: This is very crucial for feminism, because I think we have a situation where sexism, the patriarchal culture, is in many ways not really even functional for capitalism anymore. The ideology of the family, for instance, no longer serves much purpose in capitalism, but it persists as an idea because of the relative autonomy of ideology.

CJ: This is not to say that we don't accept that there are enormous gaps in all these scientific theories, which, as you say, are produced by men. We actually want to ask those questions that are in the gaps, or at least discover the gaps.

(For the last section, Laura Mulvey joins the discussion.)

AK: I'd like you to talk more about how your approach is able to describe more accurately what it is that's being done to women on the screen, than the straight content/role analysis.

CJ: First of all, there's a necessity to have recourse to some scientific notion of how myth operates in any art. The only person who has come up with a theory of myth is Roland Barthes. You have to look at women as a sign within a patriarchal order. I can't see how

---

[3] The influence of Althusser on people like Claire and Pam, heavily involved in theory, may in part account for difficulties more traditional Marxists have with their position. The London Women's Film Group as a whole clearly view themselves as Marxists, but Claire, Pam, and Laura freely admit that they have not yet satisfactorily resolved some theoretical contradictions between psychoanalysis (now a central part of their analyses) and the rationalism and historical form of Marxist thinking. In her latest essay on Jacques Tourneur (in a book of essays edited by herself) Claire Johnston attempts to formulate a position between the extreme psychoanalytic and semiological line taken by *Screen* editors and the sometimes equally extreme line taken by those opposed to the *Screen* stance. She agrees that theory must have practical application in political work and hopes to elucidate the links between her evolving theoretical position and action.

you can look at women in any other way, particularly in a visual media such as cinema.

LAURA MULVEY: I think it can be useful to do role analysis, but you tend to be just left saying that this woman is presented positively, this woman is presented unpositively; this woman is being denigrated, this woman isn't. These are all value judgments of a kind which don't come to terms with why women are like that. It leaves little more than a sense of self-congratulation that you've at last seen that women have been presented in a derogatory way, which we must all to a certain extent already be aware of. Or, alternatively, one experiences satisfaction if the role is positive in contemporary terms.

CJ: It's a process of demystification, which is essential but actually extraordinarily limited. It often isn't backed up with any knowledge of how and why. Unless you understand the processes, how can you ever hope to radically change them?

AK: But the content critics go on to talk about political or sociological matters, the Christian heritage or, if they are Marxists, property and the division of labor, as reasons for women being treated in such a way. I guess that's where you feel the methodology breaks down: you begin with an artwork . . .

LM: . . . and you're left with the whole history of Western civilization!

CJ: It's enormously simplistic. You have to look at the specificity of cinema and the actual situation of viewing. This includes the pleasure involved with watching and the way women are very much related to being watched. This seems to me to be far more important to take into account than simply "social conditions."

LM: Film shouldn't be taken as a one-to-one reflection of the world, or even of how people think in the real world. It's something quite different, isn't it?

CJ: You can have films that on a content level appear quite progressive but that at the same time, at the level of cinema, the level of the way the sign is used, are still extremely fetishistically involved with women. This is particularly true of the modern cinema where there seems to be a direct attempt by a number of liberal filmmakers, and even women, to project a free woman. Many of the films draw on reactionary myths—for instance, the myth of the suffering Madonna—in an ostensibly progressive way—woman as exemplary victim becomes the new heroine of the sixties. They are all myths. Our culture is saturated with contradictory myths of women.

PC: Claire is quite right. One has to look at film in terms of the cinema itself and not in sociological terms.

CJ: Beyond these theoretical questions, we must attempt to show what a feminist or countercinema could be, bridging the gap between theoreticians and practical filmmakers, if you like, between people who are interested in formal problems concerning the cinema and people who are interested largely in being practical filmmakers. Our film group can be a vital link between the two.

AK: It seems vital that this connection be made because you're trying to articulate a new kind of cinema, even talking about developing a new cinema language to replace the male cinema language that presented women in only very limited ways. If women continue to use male cinematic conventions, according to your whole thesis, there won't be a feminist cinema at all.

Myths of Women in the Cinema[*]

Claire Johnston

. . . there arose, identifiable by standard appearance, behaviour and attributes, the well-remembered types of the Vamp and the Straight Girl (perhaps the most convincing modern equivalents of the medieval personifications of the Vices and Virtues), the Family Man and the Villain, the latter marked by a black moustache and walking stick. Nocturnal scenes were printed on blue or green film. A checkered table-cloth meant, once for all, "poor but honest" milieu; a happy marriage, soon to be endangered by the shadows from the past symbolised by the young wife's pouring of the breakfast coffee for her husband; the first kiss was invariably announced by the lady's gently playing with her partner's necktie and was invariably accompanied by her kicking out with her left foot. The conduct of the characters was predetermined accordingly.

—Erwin Panofsky, "Style and Medium in the Motion Pictures," 1934.

Panofsky's detection of the primitive stereotyping that characterized the early cinema could prove useful for discerning the way myths of women have operated in the cinema: why the image of man underwent rapid differentiation, while the primitive stereotyping of women remained with some modifications. Much writing on the stereotyping of women in the cinema takes as its starting point a

* Excerpted from "Women's Cinema as Countercinema," *Notes on Women's Cinema,* ed. Claire Johnston, *Screen,* Pamphlet 2, 1974.

monolithic view of the media as repressive and manipulative: in this way, Hollywood has been viewed as a dream factory producing an oppressive cultural product. This overpoliticized view bears little relation to the ideas on art expressed by either Marx or Lenin, who both pointed to there being no direct connection between the development of art and the material basis of society. The idea of the intentionality of art that this view implies is extremely misleading and retrograde, and short-circuits the possibility of a critique that could prove useful for developing a strategy for women's cinema.

If we accept that the developing of female stereotypes was not a conscious strategy of the Hollywood dream machine, what are we left with? Panofsky locates the origins of iconography and stereotype in the cinema in terms of practical necessity; he suggests that in the early cinema the audience had much difficulty deciphering what appeared on the screen. Fixed iconography, then, was introduced to aid understanding and provide the audience with basic facts with which to comprehend the narrative. Iconography as a specific kind of sign or cluster of signs based on certain conventions within the Hollywood genres has been partly responsible for the stereotyping of women within the commercial cinema in general, but the fact that there is a far greater differentiation of men's roles than of women's roles in the history of the cinema relates to sexist ideology itself, and the basic opposition that places man inside history, and woman as ahistoric and eternal. As the cinema developed, the stereotyping of man was increasingly interpreted as contravening the realization of the notion of "character"; in the case of woman, this was not the case; the dominant ideology presented her as eternal and unchanging, except for modifications in terms of fashion, etc.

In general, the myths governing the cinema are no different from those governing other cultural products: they relate to a standard value system informing all cultural systems in a given society. Myth uses icons, but the icon is its weakest point. Furthermore, it is possible to use icons (that is, conventional configurations) in the face of and against the mythology usually associated with them. In his magisterial work on myth (*Mythologies*, London: Jonathan Cape, 1971) the critic Roland Barthes examines how myth, as the signifier of an ideology, operates by analyzing a whole range of items: a national dish, a society wedding, a photograph from *Paris Match*. In his book he analyzes how a sign can be emptied of its original denotative meaning and a new connotative meaning superimposed on it. What was a complete sign consisting of a signifier plus a signified becomes merely the signifier of a new signified, which subtly usurps the place of the original denotation. In this way, the new connotation is mistaken for the natural, obvious and evident denotation: this is what makes it the signifier of the ideology of the society in which it is used.

Myth then, as a form of speech or discourse, represents the major means in which women have been used in the cinema: myth transmits and transforms the ideology of sexism and renders it invisible—when it is made visible it evaporates—and therefore natural. This process puts the question of the stereotyping of women in a somewhat different light. In the first place, such a view of the way cinema operates challenges the notion that the commercial cinema is more manipulative of the image of woman than the art cinema. It could be argued that precisely because of the iconography of Hollywood, the system offers some resistance to the unconscious workings of myth. Sexist ideology is no less present in the European art cinema because stereotyping appears less obvious; it is in the nature of myth to drain the sign (the image of woman/the function of woman in the narrative) of its meaning and superimpose another that thus appears natural: in fact, a strong argument could be made for the art film inviting a greater invasion from myth. This point assumes considerable importance when considering the emerging women's cinema. The conventional view about women working in Hollywood (Arzner, Weber, Lupino, etc.) is that they had little opportunity for real expression within the dominant sexist ideology; they were token women and little more. In fact, because iconography offers in some ways a greater resistance to the realist characterizations, the mythic qualities of certain stereotypes become far more easily detachable and can be used as a shorthand for referring to an ideological tradition in order to provide a critique of it. It is possible to disengage the icons from the myth and thus bring about reverberations within the sexist ideology in which the film is made.

Dorothy Arzner certainly made use of such techniques and the work of Nelly Kaplan is particularly important in this respect. As a European director she understands the dangers of myth invading the sign in the art film, and deliberately makes use of Hollywood iconography to counteract this. The use of crazy comedy by some women directors (e.g., Stephanie Rothman) also derives from this insight.

In rejecting a sociological analysis of woman in the cinema we reject any view in terms of realism, for this would involve an acceptance of the apparent natural denotation of the sign and would involve a denial of the reality of myth in operation. Within a sexist ideology and a male-dominated cinema, woman is presented as what she represents for man. Laura Mulvey, in her most useful essay on the Pop artist Allen Jones ("You Don't Know What You're Doing Do You, Mr. Jones?," *Spare Rib,* February 1973), points out that woman as woman is totally absent in Jones's work. The fetishistic image portrayed relates only to male narcissism: woman represents not herself but, by a process of displacement, the male phallus. It is probably true to say that despite the enormous emphasis placed on woman as spectacle in the cinema, woman as woman is largely absent. A sociological analysis based on the empirical study of recurring roles and motifs would lead to a critique in terms of an enumeration of the notion of career/home/motherhood/sexuality, an examination of women as the central figures in the narrative, etc. If we view the image of woman as sign within the sexist ideology, we see that the portrayal of woman is merely one item subject to the law of verisimilitude, a law that directors worked with or reacted against. The law of verisimilitude (what determines the impression of realism) in the cinema is precisely responsible for the repression of the image of woman as woman and the celebration of her nonexistence.

This point becomes clearer when we look at a film that revolves around a woman entirely and the idea of the female star. In their analysis of Sternberg's *Morocco* (1930), the critics of *Cahiers du Cinéma* delineate the system that is in operation: in order that the man remain within the center of the universe in a text that focuses on the image of woman, the auteur is forced to repress the idea of woman as a social and sexual being (her Otherness) and to deny the opposition man/woman altogether. The woman as sign, then, becomes the pseudocenter of the filmic discourse. The real opposition posed by the sign is male/nonmale, which Sternberg establishes by his use of masculine clothing enveloping the image of Dietrich. This masquerade indicates the absence of man, an absence that is simultaneously negated and recuperated by man. The image of the woman becomes merely the trace of the exclusion and repression of Woman.

All fetishism, as Freud has observed, is a phallic replacement, a projection of male narcissistic fantasy. The star system as a whole depended on the fetishization of woman. Much of the work done on the star system concentrates on the star as the focus for false and alienating dreams. This empirical approach is essentially concerned with the effects of the star system and audience reaction. What the fetishization of the star does indicate is the collective fantasy of phallocentrism. This is particularly interesting when we look at the persona of Mae West. Many women have read into her parody of the star system and her verbal aggression an attempt at the subversion of male domination in the cinema. If we look more closely, there are many traces of phallic replacement in her persona that suggest quite the opposite. The voice itself is strongly masculine, suggesting the absence of the male, and establishes a male/nonmale dichotomy. The characteristic phallic dress possesses elements of the fetish. The female element that is introduced, the mother image, expresses male Oedipal fantasy. In other words, at the unconscious level, the persona of Mae West is entirely consistent with sexist ideology; it in no way subverts existing myths, but reinforces them.

Visual Pleasure and Narrative Cinema*

Laura Mulvey

I. INTRODUCTION

A. A Political Use of Psychoanalysis

This paper intends to use psychoanalysis to discover where and how the fascination of film is reinforced by preexisting patterns of fascination already at work within the individual subject and the social formations that have molded him. It takes as starting point the way film reflects, reveals, and even plays on the straight, socially established interpretation of sexual difference that controls images, erotic ways of looking and spectacle. It is helpful to understand what the cinema has been, how its magic has worked in the past, while attempting a theory and a practice that will challenge this cinema of the past. Psychoanalytic theory is thus appropriated here as a political weapon, demonstrating the way the unconscious of patriarchal society has structured film form.

The paradox of phallocentrism in all its manifestations is that it depends on the image of the castrated woman to give order and meaning to its world. An idea of woman stands as linchpin to the system: it is her lack that produces the phallus as a symbolic pres-

* Reprinted from *Screen,* 16, no. 3 (Autumn 1975). This essay is a reworked version of a paper given in the French Department of the University of Wisconsin, Madison, spring 1973.

ence, it is her desire to make good the lack that the phallus signifies. Recent writing in *Screen* about psychoanalysis and the cinema has not sufficiently brought out the importance of the representation of the female form in a symbolic order in which, in the last resort, it speaks castration and nothing else. To summarize briefly: the function of woman in forming the patriarchal unconscious is twofold: she first symbolizes the castration threat by her real absence of a penis and second thereby raises her child into the symbolic. Once this has been achieved, her meaning in the process is at an end, it does not last into the world of law and language except as a memory that oscillates between memory of maternal plenitude and memory of lack. Both are posited on nature (or on "anatomy" in Freud's famous phrase). Woman's desire is subjected to her image as bearer of the bleeding wound; she can exist only in relation to castration and cannot transcend it. She turns her child into the signifier of her own desire to possess a penis (the condition, she imagines, of entry into the symbolic). Either she must gracefully give way to the word, the Name of the Father and the Law, or else struggle to keep her child down with her in the half-light of the imaginary. Woman, then, stands in patriarchal culture as signifier for the male other, bound by a symbolic order in which man can live out his fantasies and obsessions through linguistic command, by imposing them on the silent image of woman still tied to her place as bearer of meaning, not maker of meaning.

There is an obvious interest in this analysis for feminists, a beauty in its exact rendering of the frustration experienced under the phallocentric order. It gets us nearer to the roots of our oppression, it brings an articulation of the problem closer, it faces us with the ultimate challenge: how to fight the unconscious/structured like a language (formed critically at the moment of arrival of language) while still caught within the language of the patriarchy. There is no way in which we can produce an alternative out of the blue, but we can begin to make a break by examining patriarchy with the tools it provides, of which psychoanalysis is not the only but an important one. We are still separated by a great gap from important issues for the female unconscious that are scarcely relevant to phallocentric theory: the sexing of the female infant and her relationship to the

symbolic, the sexually mature woman as nonmother, maternity outside the signification of the phallus, the vagina. . . . But, at this
point, psychoanalytic theory as it now stands can at least advance
our understanding of the status quo, of the patriarchal order in
which we are caught.

B. *Destruction of Pleasure as a Radical Weapon*

As an advanced representation system, the cinema poses questions
of the ways the unconscious (formed by the dominant order) structures ways of seeing and pleasure in looking. Cinema has changed
over the last few decades. It is no longer the monolithic system
based on large capital investment exemplified at its best by Hollywood in the 1930s, 1940s, and 1950s. Technological advances
(16mm, etc.) have changed the economic conditions of cinematic
production, which can now be artisanal as well as capitalist. Thus it
has been possible for an alternative cinema to develop. However
self-conscious and ironic Hollywood managed to be, it always restricted itself to a formal mise-en-scène reflecting the dominant ideological concept of the cinema. The alternative cinema provides a
space for a cinema to be born that is radical in both a political and
an aesthetic sense and challenges the basic assumptions of the
mainstream film. This is not to reject the latter moralistically, but to
highlight the ways in which its formal preoccupations reflect the
psychical obsessions of the society that produced it, and, further, to
stress that the alternative cinema must start specifically by reacting
against these obsessions and assumptions. A politically and aestheti-
cally avant-garde cinema is now possible, but it can still only exist
as a counterpoint.

The magic of the Hollywood style at its best (and of all the
cinema that fell within its sphere of influence) arose, not exclusively
but in one important aspect, from its skilled and satisfying manipulation of visual pleasure. Unchallenged, mainstream film coded the
erotic into the language of the dominant patriarchal order. In the
highly developed Hollywood cinema it was only through these
codes that the alienated subject, torn in his imaginary memory by a
sense of loss, by the terror of potential lack in fantasy, came near

to finding a glimpse of satisfaction: through its formal beauty and its play on his own formative obsessions. This essay will discuss the interweaving of that erotic pleasure in film, its meaning, and in particular the central place of the image of woman. It is said that analyzing pleasure, or beauty, destroys it. That is the intention of this article. The satisfaction and reinforcement of the ego that represent the high point of film history hitherto must be attacked. Not in favor of a reconstructed new pleasure, which cannot exist in the abstract, or of intellectualized unpleasure, but to make way for a total negation of the ease and plenitude of the narrative fiction film. The alternative is the thrill that comes from leaving the past behind without rejecting it, transcending outworn or oppressive forms, or daring to break with normal pleasurable expectations in order to conceive a new language of desire.

II. PLEASURE IN LOOKING—FASCINATION WITH THE HUMAN FORM

A. The cinema offers a number of possible pleasures. One is scopophilia. There are circumstances in which looking itself is a source of pleasure, just as, in the reverse formation, there is pleasure in being looked at. Originally, in his *Three Essays on Sexuality* (1905), Freud isolated scopophilia as one of the component instincts of sexuality that exist as drives quite independently of the erotogenic zones. At this point he associated scopophilia with taking other people as objects, subjecting them to a controlling and curious gaze. His particular examples center around the voyeuristic activities of children, their desire to see and make sure of the private and the forbidden (curiosity about other people's genital and bodily functions, about the presence or absence of the penis and, retrospectively, about the primal scene). In this analysis scopophilia is essentially active. (Later, in *Instincts and Their Vicissitudes*, 1915, Freud developed his theory of scopophilia further, attaching it initially to pregenital autoeroticism, after which the pleasure of the look is transferred to others by analogy. There is a close working here of the relationship between the active instinct and its further development in a narcissistic form.) Although the instinct is modified by other factors, in particular the constitution of the ego, it

continues to exist as the erotic basis for pleasure in looking at another person as object. At the extreme, it can become fixated into a
perversion, producing obsessive voyeurs and peeping toms, whose
only sexual satisfaction can come from watching, in an active controlling sense, an objectified other.

At first glance, the cinema would seem to be remote from the
undercover world of the surreptitious observation of an unknowing
and unwilling victim. What is seen of the screen is so manifestly
shown. But the mass of mainstream film, and the conventions within
which it has consciously evolved, portray a hermetically sealed
world that unwinds magically, indifferent to the presence of the
audience, producing for them a sense of separation and playing on
their voyeuristic fantasy. Moreover, the extreme contrast between
the darkness in the auditorium (which also isolates the spectators
from one another) and the brilliance of the shifting patterns of light
and shade on the screen helps to promote the illusion of voyeuristic
separation. Although the film is really being shown, is there to be
seen, conditions of screening and narrative conventions give the
spectator an illusion of looking in on a private world. Among other
things, the position of the spectators in the cinema is blatantly one
of repression of their exhibitionism and projection of the repressed
desire onto the performer.

B. The cinema satisfies a primordial wish for pleasurable looking,
but it also goes further, developing scopophilia in its narcissistic
aspect. The conventions of mainstream film focus attention on the
human form. Scale, space, stories are all anthropomorphic. Here,
curiosity and the wish to look intermingle with a fascination with
likeness and recognition: the human face, the human body, the
relationship between the human form and its surroundings, the visible presence of the person in the world. Jacques Lacan has described how the moment when a child recognizes its own image in
the mirror is crucial for the constitution of the ego. Several aspects
of this analysis are relevant here. The mirror phase occurs at a time
when the child's physical ambitions outstrip his motor capacity,
with the result that his recognition of himself is joyous in that he
imagines his mirror image to be more complete, more perfect than

he experiences his own body. Recognition is thus overlaid with misrecognition: the image recognized is conceived as the reflected body of the self, but its misrecognition as superior projects this body outside itself as an ideal ego, the alienated subject, which, reintrojected as an ego ideal, gives rise to the future generation of identification with others. This mirror moment predates language for the child.

Important for this essay is the fact that it is an image that constitutes the matrix of the imaginary, of recognition/misrecognition and identification, and hence of the first articulation of the *I*, of subjectivity. This is a moment when an older fascination with looking (at the mother's face, for an obvious example) collides with the initial inklings of self-awareness. Hence it is the birth of the long love affair/despair between image and self-image that has found such intensity of expression in film and such joyous recognition in the cinema audience. Quite apart from the extraneous similarities between screen and mirror (the framing of the human form in its surroundings, for instance), the cinema has structures of fascination strong enough to allow temporary loss of ego while simultaneously reinforcing the ego. The sense of forgetting the world as the ego has subsequently come to perceive it (I forgot who I am and where I was) is nostalgically reminiscent of that presubjective moment of image recognition. At the same time the cinema has distinguished itself in the production of ego ideals as expressed in particular in the star system, the stars centering both screen presence and screen story as they act out a complex process of likeness and difference (the glamorous impersonates the ordinary).

C. Sections II. A and B have set out two contradictory aspects of the pleasurable structures of looking in the conventional cinematic situation. The first, scopophilic, arises from pleasure in using another person as an object of sexual stimulation through sight. The second, developed through narcissism and the constitution of the ego, comes from identification with the image seen. Thus, in film terms, one implies a separation of the erotic identity of the subject from the object on the screen (active scopophilia), the other demands identification of the ego with the object on the screen through the spectator's fascination with and recognition of his like. The first is a function of the sexual instincts, the second of ego libido. This dichotomy was crucial for Freud. Although he saw the two as interacting and overlaying each other, the tension between instinctual drives and self-preservation continues to be a dramatic polarization in terms of pleasure. Both are formative structures, mechanisms not meanings. In themselves they have no signification, they have to be attached to an idealization. Both pursue aims in indifference to perceptual reality, creating the imagized, eroticized concept of the world that forms the perception of the subject and makes a mockery of empirical objectivity.

During its history, the cinema seems to have evolved a particular illusion of reality in which this contradiction between libido and ego has found a beautifully complementary fantasy world. In *reality* the fantasy world of the screen is subject to the law that produces it. Sexual instincts and identification processes have a meaning within the symbolic order that articulates desire. Desire, born with language, allows the possibility of transcending the instinctual and the imaginary, but its point of reference continually returns to the traumatic moment of its birth: the castration complex. Hence the look, pleasurable in form, can be threatening in content, and it is woman as representation/image that crystallizes this paradox.

III. Woman as Image, Man as Bearer of the Look

A. In a world ordered by sexual imbalance, pleasure in looking has been split between active/male and passive/female. The determining male gaze projects its fantasy onto the female figure, which is styled accordingly. In their traditional exhibitionist role women are simultaneously looked at and displayed, with their appearance coded for strong visual and erotic impact so that they can be said to connote *to-be-looked-at-ness*. Woman displayed as sexual object is the leitmotiv of erotic spectacle: from pinups to striptease, from Ziegfeld to Busby Berkeley, she holds the look, plays to, and signifies male desire. Mainstream film neatly combined spectacle and narrative. (Note, however, how in the musical song-and-dance numbers break the flow of the diegesis.) The presence of woman is an indispensable element of spectacle in normal narrative film, yet her visual presence tends to work against the development of a story line, to freeze the flow of action in moments of erotic contemplation. This alien presence then has to be integrated into cohesion with the narrative. As Budd Boetticher [a cult director of Hollywood B Westerns—Eds.] has put it:

> What counts is what the heroine provokes, or rather what she represents. She is the one, or rather the love or fear she inspires in the hero, or else the concern he feels for her, who makes him act the way he does. In herself the woman has not the slightest importance.

(A recent tendency in narrative film has been to dispense with this problem altogether; hence the development of what Molly Haskell has called the "buddy movie," in which the active homosexual eroticism of the central male figures can carry the story without distraction.) Traditionally, the woman displayed has functioned on two levels: as erotic object for the characters within the screen story, and as erotic object for the spectator within the auditorium, with a shifting tension between the looks on either side of the screen. For instance, the device of the showgirl allows the two looks to be unified technically without any apparent break in the diegesis. A woman performs within the narrative, the gaze of the spectator and that of the male characters in the film are neatly combined without breaking narrative verisimilitude. For a moment the sexual impact of the performing woman takes the film into a no-man's-land outside its own time and space. Thus Marilyn Monroe's first appearance in *The River of No Return* (1954) and Lauren Bacall's songs in *To Have and Have Not* (1944). Similarly, conventional close-ups of legs (Dietrich, for instance) or a face (Garbo) integrate into the narrative a different mode of eroticism. One part of a fragmented body destroys the Renaissance space, the illusion of depth demanded by the narrative, it gives flatness, the quality of a cutout or icon rather than verisimilitude to the screen.

B. An active/passive heterosexual division of labor has similarly controlled narrative structure. According to the principles of the ruling ideology and the psychical structures that back it up, the male figure cannot bear the burden of sexual objectification. Man is reluctant to gaze at his exhibitionist like. Hence the split between spectacle and narrative supports the man's role as the active one of forwarding the story, making things happen. The man controls the film fantasy and also emerges as the representative of power in a further sense: as the bearer of the look of the spectator, transferring it behind the screen to neutralize the extradiegetic tendencies represented by woman as spectacle. This is made possible through the processes set in motion by structuring the film around a main controlling figure with whom the spectator can identify. As the spectator identifies with the main male[1] protagonist, he projects his look onto that of his like, his screen surrogate, so that the power of the male protagonist as he controls events coincides with the active power of the erotic look, both giving a satisfying sense of omnipotence. A male movie star's glamorous characteristics are thus not those of the erotic object of the gaze, but those of the more perfect, more complete, more powerful ideal ego conceived in the original moment of recognition in front of the mirror. The character in the story can make things happen and control events better than the subject/spectator, just as the image in the mirror was more in control of motor coordination. In contrast to woman as icon, the active male figure (the ego ideal of the identification process) demands a three-dimensional space corresponding to that of the mirror recognition in which the alienated subject internalized his own representation of this imaginary existence. He is a figure in a landscape. Here the function of film is to reproduce as accurately as possible the so-called natural conditions of human perception. Camera technology (as exemplified by deep focus in particular) and camera movements (determined by the action of the protagonist), combined with invisible editing (demanded by realism), all tend to blur the limits of screen space. The male protagonist is free to command the

---

[1] There are films with a woman as main protaganist, of course. To analyze this phenomenon seriously here would take me too far afield. Pam Cook and Claire Johnston's study of *The Revolt of Mamie Stover* in Phil Hardy, ed., *Raoul Walsh* (London: Vineyard Press, 1974), shows in a striking case how the strength of this female protagonist is more apparent than real.

stage, a stage of spatial illusion in which he articulates the look and creates the action.

C.1 Sections III. A and B have set out a tension between a mode of representation of woman in film and conventions surrounding the diegesis. Each is associated with a look: that of the spectator in direct scopophilic contact with the female form displayed for his enjoyment (connoting male fantasy) and that of the spectator fascinated with the image of his like set in an illusion of natural space, and through him gaining control and possession of the woman within the diegesis. (This tension and the shift from one pole to the other can structure a single text. Thus both in *Only Angels Have Wings*, 1939, and in *To Have and Have Not* the film opens with the woman as object of the combined gaze of spectator and all the male protagonists in the film. She is isolated, glamorous, on display, sexualized. But as the narrative progresses, she falls in love with the main male protagonist and becomes his property, losing her outward glamorous characteristics, her generalized sexuality, her showgirl connotations; her eroticism is subjected to the male star alone. By means of identification with him, through participation in his power, the spectator can indirectly possess her too.)

But in psychoanalytic terms, the female figure poses a deeper problem. She also connotes something that the look continually circles around but disavows: her lack of a penis, implying a threat of castration and hence unpleasure. Ultimately, the meaning of woman is sexual difference, the absence of the penis as visually ascertainable, the material evidence on which is based the castration complex essential for the organization of entrance to the symbolic order and the Law of the Father. Thus the woman as icon, displayed for the gaze and enjoyment of men, the active controllers of the look, always threatens to evoke the anxiety it originally signified. The male unconscious has two avenues of escape from this castration anxiety: preoccupation with the reenactment of the original trauma (investigating the woman, demystifying her mystery), counterbalanced by the devaluation, punishment, or saving of the guilty object (an avenue typified by the concerns of the *film noir*); or else complete disavowal of castration by the substitution of a fetish object or turning the represented figure itself into a fetish so that it becomes reassuring rather than dangerous (hence overvaluation, the cult of the female star). This second avenue, fetishistic scopophilia, builds up the physical beauty of the object, transforming it into something satisfying in itself. The first avenue, voyeurism, on the contrary, has associations with sadism: pleasure lies in ascertaining guilt (immediately associated with castration), asserting control, and subjecting the guilty person through punishment or forgiveness. This sadistic side fits in well with narrative. Sadism demands a story, depends on making something happen, forcing a change in another person, a battle of will and strength, victory/defeat, all occurring in a linear time with a beginning and an end. Fetishistic scopophilia, on the other hand, can exist outside linear time as the erotic instinct is focused on the look alone. These contradictions and ambiguities can be illustrated more simply by using works by Hitchcock and Sternberg, both of whom take the look almost as the content or subject matter of many of their films. Hitchcock is the more complex, as he uses both mechanisms. Sternberg's work, on the other hand, provides many pure examples of fetishistic scopophilia.

C.2 It is well known that Sternberg once said he would welcome his films being projected upside down so that story and character involvement would not interfere with the spectator's undiluted appreciation of the screen image. This statement is revealing but ingenuous. Ingenuous in that his films do demand that the figure of the woman (Dietrich, in the cycle of films with her, as the ultimate example) should be identifiable. But revealing in that it emphasizes the fact that for him the pictorial space enclosed by the frame is paramount rather than narrative or identification processes. Whereas Hitchcock goes into the investigative side of voyeurism, Sternberg produces the ultimate fetish, taking it to the point where the powerful look of the male protagonist (characteristic of traditional narrative film) is broken in favor of the image in direct erotic rapport with the spectator. The beauty of the woman as object and the screen space coalesce; she is no longer the bearer of guilt but a perfect product, whose body, stylized and fragmented by close-ups, is the content of the film and the direct recipient of the spectator's look. Sternberg plays down the illusion of screen depth; his screen tends to be one-dimensional, as light and shade, lace, steam, foliage, net, streamers, etc., reduce the visual field. There is little or no mediation of the look through the eyes of the main male protagonist. On the contrary, shadowy presences like La Bessière in *Morocco* (1930) act as surrogates for the director, detached as they are from audience identification. Despite Sternberg's insistence that his stories are irrelevant, it is significant that they are concerned with situation, not suspense, and cyclical rather than linear time, while plot complications revolve around misunderstanding rather than conflict. The most important absence is that of the controlling

Amy Jolly (Marlene Dietrich) flirts with legionnaire Tom Brown (Gary Cooper) in Josef von Sternberg's *Morocco* (1930). (Courtesy Universal 16)

male gaze within the screen scene. The high point of emotional drama in the most typical Dietrich films, her supreme moments of erotic meaning, take place in the absence of the man she loves in the fiction. There are other witnesses, other spectators, watching her on the screen, their gaze is one with, not standing in for, that of the audience. At the end of *Morocco,* Tom Brown has already disappeared into the desert when Amy Jolly kicks off her gold sandals and walks after him. At the end of *Dishonored* (1931), Kranau is indifferent to the fate of Magda. In both cases, the erotic impact, sanctified by death, is displayed as a spectacle for the audience. The male hero misunderstands and, above all, does not see.

In Hitchcock, by contrast, the male hero does see precisely what the audience sees. However, in the films I shall discuss here, he takes fascination with an image through scopophilic eroticism as the subject of the film. Moreover, in these cases the hero portrays the contradictions and tensions experienced by the spectator. In *Vertigo* (1958) in particular, but also in *Marnie* (1964) and *Rear Window* (1954), the look is central to the plot, oscillating between voyeurism and fetishistic fascination. As a twist, a further manipulation of the normal viewing process, which in some sense reveals it, Hitchcock uses the process of identification normally associated with ideological correctness and the recognition of established morality and shows up its perverted side. Hitchcock has never concealed his interest in voyeurism, cinematic and noncinematic. His heroes are exemplary of the symbolic order and the law—a policeman(*Vertigo*), a dominant male possessing money and power (*Marnie*)—but their erotic drives lead them into compromised situations. The power to subject another person to the will sadistically or to the gaze voyeuristically is turned onto the woman as the object of both. Power is backed by a certainty of legal right and the established guilt of the woman (evoking castration, psychoanalytically speaking). True perversion is barely concealed under a shallow mask of ideological correctness—the man is on the right side of the law, the woman on the wrong. Hitchcock's skillful use of identification processes and liberal use of subjective camera from the point of view of the male protagonist draw the spectators deeply into his position, making them share his uneasy gaze. The audience is absorbed into a voyeuristic situation within the screen scene and diegesis that parodies his own in the cinema.

In his analysis of *Rear Window*[2] Douchet takes the film as a metaphor for the cinema. Jeffries is the audience, the events in the apartment block opposite correspond to the screen. As he watches, an erotic dimension is added to his look, a central image to the drama. His girl friend Lisa had been of little sexual interest to him, more or less a drag, so long as she remained on the spectator side. When she crosses the barrier between his room and the block opposite, their relationship is reborn erotically. He does not merely watch her through his lens, as a distant meaningful image, he also sees her as a guilty intruder exposed by a dangerous man threatening her with punishment, and thus finally saves her. Lisa's exhibitionism has already been established by her obsessive interest in dress and style, in being a passive image of visual perfection; Jeffries's voyeurism and activity have also been established through his work as a photojournalist, a maker of stories and captor of images. However, his enforced inactivity, binding him to his seat as a spectator, puts him squarely in the fantasy position of the cinema audience.

In *Vertigo*, subjective camera predominates. Apart from one flashback from Judy's point of view, the narrative is woven around what Scottie sees or fails to see. The audience follows the growth of his erotic obsession and subsequent despair precisely from his point of view. Scottie's voyeurism is blatant: he falls in love with a woman he follows and spies on without speaking to. Its sadistic side is equally blatant: he has chosen (and freely chosen, for he had been a successful lawyer) to be a policeman, with all the attendant possibilities of pursuit and investigation. As a result, he follows, watches, and falls in love with a perfect image of female beauty and mystery. Once he actually confronts her, his erotic drive is to break her down and force her to tell by persistent cross-questioning. Then, in the second part of the film, he reenacts his obsessive involvement with the image he loved to watch secretly. He reconstructs Judy as Madeleine, forces her to conform in every detail to the actual physi-

---

[2] Jean Douchet, "Hitch et son public," *Cahiers du Cinéma*, 113 (November 1960), pp. 7–15.

cal appearance of his fetish. Her exhibitionism, her masochism, make her an ideal passive counterpart to Scottie's active sadistic voyeurism. She knows her part is to perform, and only by playing it through and then replaying it can she keep Scottie's erotic interest. But in the repetition he does break her down and succeeds in exposing her guilt. His curiosity wins through and she is punished. In *Vertigo,* erotic involvement with the look is disorienting: the spectator's fascination is turned against him as the narrative carries him through and entwines him with the processes that he is himself exercising.

The Hitchcock hero here is firmly placed within the symbolic order, in narrative terms. He has all the attributes of the patriarchal superego. Hence the spectator, lulled into a false sense of security by the apparent legality of his surrogate, sees through his look and finds himself exposed as complicit, caught in the moral ambiguity of looking. Far from being simply an aside on the perversion of the police, *Vertigo* focuses on the implications of the active/ looking, passive/looked-at split in terms of sexual difference and the power of the male symbolic encapsulated in the hero. Marnie, too, performs for Mark Rutland's gaze and masquerades as the perfect to-be-looked-at image. He, too, is on the side of the law until, drawn in by obsession with her guilt, her secret, he longs to see her in the act of committing a crime, make her confess and thus save her. So he, too, becomes complicit as he acts out the implications of his power. He controls money and words, he can have his cake and eat it.

IV. SUMMARY

The psychoanalytic background that has been discussed in this essay is relevant to the pleasure and unpleasure offered by traditional narrative film. The scopophilic instinct (pleasure in looking at another person as an erotic object) and, in contradistinction, ego libido (forming identification processes) act as formations, mechanisms, which this cinema has played on. The image of woman as (passive) raw material for the (active) gaze of man takes the argument a step further into the structure of representation, adding a further layer demanded by the ideology of the patriarchal order as it is worked out in its favorite cinematic form—illusionistic narrative film. The argument returns again to the psychoanalytic background in that woman as representation signifies castration, inducing voyeuristic or fetishistic mechanisms to circumvent her threat. None of these interacting layers is intrinsic to film, but it is only in the film form that they can reach a perfect and beautiful contradiction, thanks to the possibility in the cinema of shifting the emphasis of the look. It is the place of the look that defines cinema, the possibility of varying it and exposing it. This is what makes cinema quite different in its voyeuristic potential from, say, striptease, theatre, shows, etc. Going far beyond highlighting a woman's to-be-looked-at-ness, cinema builds the way she is to be looked at into the spectacle itself. Playing on the tension between film as controlling the dimension of time (editing, narrative) and film as controlling the dimension of space (changes in distance, editing), cinematic codes create a gaze, a world, and an object, thereby producing an illusion cut to the measure of desire. It is these cinematic codes and their relationship to formative external structures that must be broken down before mainstream film and the pleasure it provides can be challenged.

To begin with (as an ending), the voyeuristic-scopophilic look that is a crucial part of traditional filmic pleasure can itself be broken down. There are three different looks associated with cinema: that of the camera as it records the profilmic event, that of the audience as it watches the final product, and that of the characters at each other within the screen illusion. The conventions of narrative film deny the first two and subordinate them to the third, the conscious aim being always to eliminate intrusive camera presence and prevent a distancing awareness in the audience. Without these two absences (the material existence of the recording process, the critical reading of the spectator), fictional drama cannot achieve reality, obviousness, and truth. Nevertheless, as this essay has argued, the structure of looking in narrative fiction film contains a contradiction in its own premises: the female image as a castration threat constantly endangers the unity of the diegesis and bursts through the world of illusion as an intrusive, static, one-dimensional fetish. Thus the two looks materially present in time and space are obsessively subordinated to the neurotic needs of the male ego. The camera becomes the mechanism for producing an illusion of Renaissance space, flowing movements compatible with the human eye, an ideology of representation that revolves around the perception of the subject; the camera's look is disavowed in order to create a convincing world in which the spectator's surrogate can perform with verisimilitude. Simultaneously, the look of the audience is denied an intrinsic force: as soon as fetishistic representation of the female image threatens to break the spell of illusion, and the erotic image on the screen appears directly (without mediation) to the spectator, the fact of fetishization, concealing as it does castration fear, freezes the look, fixates the spectator, and prevents him from achieving any distance from the image in front of him.

This complex interaction of looks is specific to film. The first blow against the monolithic accumulation of traditional film conventions (already undertaken by radical filmmakers) is to free the look of the camera into its materiality in time and space and the look of the audience into dialectics, passionate detachment. There is no doubt that this destroys the satisfaction, pleasure, and privilege of the "invisible guest," and highlights how film has depended on voyeuristic active/passive mechanisms. Women, whose image has continually been stolen and used for this end, cannot view the decline of the traditional film form with anything much more than sentimental regret.

Are Women Directors Different?*

Molly Haskell

If they do not exactly constitute a feminist renaissance, or even a *naissance*, the simultaneous success of Liliana Cavani's *The Night Porter* (1973) and Lina Wertmuller's *The Seduction of Mimi* (1972) at least affords a chance to analyze in the plural that rarest of birds, the woman director. I mean, of course, the woman as director of commercial, or narrative films. Although the area of independent filmmaking has attracted women in numbers equal to men, as have most of the other arts, commercial filmmaking remains the last stronghold—a stag nation of male supremacy. Supremacy is the right word, for it is from a lordly position that the director, like the preacher or the orchestra conductor, must give orders to groups composed largely of men. And naturally, the larger and less flexible the crew, as in American filmmaking, the less likelihood of finding a woman in their midst, and a head or two above them.

If anything, the representation of women behind the scenes—and in front of the camera, too, but that is another story—has dwindled from previous decades. With financial risks what they are, and with wheeling and dealing and bluffing and massaging consuming at least ninety percent of preshooting activity, a director must have the

* Reprinted from *The Village Voice,* February 3, 1975. Copyright © 1975 by The Village Voice, Inc.

stomach of an L. B. Mayer rather than the soul of a P. B. Shelley to survive.

Is there, then, among those who have broken through—Wertmuller, Cavani, Nelly Kaplan, Elaine May—such a thing as a "woman's point of view," a distinctly "feminine" approach to filmmaking? (This question, applied to the various arts, was the burning topic on the college symposia circuit several years ago. The fact that in literature and painting it has gone the way of the consciousness-raising session, that is, served its purpose by becoming obsolete, suggests to me that women have entered these fields in sufficient numbers to make classification by sex impossible. Not so—alas!—in film.)

Is there anything we might say of Elaine May's *The Heartbreak Kid* (1973) or the upcoming *Mikey and Nicky* (1976) that might also be true of Cavani's *The Night Porter,* or Wertmuller's *The Seduction of Mimi* and *Love and Anarchy* (1973)? Although I don't know any more about *Mikey and Nicky* than you do, I think it's safe to say these films are not about war, or football games, or motorcycles. But they *are* about men! So much for the notion that women will automatically create great parts for other women.

My own feeling, however, is that although distinctly "feminine" qualities can be discovered in each of these directors, we cannot generalize from these to a "feminine sensibility." Elaine May—witty, cerebral, puritanical, even (in the accepted comic tradition) misogynistic—actually has more in common with such male compatriots as Mike Nichols or Woody Allen or Brian de Palma than with her European "sisters," both of whom are more sensual, in their physical response to the world as well as in their gravitation toward sex as a theme.

I'd be willing to bet odds that Elaine May will never make a film exploring the sensual side of love, and that her goofy men and gullible women will sublimate sex into the various guises and disguises of comedy, or of a certain kind of farce that in a more ruthlessly unequal and antagonistic form may become the screwball comedy of the 1970s. (Those critics who hail the "adult" attitudes of contemporary films as advances in sexual maturity over the Doris Day films had better think again. People don't seem to realize the extent to which the Production Code was an expression of the norm rather than the exception, the voice from within the puritan conscience rather than an alien force. One function of both the nostalgia and disaster cycles is to avoid sex altogether.)

Wertmuller, on the other hand, tackles sex with uninhibited gusto. A well-educated Italian radical with populist instincts, she exposes, through her bumblingly yearning hero, the rearguard totems and taboos of the Sicilian working class. Cavani, too, feels no hesitation in building an entire film around a sexual relationship—the sadomasochistic love born in a concentration camp between a guard and a prisoner that is fatally rekindled thirteen years later. Wertmuller deliberately exaggerates sexual dichotomies within a raunchy, Marxist framework tending toward caricature. Cavani, dealing with it in a delirious, dreamlike manner that has confounded our more literal-minded critics, incorporates sexual psychology into a rhapsodic view of human obsession tending toward mysticism.

As different as they are, what both directors share, it occurs to me, is a certain attitude toward, and treatment of, sex that distinguishes them from their male counterparts and that—using the word with all due caution—might be characterized as *feminine*. Neither of these films—and if you don't believe me, ask the nearest man in the street—is a "turn-on." At least not in the commonly understood sense of the term in what is ultimately a masculine context. They pander to men's fantasies on neither the simple level of pure titillation, nor on the more insidious level of woman hating to which the violent forms of sex—rape, physical torture—address themselves. In fact, a man of admittedly outré tastes in these matters complained to me that he disliked *The Night Porter* not because he was morally (or aurally) outraged, but because its "kinky" sex didn't excite him. Both directors deal with sex in scenes as gamy and explicit as anything concocted in this department by men (which of course is why *these* films, and not their directors' previous ones, are box-office successes), but within total contexts—one psychological, one social—that have little to do with immediate audience gratification . . . or punishment.

Moreover, although both films place women in what, at first

Lucia (Charlotte Rampling) and Max (Dirk Bogarde) re-create the sadomasochistic relationship they shared in a World War II concentration camp in Liliana Cavani's *Night Porter* (1973). (Courtesy Avco Embassy Pictures)

glance, might be thought degraded positions—the baroquely monumental nude who engulfs Giancarlo Giannini in their lovers' tryst, Charlotte Rampling as the pale and emotionally stunted "little girl" who must obey her Nazi keeper (Dirk Bogarde)—a closer look reveals that neither film performs the ultimate act of degradation, which is to rob women of their autonomy, and both equalize, in subtle ways, the positions and responsibilities of their men and women.

Charlotte Rampling chooses to survive by surrendering to the "unspeakable" requirements of her enemy-guardian. By falling back on what is traditionally a woman's way of surviving, she reinforces with her submission his dubious sense of power. In this original act of bad faith, a perversion of the marriage of equals, she makes him, this impotent Lucifer, her lord and master, but in so doing she condemns herself to remain a little girl, a half-person consigned to the shades. Somewhere a character, another survivor, says that "to save your skin, no price is too high." But the Cavani protagonists, pitted against those who would eradicate their own guilt and start afresh, know that once they paid that price, they have acted irrevocably, and their lives must take a different course from that of other people.

The contract of love entered upon by Bogarde and Rampling—psychotic, born of weakness rather than strength—is a contract of death. It awaits only their reunion to be completed. But, as the multiple ironies of the Papageno-Pamina duet (in the "Magic Flute" scene) suggest, in the very midst of depravity, there is ecstasy and tenderness and the selflessness that is also found in "normal" love. It is this acceptance that to me gives the film its power. But it is this, and the sense of reciprocity—in love, in doom—that has apparently outraged audiences. They find that Cavani is "sympathetic" to Nazism, or "exploits it for cheap effects." But the Nazis are far less threateningly exciting than the homosexual blackshirts in Visconti's *The Damned* (1970). And the effects of a scene like the one in the cabaret are not cheap or seductive, and they are remote—distanced through the blue-gray filters of a nightmare past that holds its dreamers in thrall. Far from giving us even a perverse erotic thrill, the events of the concentration camp have a cold clamminess, coming like tentacles of the past to encircle two people in a viselike grip. Nothing less than a similar sense of consequence—but in a comic context—marks Wertmuller's film, and her treatment of the gargantuan nude.

On a purely physical level, this grandiose, lecherous woman is exaggerated to the point that she is not a sexual creature at all, a woman in whom other women are ridiculed, but an almost impersonal figure of lust. As her posterior is magnified, through lens distortion, into a jiggling mound of flesh, it becomes an abstract sculpture-in-motion. Nor does this particular part of the body seem to activate the glands in the manner of, say, the opulent uppers of Fellini's whores. The latter serve simultaneously as grotesques, projections of male fears, and overpowering mother figures for those members of the audience with lingering mammary fixations.

And Wertmuller's fat lady, apparently "abused" by the man who wants only to cuckold her husband in revenge, turns the tables triumphantly by getting herself pregnant and denouncing both men in a magnificent "aria" on the church steps! A Pyrrhic victory, perhaps, but a victory nevertheless.

It stands to reason that women, with the biological fear of pregnancy that every one of us must grow up and live with, will harbor and eventually give expression to a sterner sense of the consequences of love. This may take the form of an explicit and obsessive fear of pregnancy (the one-night-stand-and-you're-ruined-for-life fables of the old Hollywood "women's films") or merely a generalized sense of anxiety.

For instance, the most unusual occurrence in Roberta Findlay's rather routine porn film, *Angel Number 9* (1975), is not the plot device of having a man come to earth as a woman to discover "what suffering really is" (in escapades that turn out to be as boringly androcentric as ever). It is the fact that two women greet their lovers with the unwelcome news that they are pregnant. For those who are not blue-movie aficionados (as I am not; I got my information from a self-designated "historian"), pregnancy is a no-no in sexploitation movies, a definite downer to Don Juan fantasies of quickie, no-fault sex. Of course, like so many things in life, the wages of sin are exacted too late, and paid by the wrong people: the obligation of hard-core films to show what once was only simulated makes the possibility of conception considerably weaker than in old Hollywood.

What further "feminine" characteristics can we note in Cavani and Wertmuller? Are they more emotional, more intuitive? More sensitive to surroundings and decor? And while we're at it, do we observe anything—a wobbly camera, mismatched shots—that might explain why other women have such a hard time getting backing as directors? Do we notice a sudden lapse of continuity that might be explained by infirmities of a cyclical nature?

I would say that both of them, but especially Cavani, are extraordinarily sensitive to decor, to textures (remember the nubby wool of Bogarde's sweater, the material of Rampling's dress), to tactile sensations, and to architecture, but as part of a total vision. The Viennese hotel, for instance, is more hallucinatory than real, a Dantesque inferno of tiers, with its doomed inmates that Bogarde watches over and services. The awkward English dialogue that critics have objected to would be more disturbing if Cavani were operating within the laws of realism. Wertmuller, in the consciously vulgar burlesque tradition of low comedy, pushes her characters into social caricature that many people resist. But neither woman works within the narrowly realistic or autobiographical modes that we might have expected from women directors. With fully developed styles, these women will nevertheless be likely to yield a good many surprises in careers that I hope and pray can be sustained.

I catch myself, and slap my hand for using the word *expected*. For it is expectations that are at the root of the problem, prescriptive definitions of masculine and feminine that have become self-fulfilling prophecies. Better not to expect or ask for, only observe and describe. Polarities do exist, but they don't necessarily correspond to gender. All we can do is hope that women filmmakers become, like their counterparts in the other arts, merely *filmmakers*.

Bibliography

Cook, Pam, and Johnston, Claire. "The Place of Women in the Cinema of Raoul Walsh." In Phil Hardy, ed., *Raoul Walsh*. London: Vineyard Press, 1974.

Dove, Linda. "London Letter: Feminist and Left Independent Filmmaking in England." *Jump Cut*, nos. 10 and 11 (Summer 1976).

Fischer, Lucy. "The Image of Woman as Image: The Optical Politics of *Dames*." *Film Quarterly* (Fall 1976).

Giroux, Henry. "The Challenge of Neo-Fascist Culture." *Cinéaste*, 6, no. 4 (1975). [*The Night Porter*]

Godard, Jean-Luc, and Gorin, Jean-Pierre. "Excerpts from the Transcript of *Letter to Jane*." *Women and Film*, 1, nos. 3 and 4 (1973).

Kleinhans, Chuck. "A Ventriloquist Psychoanalysis." *Jump Cut*, no. 9 (October–December 1975).

Lesage, Julia. "Feminist Film Criticism: Theory and Practice." *Women and Film*, 1, nos. 5 and 6 (1974).

———. "The Human Subject—You, He, or Me? (or The Case of the Missing Penis)." *Jump Cut*, no. 4 (November–December 1974).

Martineau, Barbara Halpern. "Subjecting Her Objectification or Communism Is Not Enough." In Claire Johnston, ed., *Notes on Women's Cinema*. London: Society for Education in Film and Television, 1973.

———. "Thoughts about the Objectification of Women." *Take One*, 3, no. 2 (1972).

McCormick, Ruth. "Fascism à la Mode or Radical Chic?" *Cinéaste*, 6, no. 4 (1975). [*The Night Porter*]

McGarry, Eileen. "Documentary, Realism and Women's Cinema." *Women and Film* (Summer 1975).

Mitchell, Juliet. *Psychoanalysis and Feminism.* New York: Random House, 1975.

Penley, Constance. "Theory of Film Practice: Analysis and Review." *Women and Film,* 1, nos. 5 and 6 (1974).

Sontag, Susan. "Godard's *Vivre Sa Vie.*" *Against Interpretation.* New York: Dell Publishing Co., 1969.

Appendix
Selected Filmographies

Selected Filmographies*

Anderson, Madeline, USA
I Am Somebody (1971)

Arzner, Dorothy (1900–   ), USA
Fashions for Women (1927); *Ten Modern Commandments* (1927); *Get Your Man* (1927); *Manhattan Cocktail* (1928); *The Wild Party* 1929); *Sarah and Son* (1930); *Anybody's Woman* (1930); *Working Girls* (1930); *Paramount on Parade* (1930) [Arzner directed "The Gallows Song" vignette]; *Honor Among Lovers* (1931); *Merrily We Go to Hell* (1932); *Christopher Strong* (1933); *Nana* (1934); *Craig's Wife* (1936); *The Bride Wore Red* (1937); *Dance, Girl, Dance* (1940); *First Comes Courage* (1943). Dorothy Arzner was also director (uncredited) of *Charming Sinner* (1929), *Behind the Makeup* (1930), and *The Last of Mrs. Cheney* (1937). She edited *Blood and Sand* (1923), *The Wild Party* (1923), *The Covered Wagon* (1923), and *Old Ironsides* (1926), among others.

Ashur, Geri (1946–   ), USA
Janie's Janie (1971), with Peter Barton and Marilyn Mulford; *Make Out* (1971), with Newsreel Women's Caucus; *Village by Village* (1972), with Janet Mendelsohn; *Artists in Residence* (1973), with Nick Doob and Peter Schlaifer; *Me and Stella* (1976)

Blaché, Alice Guy (1873–1968), USA
Among the vast numbers of films credited to Alice Guy Blaché, we

* Films of women directors discussed in the text.

limit this list to selected American titles from the time she began Solax Company.

A Child's Sacrifice (1910); *Rose of the Frontier* (1911); *Across the Mexican Line* (1911); *A Daughter of the Navajos* (1911); *The Silent Signal* (1911); *The Girl and the Broncho Buster* (1911); *The Mascot of Troop "C"* (1911); *An Enlisted Man's Honor* (1911); *The Stampede* (1911); *The Hold-Up* (1911); *The Alerted Message* (1911); *His Sister's Sweetheart* (1911); *His Better Self* (1911); *A Revolutionary Romance* (1911); *The Child of Fate* (1912); *A Terrible Lesson* (1912); *His Lordship's White Feather* (1912); *Falling Leaves* (1912); *The Sewer* (1912); *In the Year 2000* (1912); *A Terrible Night* (1912); *Mickey's Pal* (1912); *Fra Diavolo* (1912); *Hotel Honeymoon* (1912); *The Equine Spy* (1912); *Two Little Rangers* (1912); *The Bloodstain* (1912); *At the Phone* (1912); *Flesh and Blood* (1912); *The Paralytic* (1912); *The Face at the Window* (1912); *The Beasts of the Jungle* (1913); *Dick Whittington and His Cat* (1913); *Kelly from the Emerald Isle* (1913); *The Pit and the Pendulum* (1913); *Western Love* (1913); *Rogues of Paris* (1913); *Blood and Water* (1913); *Ben Bolt* (1913); *The Shadows of the Moulin Rouge* (1913); *The Eyes That Could Not Close* (1913); *The House Divided* (1913); *Beneath the Czar* (1914); *The Monster and the Girl* (1914); *The Million Dollars Robbery* (1914); *The Star of India* (1913–1914); *The Fortune Hunters* (1913–1914); *The Prisoner of the Harem* (1914); *The Dream Woman* (1914); *Hook and Hand* (1914); *The Woman of Mystery* (1914); *The Yellow Traffic* (1914); *The Lure* (1914); *Michael Strogoff or the Courier to the Czar* (1914); *The Tigress* (1914); *The Heart of a Painted Woman* (1915); *Greater Love Hath No Man* (1915); *The Vampire* (1915); *My Madonna* (1915); *Barbara Frietchie* (1915); *What Will People Say?* (1916); *The Girl with the Green Eyes* (1916); *The Ocean Waif* (1916); *The Empress* (1917); *The Adventurer* (1917); *A Man and the Woman* (1917); *When You and I Were Young* (1917); *Behind the Mask* (1917); *House of Cards* (1917); *The Great Adventure* (1918); *The Painted Scene* (1918); *The Divorcee* (1919); *The Brat* (1919); *Stronger than Death* (1920); *Tarnished Reputation* (1920)

Cavani, Liliana (1936–   ), Italy
   Francis of Assisi (1966); *Galileo* (1968); *The Year of the Cannibal* (1970); *The Night Porter* (1973)

Chopra, Joyce (1936–   ), USA
   A Happy Mother's Day (1963), with Richard Leacock; *Wild Ones* (1965); *Room to Learn* (1968), with Tom Cole; *Present Tense* (1969), with Tom Cole; *Joyce at 34* (1973), with Claudia Weill;

Matina Horner—Portrait of a Person 1973 (1973), with Claudia Weill; *Girls at 12* (1974); *Clorae and Albie* (1975)

Chytilova, Vera (1929–   ), Czechoslovakia
Three Men Missing (1957); *Green Roads* (1959); *The Ceiling* (1961); *A Bag of Fleas* (1962); *Something Different* (1963); *Pearls of the Deep* (1965), episode called "The World Cafeteria"; *Daisies* (1966); *The Fruit of Paradise* (1969)

Clarke, Shirley (1925–   ), USA
Dance in the Sun (1953); *Paris Parks* (1964); *Bullfight* (1955); *Moment in Love* (1957); *Brussels "Loops"* (1958); *Bridges-Go-Round* (1958); *Skyscraper* (1959), with Willard Van Dyke; *Scary Time* (1960); *The Connection* (1960); *The Cool World* (1962); *Robert Frost—A Love Letter to the World* (1964); *A Portrait of Jason* (1967)

De Hirsch, Storm, USA
Goodbye in the Mirror (1963–1964); *Journey Around a Zero* (1964–1965); *The Color of Ritual, The Color of Thought* (1964); *Divinations* (1964); *Peyote Queen* (1965); *Newsreel: Jonas in the Brig* (1966); *Sing Lotus* (1966); *Shaman, a Tapestry for Sorcerers* (1967); *Cayuga Run—Hudson River Diary: Book I* (1967); *Trap Dance* (1968); *Third Eye Butterfly* (1968); *An Experiment in Meditation* (1971); *September Express* (1972); *Lace of Summer* (1972); *Wintergarden—Hudson River Diary: Book III* (1973); *River Ghost—Hudson River Diary: Book IV* (1973); *Geometrics of the Kabballah* (1976); and sixteen *Cine-Sonnets* in super 8mm (1974–1977)

Deren, Maya (1917–1961), USA
Meshes of the Afternoon (1943), with Alexander Hammid; *The Witches Cradle* (1943), unfinished; *At Land* (1944); *A Study in Choreography for the Camera* (1945); *Ritual in Transfigured Time* (1946); *Meditation on Violence* (1948); *The Very Eye of Night* (1959)

Dulac, Germaine (1882–1942), France
Le Soeurs Ennemies (1916); *Géo-le-Mystérieux* (1916); *Vénus Victrix* (1916); *Dans L'Ouragan de la Vie* (1916); *Ames de Fous* (1917); *Le Bonheur des Autres* (1918); *La Fête Espagnole* (1919); *La Cigarette* (1919); *Malencontre* (1920); *La Belle Dame sans Merci* (1921); *La Mort du Soleil* (1922); *Werther* (1922), unfinished; *La Souriante Madame Beudet* [*The Smiling Madame Beudet*] (1922–1923); *Gossette* (1922–1923); *Le Diable dans la Ville* (1924); *Ame d'Artiste* (1925); *La Folie des Vaillants* (1925); *Antoinette Sabrier* (1927); *L'Invitation au Voyage* (1927); *Le Cinéma au Service de l'Histoire*

(1927); *La Coquille et le Clergyman* [*The Seashell and the Clergyman*] (1928); *Variations* (1928); *Germination d'un Haricot* (1928); *La Princesse Mandane* (1928); *Mon Paris* (1928), supervisor, with Albert Guyet; *Disque 927* (1929); *Étude Cinégraphique sur une Arabesque* (1929); *France-Actualités-Gaumont* (1930–1940); *Les 24 Heures du Mans* (1930); *Le Picador* (1932), with Jaquelux; *Le Cinéma au Service de l'Histoire* (1937)

Friedman, Bonnie (1946–   ), USA
Childcare People's Liberation (1970), with Karen Mitnick; *How About You* (1972), with Deborah Shaffer and Marilyn Mulford; *Chris and Bernie* (1975), with Deborah Shaffer; *Becoming Orgasmic* series (1976); *The Flashettes* (1977)

Kaplan, Nelly (1934–   ), France
Magirama (1956), with Abel Gance; *Rudolphe Bresdin* (1961); *Gustave Moreau* (1961); *Abel Gance, Hier et Demain* (1963); *Dessins et merveilles* (1966); *Les Années 25* (1966); *A la Source, la femme aimée* (1966); *Le Regard Picasso* (1957); *La Fiancée du Pirate* [*A Very Curious Girl*] (1969); *Papa, les petits bateaux* (1971)

London Women's Film Group
Serve and Obey (1972); *Bettshanger* (1972); *The Amazing Equal Pay Show* (1975); *Whose Choice* (1976)

Lupino, Ida (1918–   ), USA
Not Wanted (1949); *Never Fear* (1950); *Outrage* (1950); *Hard, Fast and Beautiful* (1951); *The Bigamist* (1953); *The Hitchhiker* (1953); *Wanted for Murder* (1965), television movie; *I Love Mystery* (1966), television movie; *The Trouble With Angels* (1966)

Maldoror, Sarah, France
Monangambéee (1969); *The Future of Saint-Denis* (1971); *Louis Michel, la Commune et Nous* (1971), collective film project; *Sambizanga* (1972)

Mulvey, Laura, Great Britain
Penthesilea (1974), with Peter Wollen

Ono, Yoko (1933–   ), USA
Wink (1966); *Match* (1966); *Shout* (1966); *No. 4* (1967). Films made with John Lennon: *No. 5* (*Smile*) (1968); *Self Portrait* (1968); *Instant Karma* (1968); *No. 6* (*Rape II*) (1969); *Two Virgins* (1969); *Mr. and Mrs. Lennon's Honeymoon* (1969); *Give Peace a Chance* (1969); *You Are Here* (1969); *Cold Turkey* (1969); *The Fly* (1970); *Up Your Legs Forever* (1970); *Freedom* (1970); *Apotheosis* (1971); *Erection* (1971); *Image* (1971)

Reichert, Julia (1946–   ), USA
Growing Up Female: As Six Become One (1971), with Jim Klein;
Methadone: An American Way of Dealing (1974), with Jim Klein;
Union Maids (1976), with Jim Klein and Miles Mogulescu

Riefenstahl, Leni (1902–   ), Germany
Riefenstahl filmographies tend to contradict each other because of the
director's own evasiveness about her career. The editors have chosen
to print the most complete filmography.
Das Blaue Licht [*The Blue Light*] (1932); *Sieg des Glaubens* [*Victory of Faith*] (1933); *Tiefland* (1934), with Alfred Abel (completed
1944; released 1954); *Triumph des Willens* [*Triumph of the Will*]
(1935); *Tag der Freiheit—Unsere Wehrmacht* [*Day of Freedom: Our
Army*] (1933, released in 1935); *Olympia: I and II* (1938); *Berchtesgaden über Salzburg* (1938); *Schwarze Fracht* (1956). Unfinished
films: *Penthesilea* (1939); *Kriegswochenschauen* (1939); *Van Gogh*
(1943); *Das Blaue Licht* (1952), from the 1932 version; *Die roten
Teufel* (1954); *Ewige Gipfel* (1954); *Friedrich und Voltaire* (1955);
Drei Sterne am Mantel der Madonna (1955); *Das Blaue Licht* (1960),
from the 1932 version

Rothman, Stephanie, USA
Blood Bath (1966), begun by Jack Hill; *It's a Bikini World* (1966);
The Student Nurses (1970); *The Velvet Vampire* (1971); *Group Marriage* (1972); *Terminal Island* (1973); *The Working Girls* (1974)

Rothschild, Amalie (1945–   ), USA
Woo Who? May Wilson (1970); *The Center* (1970); *Safari* (1970);
It's All Right to Be a Woman, "The 51st State," WNET (1972); *It
Happens to Us* (1972); *Nana, Mom, and Me* (1974); *Amy on Her
Own* (1977)

Shaffer, Deborah (1949–   ), USA
How About You (1972), with Bonnie Friedman and Marilyn Mulford;
Chris and Bernie (1975), with Bonnie Friedman

Sontag, Susan (1933–   ), USA
Duet for Cannibals (1969); *Brother Carl* (1971); *Promised Lands*
(1974)

Varda, Agnès (1928–   ), France
La Pointe-Courte (1954); *Ô Saisons, Ô Châteaux* (1957); *Du Côté
de la Côte* (1958); *Opéra Mouffe* (1958); *La Cocotte d' Azur* (1959);
Les Fiancés du Pont Mac Donald (1961); *Cléo de Cinq à Sept* [*Cleo
from Five to Seven*] (1962); *Salut les Cubains!* (1963); *Le Bonheur*
[*Happiness*] (1965); *Elsa* (1966); *Les Créatures* (1966); *Oncle Janco*

(1967); *Lions Love* (1969); *Black Panthers* (1969); *Daguerreotypes* (1975)

Weber, Lois (1882–1939), USA

The Eyes of God (1913); *The Jew's Christmas* (1913)*; *The Merchant of Venice* (1914)*; *Traitor* (1914); *Like Most Wives* (1914); *The Hypocrites* (1914); *False Colours* (1914); *It's No Laughing Matter* (1914); *Sunshine Molly* (1915); *A Cigarette* (1915); *That's All* (1915); *Scandal* (1915)*; *Discontent* (1916); *Hop, The Devil's Brew* (1916); *Where Are My Children?* (1916); *The French Downstairs* (1916); *Alone in the World* (1916)*; *The People vs. John Doe* (1916); *The Rock of Riches* (1916)*; *John Needham's Double* (1916); *Saving the Family Name* (1916)*; *Shoes* (1916); *The Dumb Girl of Portici* (1916); *The Hand That Rocks the Cradle* (1917)*; *Even as You and I* (1917); *The Mysterious Mrs. M* (1917); *The Price of a Good Time* (1917); *The Man Who Dared God* (1917); *There's No Place Like Home* (1917); *For Husbands Only* (1917); *The Doctor and the Woman* (1918); *Borrowed Clothes* (1918); *When a Girl Loves* (1919); *Mary Regan* (1919); *Midnight Romance* (1919); *Scandal Managers* (1919); *Home* (1919); *Forbidden* (1919); *Too Wise Wives* (1921); *What's Worth While?* (1921); *To Please One Woman* (1921); *The Blot* (1921); *What Do Men Want?* (1921); *A Chapter in Her Life* (1923); *The Marriage Clause* (1926); *Sensation Seekers* (1927); *The Angel of Broadway* (1927); *White Heat* (1934)

Weill, Claudia (1946–   ), USA

Metropole (1968); *Radcliffe Blues* (1968), with Tony Ganz; *Putney School* (1969), with Eli Noyes; *This Is the Home of Mrs. Levant Graham* (1970), with Eli Noyes; *IDCA–1970* (1971); *Commuters, Yoga-Great Neck, Roaches, Marriage Bureau, Subway Lost and Found, Belly Dancing Class* (1972–1973); *Joyce at 34* (1972), with Joyce Chopra; *Matina Horner—Portrait of a Person 1973* (1974), with Joyce Chopra; *A China Memoir* (1974), with Shirley MacLaine; *Friends* (1977); 20 films for "Sesame Street" between 1971–1973

Wertmuller, Lina (1928–   ), Italy

The Lizards (1963); *This Time Let's Talk About Men* (1965); *Don't Tease the Misquito* (1967); *Giornalino de Gian Burrasca* (1967); *The Belle Starr Story* (1968); *Due et Due non fa più quattro* (1968), with Franco Zeffirelli; *Mimi the Metal-Worker, His Honor Betrayed* (1972); *Love and Anarchy* (1973); *Everything Ready, Nothing in Order* or *All Screwed Up* (1974); *Swept Away by an Unusual Destiny in the*

---

* Films codirected with Phillip Smalley, Weber's husband.

Blue Sea of August (1974); *Pasqualino Seven Beauties* (1975); *8½* (1963), assistant director to Federico Fellini

Wieland, Joyce, Canada
Tea in the Garden (1958), with Collins; *Assault in the Park* (1959), with Michael Snow; *Larry's Recent Behaviour* (1963); *Porgy's Blue Skylight* (1964); *Patriotism* (Part One) (1964); *Patriotism* (Part Two) (1964); *Water Sark* (1964–1965); *Sailboat* (1967–1968); *1933, Hand Tinting* (1967–1968); *Catfood* (1968); *Rat Life and Diet in North America* (1968); *Reason Over Passion* (1967–1969); *Dripping Water* (1969); *Pierre Vallieres* (1972); *Solidarity* (1973); *The Far Shore* (1976)

Allen, Dede, editor, USA
Endowing Your Future (1957); *Terror from the Year 5,000* (1958); *It's Always Now* (1958); *Odds Against Tomorrow* (1959); *The Hustler* (1961); *America, America* (1963); *Bonnie and Clyde* (1967); *Rachel, Rachel* (1968); *Alice's Restaurant* (1969); *Little Big Man* (1970); *Slaughterhouse Five* (1972); *Visions of Eight* (1973), episode "The Highest"; *Serpico* (1973) with Richard Marks; *Dog Day Afternoon* (1975); *The Missouri Breaks* (1976), with Gerald Greenberg, Steve Rotter; *Slap Shot* (1977)

Brackett, Leigh (1915–   ), screenwriter, USA
The Vampire's Ghost (1945); *Crime Doctor's Man-Hunt* (1945); *The Big Sleep* (1946), co-scenario: William Faulkner, Jules Furthman, from the novel by Raymond Chandler; *Rio Bravo* (1959), co-scenario: Jules Furthman, from a story by B. H. McCampbell; *Gold of the Seven Saints* (1961), co-scenario: Leonard Freeman; *Hatari!* (1962); *13 West Street* (1962), based on Brackett's novel *The Tiger Among Us;* *El Dorado* (1967); *Rio Lobo* (1970), co-scenario: Burton Wohl; *The Long Goodbye* (1973)

General Bibliography

Adler, Renata. *A Year in the Dark*. New York: Random House, 1969.

Ardmore, Jane. *The Self-Enchanted. Mae Murray: Image of an Era*. New York: McGraw-Hill Book Co., 1959.

Arvidson, Linda (Mrs. D. W. Griffith). *When the Movies Were Young*. New York: Dover Publications, 1969.

Astor, Mary. *A Life on Film*. New York: Delacorte Press, 1971.

Basinger, Jeanine. *Lana Turner*. New York: Pyramid Publications, 1976.

———. *Shirley Temple*. New York: Pyramid Publications, 1975.

Bergman, Andrew. *We're in the Money*. New York: New York University Press, 1971.

Betancourt, Jeanne. *Women in Focus*. Dayton, Ohio: Pflaum Publishing Co., 1974.

Bogle, Donald. *Toms, Coons, Mulattoes, Mammies and Bucks*. New York: The Viking Press, 1973.

Brownlow, Kevin. *The Parade's Gone By*. New York: Ballantine Books, 1969.

Burton, Julianne. *The New Latin American Cinema*. New York: Cinéaste, 1976.

Coffee, Lenore. *Recollections of a Hollywood Screenwriter*. New York: The Macmillan Co., 1972.

Cooper, Miriam, with Herndon, Bonnie. *Dark Lady of the Silents—My Life in Early Hollywood*. New York: Bobbs-Merrill, 1975.

Crawford, Joan. *My Way of Life*. New York: Simon & Schuster, 1971.

———, and Ardmore, Jane Kesner. *A Portrait of Joan*. Doubleday & Co., 1961.

Crist, Judith. *The Private Eye, the Cowboy, and the Very Naked Lady.* New York: Holt, Rinehart, & Winston, 1968.

Croce, Arlene. *The Fred Astaire and Ginger Rogers Book.* New York: Outerbridge and Lazard, 1972.

Dawson, Bonnie. *Women's Films in Print.* San Francisco: Bootlegger Press, 1975.

De Beauvoir, Simone. *Brigitte Bardot and the Lolita Syndrome.* New York: Arno Press, 1972.

————. *The Second Sex.* Translated and edited by H. M. Parshley. New York: Bantam Books, 1952.

Deming, Barbara. *Running Away from Myself—A Dream Portrait Drawn from the Films of the Forties.* New York: Grossman Publishers, 1969.

Deren, Maya. *An Anagram of Ideas on Art, Form and Film.* Outcast Chapbooks, no. 9. Yonkers, N.Y.: Alicat Book Shop, 1946.

Dickens, Homer. *The Films of Katharine Hepburn.* Secaucus, N.J.: Citadel Press, 1971.

Douglas Sirk: The Complete American Period. Storrs, Conn.: University of Connecticut Film Society, 1974.

Dressler, Marie. *My Own Story.* As told to Mildred Harrington. Boston: Little, Brown & Co., 1934.

Duras, Marguerite. *Hiroshima Mon Amour.* Translated by Richard Seaver. New York: Grove Press, 1961.

Eells, George. *Hedda and Louella.* New York: G. P. Putnam's Sons, 1972.

Farmer, Frances. *Will There Really Be a Morning?* New York: G. P. Putnam's Sons, 1972.

Firestone, Shulamith. *The Dialectic of Sex.* New York: William Morrow, 1970.

Ford, Charles. *Femmes Cinéastes, ou le Triomphe de la Volonté.* Paris: Denoël/Gonthier, 1972.

Frank, Gerold. *Judy.* New York: Harper and Row, 1975.

Friedan, Betty. *The Feminine Mystique.* New York: Dell Publishing Co., 1963.

Gill, Brendan. *Tallulah.* New York: Holt, Rinehart and Winston, 1972.

Gilliatt, Penelope. *Sunday Bloody Sunday.* New York: The Viking Press, 1972.

————. *Unholy Fools, Wits, Comics, Disturbers of the Peace.* New York: The Viking Press, 1973.

Gish, Lillian, with Pinchot, Ann. *The Movies, Mr. Griffith and Me.* Englewood Cliffs, N.J.: Prentice-Hall, 1969.

Glyn, Anthony. *Elinor Glyn.* Garden City, N.Y.: Doubleday & Co., 1955.

Guiles, Fred Lawrence. *Marion Davies.* New York: McGraw-Hill Book Co., 1972.

Goodman, Ezra. *The Fifty-Year Decline and Fall of Hollywood.* New York: Macfadden, 1962.

Halliday, John. *Sirk on Sirk.* New York: The Viking Press, 1972.

————, and Mulvey, Laura, eds. *Douglas Sirk.* Edinburgh, Scotland: Edinburgh Film Festival in association with The National Film Theatre and John Player and Sons, 1972.

Harvey, Stephen. *Joan Crawford.* New York: Pyramid Publications, 1974.

Haskell, Molly. *From Reverence to Rape: The Treatment of Women in the Movies.* New York: Holt, Rinehart & Winston, Inc., 1974.

Hellman, Lillian. *Scoundrel Time.* Boston: Little, Brown & Co., 1976.

Hess, Thomas B., and Baker, Elizabeth C. *Art and Sexual Politics.* New York: Collier Books, 1973.

Higham, Charles. *Kate: The Life of Katharine Hepburn.* New York: W. W. Norton & Co., 1975.

Horney, Karen. *Feminine Psychology.* Edited by Harold Kelman. New York: W. W. Norton & Co., Inc., 1967.

Houston, Penelope. *The Contemporary Cinema.* Baltimore, Md.: Penguin Books, 1963.

Johnston, Claire, ed. *Notes on Women's Cinema.* London: Society for Education in Film and Television, 1973.

————. *The Work of Dorothy Arzner—Towards a Feminist Cinema.* London: British Film Institute, 1975.

Kael, Pauline. *Deeper into Movies.* Boston: Little, Brown & Co., 1973.

————. *Going Steady.* Boston: Little, Brown & Co., 1970.

————. *I Lost It at the Movies.* Boston: Little, Brown & Co., 1965.

————. *Kiss Kiss, Bang Bang.* Boston: Little, Brown & Co., 1969.

————. *Reeling.* Boston: Little, Brown & Co., 1976.

Kanin, Garson. *Tracy and Hepburn: An Intimate Memoir.* New York: Bantam Books, 1972.

Kay, Karyn. *Myrna Loy.* New York: Pyramid Publications, 1977.

Koszarski, Richard. *Hollywood Directors 1914–1940.* New York: Oxford University Press, 1976.

Lambert, Gavin. *On Cukor.* New York: G. P. Putnam's Sons, 1972.

Lawson, John Howard. *Film in the Battle of Ideas.* New York: Masses and Mainstreams, 1953.

Lennig, Arthur, ed. *Classics of the Film.* Madison, Wis.: Wisconsin Film Society Press, 1965.

Loos, Anita. *A Girl Like I.* New York: The Viking Press, 1966.

————. *Kiss Hollywood Goodby.* New York: The Viking Press, 1974.

————, and Emerson, John. *Breaking into the Movies.* New York: James A. McCann Company, 1921.

Marion, Frances. *Off With Their Heads!* New York: The Macmillan Co., 1973.

McBride, Joseph, ed. *Focus on Howard Hawks.* Englewood Cliffs, N.J.: Prentice-Hall, 1972.

McGilligan, Patrick. *Ginger Rogers*. New York: Pyramid Publications, 1975.

Mellen, Joan. *Voices from the Japanese Cinema*. New York: Liveright, 1975.

————. *Women and Their Sexuality in the New Film*. New York: Horizon Press, 1973.

Mercouri, Melina. *I Was Born Greek*. New York: Doubleday & Co., 1971.

Mills, Earl. *Dorothy Dandridge: A Portrait in Black*. Los Angeles: Holloway House, 1970.

Mitchell, Juliet. *Psychoanalysis and Feminism*. New York: Random House, 1975.

Moore, Colleen. *Silent Star*. New York: Doubleday & Co., 1968.

Negri, Paula. *Memoirs of a Star*. Garden City, N.Y.: Doubleday & Co., 1970.

Parish, James Robert. *The Fox Girls*. New Rochelle, N.Y.: Arlington House, 1971.

————. *The Glamour Girls*. New Rochelle, N.Y.: Arlington House, 1975.

————. *Hollywood's Great Love Teams*. New Rochelle, N.Y.: Arlington House, 1974.

————. *The RKO Gals*. New Rochelle, N.Y.: Arlington House, 1974.

————. *The Slapstick Queens*. South Brunswick, N.J.: A. S. Barnes, 1975.

Peary, Gerald. *Rita Hayworth*. New York: Pyramid Publications, 1976.

Perry, Eleanor. *The Swimmer*. New York: Stein & Day, 1967.

Pickford, Mary. *Sunshine and Shadow: The Autobiography of Mary Pickford*. New York: Doubleday & Co., 1955.

Reininger, Lotte. *Shadow Theatre and Shadow Films*. New York: Watson-Guptil, 1970.

Ringgold, Gene. *The Films of Bette Davis*. New York: Citadel Press, 1966.

Rosen, Marjorie. *Popcorn Venus*. New York: Avon Books, 1973.

Sarris, Andrew. *Confessions of a Cultist: On the Cinema 1955/1969*. New York: Simon & Schuster, 1971.

————. *The Films of Josef von Sternberg*. New York: Doubleday & Co., 1961.

Saxton, Martha. *Jayne Mansfield and the American Fifties*. Boston: Houghton Mifflin Company, 1975.

Schickel, Richard. *The Stars*. New York: The Dial Press, 1962.

Slide, Anthony. *The Griffith Actresses*. South Brunswick, N.J.: A. S. Barnes, 1973.

Smith, Ella. *Starring Miss Barbara Stanwyck*. New York: Crown Publishers, 1974.

Smith, Sharon. *Women Who Make Movies*. New York: Hopkinson & Blake, 1975.

Sontag, Susan. *Against Interpretation*. New York: Dell Publishing Co., 1969.
———. *Brother Carl, A Screenplay*. New York: Farrar, Straus & Giroux, 1973.
———. *A Duet for Cannibals*. New York: Noonday Original Screenplays, 1970.
———. *Styles of Radical Will*. New York: Farrar, Straus & Giroux, 1969.
Sternberg, Josef von. *Fun in a Chinese Laundry*. New York: The Macmillan Co., 1965.
Turan, Kenneth, and Zito, Stephen F. *Sinema: American Pornographic Films and the People Who Make Them*. New York: Praeger Publishers, 1975.
Viertel, Salka. *The Kindness of Strangers*. Holt, Rinehart & Winston, 1969.
Viva. *Superstar: A Novel*. New Jersey: Lancer Books, 1972.
Walker, Alexander. *The Celluloid Sacrifice*. London: Michael Joseph, 1966.
———. *Stardom: The Hollywood Phenomenon*. New York: Stein & Day, 1970.
Weinberg, Herman G. *Josef von Sternberg*. New York: Dutton Paperbacks, 1967.
West, Mae. *Goodness Had Nothing to Do with It*. rev. ed. New York: Manor Books, 1970.
Wollen, Peter. *Signs and Meaning in the Cinema*. Bloomington, Ind.: Indiana University Press, 1969.
Wolfenstein, Martha, and Leites, Nathan. *Movies: A Psychological Study*. Glencoe, Ill.: The Free Press, 1950.

The Contributors

KAY ARMATAGE has taught film at the University of Toronto and helped organize the Toronto Women and Film International Festival, 1973. She is an editor for *Take One*.

JEANINE BASINGER is an associate professor of art at Wesleyan University, Middletown, Connecticut, where she teaches courses in American film. She has written three books in the Pyramid Illustrated History of the Movies series: *Shirley Temple* (1975), *Gene Kelly* (1976), and *Lana Turner* (1976).

BARBARA BERNSTEIN writes and produces for a metropolitan advertising agency. She was graduated from the University of Chicago, worked for Twentieth Century-Fox in Paris, and recently completed a documentary entitled *Silver Lining*.

PETER BISKIND, a New York filmmaker, has written for *Film Quarterly*, *Sight and Sound*, and *Cinéaste*. He is on the editorial boards of *Jump Cut* and *Radical America* and on the staff of *Seven Days*.

ALICE GUY BLACHÉ is the pioneer woman filmmaker. Her first fictional short was made in France in 1896. She died in 1968 at age ninety-five in New Jersey.

LEIGH BRACKETT has been a leading science-fiction author since 1940, when her short story, "Martian Quest," was published in *Astounding*. Her most recent screenplay was *The Long Goodbye* (1973) for Robert Altman.

LOUISE BROOKS, the American film star of the late 1920s, has written her remembrances for *Film Culture* and *Sight and Sound*.

SHIRLEY CLARKE is the independent filmmaker of *The Connection* (1960), *The Cool World* (1962), and *Portrait of Jason* (1967).

COLETTE is the honored and prolific French author of *Claudine at School* (1900), *The Vagabond* (1911), *Chéri* (1920), and *Gigi* (1942). She died in 1954.

ELIZABETH DALTON is head archivist of the Wisconsin Center for Film and Theater Research in Madison. She is the former coeditor of *The Velvet Light Trap*.

SIMONE DE BEAUVOIR is the author of *The Second Sex* (1952) and *The Mandarins* (1956), and many volumes of philosophy, fiction, and autobiography.

STORM DE HIRSCH is a New York experimental filmmaker. Her independent feature, *Goodbye in the Mirror,* was released in 1964.

MAYA DEREN is a founding mother of the American avant-garde film movement. Her works include *Meshes in the Afternoon* (1943), *At Land* (1944), and *The Very Eye of Night* (1959).

GRETA GARBO, the Swedish-born actress, starred in such Hollywood classics as *Anna Christie* (1931), *Mata Hari* (1931), *Grand Hotel* (1932), *Anna Karenina* (1935), *Camille* (1936), and *Ninotchka* (1939).

DAN GEORGAKAS coauthored *Detroit—I Do Mind Dying: A Study in Urban Revolution* (1975). He is on the editorial board of *Cinéaste*.

DIANE GIDDIS works in New York publishing. The piece on *Klute* was her first film article.

MOLLY HASKELL is film critic for *The Village Voice* and author of *From Reverence to Rape—The Treatment of Women in the Movies* (1974). She also has written for *Ms.*, *New York* magazine, and *Film Comment*.

CLAIRE JOHNSTON edited *Notes on Women's Cinema* (1973) for Britain's Society for Education in Film and Television and *The Work of Dorothy Arzner—Towards a Feminist Cinema* (1975) for the British Film Institute.

E. ANN KAPLAN is an assistant professor of English at University College, Rutgers University. She is a regular contributor to *Jump Cut* and coauthored a volume for film teachers, *Talking About the Cinema* (1963, rev. ed. 1974), issued by the British Film Institute.

MICHAEL KLEIN is an assistant professor of film and English at Livingston College, Rutgers University. He has written criticism for *Film Quarterly, Cinéaste,* and *The Velvet Light Trap,* among others, and he was a recent third-party candidate for Congress in the 1976 elections.

CHUCK KLEINHANS is coeditor of *Jump Cut.*

RICHARD KOSZARSKI has taught film history at New York University and the School of the Visual Arts. He is the author of *Hollywood Directors 1914–1940* (1976).

JULIA LESAGE is an assistant professor of English at the University of Illinois, Chicago Circle, where she teaches literature, film, and women's studies.

SARAH MALDOROR is the political filmmaker of *Sambizanga* (1972).

BARBARA HALPERN MARTINEAU is a feminist writer living in Toronto, Canada. She has completed a manuscript on women writers and directors, called *women imagine women.* She has published articles in *Jump Cut, Cinema Canada, Women and Film,* and *Take One,* and organized a program of women's films for the Toronto Festival of Festivals in 1976.

JANET MASLIN has written for *Rolling Stone* and *New Times* and was film editor for *The Boston Phoenix.* She is an associate editor for *Newsweek.*

RUTH MCCORMICK is a New York–based writer on film and politics for a number of publications. She is currently an editorial associate for *Cinéaste* and is preparing a book on film, ideology, and aesthetics.

PATRICK MCGILLIGAN is a former arts writer for *The Boston Globe,* and is author of *Ginger Rogers* (1975) and *James Cagney: The Actor as Auteur* (1975). He is writing a study of Karl Armstrong, jailed in Wisconsin for blowing up the Army Math Research Center in 1969.

LAURA MULVEY coedited *Douglas Sirk* (1972) for the Edinburgh Film Festival and codirected the experimental film, *Penthesilea, Queen of the Amazons* (1974), with Peter Wollen.

KATHLEEN MURPHY teaches film courses at the University of Washington, Seattle, and she is a regular contributor to *Movietone News.* She is completing a Ph.D. dissertation on Howard Hawks and Ernest Hemingway.

YOKO ONO is a New York–based avant-garde artist, filmmaker, and musician. She was a founding member of the Plastic Ono Band, featuring her husband, former Beatle John Lennon.

DANNIS PEARY has an M.A. in screenwriting from the University of

Southern California at Los Angeles. He has written for *Country Music* and is a frequent contributor to *The Velvet Light Trap*.

LENNY RUBENSTEIN coauthored "The Violence of Everyday Life" for the forthcoming anthology, *The City Today*. He has taught at LaGuardia Community College in New York City, and is an editorial associate for *Cinéaste*.

ANDREW SARRIS is film critic for *The Village Voice* and a professor of cinema at Columbia University. His most recent book is *The John Ford Movie Mystery* (1976).

SUSAN SONTAG is the noted filmmaker and critic. Recently she served on the selection committee of the 1976 New York Film Festival.

WILLIAM VAN WERT has a Ph.D. from Indiana University and teaches film and creative writing at Temple University. He is on the editorial board of *Jump Cut*.

ALEXANDER WALKER became film critic for the London *Evening Standard* in 1960. He is the author of *The Celluloid Sacrifice* (1966) and *Stardom: The Hollywood Phenomenon* (1970).

DEBRA WEINER is a former reporter for *The Burlington* (Vt.) *Free Press* and *The Boston Globe*. She has written for *The Velvet Light Trap* and *Focus on Film*.

JANICE WELSCH is an assistant professor of film at Western Illinois University. She wrote a Ph.D. dissertation at Northwestern University—"An Analysis of the Film Images of Hollywood's Most Popular Post–WW II Female Stars."

ELLEN WILLIS is a staff writer for *The New Yorker*, a contributing editor to *Rolling Stone*, and a free-lance writer.

STARK YOUNG was film and drama critic for *The New Republic*, and the translator of the plays of Anton Chekhov.

Index

457